Dedicated with love to Greg,
my husband, my person,
for making anything seem
possible.

PRAISE FOR
KARINA SUMNER-SMITH
AND *RADIANT*

"Inequality, economics, and postapocalyptic necromancy combine persuasively in Sumner-Smith's ingenious, insightful debut. . . . With a clean, evocative style, a clever transposition of corporate warfare into a feudal future, and a strong, complementary pair of protagonists, Sumner-Smith's Towers Trilogy is off to a captivating start."
—*Publishers Weekly*, starred review

"I love this. The writing is beautiful, the world, seen from the perspective of the have-nots, both magical and bleak. At heart it's a book about trust, loss, and the friendships that are built in spite of the bad things. It's about finding a small place—no matter how strange that place or how strange the characters (and they are)—to belong."
—Michelle Sagara, *New York Times* bestselling author of *The Chronicles of Elantra*

"Sparse, spare, and at the same time a rich tapestry of worldbuilding and the soft misery of her blighted main character Xhea, Karina Sumner-Smith's smashing debut is a page-turner of the highest pedigree. . . . Radiant is a book that is both a joy and a pleasure to read."
—J. M. Frey, award-winning author of *Triptych*

"I can't remember the last time I was as excited about the start of a new fantasy series as I am about *Radiant*, the first in a promised trilogy."
—*San Francisco Book Review*

"A first novel *Radiant* may be, but by a writer at the top of her craft. Be taken to breathless heights of imagination. Feel your heart pound until it almost breaks, then sigh for joy. This, dear readers, is the story you mustn't miss and will never forget. Recommended? No. I insist. Read *Radiant*."
—Julie E. Czerneda, author of *A Turn of Light*

"This beautifully-written page turner is topnotch. A world that comes alive, rich and magical; characters you want to spend time with; a heroine to root for; trust, friendship, and belonging—*Radiant* has it all! Fantasy not your cup of tea? You should read this one anyway; it deserves space on every bookshelf. Where's the next one?"
—Ed Greenwood, creator of The Forgotten Realms® and *New York Times* bestselling author of *Spellfire* and *The Herald*

"In penning her novel *Radiant*, Karina Sumner-Smith steps into the top ranks of a burgeoning generation of authors who are changing the face of science fiction and fantasy. With characterizations that won't let you go, deeply textured world-building, and prose that sings, she offers a book that deserves to become a classic."
—Catherine Asaro, Nebula Award-winning author of *Undercity*

"Finally! A *Bladerunner* for the fantasy crowd. Magic as you've never seen it before."
—Violette Malan, author of the Mirror Lands novels

"An imaginative and original tale of struggle, sacrifice, and friendship within a harsh cultural landscape. *Radiant* is a vibrant debut, infused with pure magic and strong characters."
—Amanda Sun, author of *Rain*

"In *Radiant*, Karina Sumner-Smith delivers a vibrant world swamped in magic and desperation, and a truly special heroine in Xhea, who is as raw and powerful as she is vulnerable. This is a must-read."
—Jaleigh Johnson, author of *The Mark of the Dragonfly*

"Long story short, you need to read *Radiant*. It's got the right blend between fantasy and sci-fi to appeal to fans of either genre, very realistic characters that you want to read more about, and enough mysteries and curiosity to leave me, at least, salivating over the sequel."
—*Bibliotropic*

DEFIANT

DEFIANT

TOWERS TRILOGY BOOK TWO

WITHDRAWN

KARINA
SUMNER-SMITH

Talos Press

Talos Press books may be purchased in bulk at special discounts for sales promotion, corporate gifts, fund-raising, or educational purposes. Special editions can also be created to specifications. For details, contact the Special Sales Department, Talos Press, 307 West 36th Street, 11th Floor, New York, NY 10018 or info@skyhorsepublishing.com.

Talos Press® is a registered trademark of Skyhorse Publishing, Inc.®, a Delaware corporation.

Visit our website at www.talospress.com.

10 9 8 7 6 5 4 3 2 1

Library of Congress Cataloging-in-Publication Data is available on file.

Cover design by Rain Saukas
Cover illustrations: Thinkstock

Print ISBN: 978-1-940456-26-3
Ebook ISBN: 978-1-940456-33-1

Printed in the United States of America

Part One

Chapter One

In the last hours before morning, silence fell, slow and inevitable as the darkness.

The party that had rocked the ballrooms on Edren's second floor since nightfall had worn down, the skyscraper's guests retiring to their rented rooms to sleep—or for other more private celebrations. No thump of music anymore; no voices raised to shout or laugh; no more drunken songs. There was only the distant clink of glasses being cleared away and the rattle of the door's heavy chain as a guard checked the locks.

As if that quiet had weight, Xhea felt it settle across her shoulders. Her ears rang with it, as did her thoughts, until it was all she could do to keep breathing, one slow and ragged breath after another.

The Edren skyscraper had been a hotel once, this cavernous space its lobby. Though the marble floors were cracked and poorly patched, and most of the walls' wood paneling had long since been stripped away, there were still glimpses of the place's absent riches. The domed ceiling had most of its original mosaic, the patterned tiles glittering faintly from the shadows above; and the main staircase, wide and sweeping, had retained its brass railings with their curlicued flourishes.

It was the stairs that held Xhea's attention—and not the ones that led up to the ballrooms and the party's remains, their thin carpeting dotted with confetti. No, it was the flanking stairs that drew her, one to either side of the main stairway, and the dusty treads that led into the darkness below.

Gray, to her—dust and brass and confetti alike. The color of her skin, the rough length of wood she clutched in her unsteady hand.

Her future.

All gray.

There was, in the end, nothing different about that. Xhea had always seen in black and white, or the grays that dominated the span between those extremes. It was only now she felt the lack, heavy like stone in her eyes and hands and heart.

At the security desk behind her the monitors flicked through their channels, the glow making shadows dance down the stairs. They moved faster than she could, these days. Faster by far.

"Tonight?" a man's voice asked from behind her, soft enough that none might overhear. It wasn't caution: there was something in this place, this hour, that asked for quiet, for softness of voice and breath—a stillness that one might only find at a funeral or in prayer. It was for that stillness, as much as the for the stairs, that Xhea had first come here on another night like this when her pain meds had worn away to nothing and her next dose was impossibly far away.

Xhea looked up, half-turning. She smiled, though it was a faint expression and faded quickly. This man, too, had become familiar—supervisor of Edren's night watch, stationed at the main desk all through these long hours when the rest of the Lower City celebrated or slept, keeping the dangers of the nighttime streets at bay. Mercks, his nametag said; she'd never heard him called anything else. Sight of his lined face and graying mustache was almost a comfort now, here where so much else seemed strange. Here in a home she thought never to have, and didn't know how to want now that it was hers.

"So I thought." Xhea shifted her weight and winced at the pain, clutching her stick for balance. She turned away, looking down the confetti-strewn stairs in an attempt to hide her expression.

She didn't know what they had been celebrating, what could possibly have required so much wine and song and confetti. Another match in Edren's arena, battles of blade and magic—entertainment for the shit-poor masses huddled on the ground beneath the City's floating Towers. Another win, another loss, another transient champion crowned.

As if any of it mattered.

"But no," she said at last, swallowing the pain. The humiliation. The anger. "Not tonight."

Perhaps not, if she was honest, ever.

Oh, she could get down the stairs, that much she knew—if not quickly nor cleanly, then at least to the bottom. But not on her feet like she wanted; not without aid of brace and stick both, and careful pauses between each step. No, for anything like speed she'd have to sit on the ground and lower herself one tread at a time, down in the dirt and crawling. And for what? In truth, it wasn't that she needed anything at the bottom of those stairs. It was that she shouldn't have had to think about stairs, or curbs, or the too-high lips of ancient doorways—had never considered them until they each became obstacles in the routines of her newly curtailed life.

She shouldn't have had to think about walking at all.

Yet here she was.

It had been more than two months since she'd injured her knee in her attempt to protect her friend Shai from the Towers who had fought to claim the ghost and her Radiant magic. Memory of the first month after that, spent in skyscraper Edren's protection, was but a haze—exhausted, indeterminable, fever-glazed days that rolled by with little to define them but pain and its too-brief absence. When the healing spells placed in her knee failed and failed again, Lorn Edren, eldest living son of the skyscraper that bore the family name, had brought a medic from the arena who knew the healing power of knives. A surgeon—or the closest they could come in the Lower City. The woman had operated on Xhea's knee, doing with scalpel and stitches what no spell had lasted long enough to achieve.

The pain had doubled after that.

Xhea had always healed slowly and badly. It was only now that such slowness mattered. Not only was her knee all but useless, but she still bore the shadows of the countless deep bruises she'd received in fight and flight: the shoulder she'd pulled in the aircar crash twinged, and the ribs she'd cracked on impact from her fall from the City ached with every deep breath. Fevers washed over her nightly, rising at dusk and receding with the sun's return, leaving her as limp and tired at dawn as she had been at the end of each long day.

The cost of saving Shai had not been too high, that Xhea never doubted. Her hand strayed to the tether that even now connected them, though the ghost was absent. But it had been a cost, and a far steeper one than she had first known.

"Well," Mercks said from beside her, his voice a quiet bass rumble, "if you need a hand, let me know. I'd be happy to help you upstairs."

Xhea smiled at his polite lie—or tried to. He knew that Xhea had no desire to climb to where the remains of this latest pointless revelry were stretched out like dogs fresh from the slaughter; he knew that she wanted to go to the one place that no one with bright magic could comfortably travel, no matter how slight their talent. He knew too that were she to accept his offer and replace her cane with the support of his strong arm, that he could stand the feel of her hand upon him for no more than a moment. For a few brief days following her fall, others had been able to touch her almost without discomfort—a consequence, she thought, of burning out her dark magic in Shai's rescue. But while the crawling discomfort of Xhea's touch had returned, her magic remained absent.

Mercks's useless offer and her quiet rejection of it were part of their near-nightly ritual, repeated often enough that there was no sting left in the words.

"I'll keep that in mind," Xhea said.

She glanced back toward the stairs, wanting . . . what? Freedom from pain, freedom from these ancient walls? So much of the life she had built for herself was rooted in the tunnels and abandoned shopping corridors that wound beneath the Lower City's streets, and if it had not been an easy life, nor a comfortable one, it had at least been hers.

This life, the life of a near-cripple, tended and useless, was not one that fit her well, for all that it came with three meals a day, clean clothes, and an endless supply of soap and water. It made her restless and angry; it made her want to smash herself against the walls of her cage. Yet there was no cage but that of her helplessness, the inevitable failure of her bones and flesh, and that was a prison she could never leave behind. There was no word, no sound big enough for that frustration, and so she stifled them, the cries and screams and tears, until, unvoiced, their echoes felt like silence.

At last Xhea turned away from the lure of the darkness at the bottom of the stairs, trying to breathe through pain and disappointment alike.

"I think," she started—and the screaming began.

Xhea started as the scream broke through her haze and the late-night silence both. The sound echoed from some distant hallway, frantic but muffled—a man's voice, she thought, but it was hard to tell. The fear in that voice, the urgency, set Xhea's heart to racing; each beat seemed to pound against the inside of her knee in a quickening rhythm of hurt.

It was only as she turned in a limping circle to pinpoint the sound that she caught sight of Mercks's expression. She stopped.

"You don't hear that, do you?"

He shook his head, his expression unreadable.

A ghost, then. A screaming, terrified ghost that only Xhea could hear. Just what she needed to finish off the night.

"Is it something I need to be concerned with?" Mercks asked, the rumble of his voice louder now. At the security desk, one of his officers glanced in their direction.

Xhea considered, wincing as the distant ghost screamed again. The domed ceiling seemed to capture the sound and hold it like an insect in cupped palms. *Maybe one of the party-goers died*, she thought. Maybe he'd fallen from one of Edren's upper windows, or had been in a fight gone too far. But it was just as likely to be an older ghost coming within her earshot for the first time.

"I don't think so," she said. "But if there's trouble, I'll let you know." She tried to sound unconcerned, but she had never been a terribly good actress at the best of times, never mind when an unknown person was screaming in terror— and coming closer by the minute.

She limped toward the noise. The muffled shouts seemed to come from one of the old hotel's back hallways— and the direction of her own small room, a former storage closet that was as far from any magical systems as possible within the skyscraper's confines. Though her magic seemed again to be no more than a dark presence in the depths of her stomach, she still feared that it might emerge while she slept—or, more commonly, slipped into the drugged semi-consciousness that was the closest she could come to sleep most days.

Xhea pushed her awkward way through the heavy swinging doors that led into the back halls, feeling Mercks's attention on her as she went. *Well, if I find a body to go with the noise, he'll be the first to know.*

The hall, long and bare and straight, led past a storage room and a side passage to the laundry before turning toward the main kitchen. The screaming was louder, though no clearer, sounding as if a madman was around the corner shouting into a pillow.

No, Xhea realized. Not around the corner, but from behind her room's closed door. She stared at her battered metal door and listened to the frantic shouting that emanated from within, pursing her lips in irritation.

"Typical," she muttered. It wasn't uncommon for ghosts to seek her out, or draw as near as their tethers allowed.

But she had little enough privacy as it was, so many people living and sleeping and breathing within these walls that it was hard to throw a stone without hitting another living thing. Hard to escape them at all. This room was her refuge—or it had been.

Frowning, Xhea opened the door.

All was as she'd left it: a small cot with its rumpled blankets was pushed against the far wall, kept company by a rusted metal shelf that held a few changes of clothing and a book. In the corner leaned a cane that had proven entirely too big for someone of her stature.

Yet now in the center of the room stood the ghost of a man, alone and screaming and so desperately unstable on his feet that Xhea thought it a wonder he was standing at all. He was younger than his ragged voice had suggested—late twenties, tops—and wore loose white clothing from head to toe. No bloodstains that she could see; no wounds or other signs of violence. It wasn't his appearance that made her blink and raise an incredulous eyebrow, but the reason for his screams' muffled sound: he had both of his hands stuffed into his mouth as far as they would go. Weaving, unsteady, the ghost stared at her as if he were drowning and Xhea was dry land, his eyes wide as he yelled urgently, desperately, into his spit-slicked fingers.

"Well," she said. "This is new."

Xhea stepped into the room and let the door slam behind her, closing out the light. She didn't bother with the overhead bulb; magic or no, she'd always seen perfectly in the dark.

He's not drunk, she decided. She hobbled slowly around him, and he followed her every move. His wide eyes were focused, intense, as he screamed and screamed and nearly fell over. *Not drunk—but something.* Once she'd met the ghost of a woman who had managed to accidentally choke herself to death, but this—this was something else. He showed no signs of quieting; if anything, he became more frantic the longer she watched.

At last, Xhea raised her index finger to her lips. "Shh," she said.

The ghost stuttered into silence.

"Too loud, my friend. Too loud by far."

The ghost started to speak—softer this time, she had to give him that.

"And your hands are in your mouth."

He stared. Listed alarmingly to one side, and barely righted himself without use of his arms. Mumbled something through his mouthful of fingers.

Xhea sighed. "If you want me to understand you, take your hands out of your mouth."

The ghost stared. Tilted. Righted himself.

"Your *hands*." Xhea wiggled her fingers in emphasis.

Comprehension dawned and the ghost pulled his hands free, strings of spit hanging between his fingers. Empty, his mouth hung open, gaping; he licked his lips once, twice and again. The ghost looked from Xhea to his wet hands and back again in growing confusion, that intensity slipping from his expression, leaving little in its wake. Then, with a cry, he fell to his knees and clutched his head, spit-darkened hair protruding from between his fingers in spikes and tufts.

Charming. Just what every girl wants to find in her room.

She watched him rock back and forth, and wondered how long this next phase of crazy was going to last. More than a minute, it seemed. More than two. Her windowless room wasn't large, but it suddenly felt far smaller.

"Hey," Xhea called. The ghost jumped at her voice then curled in upon himself further, rocking and near-tumbling to the ground.

"Hey, you. Dead guy. I'm over here." No reaction this time; she might as well have been talking to the wall. Sighing, Xhea shuffled closer and lowered herself awkwardly to the floor, the charms and coins bound into her hair chiming as she landed.

"Look at me," Xhea said.

The ghost stilled and looked up. His eyes were storm-cloud dark and afraid, but with something else behind, as if he were seeing things that had nothing to do with Xhea's tired face—a landscape far beyond this breezeblock room with its peeling paint.

She wondered suddenly who this man had been. Not just what had killed him or brought him to her, distraught and afraid, but the person he had been in life. What he had done, where he had lived, what had made him laugh. Whether this darkness—this fear and hurt and confusion—had haunted his living years. Whether someone missed him.

There was a time she would have never thought to ask such questions, nor cared enough to wonder. Now she leaned forward and asked, "Who were you?"

He sat mute, swaying.

"Why are you here?"

Still nothing. Simpler, then: "Why were you shouting?"

His eyes seemed to grow darker as she watched. Lost eyes, with something terrible hiding behind.

"Gone," the ghost whispered at last. Quiet, so quiet.

"What is?"

"Gone, lost. Find." He looked down at his hands then back to her face, his gaze as unsettled as a startled flock of birds. Afraid, Xhea thought, but not of her.

What's he tethered to? Every ghost had a tether, a line of near-invisible energy that bound him or her to the living world—a link to something that they had not, or could not, leave behind. Through long practice, Xhea had learned to sever ghosts' tethers and reconnect them to other people or things. Sometimes she had released the tether entirely, freeing the ghost to dissolve like sugar into tea. Once she'd had a knife for such tasks, an ancient silver blade that she'd carried in a jacket pocket near her heart. Gone, now; taken when another skyscraper, Orren, had captured her. Thought of that theft was still enraging—even more so as Xhea was totally helpless to do anything about it.

It wasn't until she glanced around him that she saw his tether. Most tethers connected to a ghost's heart, the center of their chest, or their head—indications of the type of connection that bound the dead to the world. This tether connected to ghost's back between his shoulder blades, as if the tether—or whatever it tied him to—had targeted him as he fled life.

Xhea shook her head to dispel such thoughts. Yet something else about the tether bothered her; she just wasn't sure what. Frowning, Xhea leaned closer, trying to see what looked—what *felt*—so different. Strong as the line appeared, she couldn't imagine what anchor would allow him such freedom of movement—especially, she realized, as the tether didn't point up into the Edren skyscraper, nor out toward the Lower City streets beyond Edren's walls, but *down*. Not sharply, not steeply, but the tether pointed ever so slightly toward the floor.

Something in the underground. But how?

She took hold of the tether. Its vibration, too, was different than she expected—lower and more intense—and its frequency increased with each moment as if drawing power from her touch. Within seconds it was akin to pain.

The ghost stopped moving, then looked up slowly. He turned to her, and his gaze was no longer confused or unsettled but sharp enough to cut.

"Run," he said.

Xhea drew back, struggling to both hold the tether and meet the ghost's eyes.

"Run." His voice was rough and raw, the word a fearful command. He saw her, of that Xhea had no doubt; he stared at her as if she were the only thing left in the world. And he said, "Run."

"I—"

"Run away. Run away."

That's what he had been screaming. Something in her chilled at the thought. The same words, over and over again: *Run away, run away, run away.* The repeating cadence echoed in her memory as the ghost's stare pinned her to the spot.

The tether's vibration increased to a fever pitch and seemed to cut into her, a narrow blade slicing into her palm. With a gasp, Xhea released it and scrambled away.

As if he were a puppet and the tether his guiding string, the ghost collapsed. A moment of stillness and then he shook, shuddered, and struggled to right himself. When he raised his head, that vital energy was gone from his eyes and expression both, leaving only darkness and confusion. Again he swayed, back and forth in an unsteady rhythm.

Xhea exhaled, and reached for the now-familiar grip of her walking stick. Run away. If only she could. Sweetness and blight, these days she'd settle for a quick walk.

"Lost," the ghost murmured almost too quietly to hear, his voice forlorn. He bowed his head toward his hands, lying limply in his lap. "Find."

Xhea lifted a hand—it was shaking, she realized. Unsettled, she grabbed the tether that connected to her sternum and gave it three sharp tugs.

She didn't know where Shai went during the long nights, though she had almost asked a thousand times. She'd followed the direction of the tether that bound them, up, up, and away, and wondered where her friend wandered, what she did when she left Xhea behind. Shai didn't seem to know that Xhea spent the nights awake as often as not, staring up at the ceiling's acoustic tiles or attempting to read the same book over and over until she fled her bed, seeking any distraction from the pain and the too-familiar tracks of her thoughts. Shai didn't know, and Xhea could never seem to tell her, taking comfort instead in the knowledge that the ghost always returned to her side by morning.

Shai's arrival was heralded by a sudden glow that cast shadows in the otherwise dark room. From the floor, Xhea glanced toward the Radiant ghost who stood looking down at the rumpled blankets in no little surprise.

"Xhea," Shai said, "you're actually—"

There was no opportunity for her to finish, for the man screamed—a raw sound that seemed ripped from his throat. Xhea swung back to face him and it was all she could do not to scramble away.

He's just a ghost. He couldn't touch her, couldn't hurt her in any way.

But it wasn't Xhea that the ghost attempted to hit, though his flailing fists passed through her in a sudden wave of cold, but Shai. He screamed again, and there was panic in expression—panic and confusion and something that she suddenly thought might be rage.

Shai gave a startled cry, and the shadows danced as she stumbled back to avoid the strange ghost's swinging fists. Another step and she would be through the wall and beyond what little help Xhea might offer. Xhea couldn't stand fast enough to stop the crazed ghost—and, sitting, his tether was beyond her reach.

Instead she shouted, "*Stop!*"

The man fell silent. No, more than silent: he had frozen mid-step, his hands still reaching over Xhea's head toward Shai. Xhea's shout reverberated through the room, a sudden sound in the silence, the ghost's scream but a memory heard only by Xhea's living ears.

"What's happening?" Shai whispered. "Where did he come from?"

Xhea could only reply, "I don't know." Then—despite her racing heart, her hands' unsteady quiver, and the tension even now thrumming between the two ghosts before her— Xhea laughed. The sound was tinged with hysteria and fatigue, yes, but no less true. This was the first truly new thing to happen in weeks, and Xhea felt almost giddy with relief.

As if the sound were a cue, the man sagged.

"Gone," he whispered. "Lost." He dropped his arms to his sides, bowed his head toward the floor. "Found."

He took a step back and another, until he slipped backward through the door and was gone.

Xhea grabbed her stick and managed to get to her feet with aid of the far wall.

"You're going to follow him?" Shai asked incredulously.

"Haven't you been pestering me to go out for days?"

"Weeks, more like it," Shai muttered. It was true: Shai had been relentless in her demands that Xhea stand up, practice her strengthening exercises, walk more, maybe speak to someone who wasn't dead.

"Well then, what's the problem?"

"I think there's something terribly wrong with that man."

"I know." Xhea laughed again, pulled open the door, and followed him into the hall. She could not see the man's ghost, but she could feel him, heading out toward Edren's main hall and away. She hurried in his wake, her boots whispering against the threadbare carpet, her stick thwacking in time to her steps. Shai followed, a steady presence just behind Xhea's right shoulder. Xhea quickly explained the ghost's arrival.

Shai shook her head. "I don't like it."

"Of course not. But you can't argue that it's not the first interesting thing to happen in weeks."

"Maybe other interesting things would happen if you bothered to leave your room."

"Yeah, like falling and reopening the wound for the third blighted time. Wouldn't that be fun?"

Mercks met them at the corner.

"Are you okay?" he asked, one hand resting on the club looped to his belt. "I heard a shout."

"Ghost startled me," Xhea said. Her chest was starting to feel tight, her breath short, and not just from the pain; this was more walking, and faster, than anything she'd done since her surgery.

"Your friend?" Mercks asked carefully. He fell into step beside her, his stride comically short as he attempted to keep himself to Xhea's pace.

Word about Shai had traveled; though none but Xhea could see her, she was nonetheless felt in Edren's halls. Even dead and bodiless, Shai produced more magic in a day than all of Edren's citizens combined. Just by being at Xhea's side, Shai had filled Edren's magical storage coils to overflowing—an unexpected influx of power that more than paid for Xhea's stay and care.

Xhea shook her head, coins chiming. "Found some crazy dead guy screaming in my room. He was headed this way."

"I felt . . ." Mercks hesitated, clearly uncomfortable. "Something cold. A chill in the hall."

"Probably him." Xhea shrugged. "Probably walked right through you."

"Xhea," Shai asked from behind her. "How do you know this man?"

Xhea didn't reply.

Back in the former lobby, Mercks called to the young guard watching the monitors; the rest were out on their hourly sweep. The guard looked up warily as they approached, his prominent Adam's apple bobbing as he swallowed. Not someone Xhea knew, though she'd met many of the guards since Lorn Edren had carried her here, bruised and broken, nearly two months before. Even so, he looked familiar. She wondered if he had been the one on duty when she'd dragged herself here from Orren with aid of a rusty length of pipe to shout for Lorn's help.

Xhea's gaze was drawn inexorably back to the stairs. She saw no glimpse of white, heard no phantom shouts or whimpers, yet knew it was the way the ghost had traveled. Down. She could feel his presence in the darkness just below, a subtle ache that urged her onward.

She tightened her grip on her stick.

Before Mercks could stop her—before she could stop herself—Xhea made a beeline for the stairs. She hopped down the first step and lost her balance, grabbing the railing to keep from falling. There was a shout from behind her— the young guard—and then Mercks called her name. Using her good leg, she lowered herself down one step and then another, breath hissing through her teeth as she knocked her braced knee against the banisters. It was only when she'd traveled beyond reach of even Mercks's long arm that she paused, panting from pain and the sudden exertion. She hadn't fallen; that was something.

"Xhea, I need you to come back here," Mercks said. There was kindness in that voice, with command beneath. She felt a pang at ignoring both; her next midnight visit was unlikely to be quite so friendly.

"I will," she said. "But not just yet."

She took a deep breath. She was hardly below ground by her standards, but already she could feel the difference. A weight had lifted from her shoulders, and her breath came a little slower, a little easier. Oh, how she missed the tunnels, strange as it seemed; how she missed the wide-open spaces that were hers and hers alone. Something in her eased as she looked down into the basement.

"Don't worry," she said over her shoulder. "If I fall, I promise I won't make you come get me." Xhea sat carefully on the tread, and began lowering herself down the stairs one slow and awkward step at a time, Shai's light a steady presence at her side.

Chapter Two

By the time she reached the bottom of the stairs, Xhea could barely breathe. She clutched her walking stick and stared at her hand as it trembled against the railing's tarnished brass.

"Seriously?" she muttered. Exhausted from one flight of stairs? Despite Shai's needling, she hadn't realized that she'd gotten so bad. So . . . *soft*.

She limped forward. Shai cast the open space at the stairs' foot in a gentle glow, yet even beyond the reach of her light, it was easy for Xhea's black and white vision to pick out details. Few had walked these halls in the years since the civil war more than a decade before. Near the stairs there were scuffs and recent lines of footprints, yet no more than ten feet beyond the dust lay thick across the floor, disturbed now only by her boots. Years living in the tunnels beneath the Lower City had taught Xhea to minimize the dust clouds her footsteps conjured; even so, she had to stifle a cough.

Here, as above, Edren showed its past: meeting rooms surrounded her, or perhaps auxiliary ballrooms, though she didn't know what anyone had needed with so many of either. This level was silent, no hint of the ghost's shouting, though Xhea still felt him like an ache at the edge of her senses. *That way*, it told her, drawing her toward the main underground complex. *That way—and retreating.*

Soon the hall opened into what had been a shopping corridor for hotel guests. The boutique shops were barely larger than one-car garages—a tourist café, a jewelry store, a women's clothing shop. Empty now, only display cases and faded signs gave testament to what had once been inside. Benches and fake trees lined the corridor's center, the trees' leaves pale with dust, the benches crazed through with cracks. Yet it was the corridor's far end that held Xhea's attention: a massive barricade blocked the hall, from floor to ceiling, from side to side; and the ghost stood before it, hands again pressed to his mouth as he shook and shuddered.

"Careful now," Xhea murmured to Shai. "If he comes after you again, run."

They crept closer—or tried to. There was no sneaking now, not with her stick clacking against the floor with her every step. *Might as well use a loudspeaker*, she thought, wincing at the sound. *Maybe add in a few firecrackers for good measure.*

The direct method, then. "Hello," she called. The hall took her words and amplified them, the echoes whispering from far corners. The ghost looked up, his white clothes bright in Shai's reflected light. He stared at her wide-eyed, and trembled.

"I'm not going to hurt you," Xhea said. She didn't want to, anyway—not until he gave her reason. "My friend isn't either."

His hands were in his mouth, but he was not screaming now. No, he was biting his fingers; she could see the tension in his jaw as he clenched down, the flash of pale teeth as he winced at the pain.

It was only as she drew closer that he pulled his hands from his mouth and held them before him to ward her away. Minutes before, his hands had been whole—Xhea remembered those long fingers reaching for Shai. Yet now his fingertips were gone, nothing beyond his third knuckle but air.

"What are you—" They had not been bitten off, Xhea realized mid-sentence. They were dissolving. As she watched, more of the flesh at his fingers' ends became indistinct, hazy and fading. The ghost shuddered and shook, hands splayed before him as he folded over as if from some blow to the gut. And again. And again.

Stranger and stranger. Something more than exertion sped Xhea's heart—though whether it was fear or exhilaration, she did not know.

Xhea stopped just outside of arm's reach of the ghost. His shaking and shuddering worsened with every moment, until it was clear he fought to stay upright, fought to stand. *A seizure? Memory of his death?* Neither seemed to fit his strange movements.

"It's his tether," Shai whispered.

Xhea moved to see the tether bound between the ghost's shoulder blades—and froze. She called it a tether—for what else could it be?—though in that moment it looked like no tether she had ever seen. It was a swirling gray, thick around as her arm and visible without squinting. So, too, could she feel its strange vibration: a deep, insistent thrum that all but made her teeth rattle.

More, it pulled on the ghost. Not like an elastic band stretched to its limits, but as if it were a living thing intent on dragging him backwards. He fought it, trembling and shuddering at every pull—but he was losing. Weakening, as if each tug on the tether took some vital part of him away.

Xhea blinked. No, the tether wasn't just pulling; it was somehow drawing away his very essence like milk through a straw. His hands were vanishing, as were his feet. He seemed now to float a few inches in the air, his blunt-ending ankles pointing toward the unmarred dust of the floor.

"Sweetness and blight," Xhea whispered. "What's on the other end of that line?"

Deep within her, something dark stirred and shifted. Xhea inhaled sharply in surprise, for she knew that sensation—her magic, dormant now these past two months, again coming to life within her. Quickly, she reached for the ghost's upraised arm, thinking to grasp him with hand and magic both.

Too late.

For a moment the ghost's gray eyes met hers, and again she saw that terrible lucidity, a focus so intense that it seemed to have a physical impact.

"*Run,*" he whispered. With a terrible jerk, the tether yanked him through the barricade, and he was gone.

For a long moment, there was only silence.

Xhea stared at the barricade's uneven surface where the ghost had been pulled through—the heavy blocks of concrete, the jumble of rusted rebar, the scrap metal sloppily welded together—as if by looking long enough she might make the ghost return. Yet there was nothing but that silence and stillness, even the dust undisturbed in wake of the ghost's passage.

"That was . . ." Shai whispered before stuttering to a stop.

"I know." Xhea's desire to laugh had long since vanished. She pressed her free hand to her stomach, feeling the faintest whisper of magic curling and coiling within, twin to her fear. She should have been relieved to find her power hadn't been entirely burned from her, and yet could only think: *Too little, too late.*

Still she stared, trying to peer though the gaps in the piled barricade and out into the empty hallway beyond. There was no movement there, no sound, no sign of life or light.

And yet . . .

Xhea frowned, stepping cautiously closer, and raised her free hand toward the barricade. Her fingers hovered but a breath away from the closest concrete block.

There's something, she thought. *Something . . .*

She did not know what. Only felt the sudden, rising desire to walk forward, touch the barrier—or pass through it entirely, as if her flesh and bone were as insubstantial as a ghost's. She shook her head, coins chiming, trying to dispel the strange feeling with the movement.

"What could have done that to him?" Shai said from beside her, voice unsteady.

"I don't know." And she didn't. Xhea had seen ghosts freed and ghosts banished, ghosts so old and weary that they had begun to fade—but never before had she seen anything like this ghost, frantic and confused in turn, disappearing in pieces. She thought of his tether, stretched beyond all thought or reason—and his anchor, hidden somewhere down here in the dark and cold—and shook her head.

"I felt like we were watching something . . . eat him."

Xhea shrugged uncomfortably; she didn't disagree. "But what could eat a ghost?"

Shai shivered. "Nothing I want to meet."

That, right there, was the reason Xhea couldn't ask Shai to walk through the barricade—little barrier though it was to one who could pass unhindered through solid walls. *There's something out there*, she thought. She saw no movement through the barrier's small gaps; heard no breath or scuff of shoes against the dirty floor. No one there, logic said. Nothing.

Instinct disagreed.

For there was something or someone to which the ghost was bound—something close. Something that called to her, urging her forward. She wanted—

Xhea shook her head. She did not know what it was that she wanted so suddenly, so urgently, only knew that it was on the other side of Edren's barricade in the tunnels beyond. Again Xhea made to step forward, and only will and pain kept her from moving.

Instead she whispered, "Do you feel that?"

Beside her, Shai looked at the barricade and shuddered, wrapping her arms around her chest as if to ward off a sudden chill. "Yes," she said. "It's awful. Xhea, we should go."

Xhea glanced at her in surprise. Strange and unfamiliar, yes—but awful?

Yet Shai was right; the ghost was beyond her help now, and whatever called to Xhea—whatever made Shai want to turn and run—was nothing they could reach. Time to make her slow way back upstairs and face the consequences that surely waited there; time to sag back into her small cot and stare at the ceiling in hope that sleep might still come before morning.

But still she stared, one hand outstretched before her. For, deep within the barricade, she saw a spot of perfect black.

It was not the dark of light blocked, not here where no light fell; neither was she seeing something black waiting behind. It was the dark of absence, the dark of nothing at all. And it, like something in the space beyond, pulled at her.

Xhea knew with sudden certainty what would happen if she touched the barricade.

Go upstairs, she told herself. *Tell Lorn, tell Mercks, tell—somebody, anybody*. But she did not move. Couldn't. For all that getting here had felt like it had taken all of her energy, she suddenly could not imagine a force great enough to draw her away.

Here, the barricade seemed to say to her. *Here, here, here*.

As if in a dream, Xhea touched the block of concrete before her. It was just a gentle touch—and yet where her fingers brushed the cold concrete, the block began to fall in on itself. Within seconds the heavy chunk had all but crumbled to nothing, as if the shape she'd seen had been nothing more than an empty façade made of sugar and sand. Nothing inside it anymore, only a hollow semblance, collapsing.

She opened her mouth to speak—but only breath came out, thin and shaking. Before her, the reaction to her touch spread like a cigarette burn widening across a sheet of dry paper, faster and faster, leaving only dust and black ash in its wake. Behind, where she had thought to see only more rubble or even the hall beyond, there was only that span of perfect black—widening, now, like a great mouth opening to swallow her down.

Xhea stumbled back and back again as the destruction spread, faster and faster—until it suddenly cascaded. She cried out as the barricade fell in a rush of sound and dust and rubble, raising her hands in a futile attempt to protect her face from the flying debris. The movement was too quick for her precarious balance. She lost her stick and tumbled to the floor.

Shai cast her hands before her and magic rushed out like a wave of sunlight. There was no shape to it, no spell, only pure magic strong enough to keep back the worst of the debris as the dust cloud rushed over them both, fast and stinging.

Curled and cringing on the floor, Xhea tried to scream— but everything was suddenly darkness and dust. Grit tried to force its way beneath her squeezed-tight eyelids. Every breath was dust and ash, her mouth thick with the taste, her ears roaring with the sound, and she choked and gasped.

She could not breathe—oh sweetness, she could not breathe.

Then the dust cloud passed and began to settle, small bits of debris hitting the ground around her like spring hail. Xhea coughed and coughed again, choking up dirt as her eyes streamed tears. For a moment, as her ears rang, she thought she could hear screams—the groan of asphalt and the creak of buckling supports—the rattle of dislodged bricks falling to the broken ground.

Memory. Only memory.

But in that instant, she was nine years old again and outside her apartment on the edge of the ruins, caught in the collapse of the Red Line subway tunnel.

She shook her head, trying to push away the memories and the adrenaline alike; tried to take a breath without choking and slow her heart's frantic beat. Yet it was not only the dust that made her tears flow.

"Xhea," Shai was saying, "Xhea, are you okay? Answer me!"

Xhea wiped her eyes and struggled to sit. Shai hovered before her, attempting to kneel, and fell silent only when Xhea moved. The ghost paused then, clearly caught between hope and despair; she reached out with one shining hand and touched Xhea's cheek as if she might wipe away the tears.

"I'm okay," Xhea murmured. It wasn't strictly true, but true enough; despite the shock and the adrenaline that even now coursed through her, she had added only minor scrapes and bruises to her tally of injuries.

Then she saw the barricade.

It had not, as she'd feared, entirely fallen. Looking at what was left, she almost wished it had.

Where she'd touched—where, so briefly, she'd seen that span of perfect black—there was now a hole bored straight the way through the barricade, taller than a man was high and wider than she could stretch her arms. And not a ragged hole, as one would expect from a tangled pile of junk, but a tunnel straight and neat as if it had been built that way.

Something had tunneled through Edren's barricade, turned it to dust from the inside out and left only the barest façade to cover the damage. Xhea could even see pieces—a sheet of metal, a heavy chair's ruined frame—that were only half-crumbled. She had the feeling that if she were to touch them, she would find them as strong and stable as the rest of the barrier itself; aged and rusted, yes, but far more resilient than anything a small girl could destroy with a touch.

Of the rest there was only dust.

"Can you stand?" Shai asked. Xhea nodded. "Then I think we need to go."

From the stairs far behind them came the echo-garbled sound of someone calling Xhea's name—but it was not that that made Xhea agree, but the feeling that grew the longer she stared at the damaged barricade. Again she felt the desire to step beyond—but now, beneath that desire, there was something else. The hairs on the back of her neck rose.

There was someone out in the darkness of the underground. Someone watching. Someone waiting.

The abandoned shopping corridors and subway tunnels that wound beneath the Lower City had always been hers and hers alone. Not anymore. Her magic shifted weakly within her, thin wisps curling and coiling at the thought.

"Have you seen my stick?" Xhea asked softly.

"Here."

Xhea retrieved it from beneath the heavy covering of debris and made her careful way to her feet. Shai only stared at the barricade and the empty hall beyond, her hands clasped and pressed hard to her stomach, her feet hovering a good six inches from the floor.

"We really need to leave," Shai said with growing urgency.

"Agreed." Xhea turned her back on the destruction, attempting to ignore the prickle between her shoulder blades. From Edren's main level the shouting increased, the sound of her name replaced by loud commands that she return.

Xhea sighed and limped as fast as she was able.

"Come on," she said. "Let's go meet the welcoming party."

It was only once they'd left the shopping corridor and returned to the hall that Xhea felt her shoulders loosen. No urge to turn anymore; no desire to walk beyond the barricade's protection. No feeling of unseen eyes on her.

A glance at Shai confirmed her suspicions. While the ghost still looked anxious, concern pinching the corners of her mouth, that restless energy was gone now—if not forgotten.

Shai met her eyes. "You know how I keep telling you to get up and actually do something?"

"Maybe once or twice, yeah."

A hint of a smile touched Shai's lips, only to vanish as she glanced behind them. "I think I take it back."

When at last they could see the base of the two sets of downward sweeping stairs from Edren's main level—and when the shouting from the top of those stairs had begun to deafen her—Xhea called out.

"I'm here," she shouted, then had to pause, coughing. She was going to be spitting dust for days.

There was a brief pause, then: "Xhea." The woman who spoke wasn't loud, but the sound carried nonetheless. Xhea cringed; she recognized the speaker all too well. "Are you injured?"

"No more than before."

"Then would you please join us?" The words were quiet, polite, but there was nothing soft about them.

"Working on it." She heard the sullen note that crept into her tone—and hated it.

Xhea looked up the stairs as they approached, noticing for the first time that a man stood partway down the flight, already closer to the lower level than he was to the top. Mercks. He clutched the railing with one pale-knuckled hand and stared down at her, eyes tight with concentration. As she watched, a rivulet of sweat ran down his temple. Xhea had to crush the sudden urge to apologize; she hadn't forced him down the stairs.

"Man," Xhea said, meeting his eyes and refusing to flinch away, "did you ever pick the short straw."

She hit the first stair and began the laborious process of hauling herself up, grabbing the railing with her left hand and her stick with the right. She wanted to just sit and push herself up backward one dirty tread at a time—but there was a crowd at the top of the stairs, and she'd be blighted if she was going to let them watch her crawl.

After all, it's only pain.

Xhea didn't look up until she reached the ground level, a sweating Mercks at her side, and even then she didn't speak. Couldn't. It was all she could do to keep breathing.

A woman waited at the top of the stairs, a small crowd of security and hastily woken officials spread behind her. She watched Xhea with careful, considering eyes.

"Sit," she said at last, gesturing. Xhea sagged onto the stairs leading up to the ballrooms, heedless of the dirt she left on the confetti-strewn carpet.

"I assume," the woman said, "that you went underground with good reason."

It was not sarcasm. Xhea looked up and up to meet the woman's eyes.

Emara Pol-Edren was tall, easily over six feet, and her whipcord-thin build was hard with muscle. She was dressed simply, casually, as if she'd been awake and working when summoned. And she had been summoned, of that Xhea had no doubt; Emara stood with the unthinking confidence of someone in charge. She managed much of the skyscraper's internal affairs, and though she wasn't in security's chain of command, that didn't change the way everyone hung on every quiet word she spoke.

"Yes," Xhea said. "Or reason enough. What I found was worse." She rubbed the sweat and dust from her forehead, then held her dirt-caked hand before her like an offering.

"This is your barricade," Xhea said, "or what's left of it."

The crowd reacted—cursing, rushing to monitors, turning to each other in dismay. Emara did not. She only stared at Xhea as if their gazes had become locked; Xhea could read the questions there as clearly as if Emara had shouted. She wanted to shout, Xhea saw, though only the tightness in her jaw hinted at the anger that boiled beneath.

"It wasn't me," Xhea said softly—so soft that even Shai, hovering by her left shoulder, could not hear. "I swear to you, this time it wasn't me."

"You will tell me everything," Emara said.

Question, command—it was all the same in the end.

Chapter Three

Xhea was allowed a quick bath and brought fresh clothes before being led to a small meeting room and grilled for what felt like forever. Before dawn broke, Xhea had told her story more times than she could count; more times, it seemed, than should have been possible in the dark hours before morning. She understood the need, even as she resented it.

The ghost and his strange behavior was her problem and Shai's, if it was anyone's—but the barricade? Its presence, and now its sudden absence, was critical to all of Edren, if only for what its loss might portend. She knew it, even though the last war in the Lower City was only a story to her told in pieces: in rumor and word of absent friends; in half-spoken tales and remembrances that trailed away to nothing; in decade-old blood feuds that even now led to harsh words, drawn knives, and worse in the Lower City's streets. Its devastation could still be seen in the scars on the walls of the underground passages—the cracked tile and black scorch marks. It was the reason for the creation of the underground barricades that protected the skyscrapers, one from the other.

The war had seen desperate days, its battles far fiercer than the combats of blade and magic that Edren sponsored within the walls of its arena. No one wanted a return to those days—or so it had been assumed. The hole said otherwise.

So Xhea told the story again and again—to Edren's head of security and his note-taking assistant, to first one Edren council member then another—dragging details from her exhausted mind and trying to sound respectful. Failing miserably at the latter, despite her honest attempts. Through it all, Emara Pol-Edren watched, noting details and asking quiet questions about seeming inconsistencies in Xhea's telling.

Soon not even Shai's patient prompting was enough to keep Xhea going; the ghost's echoes of the interviewers' questions seemed as indecipherable as the originals. Xhea's next dose of painkillers was more than welcome—as was the oblivion it brought in the wake of pain's ease. For the first time in recent memory, she did not have to fight for sleep.

Xhea woke with a headache, a dry mouth, and Shai standing over her. She blinked, pushing sleep away. For a moment it seemed that she could still hear the dead man's voice, reverberating from dream or memory.

Run away.

"They'll need you soon."

Shivering, Xhea nodded, rubbed the sleep from her eyes, and worked on standing. Dressing usually took the longest. She reached for a clean set of the loose cotton clothes—little more than pajamas—that Edren supplied. She'd worn these clothes, or ones so similar as to be nearly identical, since the day Lorn had brought her to the skyscraper on a stretcher, hurt and delirious, a distressed ghost by her side. Today she hesitated. Instead, she reached toward a folded pile of clothes long ignored on the shelf.

Long, dark pants with pockets down both legs. A light tank top as an undershirt, a heavier long-sleeved shirt on top. And a too large jacket, worn and oft-mended, with pockets on the inside and out, each filled with countless small treasures.

Warmer clothes, she thought, than she needed in the summer heat. Yet something in her eased as the jacket's weight settled across her shoulders. Shai had told her that the oversized jacket made her look smaller and younger than she was, but Xhea didn't care; it was hers.

Dressed in her old clothes, Xhea took a deep breath, sat up straighter, and smiled.

"Welcome back," Shai said softly.

Xhea looked toward the ghost, who hovered now on the small room's far side, complex patterns of magic flickering between her upraised hands like pyrotechnic fireflies. She did not pretend to misunderstand.

"Was I really so bad?" Xhea looked at her walking stick, turning it over and over in her hands.

"Well," Shai said, "never so bad that I actually murdered you. Though I came close, once or twice."

"Abelane used to tell me that I was an insufferable patient."

"Nothing's really changed." But Shai laughed as she said it.

The summons arrived shortly thereafter. "Could be worse," Xhea said when she'd read the note. "We're to go to an office on the twelfth floor at our earliest convenience."

"We? It mentions me?" Shai asked incredulously. She dropped her hands and the magic she'd held flickered as it faded to nothing.

"Yes, actually." Xhea tightened her brace, grabbed her stick, and stood. She winced as she steadied herself; her legs ached, and her arms—and not just from the new bruises from when the barricade had come down. No, she felt the ache of overworked muscles. *Soft and lazy*, she mocked herself in silence, and knew her taunts were nothing but the truth. Well, no more.

She looked up to meet Shai's surprised expression.

"Come on," she said, "it's not as if they don't know you're here. You're practically fueling the whole skyscraper." Fueling it without thought or intent. There were no spells that bound Shai to Edren, as there had been to her home Tower, Allenai; no attempt had been made to capture her for her power, as rival Tower Eridian had tried when it had abducted Shai's spirit. Yet even the faintest brush of her power against Edren's collecting spells—a pause by a magical storage coil, a walk by spelled wires—poured more magic into the skyscraper than Edren's citizens could ever provide.

"Knowing and acknowledging are different," Shai said shortly. "The summons was from Lorn, then?"

"No." Lorn Edren was the only person to have introduced himself to Shai that Xhea had witnessed. Yet despite seeing to Xhea's care and comfort—providing, even at its most basic, a level of security that she had never before known—her sometime-ally had been notably absent. She'd tried not to take that absence personally. She just hadn't tried very hard.

"Not Lorn," she said. "His wife."

Xhea made her slow way through Edren's back halls, past the main kitchen toward what had once been the rear service elevator. The halls were busier than she was used to, citizens scurrying about on tasks that she couldn't begin to fathom; yet to a one, they stepped aside to let her pass.

"I think my reputation precedes me," Xhea murmured. But then, she was used to people shying away from her as if she were poison. She kept her shoulders square and stared straight ahead, allowing the passers-by to continue on their way without feeling the need to meet her eyes.

"I think they're just trying not to knock over the tiny limping girl with the cane," Shai replied.

The service elevator was Edren's only elevator that ran entirely on mechanical parts. Her magic was no more than a whisper of dark, but even so, Xhea didn't trust herself not to short out something vital in the other lifts' workings. She could imagine many horrible things, but few beat the visceral terror of falling to her death in a magic-glitched elevator cage.

Yet when she turned the corner, it was to find the elevator cordoned off, its doors open to an empty shaft, and the sound of someone working in the darkness below. Xhea shouted over the sound of metal clanging.

"Take the stairs!" a voice called back. "Not going to be done for hours."

"Of course," Xhea muttered and made her way to the fire exit stairs. No dramatic sweeping staircase, these: they were bare concrete with a cold metal railing so often peeled and repainted that its surface rippled.

"Twelve floors. That's not so bad, right?"

Shai wisely stayed silent.

By the second flight, Shai began to ask questions—mostly, Xhea thought, to stop Xhea's incessant swearing.

"Lorn's wife—that's the woman from last night? The tall one?"

Xhea made a noise that was part laugh, part gasp as she hauled herself to the next landing. "The one and only."

"It seemed like you . . ." Shai hesitated, paused, and tried again. "It seemed like she knew you."

Xhea smiled—a pained, unhappy smile—because that right there was the heart of it.

"She visited you twice, you know," Shai said.

"When was this?" Xhea asked in surprise.

"Right after your surgery, when you were drugged. She didn't say anything to you, either. Just . . . watched."

Probably wanted to stab me in the neck. It was a thought best kept behind closed lips.

"This is not my first time in Edren," she said at last. She grabbed the railing and hauled herself upward. One step. Another.

"You don't mean when Lorn sheltered you during the night. Before that."

Xhea nodded, and Shai's brows drew down as she considered, attempting to find the words and meaning that Xhea couldn't quite say. Explaining was going to be hard, Xhea realized. She glanced around, seeing only painted breezeblock walls and bare concrete steps, and wishing she were in the tunnels nonetheless. Somewhere truly safe, with no possible risk of being overheard.

But while Shai could say whatever she wanted, Xhea had no way to make her words inaudible. She never used to worry about others' reactions when she spoke to ghosts. Truth be told, she'd rarely been around anyone long enough for them to hear more than a random sentence or two— when she'd bothered to speak to the ghosts in her care at all. Shai had changed that; Shai, and being stuck and largely immobile in a skyscraper, with the same people around her in the same halls.

And there were things that she had sworn never to speak aloud.

"You said that Edren owed you a favor, one from before I met you," Shai said at last. "You never told me how you earned that favor."

Xhea grinned. "Got it in one."

"A secret," Shai said slowly, considering. "And it had to involve a ghost, or why would Lorn have called you?"

Except it hadn't been Lorn at all.

"Oh, everyone knows that story," Xhea said, seemingly in response to a question that Shai hadn't actually asked. She leaned against the railing on the landing for balance and tried to catch her breath. Four floors—only eight to go. It seemed a small impossibility.

"The Edren family had two sons: Lorn and his elder brother Addis." Even saying the name felt strange now, so long had she kept it behind her teeth. "Lorn was wilder, then. He made a name for himself in the arena." She laughed, and gripped the railing again. "Made a name for himself in the streets, too: a man who celebrated as hard as he fought."

"That . . . doesn't sound much like the Lorn I met."

"Indeed." Xhea forced herself to keep climbing. "Addis was the quiet one. Smart, studious, good with magic—and first in line to inherit Edren's rule. Addis was as different from his brother as it was possible to be. He even had a wife: Emara Pol, arena champion and daughter of Edren's famous wartime general."

"Emara was Addis's wife?" Shai asked sharply. "But you said—"

Xhea continued as if there had been no interruption, hauling herself up another step. "One day, Lorn was injured in the arena—a deep cut to the leg with a blade spelled to speed bleeding. Illegal as hell, of course, but he wasn't in any shape to argue. Within hours, he fell unconscious and couldn't be woken.

"The same day, Addis became ill and was given a sickbed beside his brother. Rumor has it that he fell into some kind of coma."

Xhea rested again on a landing, breath hissing through her teeth. Her knee felt like a living thing inside its brace, grown large against the bars of its cage and beating fruitlessly to be free. Even her good leg ached, protesting such treatment. She spoke past the pain, forcing a casual tone: "Addis died of his illness, and of course Lorn awoke. To know more, I guess you would have had to be there."

Shai frowned in thought.

Xhea looked at the next flight of stairs, while every part of her screamed to stay still and never move again. "Of course," she added, "the experience changed Lorn. He left the arena behind, and the parties, and started training to rule the skyscraper. Trying, some say, to be more like his brother."

He's quieter now, she thought. *More studious. He even has a wife.* Willing Shai to make the connection that Xhea could not speak aloud.

"And you were there," Shai said. "So which one of them was a ghost?"

Xhea climbed in silence for a time.

"I was thinking," she said. "Given the choice, would I rather walk again without this blighted brace, or banish all stairs forever?" Xhea hit her stick against a banister and listened to the metallic reverberation echo down the stairwell. "I think I'd say both."

A hesitation, then Shai asked softly, "Both?"

"Both."

Shai's next question was one that Xhea didn't expect: "When did Emara marry Lorn?"

"Within a year." It was a well-known scandal, though anyone smart would never mention it within Emara's earshot. Her disdain of the hard partying, lustful natures, and violent tendencies so often seen in other arena fighters was notorious and sharp enough to cut. But then she married Lorn. "Most figure she wanted to maintain her power within the skyscraper. If not one brother, then the other."

The last few words were difficult to speak past her panting breaths. Sweat rolled freely down Xhea's cheeks and back, her hands shook, and her dry throat felt raw. She clutched the railing, leaned heavily against her stick, and hauled herself up. One step. Another. Another and another until she died.

And oh, she had no desire to meet the woman waiting at the other end of this journey.

"Lorn is Addis, isn't he?" Shai said. "That's what you're trying to tell me. Lorn is Addis's ghost in Lorn's body."

"Yes."

Shai stopped and stared at her from above. For a moment the light of her magic, that steady warm glow, seemed to flicker; shadows danced around them, as uncertain as the look on Shai's face.

"But he's . . . normal," Shai whispered. "How is that even possible?"

It was true: Lorn was not incapacitated, like the resurrected Radiants used to fuel the Towers above; not trapped and helpless within a foreign shell of flesh. But there was no gossip Xhea could tell, no hints or words that she could share that would guide Shai to understand that part of the story—and so Xhea only shook her head.

Shai was silent the rest of the climb.

"I am officially over stairs," Xhea announced to the young man guarding Emara's office door.

He blinked. "If you say so." He ushered her into the room and closed the door behind her.

Emara's office was small, with an attached bathroom—about what Xhea expected given the skyscraper's origins. A curtained window in the far wall let in daylight and provided a glimpse of the City above, the floating Towers, and the cloudless sky beyond. Emara herself sat at a desk that was nearly invisible beneath a weight of paper and boxes, a cobbled-together monitor flickering on the desk's far edge. Her dark hair, streaked with gray, was in thick braids that wrapped around her head like a victor's crown. A frizzy crown, now: escaping wisps formed an uneven halo about her face.

No crossed blades on the wall. No mounted knives; no trophies; no pictures of a younger Emara in the arena, arms raised, triumphant. But then weapons hardly went with the peeling floral wallpaper.

Emara looked up. She had her father's sharp features and dusky skin, with fine freckles spotting her nose and cheekbones like an afterthought. Her eyes, shadowed by short lashes, seemed to see everything and reveal nothing. It was uncomfortable to stand beneath that gaze, Xhea thought, as Emara's attention came to rest upon her. But what was a little more discomfort, a little more pain?

Emara looked Xhea up and down, clearly taking in the changes in her attire. "Well," she said, "perhaps this won't be quite as difficult as I thought."

Xhea shrugged and reached for the nearest chair without invitation, dragging it toward her and collapsing against the hard seat. She was still trying to slow her breathing.

"For you or for me?"

Instead of answering, Emara turned away and half closed her eyes as she reached one hand before her. A moment and she turned, face slightly upraised as if seeking the sun; another moment and she turned again.

"Ah," Emara murmured. Her eyes snapped open and she stared in Shai's general direction. "There you are. Hello."

Shai blinked. "She can't see me, can she?"

"No," Xhea said.

"No," Emara echoed. "I can't see you, if that's what you're asking. But I can feel you there, just a little. Thank you for coming."

"I, well—tell her you're welcome, I guess," Shai said, flustered. Xhea passed along the message.

Emara was far too magic-poor to see the light that Shai cast, unless the ghost radiated into the visual spectrum, and none but Xhea could truly see the ghost—Xhea and the night walkers, the mindless, once-human creatures that walked the Lower City's streets in darkness. Yet most could feel a ghost: a disturbance in the air, a feeling of cold or pressure, the unnerving sense that someone unseen was watching. Most dismissed such feelings as imagination or nerves—until they had been haunted themselves. Even so, most haunted individuals waited weeks, months, sometimes even years before admitting that the strange sensations were anything other than the effects of grief or nerves or flat-out craziness.

Xhea leaned back in her chair and crossed her arms, attempting with practiced nonchalance to hide her discomfort. The chair's hard wooden rails dug into her shoulder blades.

"So," she said, breaking the silence. "I made it here. What new questions do you have for me?"

Emara smiled thinly. "Actually, this isn't about your adventures yesterday. I wanted to talk about you—you and Shai both."

Xhea raised an eyebrow.

"First I wanted to discuss your healing process. You're actually up during the day and properly dressed, which is good to see, though your continued struggles to walk are somewhat concerning. I spoke with your medic. She feels that by now your healing should have advanced to the point where you no longer need the cane."

Oh, yes, Xhea could suddenly see where this conversation was going. Emara thought she was faking it— or, at the very least, exaggerating her pain and difficulties far beyond their true boundaries. And why not? Meals and a bed with fresh sheets, access to showers and bathrooms, not to mention the free meds—few could imagine that she'd want anything more. Fewer still would believe that she'd come to like the tunnels, the freedom and the safety that they provided.

Xhea just shrugged. "Easy for her to say. She hasn't so much as looked at my knee since the cast came off."

"Why should she? Her work is done; the rest is up to you."

"I can barely walk!"

"That doesn't impress me, Xhea. I've seen your injuries— I've *had* injuries like yours."

Xhea snorted. "Oh, are we bonding now? Is this where we show each other our scars, and you tell me just how much you understand how it feels to be me?"

"No," Emara said, leaning back as she stared steadily at Xhea. "This is where you stop acting like a fool—or so I'd hoped. This is where you realize that being helpless and unable to walk is the last thing you need right now."

"Do you think I haven't been *trying*?" Xhea shouted. Her anger came fast and sudden, and again she felt her magic stir deep with her: a bare whisper, but there.

"No, I know you've been trying. You just haven't been trying enough." Before Xhea could speak, Emara leaned forward again onto her desk's cluttered surface. "The healing spells don't work well for you, I get that. But I also know that you've spent most of your time in your room. You haven't been doing your exercises, and *yes*," she said, speaking over Xhea's protest, "they hurt. I know. But you can't tell me that there's nothing more you could have done—that you've given recovery your full effort and attention."

Xhea glared.

"Shai?" Emara looked in the ghost's direction. "Am I wrong? You would know better than I."

"You know she's not wrong, Xhea," Shai said softly. Xhea ignored her.

"Why do you even care?" she asked dismissively. "Let's not pretend that you've suddenly become overwhelmed with concern for my health and well-being."

Emara smiled, and something about that thin, tight-lipped expression made Xhea realize how truly exhausted the woman looked.

"Because we need you."

Xhea drew back at that, surprised. She caught herself a moment later. She couldn't undo the reaction, but she made her face relax, made herself sag back into the chair's uncomfortable embrace.

"So? Or better yet, why? If this is another attempt at an indenture contract, I swear—"

"Stop it." Only weariness in that voice, now; no command. "You know that's not what I meant."

"Then what?"

Emara looked from Xhea to the space where Shai hovered and back again, then sighed and ran a hand across her face. "You tell me," she said at last. "Have you considered the effects of Shai's presence here? At the current rate, Shai produces more magic in a day than Edren's dedicated citizenship does in eight months."

"But—but I'm not even tied to Edren," Shai protested, echoing Xhea's own thoughts; Xhea repeated the words for them both.

"I know that," Emara said quietly. "Imagine if you were. Imagine if you spent only one day generating power on Edren's behalf. Believe me when I say that the magic—the currency—you could provide is absolutely beyond anything we've ever had in the Lower City. It almost is already, and you're not even trying."

"I won't do it." Shai spoke firmly—or tried to. Only Xhea could hear that attempt fail as Shai's voice trembled.

Unhearing, Emara continued. "We've tried to suppress word of your presence here, Xhea, and rumors of even Shai's existence—but there is only so much we can do. Neither of you is a secret anymore, not in Edren—and people talk."

Xhea knew the truth in that. It was all too easy to imagine the rumors that spread from Edren like ripples across water: speculation between friends, drunken musings in the stands at the arena, conversations overheard in the market.

"The other skyscrapers have noticed," Xhea said, her voice bleak. "They've noticed, and they want Shai for their own."

"No," Shai protested. "Not again. I am not a thing to be possessed." She looked from Emara to Xhea and back again, her eyes wild as her voice rose in pitch. "Xhea, tell her—I'm not letting anyone do that to me again. They can't—"

Xhea reached for Shai's hand; caught it, the pressure of their conflicting magics feeling almost like real touch. "She knows. I know. We're going to make sure nothing like that ever happens to you again." She turned, directing those last words at Emara.

Oh, really? asked a vicious voice in the silence of her mind. *How are you going to stop them?* Barely able to walk, near incapacitated by pain and painkillers in turn, her strange magic but a whisper of dark. *If another skyscraper wanted to steal Shai—if Edren wanted to use her—what could you possibly do to stop them?*

She had but to glance at Emara's face to see that the woman knew the course of her thoughts—and that Xhea's mind had made her point more eloquently than she ever could.

"I'm not asking to enslave you, Shai," Emara said. "I'm not even asking for your service. Just think, both of you. Think what that power—what even the *potential* for that power—could do here, in the Lower City. In the hands of a single skyscraper."

"But—" Xhea started. Stopped.

Emara looked at her, steady, unblinking.

"War," Xhea said at last. Breath and word alike seemed to catch in her throat; she swallowed. "It would mean war."

No, she thought, even as she spoke the words. Clinging to denial, even if it was only in the darkened confines of her mind. But the continuance of the Lower City's delicate political balance in the face of so much power was the lie, war the seemingly inevitable reality.

What had Lorn told her when he rescued her from the ruins? The words came back to her as if from a dream. *"You don't understand what you've done, do you? You've brought a Radiant—a true Radiant—to the Lower City. Everything is about to change."*

She had expected change; had wondered over it as she lay, mind muddled with pain meds, and stared at the ceiling of her room. But change for her own life, change for Shai, change even for Edren. She had never let herself think beyond that. Had never tried.

Now she closed her eyes, suddenly unable to look at Emara's expression, or Shai's confusion and concern. Her mind whirled, thoughts turning over themselves so quickly that it was all she could do to keep from reaching out to grab the edge of Emara's desk, cling to it for dear life, and wait for the foundations to stop spinning.

Except that was the heart of it, wasn't it? Two months Shai had stayed with her in Edren—two months with the skyscraper growing stronger and richer. Two months for the other skyscrapers to notice, to plan, and to begin to act against them. For what could the careful destruction of Edren's barricade presage but an attack? An assassin, sabotage, a bomb—*something*. Stories from the last Lower City war whirled through her mind, their distant horrors suddenly all too real.

We could just go, Xhea thought suddenly. *Both of us— just vanish into the underground again.* Shai's power didn't have to go into anyone's coffers, especially not if these were the consequences. And yes, Xhea's injuries would pose a problem, but it was a problem she was already facing, even without that freedom. With Shai's help, she didn't have to scrounge and starve; together, they could build a life for themselves.

Yet that too was a lie, though a seductive one. It took her a long moment to consider, turn the tempting thought over in her mind, and push it away.

Though they might not give Shai's magic to any skyscraper willingly, each had collecting spells to gather any free power, most notably run-off from the City above. Even being careful, Shai's magic would be collected and their every move—the shops they frequented, the buildings they passed—would become a political action. At least with Edren's protection they might have more choice in what magic was given and how it was used—or was that, too, a seductive lie?

Besides, for all that Xhea had lived for years underground, it was beyond foolish to imagine that she could recreate that reality now with Shai at her side. Few had ventured below because there was little of sufficient value to justify the trip. Yet the skyscrapers had used the underground in their war, forcing themselves through the fear and discomfort and pain to use those tunnels as a method of attack and assassination. What would stop them from pursuing Shai and the almost incomprehensible magic she represented? And not just the skyscrapers: if anyone knew that the greatest treasure in the Lower City existed in the underground, a near limitless source of power and wealth, what would keep them from hunting Shai?

Shai, and the only person in the Lower City who could see her, speak to her, and convince her to do another's bidding. *Or*, Xhea thought darkly, *to be used as leverage.*

No, the underground wouldn't be a refuge, but a trap. Besieged, she couldn't imagine how they could last longer than mere months—and only that if they were clever, beyond lucky, and Xhea had full use of her leg.

Had they thought it was difficult to flee two Towers? Powerful as Allenai and Eridian were, there had only been the two of them, attempting to operate in something resembling secrecy. She could not imagine what she and Shai would do with all of the Lower City arrayed against them.

Xhea took a deep breath and opened her eyes. Across from her, Emara waited, hands folded atop the mountainous surface of her desk. She nodded as she met Xhea's gaze; nodded, Xhea thought, at the changes she could only imagine were written across her expression.

Still, intuition prodded her. "There's more, isn't there?"

"There's always more," Emara said softly. "Edren's council has been in session since early this morning. I've come to prepare you to face the Council, if you're willing to help."

"Why?" Xhea asked. But she knew why they needed her; of course she knew. "I'm the only way you can speak to Shai."

Emara inclined her head. "There is that. But also you can go underground without difficulty or preparation. Do you see why I need you to be able to walk? It took you nearly 45 minutes to respond to my summons. But if you were healthy again, or closer to it, I cannot stress enough the value that would have."

Xhea stared. She wanted—suddenly, desperately—to believe Emara's words and the reality they created; she was surprised at the intensity of that desire. To be wanted not for her knack with ghosts, but for the very thing that had made her outcast. Weakest of the weak, poorest of the poor, no way to contribute to the skyscraper's coffers, always costing more than she could generate. *That* was what Edren suddenly valued?

"Without you," Emara added softly, "we wouldn't have known that the barricade was being taken down—not until we were under attack. We grew careless, negligent, hard as that is to admit."

Xhea shook her head, forcing her thoughts back to reality. "Without me," she said, "without Shai, there would be no reason for the attack."

"Perhaps," Emara said. "Or perhaps it was inevitable. We don't know when the dismantling began, don't know the condition of the other skyscrapers' barricades. But you could tell us faster than anyone."

"Xhea," Shai said, and her hand brushed Xhea's upper arm. "This could be your chance for something good to—"

Unable to hear Shai, Emara continued. "There is also the question of your other abilities, whatever they might prove to be. Lorn has told no one of your own power—"

"No one but you, you mean."

A brief smile. "Indeed. But even so, if your magic returns—"

There was a knock at the door. At the sound, a mask seemed to slam down over Emara's features; Xhea hadn't realized the change in the woman until suddenly that stern visage looked back at her once more. Emara called for the person to enter.

Her young assistant came inside. "They're asking for you in Council, ma'am," he said, ignoring Xhea.

"I'll be right there." Emara gave a curt nod. "Xhea, will you accompany me?"

So much weight in that question; so many things left unasked, unanswered; so many consequences she had barely begun to consider. She glanced at Shai and saw the same emotions in her expression, fear and hope and something that was almost like resignation.

Xhea nodded, not trusting herself to speak, and reached for her walking stick. Again she heard the ghost's voice, so clear in her memory it felt that she had but to turn to see him.

Run away. Run away. Run away.

If only she could. She rose and slowly followed Emara from the room.

Chapter Four

In the Council meeting room, an argument was already in full swing. A dull roar was audible in the hallway; even so, Xhea stumbled back as the door opened, wincing at the assault.

Sounds just like the summertime market. Goods at their most plentiful, haggling at its fiercest, and tempers heating as quickly as the sunbaked asphalt. *Smells better, though.* Xhea tightened her grip on her stick, squared her shoulders, and limped forward.

"Councilors, my apologies for the delay." Emara entered the room with Xhea at her heels and Shai unseen behind them. Something in her calm, quiet voice cut through the shouting with the ease of a well-honed knife; in the wake of her words, her footsteps echoed through the suddenly quiet room.

Xhea glanced around the table. Lorn, she knew: a large, dark-skinned man with tattooed arms and handsome features that even now made women across the Lower City sigh after him and shout coarse jokes. Lorn glanced from his wife to Xhea and away just as swiftly. His voice had been among the loudest raised, she realized; the true Lorn had often shouted, even though Addis had not. *Appearances have to be maintained*, she thought wryly; but something about the joke seemed unfunny, even in the privacy of her own mind.

To Lorn's left, at the head of the table, sat a man who could only be his father, Verrus Edren, ruler of the skyscraper that bore the family name. She could see in that hard and weathered face something of Lorn and Addis both. The resemblance was little obscured by the man's close-shorn gray hair, or the deep wrinkles carved into the flesh around his eyes and mouth and forehead—lines that seemed worn there by every expression but a smile. It was his eyes that caught Xhea's attention: darker than his skin, they seemed almost black to her vision, black and hard like smoke-stained iron.

On Verrus Edren's other side was an absurdly tall man that Xhea knew by reputation alone: Pol. He was head of the arena, its business and its battles, and had been Edren's wartime general, known as a genius of the embattled streets. He was also Emara's father. Pol was often cited as the reason that Edren had not fallen ten years earlier, when the once-strong alliance between Edren and neighboring skyscraper Orren was broken. Yet no matter his former glory, since the war he was seldom seen outside the arena that he now managed on Edren's behalf.

Even sitting, Pol towered above Verrus, casting a shadow on the more powerful man and the son at his side. He was, Xhea thought, oddly suited to the monosyllabic name by which he was known; and if there was more to him or that name than was spoken of in Lower City gossip, she had heard neither.

Behind him was a small video monitor on a rolling stand, seemingly forgotten in the corner. Its flickering light cast harsh-edged shadows across the council table. Xhea knew a few others around that table, mostly from the seemingly endless interviews in the morning's early hours. The horse-faced councilor and his wire-thin assistant, the councilor with the cloud-pale hair, and, beside her, the one with the unfortunately nasal voice. None more than glanced at Xhea; bigger things at play here than the girl who could see ghosts. Even so, Xhea had to fight the urge to hunch her shoulders, as if making herself even smaller could dispel her discomfort or banish her sudden uncertainty.

Sweetness, what am I doing here?

Shai came to stand at her side, the ghost a glow in her peripheral vision. Xhea took a breath and let it out slowly, willing her heart to slow.

"Your seat, councilor." Verrus gestured to a vacant chair midway down the table. "The child may stand by the wall," he added, already turning away.

"Xhea has an injured knee," Emara said, cutting short the nasal-voiced councilor who had begun speaking into the silence. Xhea wished she could sink through the floor and away. "We requested her presence at this meeting. The least we can do is provide her a chair."

Verrus looked up slowly. "If you wish to stand in her stead, by all means." Concrete was more forgiving than that voice.

Xhea grabbed the edge of Emara's sleeve.

"Don't," she said. "It's fine."

Emara shook her head and made to drag her chair toward the back of the room. Her face was a perfect mask, but something in the way Emara's hands curled made Xhea think she wished she could reach for knives.

"Please," Xhea whispered; the word felt strange in her mouth. "I'll be fine, really."

Emara acquiesced with obvious reluctance, and Xhea leaned against the far wall. The conversation resumed quickly, centering on Edren's response to the threat implied by the barricade's removal. The room seemed split between calls for a quick offensive stance and continued denials while they sought more information.

Others speculated on the possible source of the attack, pointing fingers, it seemed, at each of the other four skyscrapers in turn. Someone referenced the dark history between Edren and Orren—history enough, it seemed, that an attack from that quarter was not wholly unexpected. Xhea perked up at this bit of information. It wasn't hard to believe in Orren's treachery.

Debate raged about the possible motives of Rown and Farrow. Rown was the poorest of the skyscrapers, desperate for more magic, while their reputation as an unstable political entity had been well earned in recent years. Listening to what the councilors did not say, it seemed to Xhea that they expected attack—or retaliation—from that quarter; it was only that the planning and foresight evident in weakening Edren's barricade hardly seemed Rown's style.

Retaliation, Xhea wondered, *for what?*

In contrast, Farrow—the richest and most independent of the skyscrapers—might have an entirely different motive for wanting a Radiant's power. Farrow was the Lower City's magic-merchant, home to many of the most powerful spellcasters on the ground, and the ones who had trained many more—for a price. It was one thing to have magic and the power, real and political, that accompanied it.

Farrow knew how to use that magic in ways that none of the other skyscrapers could hope to achieve.

Of the four, only Senn was more ally than potential enemy. With a recent trade agreement for food and lesser entertainments in the arena, Senn stood more to gain from cooperation with Edren than from attack. Besides, Senn's hold on the Lower City market—and the majority of the materials-trading contracts with the few Towers who deigned to do business with those on the ground—would be most destabilized with the return of conflict to the streets. While the last war had allowed Senn to consolidate its hold on the central territories, including the ancient mall that housed the market, renewed warfare could only damage its profits and risk the loss of much of the power that the skyscraper had attained in recent years.

Pol, Xhea noted, remained silent throughout the debates, as animated as a stone carving. If anything, his look was one of anger and disdain; and he leaned away from the table and Verrus Edren both.

As the conversation continued, Xhea shifted against the wall and attempted to hide her discomfort. Her whispered assurances to Emara had been but lies: her knee was a hot pain, her leg muscles ached, and she yearned for her next dose of painkillers the way she used to want the sweet hit of bright magic. Oh, for that numbness, limbs and mind alike turned hazy and indistinct—a barrier through which pain could not pierce. Pity the pills brought her no color; she struggled to remember what red looked like, or green, or blue.

A trickle of sweat ran down her cheek, and her fingers shook as she brushed it away. No, she was not fine. It was pride that made her stand. Pride that kept her upright despite her growing tremors; pride, and nearly pride alone,

that kept her from fleeing this too small council room and its
stuffy air as ever-louder words washed over her like waves.

Standing was salve, too, for her pride—knowing that
Verrus had taken her worth and dismissed it in the same
glance. He had made her stand—wanting to make her look
weak; wanting her to be at his mercy, or Emara's. Wanting
her to beg for the small comfort of a chair.

She refused.

Instead, Xhea looked toward the video forgotten in the
corner. The quality was poor, grainy and flickering, taken
by a night-vision camera. It took a moment to make out the
picture: a wide corridor with something dark at the end. A
familiar corridor, Xhea realized, with fake trees and benches
down the center. The darkness at the end was the barricade.

"Look," she whispered to Shai, and watched herself step
into the frame.

It had to be her, for all that the blurry image showed few
details. The figure's limp was clear enough, as was her mass
of braid-tangled hair. Yet that person seemed so small, so
inconsequential, one tiny person alone in the dark.

Neither ghost was visible, nor was Shai's light. Xhea
watched her image limp down the corridor in a direct line
to the barricade; watched herself pause, reach out—and
stop. That was when the ghost had been pulled away,
and yet even to her it looked different. It looked like she had
been about to touch the barricade.

She stared, a sinking feeling in her stomach, knowing what
came next. In the video, her grainy self stared unmoving for
a long moment. There was no way to hear what she said to
Shai, no glimpse of her face; only the unexpressive expanse
of her back and the slight movement of her charm-bound
hair. At last her image lifted her hand once more, reached
farther, and touched the barricade. For a moment, nothing.

Silence, stillness—not even a glimpse of the slow crumbling of the concrete block that had stood before her. Then a cloud of dust and debris billowed outward, obscuring Xhea's image and filling the corridor entirely.

The image flickered and went dark. The video loop began again.

"Well," she muttered under her breath. "That looks bad."

As she looked away from the screen, Xhea realized the room had fallen silent and the councilors, one and all, were turned toward her. Desperately she cast her mind back, trying to recall the echoes of a question that she had not truly heard.

"Verrus Edren asked what you thought of the video," Shai prompted.

Xhea turned to meet Verrus's iron-dark eyes, the clink of her hair the only sound. Lies or misdirection—neither would work with this man, and his was the only opinion that counted.

Step lightly. Her sweaty hand tightened around her walking stick.

"It looks like I knew where to touch to make the barricade fall," Xhea said. She kept her words bare and direct, and managed to hold his gaze. "It looks like I walked directly to the point of weakness. Like that's what I was there to do."

"It does," he replied. Only that.

It was the horse-faced councilor from the table's other end who asked the question: "Why did you sabotage Edren's barricade?"

Xhea looked toward him with a glare that said exactly how stupid she found that comment. "I didn't, I only touched it."

"Let me rephrase the question," horse-face said. "Who paid you to bring down our barricade?"

"*What?*" Xhea said. She looked from one serious face to another. "No one! I've said what drew me there."

"Another ghost," said a different councilor, skepticism clear in her face and tone. "A story that is nearly impossible for us to verify."

"Councilor Lorris, Councilor Suriel," Emara interjected, halting Xhea's reply. "Xhea has been in our care for two months and has rarely left her assigned room. Security has kept a watch on her, day and night. When, exactly, do you think someone was able to hire her? Unless, of course, you are suggesting she was hired from within."

The news that she'd been under security watch made Xhea cringe. She could only wonder if Mercks would have been so kind were it not for his orders.

"That supposes that the girl's injuries were not a pre-arranged part of the plan."

Xhea straightened at that—or tried to. "As if I'd cripple myself to get at your barricade," she spat. "Why would I sabotage it from here when I could have approached from the other side at any time, unseen? And that's *if* I had any idea how to turn solid objects into dust, which I don't."

Again, deep in the pit of her belly, Xhea felt her magic stir and turn. It was all she could do to keep from clutching her stomach, though whether from fear or surprise or a sudden fierce gratitude at its return, she could not say.

Emara rose, placed her palms flat on the table, and leaned forward as she spoke. "For all the inelegance of the segue, Xhea has struck upon the reason that I requested she join us today. Councilors, as the video demonstrates, Xhea has the ability to go underground without preparation or long-term consequence. The debate about who damaged the barricade and their direct motives for doing so is a necessary one—but we need more information. I assume we have not heard formal word from our rivals?"

"Not yet." Lorn spoke for the first time, his voice a bass rumble. "Though they know of the attack. Our various guests and partygoers from last night's celebration were all too happy to spread news of the barricade's fall. We are the talk of the Lower City."

"As we were before," Emara said with a nod. "The warehouse district aside, our recent contract renegotiations and attempts to claim our rivals' City contacts have not gone unnoticed. We have been making enemies, councilors, and clumsily at that."

The warehouse district? Contract negotiations? Xhea frowned. *But what—*

The blood drained from her face as she understood. What good was magic merely filling Edren's coffers? For that's what she'd imagined: storage coils almost overflowing with Shai's power . . . and then left there. As if Verrus would let power sit idle. If Emara spoke openly of attempts to steal other skyscrapers' trading contracts, Xhea could only imagine what they had been doing in secret.

Edren had never been the most powerful of the skyscrapers—until now.

Emara continued, "As news of our vulnerability spreads, the other skyscrapers will be all too happy to take advantage. We need to understand what's happening below ground, and we need to know now."

"But we have the ghost girl's power," someone said. "Can't we just make a spell for that now?"

Only Xhea heard Shai's indignant sound of disbelief.

Verrus glanced toward the councilor and she pulled back from the table, shutting her mouth so quickly that her teeth clacked together. Verrus turned away, once more pinning

Emara with his flat stare. "Make up your mind, councilor," he said dryly. "Either the girl is too injured to have sold us out, or she is well enough to be useful."

"I fail to see the two as mutually exclusive." Bare words stripped of all emotion. "Her condition has been serious, but she is well enough now to be of assistance. And my suggestion is not to use Xhea to examine our barricade, but those of the other four skyscrapers."

Verrus's eyebrow rose—the only movement in his otherwise impassive expression.

"Further," Emara continued, "the attackers may have left some evidence, which Xhea may be able to identify. As my colleague said, we could 'just make a spell for that now'—but I think Xhea will know what to look for better than any of us. This is a far better use of still-precious resources, should tensions continue to escalate."

"And they will," said a new voice, low and filled with gravel. Pol. Xhea turned to stare at the tall man, so long silent at Verrus's side. He seemed no happier to be here, nor had his body language changed; if anything, the words he spoke were a challenge. "We should send the girl below."

Verrus met the general's eye. *Knives*, Xhea thought. *A dagger in the back.* Each would be gentler than the look that passed between them.

At last Verrus nodded. "Agreed. But not alone."

"But I—" Xhea interjected.

"Be silent," Verrus said without a glance. "Lorn, have the watch accompany the girl. One guard should be sufficient. How long to have someone ready?"

Xhea thought of the presence that both she and Shai had felt waiting beyond the barricade—the watching presence, and the strange draw it had on her. That part of her story she'd not told to Emara, or to anyone.

Again she felt that thin wisp of dark magic within her, responding not to anger now, but to fear. It was a far cry from the torrent of dark she'd known two months before—but already it was steadier, stronger. As that power trickled through her, she felt something in her ease, even as her shaking grew worse. A slow rivulet of sweat ran down from her temple; another rivulet, slower, traced a path down her calf from her injured knee.

"No, listen," she started, and was again cut off.

"You will be silent when told." Something in Verrus's tone made Xhea's blood run cold.

"No sooner than this evening," Lorn replied, as if there had been no interruption. He, like his father, did not so much as glance at Xhea. No smile, no nod, no hidden gesture to acknowledge her presence, unsteady and upset against the far wall. So much for her one-time rescuer.

"See to it." Verrus rose. "We will have a ten minute recess." As if the words were a command, the councilors pushed their chairs back and began to file from the room. Pol left last, his posture stiff and angry; he didn't speak, only gently touched his daughter's shoulder as he walked past. Only Emara and Lorn remained in the stuffy room. Xhea looked from one to another, all but grinding her teeth in frustration.

"And what, exactly, was the point of that?" she said at last. "Other than humiliating me."

More humiliating still: her hands were visibly shaking now, her right fist trembling with her stick in its white-knuckled grip.

"They needed to see you," Emara said. "They needed to know that you are not a threat."

See that she was too small and weak and injured to have sold them out, she meant; see that she was too stupid to have even thought of such a plan.

"Fine. You got what you wanted." In truth, Xhea had also gotten what she thought she'd wanted: the opportunity to go below, investigate the mystery of the disappearing ghost, and see what else had been wrought in the tunnels beneath the Lower City in her absence. But this hardly felt like success. "Happy now?"

"Xhea," Emara started.

"No, leave it," Xhea said, ignoring everyone as she limped to the door. No one moved to stop her, nor spoke until the door slammed at her back.

"I wish we could go home," Shai said at last.

"Me too."

If only she knew where that was.

Chapter Five

Xhea was exhausted by the time she reached her small room, and her anger had fled with her energy. She sat on the edge of the bed and put her head in her hands.

Shai, in contrast, had only grown angrier the farther she got from the meeting room, her usual steadiness giving way to frustration. She paced back and forth before Xhea's bed, the rant that had begun floors above still going strong.

"And the casual way that woman just mentioned using my magic? Like it was just assumed that I'd give it to her— to any of them? I'm not even a person to them, am I? Just some sort of *resource.*"

Xhea wanted to lie down, but she couldn't, not yet. Instead, heart in her mouth, she carefully rolled up her pant leg, wincing as the pockets' stitching caught on her knee brace. The fabric was dark green, she thought— dark enough, anyway, that it hid most stains.

Ignoring Shai's ranting, Xhea opened the brace and pulled it from her knee, hissing as it tugged on the flesh around the bandages. The bandages were next, the thin gauze wrappings stiff and crusted dark.

Xhea sat back and regarded the renewed ruin of her knee.

The swelling and mottled bruising were the same as they had been that morning, yet her skin was now smeared dark with blood. The medic's cut across her knee had reopened, splitting along its length to gape like a slack-lipped mouth.

Shai had gone quiet. "What happened?" she whispered. Her anger, so fierce and sudden, had fled as quickly as it had come. The ghost knelt by Xhea's bedside and reached for her wounded leg with one tentative hand. "It was better than this before. I saw it this morning—that wound was healed."

Not healed, but it had been closed, the stitches removed. She could give the easy answer, she knew: that she had overexerted herself, stretched the new skin too hard in climbing the stairs. It was, after all, the answer she would give to Emara or Lorn or the medic who had treated her—the answer for anyone who would not know her steady, calm words for lies, or hear the panic, carefully suppressed, that lay beneath.

To Shai and Shai alone she said, "It's returning."

Shai met her gaze. Her silver eyes, her gentle face and long pale hair, seemed to fill the whole of Xhea's vision.

"Your magic."

Xhea nodded. "Last night, before the ghost got pulled through the barrier, I felt it. Just a little bit, but there. And again when I got angry in Emara's office, and in the Council meeting. That's when I felt my knee start bleeding."

Shai rose from the floor and moved to sit at Xhea's side, close but not quite touching. For a moment Xhea closed her eyes, feeling the chill of Shai's presence and the warm glow of her magic.

She missed the painkillers' haze. Missed, if she were honest, the cocooning blanket of misery and despair in which she'd existed these past few weeks, and the artificial distance it had created. Awake now and aware, she could not keep the fear at bay.

"I think that this is what it does." Xhea stared at her knee and its traceries of blood and sweat, its storm-dark swirl of bruises. "My magic. Whatever this power is, it's the opposite of bright magic—the opposite of your light and life and growth. I've been turning it over in my head, hours and hours just staring at this blighted ceiling—what this magic is, what it does. Now it seems like the stronger this power gets, the more damage it will do."

"So—what are you saying? That you'll never heal?"

Xhea smiled. It was a pale imitation of her normal grin—but then she felt like a pale imitation of her normal self. "Maybe not. Not on my own, anyway."

Shai opened her mouth to protest and Xhea cut her off with an impatient wave of her hand.

"No, stop. Listen to me. My magic, whatever it is—it *kills*. More than anyone, you know that. It kills and unravels spells, turns everything to black and ash. How can that power flood through me and not do any damage?" Xhea looked back to her knee; a bead of blood glistened as it rolled down her shin, a slow and dark tear.

When she spoke again, her voice was low, haunted. "Look at me, Shai. I'm fifteen, probably older, and I look— what, maybe twelve? If I'm lucky. I'm too small. I never grow. And I don't heal—not quickly and not well."

"You're hardly the first to be small for your age . . ." Shai said, yet the words trailed away, and, it seemed, the ghost's will to speak them. She looked again at the bleeding ruin of Xhea's knee, her expression a slow study in despair.

Xhea carefully took off her boots, letting them thump to the floor. She wore socks day and night, despite the summer heat. Only now did she draw the sock off her right foot, showing Shai what she had hidden: a foot bruised black with blood. Such bruising was normal right after surgery, when the blood from internal incisions were pulled down by gravity—but this, like all else, should have been long healed. It wasn't just the external wound that had re-opened; her knee was bleeding on the inside.

"I know that you and Emara were just trying to motivate me to try harder and . . . you weren't wrong." Xhea smiled sadly. "And you were. No, I wasn't trying as hard as I should have been, I know that—and yet my knee isn't healed. Exercises can't help a gaping wound. Now that my magic is returning, I think . . ." Her throat suddenly felt tight; she forced herself to continue. "I think it's only going to get worse."

"But what you said in the meeting—what we're supposed to do—"

"I know. But what choice do I have?"

Verrus Edren had allowed her to stay within Edren's walls only because of her link to Shai; she knew that now. He had no use for her and would toss her back on the streets without pause or regret if only he could do so without losing Shai's power.

Xhea had to prove her worth, no matter how small that worth might be. Perhaps they could find her a wheelchair or a walker, something to help. Even considering that option felt like another bruise to her pride. The shame at being made so helpless, so dependent, *burned*; and no amount of logic, nor mental reassurances, made the feelings any weaker. If there was any other option . . .

She took a deep breath and asked, "The healing spells on my knee—did you get a good look at them while they lasted?"

"I, well . . . yes. For the reinforcement." Shai had attempted to fuel the medic's healing spells to slow their degradation. Yet the spell lines had been overwhelmed by Shai's power, weak and inexpertly wrought as they were. Despite her skill and practice, there was only so much a magic-poor Lower City medic could do.

"Do you remember the spell's shape—the lines of intent?"

Shai looked at her then, the sudden directness of that gaze telling Xhea that the ghost knew all too well what she was going to propose. For all her magic, Shai had never learned complex spellwork, being used instead for raw power rather than any skill with the energy she generated. But that didn't mean she lacked the ability—or, at least, the potential.

"You said yourself that healing spells don't work on you."

"I said that they never *last* long enough to work. They . . . unravel, dissolve, whatever. But they do work. When I was trapped in Orren, a medic-in-training helped heal some of the damage done to my knee when I got tangled in that entrapment spell." She'd been able to move her leg again and stand, if barely. Never mind that her crash-landing in Eridian and fall from the City had undone what good Lin's spells had wrought, and worsened the damage by far.

"For a spell to work, it would have to be continually recharged by the original caster—which I could never pay for, even if I could find someone willing to touch me long enough to set the spells. But if you created the spells *and* fueled them . . ." Xhea let the words trail away, looking at Shai. Trying to keep the sudden, desperate hope from her expression.

"What about the pain?" Shai asked quietly. "You reacted so badly to even a spark of magic. Now you want me to . . . what, set a spell and keep pumping magic into it, no matter what?"

Xhea laughed thinly. "Pretty much."

Shai shook her head and looked away. "I don't know if I can."

"I think this is my only chance, Shai. Here. Now." Xhea looked back at her knee—at the thin trails of blood down her leg, her blackened foot—and bowed her head as if in penitence. "If my magic is returning, then my reaction—and the pain—will only get worse if we wait. I'll destroy the spells faster. If I'm ever going to be anything but the walking wounded, then it has to be now."

"Yes, but I—I don't know that I can do it," Shai confessed. "I saw the spell, I remember it, but . . . it's more complicated than just magic, Xhea. I've read books, too, but that doesn't mean I could recreate them from memory."

"No, but . . . you could do *something*, couldn't you? Anything."

Shai looked away, looked to her hands, looked anywhere but at Xhea's face. Her expression seemed almost ashamed, Xhea thought; but, try as she might, Xhea could think of no reason for either the ghost's hesitance or her shame.

"Please, Shai," Xhea whispered. "Won't you at least try?"

Silence was the only reply.

At last Xhea muttered, "It was a stupid idea, anyway." She waved a hand dismissively as if the request didn't matter, couldn't matter; as if she didn't feel the weight of despair settle once more like a yoke across her shoulders. "I shouldn't have asked."

Xhea reached for fresh bandages from the nearby shelf, fingers fumbling for purchase. *No,* she told herself as she grabbed first the bandages and then a bottle of water, *the real mistake was allowing yourself to hope.* To believe, however briefly, that things might be different.

She wet the cloth and dabbed at the reopened wound's edges. She showed no reaction to that pain, though it stung and the skin was tender with fresh swelling. There was no need for theatrics.

To distract herself, she cast her mind forward. Her walking stick alone would not be enough to travel to each of the skyscrapers' barricades, not in the shape she was in. There was something to the idea about the wheelchair, much as it pained her to admit it. She wanted to walk under her own power, yes—but practicality and survival had to be her priorities. Right now she needed Edren's protection more than she needed her pride or independence.

Xhea forced out a breath, blinking back tears. *Just the pain,* she told herself. She leaned down to look at the wound. With the blood washed away, it didn't look quite as bad as she'd feared. New stitches might have helped, but she wasn't going to attempt that herself. She readied the bandages.

"I'll do it," Shai blurted.

The ghost wasn't looking at Xhea but at the floor—and the little dark spots where Xhea's blood had dripped.

"I'll do it," Shai repeated, her voice catching. "I'll try. Just . . . sit back. Quick, before I change my mind."

Xhea hurried to comply, supporting her knee with her hands and turning awkwardly until she could stretch both legs along the length of the cot and lean against the wall.

"You can do this," Xhea whispered. But as the ghost's trembling hands hovered above her knee, she wondered whether she meant the encouragement for Shai or herself.

Shai reached until her hands were but a whisper away from Xhea's flesh, and let her power flow. Xhea jerked as the magic flowed over her knee, through it, feeling like fire and ice combined. Then the pain came, an ache that seemed to anchor itself to the ends of her bones before blossoming beneath her kneecap. Nausea rose in its wake.

It's not so bad, Xhea thought, even as she shivered and fought not to shy away. She grit her teeth and focused on her breathing.

"Okay," Shai said at last, "I've set the spell anchors. You ready to begin?"

"That wasn't—" Xhea stopped herself. Of course Shai hadn't started the real spellwork yet. She swallowed and nodded. "Let's do this thing."

Again Shai's hands glowed—brighter this time, like noonday sunlight; brighter, like spotlights turned on full; and brighter still. This time when Shai's magic touched her, Xhea could not help it—she screamed. Her back arched and her muscles seized, her body locking into a twisted arc.

Shai recoiled, her magic vanishing, and Xhea collapsed onto the cot.

"Are you okay?" Shai cried.

Xhea's hands shook, and her legs, muscles spasming as if in reaction to extreme cold. She managed to nod. Forcing her eyes open, she could just make out Shai's face, a pale light in the darkness. Everything else seemed dim and distant, blurry shapes far beyond her reach.

"I'm okay," Xhea whispered. She rubbed her eyes, but could not seem to clear her vision. No color now, only darkness, blurred and indistinct. No matter; she kept her eyes closed and grabbed the sheet, twisting one end into a makeshift gag.

"Okay," she said, teeth chattering. "Start again."

"*What?* Are you insane?"

"Slower this time," Xhea said. "Give me time to adjust."

"Xhea, I'm not—"

Xhea opened one eye and looked at the smeared, glowing shape that was Shai's face. "Nothing has changed," she said, fighting the urge to beg, to plead.

Xhea was almost glad that she couldn't pull Shai's features into focus, for it meant that she didn't truly have to face the ghost's glare; only saw the flickers as Shai's magic shifted and guttered like a fire in the wind. At last Shai moved—a jerk that Xhea could only assume was a nod— and reached out again.

"Slowly this time," Shai agreed quietly.

It was not better, Xhea thought, having that magic come upon her slowly, the pressure increasing like the tightening grip of some heated metal vice. It was just easier to control her reaction: she bit down hard on the gag, and smothered the cries that threatened to force their way past her clenched teeth. Her hands, too, gripped the sheet, tightening to fists so Shai wouldn't see them shake—and so she wouldn't strike out, hit the wall or the ghost or her own flesh to stop the pain and the pressure that built and built and built.

She could feel Shai's magic working inside her knee, as if that power were a thousand small fingers, moving, twisting, prodding—every one of them red-hot and burning like a live wire. Nausea washed over her, numbness eddying in its wake.

When at last Shai drew her hands away, it was all that Xhea could do to pull the spit-sodden sheet from her mouth and sag against the breezeblock wall.

"Will it hold?" she gasped.

"For now," Shai said.

Xhea nodded, breath slipping from her in a sigh of relief, and surrendered to darkness that came too fast, too hard, to be sleep.

Xhea's first thought upon returning to consciousness was not of pain or discomfort—though there were enough of both to spare—but *yellow*. Soft and golden and dim, yellow light seemed to wrap around her like a warm blanket. She took a long, shuddering breath, as if that light were a tangible thing that she could draw inside her.

"Xhea? Are you awake?"

Not Shai's voice. Struggling up through disorientation and the waves of yellow, it took her a moment to place the sound.

Lorn. After all this time.

She turned toward his voice, and only then realized that the yellow was not a hallucination, but light in truth. The room's bare bulb was switched on—or at least she thought it was. There was a sharper patch of brightness above her where the ceiling would be, blurred and indistinct. She blinked. There was a large patch of darkness beside her, a hulking shadow in the shape of a man, with a glowing figure standing behind.

Slowly, oh so slowly—moving hurt, every joint aching in protest, never mind the fiery pain that was her knee—Xhea raised a hand to rub her eyes. Blinked away tears. Rubbed again.

At last her vision cleared enough for her to see. Lorn sat at her bedside, leaning forward in evident concern, while Shai paced the small room at his back.

"What'd I miss?" Xhea managed.

"We have a guard prepped, and you didn't respond to summons. What happened to you?"

Xhea looked over Lorn's shoulder in inquiry.

"You've been out for five hours," Shai said shortly, angrily. Afraid. "I stopped the flow to the spells when Lorn arrived so you would wake."

"Am I better?" she mumbled.

Shai turned and met her gaze, eyes narrowed and brimming with tears. "I don't know."

Lorn was watching, waiting. Xhea pushed herself toward sitting, and struggled with the sheet that again covered her injury, flipping aside the sheet's edge to reveal her knee. Lorn jerked back when he saw the swollen joint. Xhea had to admit, even slightly unfocused, the wound seemed far more impressive in color, her dusky gold skin streaked red with blood, the mottled bruises almost . . . festive.

The line of the medic's cut was closed, a neat line of pink, healing flesh in the middle of so much dried blood. Xhea probed the joint with careful fingers. Swollen and tender—but better. Cautiously, she drew her leg toward her, bending the knee. She stopped quickly, hissing between her teeth—but even that much movement told her what she needed to know. It hurt, but it was a different hurt than the one she'd spent the past two months enduring. Not that raw pain of flesh tearing with every movement.

Not healed, she thought. *But healing.*

She smiled at Shai. "You did it. It's working." Her words were colored by hope and awe—stronger, both, than the nausea and pain. But Shai's eyes were bright with tears as she nodded tensely and turned away.

Lorn waited for Xhea to explain. She struggled to do so, not knowing where to start—the wound itself, her nighttime struggles to walk, Emara's request, or maybe just the effects of her slowly returning magic?

And sweetness and blight, why couldn't she *focus*? Her vision and thoughts alike swam and blurred. She gazed at the yellow bulb overhead, the deep brown of Lorn's skin and the black marks of his tattoos, the light-flecked amber of his eyes. All the while, her stomach churned. *Of course,* she thought. Even if her body processed bright magic differently now, it had the same impact on her mind.

Lorn sat back as Xhea finished her fumbling explanations. "You should have told me," he said.

Xhea raised an eyebrow. "And when, exactly, was I supposed to do that? No," she said when Lorn made to protest, "don't pretend that not knowing was any fault of mine. You abandoned me, Lorn."

"I thought your magic was gone." He spoke quietly. "I held your hand for an hour or more when you were waking from the anesthetic—do you remember? It didn't hurt. You said yourself that you thought you might have burned out your power when you saved Shai."

"So, what—you only care about my magic?"

Lorn sighed and rubbed his face as if to push away his weary expression. When he spoke again, his tone had lost some of its habitual edge. His words were softer—and infinitely more tired. Addis's voice, not that of his brother.

"No," he said. "But I didn't want you to come to my father's attention. It was better if he took no notice of you at all. If he so much as imagined that you had even a wisp of dark power . . ."

"Why?" she asked. "This magic—you know what it is, what it does. Tell me."

"Xhea, I—"

She knew avoidance when she heard it; no need for him to utter the rest of that sentence.

"*No.*" He looked at her when she spoke; she felt his gaze as a physical thing. Assessing, reviewing—condemning. "You want to use me to go underground? You want my help? Then give me something back, Lorn.

"Besides," she continued. "You promised. Before I went to Eridian to get Shai, you said that my magic was a worse threat than a knife to your throat. You told me you'd explain, but instead you just left me here alone."

He stared, his expression bleak.

"What am I, Lorn?" Xhea held up her hands to that yellow light, already imaging the smoke-like darkness that would once again curl and coil around her fingers. Her vision blurred further—tears, Xhea thought in frustration. Still she asked, "What am I becoming?"

Lorn's voice, when he spoke, had gone quiet.

"In living memory, the Lower City has seen only one person who had something like your power. We don't know who he was, for he was always fully covered, even his face, but he fought for Farrow in the war."

"A soldier?"

Lorn's smile was edged. "An assassin. We lived in fear of him. It seemed he could go anywhere, find anyone. One of Senn's leaders died inside a locked room, no signs of a struggle—just fingerprints burned into the skin of his arm. Those killings that were witnessed, the witnesses all said the same thing: that the killer had some kind of strange smoke around his hands that poured inside the victims until they fell dead."

For all her skepticism, Xhea had once killed a man—a night walker—in much the same way.

A pause. "I was one of those witnesses," Lorn added. "He killed my grandmother. Back when the skyscraper was under her leadership, relations with Farrow were . . . tense."

Xhea didn't know what to say to that. "How did you know it was magic?" she asked at last.

Lorn shook his head. "What else could it be? And that was what my father told me back then. He knows more, I think—not that I've asked."

"What happened to him? The assassin."

"I don't know. He vanished a little before the end of the war. Died, I can only assume; I don't know how. But I saw his power, Xhea—power enough to kill a person in mere moments, not a drop of blood spilled—and it was nothing, *nothing*, compared to what you did in the street outside Edren that day. He had wisps of thin darkness, and you?" Lorn shook his head, suddenly unable to meet her eyes. "I'd never seen anything like it before. If I didn't know you—if I hadn't realized you didn't understand what you'd done—I would have barricaded myself and every Edren citizen inside and bombed you from the rooftops where you stood."

He gave a snort that was almost a laugh, yet Xhea knew he was not joking. If that much power—that swirl of dark that she'd spun about her head and swallowed back down—were enough to cause such fear, she was glad that he had no way of knowing what she'd done in Eridian: that flood of black, thick and dark, cast against the Tower's living heart.

Pushing the memory away, she asked, "Who knows about that morning? You and Emara . . ."

"Yes. And—" He hesitated, chewing over the words. "—and one more."

"Mercks." Head of the night watch—and so careful to keep an eye on her these past few months, even when she was weak and drugged and barely able to walk.

Lorn nodded.

Xhea had questions—she could feel them tumbling over and over in her magic-addled brain, questions birthing questions, more than she could voice—and knew that there was not time. Not now; not yet.

"When am I supposed to go underground?" Xhea asked.

"Our guard is ready," Lorn said—all trace of Addis vanishing from his voice. "Are you?"

Xhea shrugged. "Only one way to find out."

Already she could feel Shai's spell burning out, the magic destroyed by its contact with her flesh—but it was far from gone entirely. Yet while the knee injury was still new to her, being high on bright magic was something with which she had a great deal of experience. She moved slowly, keeping her head as still as possible as she pushed herself up. The world tilted and whirled, and a low, grinding nausea roared to life within her. *Only a matter of time before the cold sweats kick in*, Xhea thought, and pushed her legs over the edge of the mattress.

Lorn turned away to allow her to dab the dried blood from her legs, re-fasten her brace, and struggle to pull her pant leg down over the whole mess. At last she took a deep breath.

"Moment of truth."

Lorn and Shai both turned at the words, their near-identical movements making Xhea snicker as she gathered her strength. *Laugh while you can.* She forced herself to stand.

For the first time in months, Xhea's first concern was not the pain in her knee but her stomach's sudden rebellion. Only her hours unconscious saved her—with nothing but bile in her stomach, she managed to press her lips into a tight line and keep everything down.

"Xhea?"

A deep breath. Another.

"I'm all right," she said. She blinked and looked toward Shai, her blurred vision suddenly due more to brimming tears than the lingering bright magic.

"I'm all right," she said again, and could have wept for joy.

Standing, the pain was greater—but even so, it was a pain that didn't steal her breath and leave her gasping; it didn't sap her will and make her want to collapse into some dark corner and never, ever get up again. Shai watched, still angry, still upset—but her eyes widened as she watched Xhea stand without falling.

"I did it?" Shai whispered. "Truly?"

"Yes." Xhea was struck by the sudden, strange urge to reach out and hug the ghost—or try. Instead, she ducked her head, rubbed the tears from her eyes, and pushed her tangled hair from her face, coins and charms chiming.

Lorn held out her stick, the question clear in the movement. She took it gratefully. Only so much a few hours could do, no matter how much magic Shai had pumped into that spell.

Xhea limped forward, Shai a shining presence at her side.

"You ready? I think it's time to go stop a war."

Chapter Six

Xhea stood at the top of the stairs in Edren's lobby, staring down into the darkness below. There was no party, and the main doors were closed—if they'd ever been opened at all. No crowd here, no curious onlookers, just the few who knew of this excursion and had some responsibility to see it turn out right.

Beside her, Mercks settled a pack across his shoulders, then stood as one of his guards tied a wheeled wooden sledge on the back. From the stains on the thing—and its smell—Xhea suspected that it was used to help haul waste to one of the midden heaps a few blocks away. A sad and sorry excuse for a wheelchair. *Better than nothing*, Xhea thought sourly, and tried to believe it.

"How'd you get stuck with this gig?" she had asked Mercks incredulously on her arrival.

"It's my job," he'd said simply. As if the supervisor of the night watch was an obvious choice for this excursion. Given how far he'd made it down the stairs the day before, she didn't doubt that he was among Edren's poorer citizens—yet she suspected that there were other reasons he'd been chosen. Or had volunteered. She'd shrugged and looked away, as if such things hardly mattered.

She tried now to listen as Lorn reviewed their instructions: Document as much as possible. Find what evidence they could without putting themselves at risk. Remain in contact with Edren. Remain together. Flee at any sign of danger.

"Got it," Xhea said. "Don't die."

Mercks just nodded and stared at the stairs like a man looking at his own grave, clutching a flashlight in one white-knuckled hand. Looking at his hopeless face, Xhea wanted nothing more than to apologize. But then she hadn't damaged the barricade; only touched it and watched it fall. She hadn't wanted this—not any of it.

Yet she felt as much as saw Shai by her side, that so familiar presence and the tether that joined them, and knew that wanting had nothing to do with it. Xhea was here because of Shai, and Shai was here because of her, and Shai's Radiant magic had disrupted so much in the Lower City so very quickly—so maybe it was all her fault in the end.

Mercks turned to her and something in his stark expression softened.

"Tonight?" he asked, gesturing to the stairs—the same question he'd asked every night. For an instant, she forgot the watching onlookers—forgot the pack and the sledge and all the unknowns that waited—and simply smiled.

"Yes," she said. "I think so." She reached out and gripped the brass railing.

"I always said I'd give you a hand, didn't I?" Mercks laughed then, genuine amusement beneath the strain. Night after night, and neither of them had ever imagined this.

Together, they descended into darkness. Xhea could not walk quickly or easily—the still-sharp hurt, despite Shai's healing, kept her from even trying—but she was on her feet. At her side, Mercks moved just as slowly, his breath already short despite the drugs.

The temperature dropped, step by step, as if they left summer in Edren and descended into another world. A world colder and darker, the air no longer thick with heat and humidity, but chill and damp and smelling of dust. Despite the chill, a pressure lifted from Xhea nonetheless as she took her first breath of the underground's dusty, closed-in air: tension of which she hadn't even been aware loosening its grip on her chest and shoulders, brushing away the fog from the inside of her brain. The fog—and the last of the spell's bright magic. The gleam of yellow vanished from the beam of the flashlight Mercks held, leaving only gray.

Home, she thought unbidden—and just as quickly pushed the thought aside.

Beside her, Mercks felt no such ease. Even through his drug cocktail, his discomfort was evident. With effort, he pried his white-knuckled hand from the stairs' railing and took a heavy step forward.

Once his reaction would have made her laugh, such fear and the weakness of which it told a sharp contrast to the ease with which she traveled below. Now, nothing in his fear or pain was amusing. They were each slamming up against their bodies' limits, she knew; each pushing past with will alone. Perhaps she could make this journey easier for him, as he had made her long nights of painful exercises and the inevitable failures of her wounded flesh easier for her.

A noble concept; if only it made words come to lips or mind.

Shai watched Mercks, and it seemed her thoughts followed a similar path—or, at least, ended at the same destination. "Say something," she said.

Xhea swallowed and said the first thing that came to mind. "When was the last time you went underground?" The image of him pinch-mouthed and sweating halfway down the stairs loomed large in her mind's eye, and she winced. "Before yesterday, I mean."

"Two months ago," Mercks said. He visibly struggled to slow his breathing. "We hold regular attack drills."

So much for drills. Xhea just managed to suppress the snort that accompanied the thought. She'd seen how far the guards' footsteps made it into the underground— barely at all.

Mercks played the harsh white beam of his flashlight across the walls, the ceiling, the crisscrossed pattern of footsteps across the floor—looking, Xhea could only assume, for some evidence she didn't know how to recognize. At the same time, Xhea tried to feel whether there was anything different—whether she might feel the faintest hint of either that strange pull or the unease that had come in its wake, or the feeling of being watched. Goosebumps rose on her arms, and she shook her head. *Only the cold.* All else felt as it should.

At last Mercks started toward the barricade, leading the way.

"My record was twenty-five minutes below," he added quietly. "This, I think, will be longer."

At their creeping pace? Of that Xhea had no doubt. The sound of her stick against the floor echoed around them like a heartbeat.

They were almost to the turn toward the small shopping plaza before Xhea spoke again. In the quiet, even her soft words seemed loud.

"This is the hardest part, you know."

"The hall?"

"The fear." She smiled grimly. "Anticipating pain makes everything worse. When the pain comes? Then it's just a matter of dealing with it." Story of the last two months wrapped up in a neat little box, that was.

Mercks made a sound that could have been a laugh or a grunt or nothing at all.

Another step. Another.

"How do you know him?" Shai asked. The same question she'd asked the night before.

Xhea glanced at her. The ghost's voice had been quiet, her face impassive—but the anger there was poorly hidden. New anger, old anger, and hurt beneath both. Xhea didn't understand; the healing she'd asked for had been a risk, but a worthwhile one. Shai's magic had *worked*, if imperfectly.

Xhea shrugged. "I don't sleep much these days, and he supervises the night watch. I used the main stairs for my knee exercises—or tried to. I walked the halls." Again she shrugged, as if the admission and its heavy subtext came easily.

That's how I spend my nights, Xhea wanted to say. *Where do you go?* Hurt, too, in those words; the hurt of night after night spent alone. But now, she knew, was not the time to ask.

Shai looked surprised. "I didn't know . . ." she started, but Mercks spoke over her hesitant words.

"Your friend?"

Xhea nodded. No time for anything more: they turned the corner and the barricade was before them.

They stopped, staring. Before, this corridor had been untouched, pale dust coating every surface like winter's first snow. Now everything—from the benches and fake trees to the floor and the gaping holes of the light fixtures—was coated in a thick layer of grit and debris blown out from the collapse. The barricade itself loomed at the hall's end, the hole through its center like a dark, gaping mouth.

Mercks played his flashlight over the damage, and made a sound of disbelief. The video, she supposed, had done little to capture the truth of the collapse. The shape and the fact of it, yes, in grainy black and white; but not the feel in the air, heavy and cold; not the smell, or the sheer size of the destruction. But it was not the barricade's appearance that made her stare, nor Edren's request that made her step forward.

As Mercks used his radio to call back to those waiting above, Xhea moved carefully toward the barricade, Shai at her side. The ground was treacherous underfoot, covered in shards of debris and chunks of concrete; more than once Xhea's walking stick was the only thing that kept her upright. When she stood in the half-clear patch that marked the place where she'd fallen the day before, Xhea paused and extended her free hand toward the barricade. Her hand trembled.

"You feel it too?" Shai asked. Her anger seemed forgotten: now there was only fear. The ghost looked like she wanted nothing more than to turn and flee the way she had come.

Xhea nodded. Except she had no words for what she felt, no name for the sensation that played across her fingertips and made her stomach twist and roil. At first it had felt almost like Shai's light on her face: something so faint as to be all but unnoticeable until she trained her attention on it. Except instead of the warmth and light she had come to associate with Shai's presence, this was something cold and still and dark.

And it drew her.

The fear that Shai clearly felt, that dread that made the light of her magic flicker and flare—Xhea felt none of it, only that pull urging her forward once more.

No, more than urging—it seemed to drag at her, yanking at her thoughts and body alike, stronger and stronger with each passing moment. Xhea took a step without meaning to, and another, stumbling closer until she stood just inside the barricade. It was only then that she saw the reason for the new tunnel's perfect darkness: something blocked the tunnel's far end, a wall of solid black that even her vision could not pierce. Though the light of Shai's magic played across the barrier's broken ends—severed pipes and shorn-clean edges of metal doors, concrete and oil drums and bicycle frames—it did not touch that black.

Say something, Xhea thought. *Anything*. But it was all she could do to keep breathing.

Another step, another, and she walked through the tunnel toward that impenetrable darkness. Her hand clutched her stick, cold and sweating. Her heartbeat was so loud that though she could hear Shai's voice—suddenly, urgently—she could not understand the ghost's words through the staccato beat.

Still that darkness drew her, closer, closer. It was flat black: no sheen to it, no depth; only a span of perfect dark. As if in a dream, Xhea reached out and touched it.

Everything stopped.

Xhea was touching the black and that black touched her, and something that had neither shape nor substance felt as whole and real as her own flesh. It was cold, yes, like dipping her hand into fresh snowmelt—but it did not hurt. Or perhaps it was only that pain was such a constant now that in that moment it was impossible to tell pain from pleasure from the absence of each.

Oh, she wanted to close her eyes; wanted to release her hand from her walking stick and just fall, boneless, as if this darkness could embrace her, enfold her, and never let her go.

A sudden flash of light broke her trance—a surge of bright magic—and Xhea gasped, stumbling back.

Shai was calling, high and urgent; over and over, she shouted Xhea's name. Her hand, too, was outstretched, light again building around her fingers.

Xhea struggled to think, struggled to breathe. She grabbed the barrier to keep from falling, her hand grasping a sharp metal edge. It sliced into her palm, and then, only then, did she gasp and shake herself awake.

The black before her was gone. She could see the hall beyond the barricade: a span of dirty linoleum and the hulking shapes of parts of the barrier dragged carefully aside.

Heart still pounding, Xhea looked at her hand. The cut wasn't deep, but it was ugly; already blood pooled in her palm and dribbled over the side of her hand, dripping in black droplets to the dusty ground below. Black on gray— no hint of ruby, no sign that her eyes had ever known color.

But it was not the blood that caught her attention, nor the wound from which it flowed, but the darkness that even now surrounded her upraised hand in a swirling cloud— the only remnants of the black wall she'd seen before her. She knew this darkness, this shape that moved like living smoke; she knew it as she knew her own self. It seemed to sink into her; at its touch, she felt something deep within her stir in response. Yet she could not feel the lingering smoke that twined through her fingers and rose, spiraling, into the empty air; she had no sense of that power as anything other than something outside herself.

As she watched, the swirling darkness dissipated—fraying, tattered, gone.

"Xhea," Shai said, louder now, more urgent, and she felt the ghost's hand on her shoulder. She turned, stepping back until she was clear of the barricade, and looked toward Shai. The ghost stared back, wide-eyed.

"What was that?" No sign of Shai's earlier anger, now; only fear.

Xhea looked from the barricade to her hand—bare and bloody—and curled her fingers into a fist in a vain attempt to stop the bleeding. She was not shaking, now; she was not afraid. For the first time in months, her head felt perfectly clear.

"Magic," she said. Dark magic, and it had not been hers.

Run away, some distant part of her mind screamed. Yet she heard the wonder in her own voice, felt tears sting her eyes and run hot down her cheeks, and knew that she would not.

"Xhea?" Mercks's voice. She had almost forgotten him. "Xhea, what's wrong, what do you see?"

She looked to the guard. She should tell him, she knew—it was, after all, why she was there, to explain the things only she could see. But doing so, she realized, would put her at risk.

She had said she knew no way to bore a hole through the barricade, no way to turn solid objects to dust—and understood, now, that she'd been wrong. Of everyone in Edren, she was the only one who might have done this damage, had her magic been strong enough. When her power was ascendant, she'd turned petals and leaves to nothing more than fine-grained ash, rotted away a silk scarf in mere moments. It was easy, now to imagine it: a flow of power in the shape of a tunnel, destroying everything from the inside out—and just waiting for that little push to send everything tumbling down.

It didn't matter that she was blameless; to say anything of what she had just seen would necessitate revealing her magic, and doing that would make her a suspect, a spy. The control evident in the shape of the damage spoke of one with far more experience than her—yet she doubted few would care to debate the difference.

"Don't touch the barricade," was all she said, holding up her bloody palm in explanation. "Blighted thing's sharp."

Let him think the cut was the reason for her tears. She almost wished she believed it herself. Inwardly, she reeled: there was someone else with her power—not just a story, like Lorn's, but someone living, someone *here*. If the screaming ghost from the night before was any evidence, dark magic and the ability to see ghosts went hand in hand.

And the spell? For she knew not what else that span of solid black might have been but a spell wrought with dark power. *What was that for?*

She shook her head, the charms in her hair clinking softly in the silence. She had no way to know. She would just have to be cautious, that was all; keep every sense trained for evidence of whoever this dark magic caster might be, and what they might want of Edren—or of her.

Mercks finished his cursory examination of the barrier and gestured toward the tunnel with his flashlight beam. "Let's get this over with," he said. His hands were already trembling, his breath short.

"Be careful," Xhea whispered to Shai. The ghost nodded. One by one they filed through the tunnel, out of Edren and into the underground.

In the hall beyond, there was no movement as far as she could see in either direction. Mercks played his flashlight across the floor, checking as Xhea had done for any sign that they were not alone. Xhea took a long, slow breath; it was just the underground, dark and quiet and familiar as the sound of her own voice.

She had expected dust to be thick on the ground, here as in Edren. It was not. Whoever was responsible for the destruction had left neither note nor signature; but beyond the wash of dirt from the collapse, the ground was patterned with countless footprints, and smeared with the heavy trails of objects dragged across the floor. Most of those tracks led down the hall to Xhea's left—the direction, she knew, of both Orren and Senn.

Mercks untied the sledge and set it down, then crouched to examine the marks; but there was little point, Xhea thought as she looked around with a critical eye. Just more of the same: more rubble, more things cast aside, more signs that something was not right. She searched nonetheless, looking for evidence that Mercks would never see: signs of ghosts.

Or, more specifically, the ghost from the night before. She heard no hint of his muffled shouting, nor his words. No sign, either, of to what—or, rather, to whom—he might have been tethered.

But there was something here, she realized. Something that lingered just on the edges of her senses. Xhea frowned, peering down the hall into the darkness beyond.

"This was a bad idea," Shai whispered. The ghost raised a hand before her as if feeling for heat. "Do you feel that? There's someone here. Someone's watching us."

Xhea remembered the feeling from the night before, that prickle between her shoulder blades as if someone were targeting her from the darkness. Now there was nothing—nothing but the song that even now played on the edges of Xhea's hearing, drawing her forward, calling her on.

Song? Xhea frowned. Why had she thought that? She shook her head as if to dispel such thoughts and the strange feeling that had settled in their wake. There was no song, no sounds at all but Mercks's increasingly labored breathing and the rhythm of her own uneven steps.

Tap-scuff. Tap-scuff. Tap-scuff.

Her cane sounded loud against the floor. So, too, did the scuff of her boots' heels against that dirty ground. She did not remember starting to walk, only realized that she'd traveled half the length of the hall—and that Shai and Mercks were even now scrambling to catch up.

"Xhea?" Shai asked. "What is it? Xhea, no—*stop.*"

Because this was not her careful, limping walk. Within the limitations set by pain and under-used muscles, she was all but running.

"I can hear . . ." Xhea said, glancing back, but could not finish the thought.

Mercks said something. Xhea tried to understand before letting even the memory of his voice slip away to be drowned beneath something that was—and was not—sound. He hurried to catch her; as he entered her peripheral vision, she saw him reach with shaking hands for his belt and the weapons secured there.

That means—

She let the thought go. It did not matter, could not matter. She just had to keep walking. All else was buried beneath the sound.

And it was a sound—how could she have ever thought otherwise? It sounded like—

Like—

Xhea kept walking. *Tap-scuff. Tap-scuff. Tap-scuff.*

She reached the old metal doorframe, its paint peeling in long curls, that marked the transition from the corridor to the warren of tunnels and plazas beyond. Xhea paused there, her bleeding hand on the doorframe, as she looked at the paths stretched before her.

The leftward passage led toward Orren and Senn. It was a direct route—and the direction that many of the footsteps led. Yet Xhea turned away, dismissing her old enemy—hers and Edren's alike—with little more than a glance.

The rightward passage, its walls lined with old advertisements, went toward a food court. From there, passages branched out: a path to the nearest subway station, a set of doors that led to part of the main underground mall, and a dead escalator that led to the surface. And the song.

"This way," she said, and turned.

There was a curve in the hall, then five stairs and a wheelchair ramp that led to the food court. She had to get there. She had to hurry.

Mercks called to her, but it was Shai's voice that cut through the haze: "Xhea, *stop!* Don't you feel it?"

Xhea reached the ramp and grabbed the rusted railing, yet even as she pulled herself up, some part of her understood Shai's meaning. For underneath the urgency, there was a feeling that crawled down her spine and settled in the base of her stomach where her magic lay, weak and quiescent. A sense of slow and certain dread.

But the song . . .

"I can hear—" Xhea said, and stumbled to a stop.

She couldn't hear anything. There was nothing: no song, no sound, nothing but the echoing silence of these dead and empty passages. Xhea looked down at her palm. It was dark with her blood—and something more. As she watched, a thin wisp of black lifted from her palm, curling up and away. Xhea gasped as the last of the foreign magic fled from her, vanishing into the air.

Dread. It hit suddenly, like a weight in her stomach, a quiver in her muscles that had nothing to do with fatigue. This was what Shai had meant—this feeling, its weight in hands and heart. Dread that felt every bit as strong as the inexplicable attraction that still drew her forward, step by step.

There was something here, she knew with a cold and sudden certainty. Something watching. Something waiting. The dust-coated tables seemed undisturbed, as did many of the old counters—but footsteps marked the passage of more than one person across this ground. Yet she saw no movement, nothing to betray what pulled and repelled her in equal measure.

"What happened?" she whispered. She glanced around, trying to orient herself; the past few minutes felt like a dream from which she struggled to wake.

This, she thought in echo of Shai, *was a very bad idea.* The back of her neck crawled as if there was an unseen target painted between her shoulder blades. She was unarmed, unable to run, and had a drugged and semi-incapacitated man at her side. They should have sent a whole group of guards; they should have sent the arena's best fighters with their spelled weapons and blade-scarred armor; they should have boarded up the stairs, barricaded the entrances, and prepared for whatever disaster was even now bearing down upon them.

They should never have let her down here.

Mercks struggled to climb the stairs. "I don't know, you just—" he started, when an unknown voice interrupted.

"I called you," someone said, the voice high and child-like. Xhea looked up as a small figure stepped out from behind a food-court counter.

Xhea blinked, staring. Not just child-like, but a child. A boy.

He walked away from the counter that had concealed him and out into the maze of tables bolted to the dusty floor. His hands were loose by his sides. His hair was pale, tousled like it wanted to curl, and a spray of freckles patterned the fair skin of his nose and cheeks. His clothes, Xhea noted, were dirty and mismatched—but beneath the evidence of poor treatment, they were hardly worn. Almost new.

He looked no more than six years old.

Like Xhea, he stood here easily, no sweat across his face, no tremor in his hands. His pale eyes were clear and steady, without the glazed look of drugs; he bore no chains or wounds or other evidence of coercion. He showed no pain. When Mercks trained the beam of the flashlight full on his face, he barely flinched from that light—nor did he have a light of his own. Like Xhea, he needed none.

Xhea opened her mouth, but could not speak; only stared as the implications of what she saw crashed and cascaded through her mind. The attacker—the dark magic caster she had so feared—was a *child*?

Mercks showed no such hesitance. Though he had his light trained on the boy, and his weapon still in his hand, he spoke with the gentleness Xhea remembered from her first few nights limping through Edren's halls.

"Son?" he said. "What are you doing here? Are you all right?"

The boy turned to Mercks, and Mercks stopped speaking mid-word. There was a long moment of silence, and then Mercks began again to shiver. Lightly at first, then harder, his muscles spasming as if he were not experiencing a simple reaction to pain and cold, but heading toward a seizure. The beam of his flashlight slipped from the boy's face to dance across the dirty floor; the point of his weapon, brought to bear, dipped as his shaking fingers attempted to keep their grip.

"Mercks?" Xhea asked. She reached a hesitant hand toward him, but would not—could not—touch him. Not unless she could somehow help; otherwise, she'd only make his reaction worse.

The boy just looked at him, watching as Mercks stumbled on the top step and fell to his knees, gasping for air. A cloud of dust swirled at the impact. Xhea turned to Shai for help, and only then did she realize Shai wasn't with her. She reached with mental hands, following the tether that joined them, and could feel the ghost just out of sight beyond the hall's curve. Xhea glanced back, but even Shai's light was dim; only the faintest glow betrayed her presence.

She had heeded the warning, that feeling of dread—a warning that Mercks hadn't felt at all, and Xhea had ignored. The boy was small and skinny, and something in his careful movements made her think of someone afflicted by long illness; surely he was no threat. Still some instinct told her to flee from him, as fast and as far as she could.

"Why'd you bring him down here?" the boy asked. "It's hurting him." He looked up and met Xhea's eyes, his head tilting in sudden question. "He is yours, right?"

"Mine?" Xhea blinked. "What, I—no. He's not mine."

At that the boy seemed to perk up. "Oh! Can I have him?"

"For what?" she asked incredulously.

"I'm hungry."

Xhea stared.

Even from twenty feet away, Xhea did not disbelieve him; there was something in his expression that spoke of hunger. Yet despite his skinny frame and the hollows of his cheeks, she knew he was not starving. She had seen starving in the Lower City streets. She had felt starving, the way that hunger turned to pain and then only to absence, a lack so great that it stole sleep and thought and strength.

No, what was writ large on those young features was *wanting*. But there was no food here, only a man collapsed on the dust-coated tile—and it was that man, weak and shivering, that held the boy's gaze. Xhea watched as the boy lifted a hand toward Mercks as if, even so far away, he was a bit of fruit on a plate, unwatched and ripe for the taking.

As he reached out, Xhea saw tangled in his fingers the finest thread of a tether. She squinted, following the near-invisible line to its end between the shoulder blades of a ghost. Or, she thought, what had once been a ghost.

Ghosts, to her, had always looked like people: if not always as strong or intense as the living, then every bit as real. This figure, pulled in the boy's wake, was nearly as invisible as the tether that bound them—a shape more felt than seen.

Xhea could just make out the rough outline of features: a tangle of hair, a slash of a mouth, two darker shadows in place of eyes. Still, she knew him; knew that slumped posture, the defeat of his pose. His hands were no longer in his mouth—for his hands, she saw, weren't there at all. Nor were his legs. He was but an impression of a person, his limbs—his very self—vanishing into nothingness.

Gone, she thought. No movement in the figure now, neither that frantic energy nor the confused wandering that she had seen the night before, nothing more than a gentle sway like fabric caught in a sluggish breeze. No words, whispered or screamed or otherwise. No face.

Xhea looked again to the boy. *Eater of ghosts*, she thought in shock, and shuddered.

Her shudder caught his eye. Again, the boy looked at her—then his expression changed. He took a step toward her, and another, his face suddenly alight.

"You don't have a bondling?" he asked.

Xhea shook her head, not understanding. "What do you mean?"

Closer he walked, his steps mere whispers against the ground. "You have no binding. You've claimed no one?"

"No," she said, confused. "I—"

He reached for her.

No, she thought in sudden understanding—not for her, but for the tether that joined her to Shai. Xhea stumbled back and back again, her stick clutched like an awkward weapon, her hand raised as if magic might pour from her fingers at her desperate call.

She had thought her power gone. Not gone, she realized now as she felt the magic curl in the depths of her fear-clenched stomach; never gone, but exhausted. *Dark magic*, she thought. *Death magic*. A power of ash and endings.

And oh, what use was that power against one so much more skilled at its wielding? For already she could see dark power twining around his fingers—and not the drifting, aimless smoke with which she was so familiar, but a coil of dark that moved with purpose and intent.

It wasn't the boy she needed to fear, but the sound that his movement—the sounds that her own ragged breath, and Mercks's—had concealed. Shai cried a warning from her hiding place.

Too late.

Xhea turned to see two men clad in dark, mismatched clothes come around the corner, goggles over their eyes to let them see in the dark. Mercks struggled to his feet, gasping and trembling, to face them. The shorter one kicked the flashlight from his hand, sending it spinning across the floor, while the taller one wrenched the weapon from Mercks's hand with a single, wicked twist. Even so, Mercks stood, trying to put his body between the attackers and Xhea.

The taller one grabbed Mercks, twisted him around, and pulled him close to his chest. "Sorry, friend," he murmured into Mercks's ear. "Wrong place, wrong time."

Xhea only saw the blade in the shorter man's hand as it plunged into Mercks's side. Mercks did not scream, only groaned as he curled in on himself, folding over the wound. The taller one released him and Mercks sagged, sliding off the blade as he tumbled to the floor and down the stairs.

His hands shook as he pressed them to the wound, sliding, fumbling. To Xhea's eyes, his hands were already black with blood.

"No," she whispered. She moved toward him—only to have the attackers turn their attention to her. Their goggles obscured their faces, but she knew that voice, she knew those hands. They were Rown hunters, and one of them was female.

Leaving Mercks on the floor they came at Xhea, one on either side of her, blocking her escape as they reached for her. They grabbed her by the arms, their heavy gloves enough to make them no more than flinch at her touch. Her walking stick clattered to the ground.

"Well, well," the man said. Xhea could hear the smile in his voice. "Would you look who it is? Imagine seeing you down here."

The other said nothing at all, just wiped her bloody knife on the sleeve of her coat.

"Hold her still," the boy said, coming closer, and reached once more for the tether.

"Stay back," Xhea cried—not to the hunters, nor the boy, but to her friend. "Shai—*run!*"

Xhea felt the moment the boy's hand closed around the tether. There was a sudden, wrenching jerk, as if the tether itself had come alive and tried to force the boy's hand away—to no avail. There came a wave of cold, and a sense of invasion so strong that Xhea could do nothing but cry out.

Again she tried to call her magic, but the boy was stronger. His magic—dark magic, death magic—rose around her in a cloud. She opened her mouth to scream but the magic just poured into her, mouth and nose, eyes and ears, and suddenly all she knew was darkness. She felt herself stumbling, sagging, as unconsciousness came to claim her.

"Shai," she tried to say, once, desperately.

The tether binding them snapped.

Part Two

Chapter Seven

In the darkness, Shai listened.

She told herself that it was caution that slowed her steps in Xhea's wake; caution that bid her pause out of sight of whomever or whatever she could feel waiting beyond the hall's curve. Only caution that made her draw her power to her and damp it down tightly, restricting her magic and its ever-present glow until its pressure within her felt akin to pain.

Caution sounded so much better than fear.

But caution did not make one's hands shake or breath become short—physical habits both that even death hadn't broken. Caution did not make one cower in the darkness or want to flee, leaving everyone else behind.

Fear did that. Fear and cowardice and the terrible weight of helplessness.

Why aren't you doing anything? she thought as she hid and cringed away. Knowing that there was nothing, *nothing* she could do to stop what she heard happening.

Shai covered her mouth with her hand, fingers shaking. Her life had been short; her time in the Lower City shorter still. Even so, she recognized the sound of a knife being drawn; knew what pain sounded like, and the sound of a grown man falling to the floor. Shai knew, too, what Xhea sounded like when she was afraid: that edge to her words— and, between them, that low, almost inaudible sound that not even her clenched jaw could hold back. A whimper that the girl refused to voice.

Absent gods, Shai thought. *Please, please . . .*

"Stay back," Xhea cried. "Shai—*run!*"

Yet Shai stood frozen, quivering, as if her incorporeal self had become part of the wall; as if her tether bound her not to Xhea, but to this place, this moment, this sick dread and terror.

Something grabbed her tether. Shai gasped, recoiling— but the tether held her tight.

It was not Xhea; that Shai knew in an instant. Dark though her power was, Xhea's touch never felt so sharp or so cold—nor would Xhea force her to act against her will. But Shai could feel the tether now attempting to do just that, commanding her to step forward when she wanted to pull away, and she fought it for all she was worth.

Since her death, the tether had felt as much a part of Shai as her hands or legs; yet at her resistance, it writhed and twisted like some wild creature, turning against her. It slowly, slowly, dragged her forward. She struggled against it, frantically, desperately; she grabbed for the wall to hold herself in place and her hand passed through without stopping. There was nothing she could reach, nothing she could hold, yet still she fought for purchase, flailing against the empty air.

Dark magic rushed through the tether and washed over her, *through* her, sharp and cold. Everything around her went black.

"*No!*" she cried as that chilling black stole the world from her. She screamed and screamed and could not hear her own voice. She reached with desperate hands to grab something, anything—but suddenly she could not see her own self, nor could she feel anything against her hands or skin—

No ground beneath her feet, no light of her magic—

No heat nor chill, no sight of anything at all—

Only a howling black *nothing*, and that nothing yawned wide to swallow her whole. She was dissolving, unraveling, and she screamed and screamed in silence.

In her terror, her magic flared. Light shone from her, brilliant as sunlight, pushing back the darkness that dug into her like claws—and, somewhere distant, a spark flared in echo. Shai saw the light, and reached for it, clutched at it—held tight with her whole being, all her fear and wanting and the desperate need to exist, and *pulled*. For a moment, she was caught between life and that chill hunger, being torn into a thousand pieces to be scattered wide.

There came a rush of emotion, a surge of pain and anger and regret—emotions not her own. Emotions that suddenly stopped, that torrent replaced only by echoing silence. Still Shai pulled against the darkness that dug into her, fighting desperately to be free.

The tether connecting her to Xhea snapped.

Shai flew, fell—she did not know, only gasped as reality crashed upon her in a wave of light, sound, and sensation. She collapsed, limp and exhausted, unable even to open her eyes. She was in the underground once more, sprawled on the chill and dusty hall floor, and for a moment she could do nothing but quiver.

"What was that?" she whispered at last, dazed and hurting. It felt as if those dark claws had begun pulling her apart in truth; her body, her very existence, felt as tenuous and scattered as her thoughts. The words, as she spoke them, felt like an anchor: something real to cling to, their sound echoing in her ears. "Oh, absent gods, what was that?"

Not death—true death—nor what might wait beyond, no matter her fears that she was but skirting the edge of oblivion. No, not death, but something real and vast and hungry.

It was the boy, she thought in sudden realization. The child she'd heard—she'd felt—waiting for them in the underground, the boy whose presence alone had made her flee. In spite of everything, he had nearly caught her.

And Xhea—

It was only then that Shai understood what she had felt but moments before, caught between that darkness and the light she'd used to haul herself back into the living world, screaming in pain. Understood that snapping recoil against her sternum, the shock that even now echoed through her.

Understood the ache of sudden absence.

Xhea. Beyond, Shai could hear voices, scuffing feet, the sound of Xhea's stick rolling across the floor. Footsteps walking away. No sound of Xhea's voice; no one walking, or limping, towards Edren.

Shai forced her eyes open. There was no sign of the spark of light that she'd used to return to the living world, only a wall before her. She blinked as she realized it was Edren's foundation near the damaged barricade, a full hall's length from where she'd been standing. Even now she held tight to Edren—and not just with her spectral hands, fingers splayed against the dirty wall, but with her magic, her whole self. Power flowed from her unthinkingly, bathing the wall, the ground at her feet, the dusty air around her in a soft, golden light.

Power that reached into the skyscraper—and only there did she see the light that she had grabbed to haul herself away from that hungry grasp: magic. Edren's magic—no, *her* magic. Because the energy that flowed through the skyscraper and fueled its myriad spells was all touched by her signature.

Shai shook her head. Didn't matter, couldn't matter.

"Xhea," she whispered, and tried to stand. There was no response, no tether to which to cling; only a sudden, aching absence. Her hands trembled as they slid through the wall and the floor, finding no purchase. Perhaps something of her had been stolen after all, for she felt so transparent that it seemed light should shine through her like glass. Shai struggled to pull herself up, struggled to rise—struggled to do anything but cling to this bit of reality and try to hold on to her very existence.

Xhea's all right, Shai told herself. *She has to be.*

The broken tether told another story.

Get up, she commanded, her anger growing to equal her shame. She had abandoned Xhea to the boy and the silent attackers, not even trying to help. No more.

Get up. For the pain she felt, the disorientation, was not real: she had no body to hurt, no weakness of muscle or mind. No, if she were weak, it could be no more than weakness of will, weakness of the self.

It was hard to pull her hands from the wall of Edren's foundation, as if each had been bound by the palm to the aging stonework; hard, too, to step away from that wall and leave it behind her. Shai's breath became short and her knees felt weak, and she told herself that her physical symptoms were nothing but her imagination.

Her imagination hurt.

She stumbled down the hall. This time she did not hide behind the corner but continued toward the dusty food court that lay beyond.

"Xhea?" she called. Her voice was but a whisper. She forced herself to be louder: "Xhea, where are you?" There was no one there, only silence and stillness. No body where she had fallen; only her walking stick, abandoned near a wide scuff in the dirt on the floor.

I have to find her, Shai thought—but she could not look away from the floor. She who needed no air suddenly could not breathe.

Shai stepped closer, hesitantly, fearfully, and knelt where Xhea had fallen. That wide scuff in the dirt was marked red with smears of Xhea's blood. She reached out, fingers hovering but a breath away from those marks, as if the blood were a story she might read by touch alone.

They had hurt her somehow. They had hurt her, and she had cried out, and then—

And then—

The tether had snapped.

Shai drew back and pressed her hand to the center of her chest where the tether had connected, thinking of that surge of emotion, all that fear and pain and regret. She, more than anyone, knew what a broken tether meant— and it had broken, that much she had felt. Not dissolved naturally, the ghost's purpose in the world completed; not cut, as Xhea might have done with her silver knife; but snapped, suddenly and roughly and finally. Xhea had told her herself: tethers only snapped when the living anchor to which they were joined died.

No, Shai thought desperately. *It's not true. Maybe she just cut the tether by accident. Maybe she was just trying to protect me. And then the attackers abducted her and—*

She looked around, half panicked. Footsteps in the dust crisscrossed this space now, leaving no clear path for her to follow. She didn't even know where these paths went—she'd never traveled here with Xhea. But she would follow every path, every footstep—she would search for the smallest drop of blood. She would—

Shai's breath caught in her throat and she stopped, struggling in a vain attempt to stop her tears from falling. For she knew her words for lies, her hopes for ashes.

Shai had been here before, had clung to denial, had nursed this same awful hope—and for nothing. The tether that had connected her to her father had snapped, and it had felt the same then, the exact same. Though she'd found that whatever had been done to her father had not killed his body, she could not say that he lived. Only an empty shell was left, no spirit inside. There were some fates, she knew, that were worse even than death, and counted his among them.

Two tethers snapped. Her father was dead, and now Xhea—

Oh, Xhea.

The unknown attackers had killed her—for what else could have broken the link between her and Shai? They killed her and took her body and Shai—

She had let them. Sweet, absent gods, she had let them.

Tears slipped down Shai's face and fell, glittering with magic, toward the floor below. Shai curled in upon herself

in the darkness, weeping, and never—not in life nor death—
had she ever felt so weak or helpless or alone.

It was a sound that broke Shai from her misery. She startled
and turned.

Ignored in the darkness behind her huddled a form at
the bottom of the short flight of stairs. Not a discarded pack
or heavy patch of shadow, as she had thought, but a man.
The guard.

She moved hesitantly toward him, wiping away her
tears. *Dead*, Shai thought as the light of her magic fell upon
him—the man that Xhea had seemed to know. But no, even
as she watched he shifted and the noise came again, his
breath escaping in something that was almost a groan.

Not dead yet, but soon. Blood surrounded him: brilliant
red against his fingers, pooling beneath his shuddering body,
staining his uniform a deep, wet black. Again he curled in
upon himself as if all his muscles had contracted at once,
before he struggled again to raise his head. Struggled to rise.

"You couldn't stop them either," Shai murmured. It
was cold comfort. He, too, was paying for that failure—his
failure, and hers. Maybe he, like Xhea, would have lived if
only Shai had shouted her warning faster; if only she had
kept watch instead of cowering, useless and afraid.

Shai knelt and reached for his face with one glowing hand.
He did not react—of course he didn't. But she looked into
his face, his expression twisted by pain and panic; his eyes
were wide, staring blindly. It was dark for him, she realized.
Magic-poor and wounded, he could not see her glow, could
not see the faintest glimpse of daylight from above—could
not see anything at all. The attackers had taken his flashlight,
the pack from his shoulder, and all his supplies; only the

sledge remained. As far as he knew, he was alone and helpless in the dark, and no one was coming to help him.

He wasn't wrong. For without Xhea, what was Shai but magic that remembered once being a person? Not real, not even really *here*, just . . . existing. And struggling, now, to do even that.

Her fingers touched the guard's cheek and passed through; she felt only the slightest tingle as her hand moved through his flesh, and from his reaction he felt her not at all. Perhaps her touch was nothing but a chill whisper against his skin, less noticeable than the tears that ran to catch in his mustache and slide across his stubbled chin.

"I'm sorry," she whispered, for all that he could not hear her. "I should have . . ."

She could not finish.

She should go, she knew. Somewhere in these underground passages the attackers still walked, carrying Xhea's body. Maybe she could get one last look at her friend, see how she had died. Understand where they were taking her body, and why. Stare at the reality of that death until it felt like anything other than a horrible, surreal dream.

But what she wanted beyond any thought or reason was to lie down beside this man in the dirt and the blood, and close her eyes. She had clung to life—to living, or its semblance— once and again; now she could only wonder why. Why stay here, why stay *anywhere*, if this was all there was? If the things for which she had lived could be taken from her, one by one.

Her father, and his love. Her faith in her mother, and in Allenai; her responsibilities to her people. Her place in the world. Her life.

Xhea. Her friend, her ally, the anchor for her very existence. The anchor, in truth, for her heart.

She could just...stop. She knew it now. All the desperation with which she had clung to this reality but moments before was gone entirely, as if it had never been. She could just lie down, and close her eyes, and try to believe that when she slipped from this world she would find more waiting for her than a space of unending nothingness.

Beside her, the fallen guard groaned again. It was not a loud sound; but Shai remembered making such a sound, time and again, unbidden. She knew the kind of pain from which it had been birthed.

She could go, one way or another; she could chase fruitlessly after her dead friend's body, or slip from this world—but either way she would leave this man to die in pain, alone in the dark. She remembered dying, all the hurt and fear that had preceded her death, and could not imagine how she might have faced it without her father at her side. Without Xhea.

Shai took a long, shuddering breath.

A *light*, she thought at last, looking down at the man—a true light, one that he could see. Surely she could give him that much.

It was a simple spell, one that she'd used since childhood when she'd hidden beneath the covers to read long into the night. She had failed at nearly every new spell she'd tried to learn since her death, tangling the lines of intent, overpowering the spells' weave with sheer force of magic—but this one she knew.

Shai cupped her hand as if light were a liquid she might hold in her palm, and wove the spell within it. *Just a small light*, she thought. *No bigger than a candle's flame.* She felt a spark of satisfaction as the light kindled to life. Dim as it was, the guard recoiled as the light appeared, crying out and lifting one weak and bloody hand to shield his eyes.

"Who's there?" he said—or tried to. His voice was thin, his words slurred; and his eyes, when Shai bent to look, were glazed and glassy. Shai did not reply—could not—only drew slowly closer, lowering the hand holding the light toward the floor.

As his vision adjusted, the guard's eyes widened as he realized that the light hovered unaided in midair.

"Xhea's . . . friend?" he managed. And oh, that voice; the fear and hope that laced his words in equal measure. Was it worse to be alone in the dark, or kept company by the dead? Down in the blood and dirt, it seemed hope won out in the end.

Shai raised and lowered her outstretched hand, making the light bob in assent.

"Xhea . . . ?" He struggled once more to push himself up with a single hand, the other pressed hard to his wound, as he looked toward where Xhea had fallen. Blood flowed over his fingers and he cried out, slipping back to the tile. But it had been enough: even in Shai's faint light, he had seen that there was no one else there, only Xhea's stick abandoned on the floor.

His eyes fluttered; he was losing consciousness. *It won't be long now. Unless . . .*

Shai froze, staring. *No. I couldn't . . .*

Yet she reached toward the wound in his gut, because suddenly, foolishly, she found herself thinking of the spell she had worked on Xhea's knee. A healing spell.

Despite her power, Shai knew little of the art of magic-work. She knew only basic spells—how to turn on a light or open a door, how to press her signature into objects, how to transform her power into renai. She hadn't *needed* to know anything more; and now, looking back, she could see the bitter truth: no one had wanted her to have that knowledge. Every bit of power that she had used or shaped was magic that had not gone to Allenai, power that had not filled the Tower's coffers or fueled their spells or kept the great structure aloft, dancing the slow political dance of buildings across the sky.

She could *read* spells, quickly and with ease; she could discern meaning in intricate spell-patterns the likes of which the Lower City people around her could not even see. Yet it was as if she had been a taught a language as text only. Her eyes could dance across the words and pull stories from their shapes, while her mouth, her clumsy tongue, could but fumble in ignorance, unsure how to voice words she'd never heard spoken.

Xhea had not known what she was asking, and Shai hadn't had the courage to tell her. She'd been ashamed, that was the truth of it—ashamed and angry that Xhea had backed her into that corner, had asked her to do something that she felt she had no right to refuse. Worse had been watching Xhea lie unconscious, whimpering and quivering with pain, for hours. Five long hours.

Had Xhea seen the shape that Shai had wrought within her flesh—had any true healer seen the clumsy working she'd tangled in Xhea's broken mass of torn ligament, damaged cartilage, and bone—she would have been appalled. Even that had been mere mimicry. Shai had seen earlier attempts to heal Xhea's injuries, and if the spell-casters had been weak, their spell-lines simple, she was not so foolish as to mistake simplicity for lack of skill.

But here? Here she had nothing, no guide, only blood and light and a man dying as she watched. Nothing, she realized, left to lose—and much for which she must atone.

"You've seen the dancer on the stage," Shai whispered as the man groaned again, weaker. "You've seen her perfect grace. Now all you have to do is dance. Just dance."

Magic shining, Shai reached for the guard. Beneath her hand, he was little more than a faintly lit figure—his magic, so dim as to be all but invisible inside him, faded as she watched. She poured pure magic into him, bolstering what power remained. It did nothing for the blood loss, nor the deep stab wound in his side.

I can't. Shai pushed the thought aside. Failure could be no worse for him than the fate he already faced. He was drifting in and out of consciousness now, and his skin had become waxen.

Don't think, she told herself, and let her power flow.

Shai did not know how to make a true healing spell; for of all the ones she had seen, in this dark and empty place she could remember none of them. Still she worked, pouring her light into the man's wound and shaping it, willing it to work as she bid. Minutes passed before Shai realized that she was humming. It took a moment to recognize the song: a simple, foolish tune from her childhood about a man who made a net of magic to pull his daughter down the stars. Her father had sung it to her when she was but a child—and again, later, as she was dying and he thought she was asleep.

Comfort, the song said to her. Comfort and warmth and wholeness. Some days it was hard to remember anything of her life but the pain—but now, here, she remembered what it was to breathe. She remembered the feel of blood and of flesh, the warmth of a living body. She remembered what it was to live. She did not think nor question the thoughts as they surfaced, only wove them, one by one, into her spell.

At last, she finished. Beneath her, the man was still. Sometime during her working he had lost consciousness entirely; his face was no longer tight with pain, but soft and somehow blank, like a discarded mask. Yet as she watched, his chest rose and fell—shallow breaths, but steady.

She could not move his protective hands, nor open his bloody shirt to see the skin beneath. She felt that her spell had worked—it was a crude healing, but perhaps just enough to get him back to Edren alive.

The realization made Shai look from the man to her glowing hands and back again. She had done it—if not perfectly, nor well, if not even in a way that she quite understood, she had nonetheless succeeded. She shook her head mutely in disbelief.

The guard regained consciousness slowly. "Hello?" he murmured, disoriented and afraid; his voice cracked on the word. "Are you still there?"

Shai kindled another light and sent it to his hand. She should go. Every moment took Xhea's body—Xhea's attackers—farther from her. Farther, too, from any hope of understanding why. The guard would be fine now; he just had to get himself back to Edren. A slow process, to be sure, but he had the sledge to help him.

Yet his face was gray, and his limbs weak. Though she had stopped his bleeding, her work had done nothing to undo the damage done by blood loss, nor address the risk of shock. Neither had her work changed the effect of being underground. Again the guard trembled, his hands and arms and lower lip. He fought against the shakes as he struggled to rise, slipping and sliding in the smeared puddle of his own blood.

"Get up, old man," he told himself. But his voice had lost whatever strength it had once had, and despair tinged the words. She watched as he struggled to rise, once and again, cursing himself and his weakness with every motion. Every time he fell back it took him longer to try again.

Shai looked around—at the footsteps in the dust, at the spots of Xhea's blood—caught in a moment of terrible indecision. How long had she spent clinging to Edren's foundation as if the skyscraper were her only hold on life? More than a simple minute or two. *Admit it. They're long gone.* The attackers and the strange boy would be out in the Lower City by now, or down a subway tunnel, or in another skyscraper, or—absent gods only knew where.

Shai bit her lip. She felt like she was abandoning Xhea once more. Yet she couldn't leave this man here alone to die. At last she returned to his side, trying to push away the grief and guilt that threatened to overwhelm her.

As she drew closer, Shai watched as the man's shaking eased. It did not stop—and his face remained the color of curdled cream, his skin damp with sweat, his pupils dilated wide. Even so, he seemed stronger as the light of her magic fell upon him, as if even that slight touch of power eased his pain. Or, she thought, as if her magic pushed back the pain and the pressure that the underground caused, creating a bubble of safety—if only for a moment.

She extended her hand and sent a stream of magic toward him. Magic was power and money, yes—but more than either, magic was life. It was the light of living, the light of growth and health and strength.

He gasped as her power washed over him, and his face flushed pink; his hands stopped shaking long enough to grab the edge of the wheeled sledge and drag it toward him. Slowly, awkwardly, he pulled himself atop the board. A moment for breath, and then he pushed with his feet; the wheels squeaked as he inched down the hall back toward Edren.

Carefully, Shai expanded the aura of her magic to encompass him, bathing him in her radiant glow. With her free hand Shai lit another light, that he might know she was beside him, however long or slow his journey might be.

"It's okay," Shai murmured to him, knowing he could not hear her and speaking nonetheless. "We'll go together."

Chapter Eight

Water hit Xhea's face: drip, drip, drip.

She flinched, squeezing her eyes tight against the drops, and tried to turn away. Her neck felt weak, her head too light and swollen like a balloon, and she ended up only thrashing ineffectually against the pillow.

"Hey," a voice said. A weight settled across her chest. Again came the water: drip, drip, drip, against her closed eyes and the bridge of her nose and in the exact center of her forehead. "Come on, wake up."

Xhea blinked and looked up into the pale face that hovered above her own, blurry and indistinct. Again she blinked, water running like tears down her cheeks, and her vision cleared. For a moment she stared at the boy above her: pale skin with a smattering of freckles across his nose, a tangle of poorly cut hair falling into gray eyes that she guessed were blue. He leaned across her body, his right forearm and most of his weight resting on her collarbones, his left hand raised and dripping.

It's the boy, she thought in sudden recognition. The dark magic child, eater of ghosts—the one who had stolen her away. She remembered that power washing over her.

He met her gaze, smiled, and flicked water from his dripping fingers across her face. Laughed.

"Enough sleeping," he said. "Come on, get up."

She remembered Shai's tether snapping.

Xhea flailed, pushing the boy roughly aside and placing her splayed-fingered hand across her upper chest, reopening the wound on her hand. Beneath the layers of her shirt and jacket, she felt only the hard bone of her sternum, her collarbone, the arches of her ribs. No tether.

"Shai?" she said aloud, trying and failing to hide her growing panic. "*Shai?*"

No answer. The boy just frowned as he sat back, his hand poised over a glass of water as he considered whether to splash her again.

If Shai wasn't here, if her tether was gone, then she—

Then the boy—

No.

"What did you do?" Xhea hissed. "What did you do to Shai?"

"Who?"

Xhea reached out to grab him, heedless of her bloody palm, but he scrambled away, eyes wide. The glass he had been holding slipped from his grasp and fell to the floor, spraying water across the small room.

"The ghost! The one bound to me."

"She wasn't bound, you said so yourself," he protested. At her look, he raised his hands in innocence. "I didn't do anything. Bright magic broke the tether."

"Bright magic . . . ?"

The boy misunderstood. "I know, right? *Weird.* Don't know who did it, but it wasn't me, I swear."

Shai's okay, Xhea reassured herself. She had to be. If she had somehow used her power to cut the tether that joined them, then she had escaped the boy and whatever it was he had attempted with that sudden surge of dark magic. Shai wasn't like other ghosts, who simply vanished from the world when their tethers were cut; she had been untethered before.

Despite her mental reassurances, Xhea felt sick. Xhea had been the reason for Shai's death, no matter that it had seemed a kindness; she couldn't imagine if her carelessness had banished Shai from the living world entirely.

She's all right, Xhea thought again. *Just smart enough to stay far away from this boy.*

Carefully, she looked around as she pressed a bit of her sleeve to the cut in her hand. Small room with stained breezeblock walls, the narrow bed on which she lay pushed into one corner, with another bed against the opposite wall. Thick, plump pillows beneath her head; a warm, fuzzy blanket pulled over her legs and chest—the bedding wholly at odds with the room's signs of neglect.

It was only then that Xhea realized that the boy had not just known a ghost had been tethered to her, but had been sitting beside her. Leaning *on* her. Splashing her in the face with his bare hand.

He'd come closer again, peering down at the glass and the puddle of water on the floor.

"I'm not cleaning that, you know. It's your fault."

Xhea grabbed him by the wrist. He was tinier than she had expected; even her small hand could close around his arm with ease.

"Hey," he protested, startled. He tried to pull away.

Even weak and disoriented, Xhea was far stronger. She stared at her hand closed around his wrist, touching skin to skin. No shock in that touch. No discomfort. For all the reaction—his or hers—she might have been touching her own flesh.

Nor did he have any reaction to being underground—and they were underground, she knew. She did not know this place or these walls, but she knew the smell of air rarely stirred, of dust and damp and closed-in spaces. She knew this type of silence, echoing halls where no other footsteps fell. She knew, too, the way that being underground seemed to lift a previously unfelt weight from her shoulders and loosen the invisible bands that constricted her breathing.

And here the boy sat, his wrist in her hand, showing no more discomfort than she did.

Xhea opened her fingers, letting him slip away, and struggled to sit. It was dark in this room, no light nor distant glow from beneath the closed door. Yet he looked at her, he met her eyes.

"*What are you?*" she asked.

He shrugged, the movement so much like her habitual gesture that for a moment Xhea could but stare. The boy crossed the room to the bed that stood against the other wall, twin to her own. He flopped down on the sheets and stared at the bare concrete of the ceiling.

"Bored," he said at last, as if that were a reasonable response. "Hungry."

Sitting, the world seemed to swing and sway around her, but that was familiar enough. Xhea breathed slowly until the dizziness passed, then maneuvered her legs out from beneath the blanket, grateful her knee brace hadn't been removed while she was unconscious. A moment longer and she was able to push herself carefully to her feet. With no stick to support her, and muscles vehemently protesting their recent overuse, walking was a slow process—but that, too, was familiar.

She reached the door and tried the handle. It turned, but when she went to pull the door open, it only rattled. The sound, she thought, of a padlock on the door's other side.

"They locked it," he said, as if that should have been obvious. "They always do."

"They?" Xhea asked. Her abductors had been from skyscraper Rown, that much she knew without question—but had they been acting on behalf of their skyscraper, or only hired to do another's job? This room, clean and neat for all that it was underground, didn't look much like the decaying, half-flooded tunnels that she knew near Rown; but who knew what the foundations of the skyscraper itself looked like?

Again she rattled the door, harder this time, until it shook on its hinges. She wanted, suddenly, to scream or pound her fists against the door's surface. Weak magic stirred in her stomach; she wished for power enough to destroy the door and handle both, leave them nothing but dust and ash.

"I used to have a room up high," the boy said, ignoring her question. "Nicer than this, I guess, though everything here's pretty crooked. No locks on that door."

He looked at her then, face so open, almost eager, just waiting for her to ask him why he'd been moved, why he was kept now behind locked doors. He sighed dramatically when she remained silent, and continued anyway. "I'd used up my bondling, see, and no one understood that I *really* needed a replacement, and so I just,"—again, that shrug—"took one. He's gone now, too, and the people here are almost empty." He said this as if it were proof of some great trial.

Xhea glared at the door before limping back to the bed on which she'd woken. Glared at the boy, too, which he appeared not to notice. Gone was the dread she'd felt in the hallway, once and again, at his presence. Gone, too, was that strange pull, as if she were nothing but iron drawn toward a magnet.

Except...

Xhea frowned, considering. Even when she turned her back to the boy she could feel his presence, almost as if he were a ghost. Almost—but not quite. For all the familiarity of the sensation, that awareness of someone, some*thing*, outside herself, she would never have mistaken him for a bodiless spirit.

He felt somehow darker, colder—as if her touch against his skin would find not warm flesh, nor a ghost's subtle chill, but something sharp like ice. Was this, she wondered, the sensation that others complained of when they touched her?

She was not the only one with dark magic; it should have been a revelation. As it was, Xhea found herself wishing she could throttle the kid, if only it would stop his incessant sighing and eye rolling and the grating irritation of his superior tone.

Carefully, she limped back to her bed and sat, trying to catch her breath.

"What do you mean, 'bondling'?" Xhea asked at last.

The boy gave her an exasperated look. "I know what you are," he said.

"What I am?"

"Maybe you can hide it from the rest of these people," at this he gestured about the empty room dismissively, "but not me. Weak as you are, I still know."

"Weak?" she asked quietly, dangerously. Throttling him seemed more appealing by the minute.

Again, that look. "Well, you can't exactly be very strong, can you? You're older than me, that's for sure. Older by far."

Xhea snorted. "And how old are you?"

"Eight," he said proudly. She blinked at that; he looked smaller, younger. Even Lower City street kids looked older than he did, scrawny and underfed as they were. But when Xhea didn't reply, his shoulders slumped and his gaze dropped to the floor between them. "Okay, fine. I'm ten."

As if those two extra years were a source of shame.

After a pause, he said, "This is my last job, this lifting. A few weeks, maybe a month or two, and then . . ." He shrugged and closed his eyes. "Maybe faster if all the ghosts down here are so insubstantial. How do you do it? Live like this?"

Xhea didn't answer; something in the finality of those words had caught her attention. She looked at him then, truly looked, ignoring the mask of his expression, the veil of his tousled hair. She remembered her thought when she'd first seen him, that he had been wasted by some long illness. Now, he rested on the bed as if his burst of energy had been exhausted; his face glistened with sweat. His skin was not just pale, she realized, but sallow, and his breath came short and fast.

"You *are* ill," Xhea said.

The boy just looked at her, his expression something that she could not read, before he nodded. Xhea made to speak—but whatever she was going to say went unvoiced, for from the hall came the sound of footsteps. She tensed and eyed the door, listening.

Two sets of footsteps, a rattle in the lock, and then the door swung wide to reveal two dark-clad figures, each with a flashlight in hand. The two who had grabbed her in the corridor beyond Edren's barrier, and dragged her here. Except their goggles were off now, and their gloves.

"Oh, good," the taller one said to the boy. "You didn't kill her. That's a pleasant surprise."

Xhea was on her feet before she thought, and not even the sharp pain in her knee stopped her from flying across the room and grabbing the taller figure by the arm. She wrapped both her hands around his wrist, one atop the other, and squeezed hard so that he could not easily shake her off. Magic rose with her anger, and thin and weak though it was, it flowed fast through her hands to her kidnapper's skin. He'd only flinched when she touched him—but now, her magic soaking into him, he cried out in true pain.

But it was the boy who moved, leaping forward to pull her away. She clung for a moment, appreciating the sound of the man's cry and its echoes, before releasing her hold, leaving a bloody handprint in her wake. Even now, she thought, with dark magic swirling about her fingers, the boy did not flinch from her touch, did not recoil.

"What are you doing?" he cried, incredulous. "Are you trying to kill yourself?"

Xhea just shook her head and hands both, flicking away the smoke-like whispers of black that trailed from her fingers.

"Hello, Torrence," she said, low and vicious as she glared at the pair in the doorway. "Hello, Daye. How nice to see you again."

That's for abducting me, she thought to them, staring daggers. *That's for Mercks.* And, if she had her way, it was only the beginning of her retribution.

Torrence stared, holding his arm. Beneath the bloody smear, Xhea could see the white imprint of her hands against his tanned skin. Not dead flesh, she thought, not after so slight a contact—though she realized some part of her would not have cared if he lost the hand. It would have served him right.

Sometimes pawns fight back.

Despite everything, Torrence looked at her, looked at his arm, and laughed. It was not a mean laugh, not mocking, but Xhea still stiffened in response.

"It seems our darling girl has teeth after all," he said, and smiled his broad, white smile as if nothing in the world were wrong. He rubbed the whitened skin on his arm once more, then pulled down his sleeve.

From behind him, his partner, Daye, made a sound that was very much like a snort, pushed past Torrence, and slammed the door shut in their wake. Where Torrence was tall and blond, handsome and always wearing his carefully crafted façade of friendliness, Daye was short and firmly muscled, with a stern mouth that never smiled and a hard face framed by short, dark hair.

They were not—had never been—Xhea's friends; yet she had worked with them over the years until they had the sort of easy camaraderie that was the closest Xhea had ever come to friendship. Both were near as magic-poor as Xhea had once assumed herself; both generated so little magic as to barely have a magical signature, never mind the ability to work spells. They, too, had turned that weakness into a strength. With the right preparation, both could travel underground, searching the ruins and underground passages for salvage. When the materials they had been hired to find ran too deep, they'd hired Xhea.

There had been months that she'd eaten only because of that work.

Not that it mattered now. As far as Xhea was concerned, their business relationship had been permanently severed on the day they accepted a contract from Tower Eridian to track and kidnap Xhea by whatever means necessary. Eridian had only wanted Shai and her power, and had seen Xhea as the easiest means to get her. That Torrence and Daye had failed in those attempts at capture two months before did absolutely nothing to endear the pair.

Especially not now that they had at last succeeded.

Xhea looked from Torrence to Daye, seeing in their eyes the too bright gleam that she associated with the drugs they took to numb them to the pain of the underground. Recognized, too, their clothing, that mottled collection of dark. In some places the cloth had been patched and re-sewn; in others, the fabric thinned to mere threads, edges torn and trailing. On that fraying backdrop, Rown's mark had been stitched.

Xhea felt a wave of tiredness wash over her, leaving her feeling too hot and too cold, and making her knee throb. She hated to look weak in front of the bounty hunters, but there was nothing for it; glaring over her shoulder, Xhea staggered, dizzy, back to her bed. The boy followed in her wake, apparently satisfied that she was not going to attack their guests again.

"What are you here for, anyway?" Xhea asked Torrence and Daye. "I'm here; your job is done. Shouldn't you be upstairs collecting your renai?"

Torrence ignored her and instead smiled down on the boy. "Ieren, my boy, feeling any better?"

The boy—Ieren—shrugged. "Still hungry." For a moment Xhea saw something flicker in his eyes, a pale shadow of the craving that she'd seen writ naked across his expression before. Xhea shivered. *Just the chill*, she told herself. *Just the aftereffects of the magic.*

She'd never been good at lying to herself.

"Then I have good news for you, my friend," Torrence said. "The boss has cleared you to make a little visit to the medic. Sound good?"

At that word, "medic," Ieren leapt up from his bed and stood swaying, face eager. "Can we go now?" he asked. "I'm so hungry."

Torrence gestured toward the door, allowing the boy to walk ahead of him. Xhea could just stare. *The medic*, she thought. *He's going to visit the medic to eat.*

And oh, would that she did not understand; would that her anger or her magic or the renewed spinning in her head clouded her thoughts so that she did not see what was about to happen. Though she'd never been to visit a Lower City medic, nor sat as a patient in one of their clinics, no matter how crude, she'd felt what was inside. Or, rather, who.

People who stayed in the living world were bound to their unfinished business, whether that was a place or a person. "Unfinished business" could be great and noble things: love, sacrifice, duty. It could be hard and vicious things, like hatred or the desire for revenge. But just as often, it was something small: the desire to rest, a hope for pain's ease, a simple denial of the inevitability of death. Places where people died were often thick with ghosts, and unless someone was paying her, Xhea avoided them like the plague.

Eater of ghosts, she thought again, and shuddered.

If Torrence knew why Ieren wished to go to the medic, whole and unwounded as the boy was, he gave no sign.

"Play nice, darlin'," he said to Xhea, and though he smiled, she saw all too clearly the threat behind his pleasant expression. It was easy to remember to be wary around Daye—the woman's cold expression, heavily scarred knuckles, and easy access to the knives on her belt guaranteed that—but Torrence? She'd once seen him smile and joke with a man for a good ten minutes, only to bring a brick down on the man's head the moment his back was turned. He'd cheated them a while back, Torrence had explained; Daye had just shrugged, rummaged through the man's pockets, and rolled him into a nearby alley without once checking whether he was still breathing.

Xhea lifted a hand palm-up, gestured slightly with her fingers, and pretended to blow smoke from her palm. Magic-blind as he was, Torrence had no way of knowing that there was no magic in her hand, no dark power. Xhea's edged grin matched Torrence's own.

"Be careful," Xhea heard Torrence mutter in Daye's ear as he passed. Maybe he'd be a bit more cautious of her now—or at least cautious of her magic.

Daye did not close the door, only waited as their footsteps receded before turning to Xhea. Despite the drugs that Xhea knew were coursing through the woman's system—despite the sheen of sweat across her brow and the slight tremor to her fingers—Daye's eyes were cold, her expression unsympathetic.

"What now?" Xhea asked.

All too easily, she could imagine the myriad fates that might await, from questioning to staying locked in this room to being traded to some rival skyscraper. But Daye said only, "Dinner."

Daye spoke rarely; her voice, those few times that Xhea had heard it, had always come as a surprise. It was soft and undeniably feminine, and, though there was nothing gentle in her tone or in the clipped edges of her words, it nonetheless made Xhea think of a lullaby. Though Daye was the last person she'd want singing her to sleep.

When Xhea didn't move from her perch on the bed, Daye inclined her head toward the door. "Get up," she said.

"Or what?"

Daye raised a single shoulder and tilted her head, both movements so slight as to be all but unnoticeable. Her version, Xhea thought, of a shrug. Then she just watched Xhea, as if to say, "Why don't you find out?"

Xhea forced herself off the bed and limped to the door. There she paused, seeing if Daye would walk ahead of her with her flashlight—allowing Xhea the slightest chance to slip away into the darkness—but Daye only waited, expressionless and clearly not amused, until Xhea sighed and stepped into the cold hall.

She did not recognize the hall, nor the one after it, though she paid attention to the patterns on the stripped concrete walls, listened to the distant drip of water, looked for evidence of paint or carpet or the marks where drywall may have been torn away, hoping for clues as to her location. Seeking hints as to the direction of her escape.

Maybe Shai could find her, too, now that Ieren wasn't there to scare her away. She tried not to hold too closely to the thought; without the tether joining them, it might take the ghost hours or more to track her down.

The healing helped, Xhea thought as she stumbled forward; even so, she missed her walking stick. Without its aid, there was no way she could hide the unevenness of her gate, nor her winces as her braced leg bore her weight. There was a time when pride would have made her struggle on regardless, head up and shoulders back as she walked, doing everything in her power to mask the extent of her injury. Perhaps here, in enemy hands, she should have dredged up the will to pretend one more time.

But oh, her pride was long gone, bled out and discarded with yet another tangle of post-operative bandages. She only had so much strength—and would need it more for whatever lay ahead than for masking the pain when only Daye was present to see. Xhea held to the wall and made her steps small and careful. Daye did not protest, only kept pace just behind and out of Xhea's line of sight, her flashlight a steady white glow. The only sound between them as they walked was the clink and chime of the charms bound into Xhea's hair.

No stairs this time; Daye directed her with the flashlight's beam toward an elevator. Mechanical—no glimmer of magic on the call button, no gleam of spellwork in the elevator shaft beyond. The elevator, when it arrived, looked as bashed and battered as a tin can used for a children's kickball game, but it worked. Daye pressed the button for the highest floor and they rose in silence, the elevator vibrating all around them. Daye did not relax as they rose from underground; yet something in her eased with each moment, the corded tension of her jaw and shoulders softening.

It wasn't Daye that gave Xhea pause, though, but the elevator itself. *There's something . . .* she thought. Not the threadbare carpet nor the scraped and dented walls, but something . . . The floor buttons, she realized: there were rows upon rows of them. Far more than were needed for Rown's thirty-five stories.

The elevator jerked to a stop and the doors creaked as they opened into a room filled with the light of the setting sun. Xhea drew back, blinking; it was only Daye's quick, hard shove in the center of her back that made her stumble forward.

Xhea ground her teeth. Her payback, when it came, would be something that neither Torrence nor Daye would ever forget. Sometimes betrayals were just about business, Xhea knew that. This had crossed the line.

She found her balance and looked around the huge room. There was a heavy wooden table in the center—real wood, polished to a mirror shine—and two chairs pulled up to the table's sides. Platters of food had been set in the center, steam rising from around their edges. The walls to either side were clean, the drywall showing only the barest hints of water stains around their corners and edges, while the remains of a staircase led to a loft-like second story.

But it was the windows that held her attention, wide panes of glass that seemed to stretch the length of the building, with only a few cracked or patched or boarded over. They looked across the Lower City, the huddled structures bathed in the setting sun's light—a thousand shades of gray to Xhea's eyes. In the distance, she could see Edren and Orren and Senn, the smoke from the market generators rising in a thick pall between them.

Xhea swallowed. Sweetness and blight, she hated heights.

Above was the Central Spire, the vast needle that marked the City's center. The Spire was massive; it stretched from the City's bottom to its peak, managing to all but touch the ground and pierce the very sky at once. Around it spun the Towers, each seeming to dance against the brilliance of the setting sun, light sparking from their sides as they rose and fell, sliding on air.

Closer, Xhea saw the dark, squat shape of another skyscraper.

This isn't Rown. Xhea took a step toward the windows. This wasn't Rown, for Rown was right there, the dark-stained skyscraper sitting in a patch of shadow cast by the overhead Towers, ratty flags and mottled pennants flying from its uppermost level.

Not Rown at all, but Farrow, the tallest skyscraper—and the Lower City's dominant power. This room was the former condominium's penthouse suite.

It was only as she moved cautiously forward that Xhea noticed the man that stood to one side, hands behind his back. He stared across the Lower City and all the structures huddled near Farrow's base as if he owned them all. Perhaps he did.

He turned, casting his face in shadow. He met Xhea's eyes and smiled.

"Hello, my dear," he said. "Welcome home."

Chapter Nine

The rescue team found them near the barricade. The guard's progress had been slow and painful, minutes marked by his labored breath and the squeal of dust-clogged wheels against the floor. When he had been whole and healthy, his progress underground had been a matter of will, each step paid in hurt. Now, Shai could not imagine what gave him the strength to keep pushing forward.

Perhaps it was the sound of his own breathing, or the masking thud of his beating heart; perhaps it was that shock had made the world around him seem distant and dim. Whatever the reason, he did not hear the rescue's approach, only lay there, exhausted and despairing, trying to gather the strength to push himself forward another few inches.

There was only so much one spell, a small light, and a bubble of unshaped magic could do—but she had tried.

The thought was little consolation.

Even so, as Shai saw the approach of the rescue team's red-shielded flashlights, she closed her hands around her spell and absorbed what was left of the magic. The guard looked up as, to his eyes, all went dark but for the pinprick light she'd attached to his hand. A light that glowed dimmer by the moment.

"Please," he whispered. "Don't leave me."

Then a young man crept through the tunnel bored through the barricade, and his flashlight's red beam fell upon the fallen guard.

"Mercks!" he exclaimed, before cringing at his own volume.

There was another man, little older than the first, and both were clearly drugged halfway to insensibility. They showed obvious signs of discomfort with being underground, sweating and shuddering as they hurried to get Mercks more fully on the sledge and drag him back to Edren. No coordination in their movements: they fumbled and nearly fell over themselves in their efforts.

Shai stepped back and back again. Edren thought they were ready for an attack; they believed they could defend their skyscraper. Yet even her inexperienced eyes saw only poorly organized chaos and old training too rarely practiced to be useful.

They don't know what's coming. But then, neither did she. She only had a sick feeling that it would be something far worse than Edren was expecting. A storm was building, and they could only see its edges.

The rescuers helped the guard—*Mercks*, Shai corrected—farther onto the sledge. One dragged the sledge forward while the other covered their journey back into the skyscraper's basement, weapon raised, bloody-beamed flashlight shining into every corner.

Gone, she thought to them. *They're long gone. You're far, far too late.*

The guilt that came with that thought bowed her head with its weight.

Even so, Shai expanded the bubble of her magic to encompass them all. Unseen and unnoticed, she trailed behind them, easing their pain as they struggled back to the stairs.

They had reached the hall leading to Edren's main staircase when Shai's magic ran out. There was no warning. One moment she held a bubble of pure magic around Mercks and his two sweating rescuers, and the next . . . nothing. The magic vanished as if it had never been; even the pinprick light spell that clung to Mercks's hand guttered and died like a candle flame. The hall plunged into darkness broken only by the weak red lights of the rescuers' flashlights.

Shai gasped and staggered to a stop, staring at her hands. The guards swore, suddenly feeling the pain and disorientation of the underground once more. Even Mercks groaned, a sound low in his throat. But they were distant sounds that seemed to echo to her from somewhere impossibly far away.

Shai's hands were just . . . hands. In the faint red light, she could see her pale skin, the shadows of her fingers, and nothing else. No magic shone from within her—not even a glimmer of the power that had been hers since birth.

A wave of exhaustion rushed over her, and Shai sank to her knees—then farther, until she felt the floor's tile and concrete sliding through her incorporeal self. What, she thought in sudden fear, would keep her from sinking through the floor or the soil below? What would keep her from sinking and sinking until she was lost forever within the darkness of the earth, unbound and buried? Nothing, nothing. So she tried to cling to the ground with those pale and helpless hands, and prayed to absent gods that the weakness would pass.

When she could open her eyes again, Shai looked around. There was only darkness—the guards had staggered onward, leaving her behind—but she had practice enough seeing in the dark. After a moment of disorientation she saw again the walls around her, the floor, the distant glow that filtered down from the lobby. She forced herself up and forward, only just noticing that her feet hovered off the ground and her legs' movement was unconnected to her momentum.

Just like the early days, when Xhea used to laugh at me. The memory felt sharp enough to cut.

Then, she'd just been getting used to being dead. Now it was a measure of her distress. She'd never been anything but Radiant, never knew an existence in life or in death where she did not feel magic flowing from her center, through her body and out into the world beyond. Hadn't even known how central that sensation was to her concept of self until it was suddenly and inexplicably gone.

And Xhea . . .

Too much, even, to think about. She pushed herself onward, weak and disoriented.

Shai found the rescuers near the top of the stairs. They'd abandoned the sledge and now struggled to carry Mercks's weak and bloody form between them as they staggered upward. From the main level, other black-clad security members ran down to help, ignoring the discomfort to help drag Mercks to safety. Shai rose unseen in their wake, feeling as desperately unsteady as they looked.

They laid Mercks on the floor; Lorn and Emara stood nearby, tense and visibly upset. It was hot here, and humid.

In the afternoon sunlight that streamed through the lobby's upper windows, all Shai could see was the blood: dark and shining on Mercks's dust-caked uniform, smeared stains on his face and neck, his hands so red and sticky that she could not see the skin beneath.

Within seconds, the medic was at his side, grabbing for scissors and bandages and offering terse commands to a seemingly unflappable young assistant. Emara went to her knees and took Mercks's hand, out of the medic's way, while to the side one of the rescuers retched into a bucket.

"Where is she?" Lorn asked, over and over again. "Where is Xhea?"

Emara was quieter, steadier. "Mercks," she said. "What happened?"

"Gone," Mercks whispered. His eyelids flickered, but he clung valiantly to consciousness, forcing out the words. "They came at us in the tunnels. Two men and a boy. Rown's sigil on their shoulders. Took Xhea. Stabbed me."

Gone, taken. If only. Shai pressed her hand to her sternum as if force of will could make the tether reappear and Xhea with it—whole and healthy and alive.

"They killed her," Shai whispered, just to hear the words. Just to know they had been spoken—though speaking made them feel no more true.

The medic had cut through Mercks's uniform jacket and now sliced away the bloody mess of his shirt, tossing the fabric aside as he looked for the wound.

He froze. Around him, the crowd fell silent. Staring.

"What . . . ?" the medic said. He took some water from his assistant and poured it across Mercks's chest and lower torso. The water ran red, pink, clear, as the medic carefully bathed the wound.

Or, rather, where the wound had been.

Shai came closer and peered down at Mercks, sprawled on his back on the cracked marble floor in a puddle of blood and water. At last she could see the effects of her spell. There was no wound anymore—not even the deep pink mark of a wound recently healed. Only a thin, puckered scar marked where he had been stabbed, so pale that it looked years old.

Around them, the onlookers stared, their stunned silence broken only by the sound of the ill rescuer's retching.

"The ghost saved me," Mercks said, and fainted dead away.

Then: light.

Shai gasped and stumbled back as her magic rekindled inside her. She lifted her hand and watched as her skin seemed to glimmer, then to glow, light shining from her once more—weak, now, but growing stronger by the minute.

She would have said that her magic didn't have a feeling—would have said she couldn't feel its presence at all. It was only in the wake of its sudden absence that she knew the error of such thoughts. Magic felt like the sun on a chill day, when the clouds parted and warm, golden light poured down like a blessing.

It rushed through her, suffusing her, and she closed her eyes. For a moment, she almost forgot what had happened, what was happening all around her; she just let the magic flow through her, purify her, wash clean her heart and thoughts alike.

For a moment.

Then reality crashed back in, and no amount of magic was enough to banish it.

Around her, the lobby had become chaos. The security manager, Lorn, Emara—each called people to their sides, made requests, and issued orders. The medic had moved Mercks to a stretcher and was carrying him away, leaving only puddles and blood smears on the marble flooring. Mercks was going to live because of her spell. She should have felt—what? Pride? Joy? Beneath her surprise and the almost dizzy rush of her power returning, she felt only dazed confusion. All else seemed buried beneath ash.

Plans, protocols, calls for emergency meetings—Shai stopped listening. She just let people and words alike flow around her, through her, and closed her eyes. Opened them. What difference did it make? Countless things to be done, and none of them needed her.

No one needed her. Only her magic.

If she could, she would hollow out that power and hand it to them, just to be done with it. All of it.

So much magic, she thought as she shone brighter and brighter. Her sudden feelings of weakness, of exhaustion, eased; and she felt no better for their lack. *So much magic, and what does it matter?*

Whatever brief spark of hope she'd felt was gone now, gone and buried. She could not stop thinking about the rush of emotion that she'd felt from Xhea—and, worse, the instant of echoing silence that had followed—right before the tether had snapped.

She'd felt guilty when her father had been killed, knowing that he was only targeted because he'd tried to save her— guilty and shocked and sad beyond words. During the day she'd almost been able to push the feelings away, distract herself; yet at night, loss felt like a physical weight, as real and strong as gravity. She'd all but staggered beneath it as she wandered the Lower City's nighttime streets alone, searching for her father's empty, still-living body.

But this? This was different.

Her father had died trying to protect her—but he was her *father*. Of course her daddy tried to keep her safe. It was a child's reaction, yes, but no less true.

Xhea had only been her friend; in the end, she'd owed Shai nothing. And yet she had risked everything—had endured pain and injury, had faced death—to save her. But when Xhea was the one who needed saving, Shai had failed. Truly, utterly failed, beyond any hope of redemption.

Shai stared at her shining hands, still spread before her, and wondered why she hadn't just let herself dissolve into air and nothing. She shook her head, trying to push back the tears that once more threatened.

She wanted to rest, to sleep, to close her eyes and just *stop thinking*. Stop remembering.

Just . . . stop.

Instead she turned and staggered back towards the stairs and the darkness below, her movement slow and uneven as much due to the tears that half blinded her as to her lingering weakness. Voices rose and fell around her as she went— orders and conversations and whispers—as Edren prepared for whatever was to come. She could not help but hear.

Rown. That was the word said over and over again. *Rown* and *attack* and—against all expectation, mentions of a warehouse district.

Shai slowed, hesitated. Listened.

It took her a few moments to piece together the meaning from a dozen disparate half-heard conversations between the security personnel, Lorn and Emara's aides, and even the cleaners sent to mop up the pink-tinged water from the floor. Some thought the attack was orchestrated by skyscraper Orren, in revenge for Edren's betrayal and killing of the Orren family at the end of the last war. Yet more pointed the finger toward skyscraper Rown—and not just because of the sigils Mercks had seen on the hunters' sleeves, but because the day before Edren had conducted a covert attack on Rown's territory in an attempt to claim the warehouse district for their own.

Shai blinked at that, then followed a passing security pair who muttered as they took up their posts at the top of the stairs; she was certain she'd misunderstood. But no: for all the debate and whispers, everyone agreed that the attack held at dusk the night before was the cause for retaliation.

An attack, Shai realized, whose aftermath had been hidden by a wild party within Edren's walls—a party, like the fight held in the arena itself, that she suddenly suspected had been nothing but a distraction.

But why would Rown hurt Xhea? Because the ghost and the dark magic spell seemed designed to draw Xhea's attention, and her attention alone.

Again Shai looked to the stairs and the evidence she knew remained below. Hesitated, shame once more rising up her throat like bile, then turned and rushed after Lorn as he vanished into the elevator.

Emara was with him, their argument already in full swing. Shai slipped in beside them, pushing herself against the far wall in an attempt to avoid notice; yet each stared at the other as if there was no one else in the world.

"A weapon?" Emara was saying, her frustration evident. "If you think Xhea will turn on us, you don't know that girl half as well as you pretend to."

Lorn shook his head. "The risk is still there."

Emara crossed her arms to hide the way her hands curled into fists. "So you mean to tell your father?"

"No, we can't. You know what he'll do. And the council's a sham—that lot doesn't piss without his say-so." He ran a hand over his face, weary and frustrated.

"What, then?" Emara asked.

"I don't see that we have a lot of options—but, love, we're heading for war. The others have been creeping around Edren's edges since the first rumors of the Radiant's magic spread. Now, with what my father's done? The attacks on Rown's warehouses, the attempts to take Senn's trading contracts, that nonsense posturing against Farrow—it's just a matter of time."

"We can't let that happen." Emara's voice had gone hard. We won't.

Lorn reached out and hit the stop button; the elevator jerked to an unsteady halt. "Do you see another choice?"

"You don't understand. The only scars Lorn's body—your—" Emara stopped, took a deep breath, and tried again: "The only scars your flesh bears are ones from the arena. Not mine. Fighting as one of Edren's troops was vastly different than what you experienced—you and your father and your brother, all safe and sound within these walls."

"That's not fair," Lorn protested quietly. "I didn't spend every moment safe inside—no one did."

"It's not the same." Emara shook her head, expression haunted. "You think of the war, and you think of the skyscrapers clashing. Politics gone wrong. Threats, posturing, tactical movements. One of your father's cold cost/benefit analyses."

And oh, the anger in those words, the hurt and frustration and despair.

"I think of the war, and I remember kneeling in the street holding a child stabbed with a blade spelled for pain as she bled to death, crying for her mother." Emara had to stop, then; she closed her eyes and struggled to steady her breathing.

When she spoke again, her words were quiet and deliberate, if no less powerful. "I will not fight your father's battles. I will not help him start another war. I will fight for many things, but not this. Not this senselessness."

"You're a citizen of Edren, under his rule. He won't give you a choice."

Emara's expression was bleak. "I know." She took his hand, clasped it in her own as if she walked a cliff's edge and he was her only stability. "Give me another option."

"I—" He would have looked no less shocked if she'd struck him.

"Edren needs a real leader," Emara murmured. "This is the best time. The only time."

"The best time," he said at last, "or the worst. Either way, this is not the place to discuss it." He glanced meaningfully at the elevator's metal walls, then reached out and pressed another button. The elevator ground slowly upward once more.

"We're only going to be given so many chances, beloved," she said. "You and me and this skyscraper. Addis and I had a dream about what Edren could be when he was at last in command. Things that Lorn would never do, for all his strength and rage and bluster."

Emara smiled then, a slow, sad smile. "I think the time has come for you to decide: who are you going to be?"

Again she squeezed his hand, and met his eyes; she lifted her free hand to gently touch his cheek. When the doors rolled open, she released him and quietly walked away.

Lorn—Addis—stood staring after her, his expression a study in hope and despair.

Shai followed in Emara's wake. Some choices could only be made alone.

Chapter Ten

Xhea stared at the man who stood before her smiling, the setting sun sparking highlights from his hair. She did not know him. Did not, in truth, know this skyscraper any more than she did Rown.

What she knew of Farrow was only common knowledge: that it was the tallest, and—against all odds—the best kept of the skyscrapers, standing some space distant from the Lower City core. Farrow controlled the contracts with more than a dozen Towers out on the City's edges; and in the battles ten years past, least of all the Lower City's spilled blood had been theirs, while they had collected the spoils.

The market, the arena, Senn's trading contracts—what use were those to Farrow? They traded in a truer coin, one far more useful in the City, Lower and proper alike: magic.

Farrow was the home of the Lower City's best casters, the magic-workers, and those powerful enough to train them for such work. This man—to be here, in charge? If he was not a caster, not a magic-worker with quick hands and clever spells, he would nonetheless be a power—or the closest thing they had in the Lower City.

Though she had to wonder whether being here, talking to her with this dish-laden table between them, spoke to a higher status or a lower one. Who was she in this political tangle? A pawn, that much she knew; but perhaps it was known that, on this strange chessboard, she was a pawn tied to the power of a queen.

Or had been. She simply wouldn't mention that she and Shai were no longer joined.

She'll find me. Soon.

So Xhea stepped toward him, hiding her limp as best she could, until she reached the table and placed her hands flat upon it. *Welcome home,* he had said. Xhea looked into his eyes, making her expression as cold as her voice as she said, "I don't know you, and I don't know this place, and this is not my home."

The man's smile slipped as he made his way to the table. Away from the window, the setting sun no longer making his gray-streaked hair gleam like metal, he seemed smaller somehow, older and more human.

He made to speak, and Xhea gestured sharply.

"No," she said. "*Home,* as you said, does not steal you away. *Home* does not attack your friends and leave them to die in the dark and the cold. *Home* does not lock you away, injured and alone. So whatever your welcome, this is not my home." For all her fatigue and lingering dizziness, her anger felt good—simple and pure. Though she kept her weakened magic contained, again she felt it black and cold in the pit of her stomach, and was stronger for it.

"My apologies." He inclined his head. "I misspoke."

Xhea raised a slow eyebrow. "As if the words were the offense."

He looked to Daye, who loomed behind Xhea like a shadow. Noticed, perhaps, the dark stain on her sleeve where she had wiped her knife clean. "You needed to use force? Ieren's approach did not work?"

Xhea did not so much as glance at the bounty hunter, but she heard the whisper of fabric and could imagine the woman's shrug.

"She's here," Daye said flatly, as if that were the only explanation needed.

"You didn't *need* to do anything," Xhea said.

"You were not being held against your will?" he asked. Xhea looked at him incredulously. "Again," he said, "I apologize. You were not supposed to be abducted nor locked away, and if anyone you knew was hurt trying to stop you from being taken, you have my personal assurance that amends will be made."

"Your assurance?" Xhea snorted. "And who are you?"

"My name is Ahrent Altaigh."

She did not know him; and though she could not bring the name of Farrow's current leader to mind, she'd recognize it if she heard it. No, he was not in charge—but not far from the seat of power, unless she missed her guess.

A caster, then. But what use was she to a caster? What use was she to anyone? Anchor to a power plant, an unending fountain of renai, that's all—and she already knew how Shai's power might be used.

Her thoughts must have shown on her face. Ahrent Altaigh, whoever the blight he was, smiled and raised his hands palm-out as if in surrender.

"Allow me to explain. Please," he said, and gestured to the heavy wooden chair nearest to her. "Sit. Make yourself comfortable."

She heard no threat hidden in the words, despite Daye's continued presence. As he spoke he drew out a chair, settled himself and placed a napkin in his lap. *How civilized*, Xhea thought, dark and unhappy.

She stared for a long, silent moment, watching the man, watching his calm, easy movements. Some part of her wanted to strike out, to shout at him, to turn and run away as fast as she could. There was a time she would have tried, no matter that closed doors barred her escape. Her anger, now, was no less—but oh, the weight of fatigue. Her will to move seemed to drain from her by the second, her reserves long since stripped from her by weeks of pain and drugs and very little sleep. It was so hard to stand defiant when all she wanted was to lie down, close her eyes, and rest.

Behind her, she felt the weight of Daye's silent regard. Some time and planning had gone into attracting her attention, drawing her out from the safety of Edren's walls, and bringing her here, Xhea realized; some expense, too, to pay the bounty hunters and create the dinner arrayed before her.

Run, Xhea thought. *Run away.* But what was there left to run to?

Xhea sat. There were only two plates at the table, yet she counted ten large covered platters. As she watched, Ahrent Altaigh drew the covers from each, releasing puffs of fragrant steam, then began to serve them both.

"Please," he said again, pushing a laden plate towards her. "Eat."

Xhea stared at the plate. It was a bribe, she thought—or a display meant to impress. Because oh, sweetness, she'd never seen such food.

There were steamed greens on a bed of fluffy rice; soft buns cut open to reveal a thick, spiced filling; and long fried pastries dusted in sugar. There was *meat*—and not just the bits and scraps that Xhea knew from her better meals, meat scrounged or hunted from the few animals that still roamed out in the badlands, but real, thick slabs of meat, spiced and covered in a shining glaze. There were foods she couldn't recognize, never mind name.

Not Lower City food, not any of it. This was food from the multi-tiered growing platforms out on the City's edges. Food not burned, nor gritty from the sand mixed into the spice; food not half-turned, wilted, or cooked a week or more earlier.

At a faint noise, Xhea glanced back at Daye. Though the bounty hunter stood unmoving, her stone-gray eyes watching everything, she had a pinched look about her mouth. The drugs Daye used to go underground made her nauseated, Xhea remembered—sick, then shaky, then so hungry she could eat a normal dinner three times over and not be full.

Still in the sick phase. Xhea snorted in amusement. *Serves her right.*

Not that Xhea felt much better. Magic, anger, and the aftereffects of painkillers had left her stomach a twisted knot. But it was not her stomach that made her pause and then fold her hands deliberately on the table, ignoring the food, but the man before her. He wanted her to eat, and so she would not.

Ahrent Altaigh ate a few bites, each slower than the last, before dabbing his mouth with the napkin. "I brought you here," he said, "to offer you a job."

"Generally, job offers are not preceded by abductions."

"No. Rarely are such extreme measures necessary." He smiled at her expression. "Surely you did not think my first attempt to contact you involved hired muscle?"

Xhea stared, her gaze never wavering, because of course that was what she'd thought.

He continued: "I left notes of introduction with your known contacts, but was told that you hadn't been seen for two months. I hired people to investigate. Later, when I found you were in Edren, I sent messages to you directly. You did not receive any of my notes, did you?"

"You sent them to Edren?" she asked slowly. "Addressed to me."

"Yes. More, even, than I can count, though I received not so much as an acknowledgment in reply. My messengers were told that they could not speak to nor see you, and that any attempt to force a face-to-face meeting would be seen as an act of aggression." He gestured with one hand. "It was entirely believable when my contacts said that you were in Edren against your will."

"Contacts? You mean spies."

He did not debate the point.

As for being held captive—well, it was true that she had barely stepped outside in the two months that she'd been in Edren, though that was due to her injuries and inability to walk, not Edren holding her there. And yes, once or twice she'd tried to walk out the front door only to have security stop her. She'd been asked to wait until someone could accompany her, asked her to use another door—and by then she was usually too exhausted to argue, trembling with pain and fatigue. Returning to her room had been the easier option.

But they hadn't actually been holding her, hadn't . . .

"Sweetness and blight," Xhea muttered. Because she suddenly had no doubt that Verrus Edren would have ordered her restrained and kept in the skyscraper if that's what was required to keep Shai nearby. *Lorn wouldn't have let them,* came the thought—or had his knowledge of the orders to keep her captive been just one more reason for him to avoid her?

She looked at the piled plate before her. She thought of Shai's fear of the dark magic boy. She thought of Torrence grabbing Mercks, and the flash of the knife as Daye drove it into Mercks's side. She thought of that wave of dark rolling over her; that feeling of helplessness as she fell to the ground, unable to stop what was happening.

She thought again of the tether snapping—not so much a sound as a feeling that had reverberated through her. A sudden, echoing absence.

She thought of her so-called allies, and darkness swirled within her.

Oh, no, her rage had little abated. She took a deep breath to steady herself, and tried to think rationally.

"So I'm not a prisoner?" she asked, daring him to contradict. "I could just get up right now and walk out of here, and you wouldn't object?"

"I would be disappointed," Ahrent Altaigh said, "especially given the time and effort I've already invested, but yes, you could go. I hope, though, that you'll at least hear out my proposal."

She wanted to tell him what he could do with his proposal. She made to rise.

Yet even if she stormed—limped—from this place, made her slow and painful way back to Edren, then what? *Shai*, she thought—and yes, perhaps the ghost would return there too. But if Ahrent Altaigh's suspicions were true, and Edren had been keeping her captive—and she'd just been too hurt, too exhausted, to notice? She'd be a fool to walk willingly back into that trap.

If not Edren, there were always the tunnels. Her old ways of living. Maybe, with Shai's healing, returning to that life wouldn't be as difficult as she had imagined. And when she found Shai, she could ask her to re-create the healing spell. Perhaps, if her magic stayed quiet, if she could just endure the pain, she could be whole and strong again.

If, if, if. The uncertainties piled higher and higher—and any way she looked at it, Shai's power painted a target on her back.

Xhea lifted her fork and ate a slow and deliberate bite, and another. She chewed and swallowed mechanically as if the fine spices and rich sauce were nothing to her, as if she ate tender meat and fresh vegetables every day. The food seemed to drop a long way before it hit the cold pit of her stomach. Silence settled across the table as she ate.

"What's the job?" Xhea asked at last.

Ahrent Altaigh hesitated, considering. "Are you finished?" He gestured to her plate, emptied twice, little though she remembered eating. She nodded. "Then there's something I want to show you. Many things, actually, but I think this will help make my offer make sense."

Xhea met his gaze, her expression mimicking Daye's. "Just tell me. Is the job that bad—or can you not pay?"

"Citizenship, Xhea. I'm offering to renew your full citizenship in Farrow—and that's just to start."

"Renew?" Xhea scoffed. "I never lived in Farrow." She'd never even been a citizen of Orren, for all that she'd lived within Orren's crooked walls and still had their indenture contract hanging over her head.

"You did," Ahrent said simply. "You were born a citizen of Farrow. You lived here with your family until you were taken from us."

"Don't lie to me." Xhea's voice was cold and hard and flat. "I never lived here. I don't have a family. I never did."

"You did. And I can prove it."

His opening words came back to her, echoing through her mind as if from somewhere impossibly far away: *Welcome home.*

She wanted to speak some hard, flat denial. She wanted to roll her eyes, and push back in her chair, and wave her hand dismissively as if to knock his words from the air like flies.

But all she could do was stare. Her whole body had become strangely light, as if she were but a ghost barely tethered to her ailing flesh. All her words, all her thoughts, had drained from her, leaving her empty and echoing.

When at last she could speak, all she said was, "Show me."

It took a very long time to walk to their destination, some ten stories and two very long hallways away. They went in silence, and even Xhea did not complain at the pace.

She had been on her feet too long, and even longer without painkillers. She wanted to walk tall, strong, confident. Yet no amount of will was enough to straighten her shoulders or lift her head; and her feet, as she walked, all but dragged along the worn carpet. Every movement hurt.

Even so, she felt the weight of Daye's attention upon her, as if the bounty hunter expected her to suddenly run. *No flight risk here*, Xhea thought irritably.

At last, Ahrent unlocked an apartment door and gestured her inside. Xhea stepped cautiously into the shadowed space.

There was a sagging couch in one corner and a knotted rug spread across the floor. A single low table made from bricks and a warped board stood in the center of the room, upon which rested a chipped teacup. The next room was a kitchen, which even had a few cupboards left; and there was a narrow hall, down which Xhea could catch a glimpse of two more doors.

No beds on the floor; no sign of small personal spaces claimed in corners. One person lived here, or two. In Orren, a space like this would have held ten people or more; only the skyscraper's most powerful families had anything like this kind of personal room.

It was nice—beyond nice. Never mind her tunnel corners or the back room in Edren with its rusting cot; this was luxury. Yet as she looked around, Xhea felt a kind of empty disappointment.

"It's nice and all," she said with a shrug, "but I don't really see . . ."

"Here." Ahrent crossed the room and pulled a photo from the wall. He handed it to her.

She saw the back first. *Ennaline and Enjeia, age 4*, said the hand-written words.

"This isn't me," Xhea said as she turned it over. "That's not my—"

Suddenly, she couldn't breathe.

It was not her name, no—at least not any name she remembered—nor was the child in the picture in any way familiar: a small girl with dark, tangled hair, dusky skin and a slight upward tilt to her eyes. It might have been her. Then again, it might have been any number of young girls who roamed the Lower City streets, then or now.

But the woman in the picture . . .

If asked, Xhea would have said that she remembered almost nothing of her life before Abelane found her on the streets. She had only snatches of memory, incomplete fragments with edges so sharp she had little desire to handle them. The cold. The thick, wet mud that clung to her bare feet like heavy shoes. Hiding curled in an alley behind piled refuse, shaking and shivering and staring at the Towers above so she would not have to see whether the man who had tried to grab her had found her dead-end hiding spot.

Nothing good. Nothing, in the end, worth remembering.

Except when she saw the photo, she felt a pang go through her so sharp it might have been Daye's blade. The picture blurred and wavered before her, and only then did Xhea realize she was fighting back tears.

In the image, an older woman held a small child on her lap, wrapped in patchwork blankets. The woman had dark skin that creased into well-worn lines around her eyes and mouth, and her face was framed by a round halo of cloud-white hair. The child stared at the viewer, dark eyes wide and serious; but the woman was laughing, her smile wide as she looked at the girl in her arms as if she were the most precious thing in the world.

Xhea couldn't speak; didn't know what words she would shape even if her pressed-tight lips allowed the attempt. She knew this woman. Knew her in a way that bypassed all thought or memory.

"Ennaline was your grandmother," Ahrent said quietly.

"Was?" Xhea choked out.

"Yes. I'm afraid she died just a little over a year ago."

A year. A year ago, Xhea had been but streets away from this place. She had passed the skyscraper as she went about her business, sat in the shade that Farrow cast, and never once had she thought—never once had she imagined—

"I didn't..." Her thoughts tumbled over themselves, twisting, tangling. "I never knew my family," she managed.

Didn't, in truth, believe that she'd ever had a family. She'd been born to someone, and had been orphaned or cast aside, it mattered little which. Even that word—*family*—didn't feel right in her mouth, as if she had no claim to it.

She'd only ever had Abelane, only ever had Shai—the family that she'd found and chose and clung to desperately with both hands.

But this—a grandmother. A woman who had held her through blankets' protective swaddling; a woman who had smiled at her, laughed with her. Loved her. It was more than she knew how to process.

She needed, quite suddenly, to sit down. Xhea stumbled to the couch and all but fell into its worn cushions. For a long moment, she struggled to breathe as darkness seeped in around the edges of her vision. When the dizziness faded, she carefully looked around: there were more pictures pinned to the wall, photos and drawings and images in small, handcrafted frames of sheet metal and wood. A child's clumsy drawings. Photos and hand-drawn images of a little girl's face.

Enjeia.

Xhea had to look away. Her gaze caught on the cup on the table before her—a cup that still held a splash of a deep gray liquid that she thought to be tea.

"Someone lives here," she said quietly.

"Yes. Marna—your grandmother's partner—still lives here, though she wants to leave the place to you. If you want it." Ahrent Altaigh walked toward the couch and, when Xhea did not protest his presence, sat carefully on the far end, a meaningful gap between them.

"Why would she . . . I mean, but she . . ." No matter what she did, the words would not piece together, nor her thoughts.

Get it together, Xhea. She took a steadying breath.

"Why are you doing this to me?" she asked. Xhea turned, met his eye. "Showing me this. Telling me this. Even if it's true, you can't pretend it's for my benefit. You're not doing this out of the goodness of your heart."

"No, of course not." At least he didn't bother to lie; for that much, at least, Xhea was grateful. "But I needed you to understand some small element of what I'm offering you in all seriousness so that you understand the importance of what I'm doing."

An apartment would have been an unthinkable payment, as would citizenship and all the privileges that came with—especially given that she had no bright magic to contribute to the skyscraper, nor skills that would improve Farrow's wellbeing.

And the rest? Home. Family. They were hooks, nothing more; hooks she knew had become embedded deep in her flesh, despite everything. Caution, wariness; they might as well have been nothing, so much sand and ash. For Xhea looked again at the picture in her hand, that woman smiling outward, that small, cherished girl, and something in her broke and was mended at the same time.

"I knew of no one alive in the Lower City who had your talent. But when I heard a rumor of what happened to Allenai and Eridian—when I heard the stories—I understood. I knew I had to find you."

"Ah," Xhea said. She leaned back and briefly closed her eyes. The anger drained from her, and the hope. "It's not even me you want, is it? It's Shai." At his confused look, she clarified; "The Radiant ghost."

If that's why she was here, so he could take Shai from her and bind her to Farrow, there was nothing he could offer her that would make her agree. Not even this.

Ahrent Altaigh took a long breath and let it out slowly. "A Radiant? You truly . . ." He rubbed a hand across his face. "I'd thought that rumor exaggeration or lies, no matter how much Edren started swinging around their newfound wealth. So few people here even understand what a Radiant is, I never . . ." Again, that breath. "But no, Xhea. As much as I'd dearly love a Radiant's support, it's you that I'm after. You that Farrow needs."

He laughed softly at her expression. "You don't know how valuable you are, do you? Worth more than a Radiant a hundred times over."

Xhea blinked at that, then shook her head. His words made no sense.

"What do you want?" she asked instead. "You . . . have a ghost?" What other use had anyone ever had for her?

"No," he said. "I have a plan. A brave and crazy plan to save thousands of people in the Lower City, and give them the life we never had—and I need you to help me make it real."

He had to be mocking her, yet she saw no amusement in his face, no mirth. But there was a light in his eye as he spoke; a spark, like fire, that told of some burning passion.

"Tell me."

He smiled then and said, "I'm going to transform Farrow into a Tower."

Chapter Eleven

"You're insane," Xhea whispered. The words just slipped out; spoken, they seemed to hang in the air between them.

Ahrent Altaigh inclined his head. "Perhaps," he admitted. "Ambitious, at least, beyond anything the Lower City has known these past years. So many petty fights and squabbles down here in the dirt—and for what? Just more of the same. It's time, I think, to change that."

Xhea looked from Ahrent to Daye, who stood just inside the apartment's closed door. She didn't know what she expected: disbelief, incredulity twin to her own—or even passion, that fire and light that seemed even now to burn from Ahrent, filling his words and face and every gesture. Yet Daye just watched, still as stone, her face impassive.

Xhea turned back to Ahrent.

"Have you never wondered where the Towers came from?" He met her eyes; he seemed, Xhea thought, genuinely curious.

Xhea's mind felt so full of words, of thoughts, of shocks and absence, that she could not keep them all straight. So many that their weight felt like silence. Even so, it was not hard to consider his question. Where had the Towers come from? Where had the sky come from, or the clouds, or the ground beneath their feet? From whence had the sun been birthed, and what filled the darkness between the stars?

Useless questions, all. Of course she'd never wondered. Mutely, she shook her head.

"Few do," he said simply. "But think, they didn't just appear in the sky. They were created. Farrow will be the first wholly new Tower in more than a hundred years."

"You can't," Xhea protested. "Towers aren't just made, they're—" She stopped. Frowned.

She had been about to say that Towers were born, though that couldn't be right. In all her years looking skyward, she'd seen Towers merge and change shapes, seen them rise and fall, but never once had she seen a Tower born.

Yet the Towers were alive. She'd always known it, but it was only in Allenai's forced takeover of Eridian two months before that she'd experienced that truth. She'd seen the walls and floors and everything around her move and quiver like the inside of some great beast; she'd seen the power of the Towers' magic, the beat of their flaring hearts. She'd heard the Towers *singing*.

"Skyscrapers are just metal," she said instead. "Concrete and iron, glass and rebar . . . dead things. *Heavy* things." She shook her head at the thought of Farrow leaping aloft. "It's impossible."

"Maybe. But I'm going to try. *We're* going to try. Once, the Towers were buildings—real structures here on the ground, anchored to earth. Have you never wondered why there are only five tall buildings left here? Of all the buildings of the city that came before, only five not cut down to within mere stories of the ground."

Oh, the things she could tell him to do with his "have you never wondered" nonsense. She'd wondered about plenty, most of it involving where she was going to find food and shelter, how she was going to live through the winter, how to find or make a new water catch-basin after some fool stole one of hers for the thousandth blighted time. In comparison, the greater workings of the City held little interest.

Again, she shook her head. She knew what he wanted her to think: *Towers. They became Towers.*

"Here." Ahrent drew an object from his pocket and held it flat on his palm. "With your magic, you may not want to touch it. But look."

Xhea leaned forward, steadying herself on the couch cushions as she peered at the object. It was a small sculpture made from gray metal in the shape of a long, thin animal. The creature was curled into a circle, head resting on its clawed front legs, with bat-like wings folded across its back. There was an indentation where the lizard-thing's eye should have been where once a bead or jewel might have rested.

Xhea had spent enough time combing through the ruins to know an artifact when she saw one. Its edges were rounded, its patterned scales worn almost smooth, while nicks and scratches marked the creature's folded wings. If she'd found it herself, she might have offered it to Wen, the collector and artifact trader with whom she'd worked most often, though she doubted it would have earned her much renai. Junk, mostly—but it was pretty, too, in a strange way. Maybe she would have kept it.

"I found it when I was a child, and have kept it in one pocket or another for most of my life." Not unlike Xhea's knife, if far less useful. Ahrent continued, "I'm a spellcaster—one of Farrow's strongest—and that means I use a lot of magic, day in, day out."

"But what—?"

"Keep looking. Truly look."

Xhea stared at the little gray thing on his gray hand until she felt her eyes tear and blur—and then her focus shifted, like when she wanted to see spells. Suddenly, the little figurine glowed. She blinked and looked closer.

It was not alive, Xhea decided, but it was not exactly dead, either. Not just metal, not anymore. Deep within it, magic glowed. It was not a spell; look though she might, she could find no lines of intent, no spell-anchors, no signs even of a former spell's decay. Yet there was power there, centered at the little sculpture's core and radiating outwards.

She reached hesitantly toward the figurine, though stopped short of touching it. Even so, she imagined that she could feel a whisper of magic against her fingertips—or was that power only from Ahrent's hand, below the creature? Still, Xhea drew back, suddenly wary, as if the little creature might uncurl, stand up on its clawed legs and stretch its long neck, raise and flap its pewter wings. As if that empty eye socket might fix on her and stare unblinking.

"Enough magic changes a thing," Ahrent said quietly. "Even little things like this. Magic is the power of life. With enough magic and enough time, things begin to change—to become something more than they were. Eventually, even metal or glass or stone can begin to awaken."

Awaken. As if inert things were only dormant, awaiting spring.

She did not want to believe him; did not think, even staring at the pewter sculpture that he placed in his pocket once more, that what he said could be true. Yet she had seen the Towers for as long as she could remember; had seen them shift and change, as if the metal and stone of their structures was liquid; had seen them grow, larger and larger, as if each were a great tree, its defensive spires like roots and branches reaching for sun and soil.

If what he said was false, what explained the Towers themselves? Yet, if enough magic could wake a sky-borne structure, why not a curled figurine of a dragon? Why not this crumbling skyscraper, this ruin from another time?

If his words were true, she was not fool enough to miss their implications. *Enough magic*, Ahrent had said. *Enough time.* Time was plentiful enough to one willing to wait—but magic? Xhea felt cold. Because she knew, as few others did, the true power required to keep a Tower aloft, living and growing and changing. Bound to every Tower, there was a Radiant—perhaps more than one, perhaps many more—whose power fueled the Tower's daily life. Radiants were more than just the most powerful magic-users in the City; they were a wellspring of magic that knew no end.

Bright magic was the power of life and growth; but life and growth unchecked led inevitably to mutations, to cancer, and to death. Because they needed every Radiant's magic, Towers bound their Radiants' spirits to their ailing bodies—or made those spirits inhabit foreign flesh—just to keep their power flowing. For all their magic, Radiants were trapped, forced to live long past the time when death would be a mercy, helpless in a cage of immovable flesh.

Radiants like Shai.

Ahrent Altaigh might be a powerful Lower City spellcaster; he might even be strong enough to be a citizen of a Tower above, had he desired it. But the strength that made him a power here was nothing in comparison to the strength of the City's best casters—and even their strength paled in comparison to a Radiant's.

"You don't have enough magic," Xhea said. "For something small, maybe. But a whole skyscraper? No one here has that kind of power to spare."

"No," he said. "But we've been working toward this for a very long time. It's easiest, I think, if I just show you."

Xhea shook her head. "And me?" she asked. "Why do you need me?" Again she looked around, seeing not only this room with its wall hangings and pictures, not just the images of a little girl that she struggled to believe might once have been her, but the whole skyscraper. She imagined the structure all around her, a tall and slender building stabbing toward the sky.

Again he said, "Let me show you." Then he looked at her, and seemed for the first time to see the weariness and confusion that underlay her every word and action. "Let me see if Ieren has returned," he said then. "Perhaps you'd like a few moments of quiet before I show you more?"

No—what she wanted was for it suddenly to be yesterday again, a day defined only by pills and their absence. What she wanted was to be gone from here, gone as if she'd never been. What she wanted was for this to make *sense*.

But then, she'd never really gotten what she'd wanted. Desire, it seemed, existed only to be thwarted.

Yet Xhea hadn't realized how short her breath had become until, at Ahrent's quiet offer, she felt like she could inhale again. No words: she only nodded. He rose, murmuring that he would return shortly, and gestured Daye to follow.

The door clicked shut.

Quiet.

Seconds passed. Minutes.

She was not alone; Xhea was not so much a fool to believe that she would be left untended. Daye had gone no farther than the hall, and now stood guard in silence.

Let her stand.

Yet even that presence seemed muted, the few steps and the closed door between them like a vast and echoing space. A welcome space at that.

Xhea slowly looked around the apartment. She could not bear to face the pictures that so liberally scattered the walls, nor their import; her eyes skimmed over them and landed instead on tiny, insignificant details. The scuffed doorframes, bare patches testament to the years upon years of hands that had rested upon them; the teacup on the makeshift table and the near-invisible print left by lips upon its rim; the faint smell of lilacs in the air.

Welcome home.

She did not feel like she was home. No comfort, here; no warmth nor joy nor safety. If anything, she felt more hopelessly off-balance than she had locked in Edren's halls, struggling to walk again.

What Ahrent Altaigh had said did not make sense—not her birth here, not Farrow's transformation, not any of it. Yet she could not deny her shock, nor her feeling when she saw the older woman in the photo. She had no name for that emotion, nor could she say what she felt now. Only that she struggled to breathe, to focus, and wished for the willful oblivion of sleep or drugs with all her being.

Because what Ahrent Altaigh had said did not make sense—but if it were true? Oh, dangerous thought. She could not help but imagine it—and not just meeting the family that Ahrent assured her she'd once had, but knowing them. Never having lost them at all.

To have grown up within these walls, in this very place; to have her image on the wall, a picture for every year of her life. To have the memories, good and bad and in-between; so many memories that she could spend all day staring, thinking, and never go through them all.

To have had a home.

She would never have known Abelane, nor lost her; she knew that. She might never have learned she could travel underground. She would never have met Shai. The sharp, precious joys of her life would never have been—gone, unmade, as surely as all the difficult times.

But it was not those memories on which her thoughts lingered—not the memories, true or imagined—but the thought that lay underneath them all: to be *wanted*.

Oh, to be wanted.

Shai, she thought, pressing a hand to her sternum. *Where are you?*

Xhea sat on that battered couch, let the moments pass around her like water, and tried not to cry. What Ahrent had told her could not be true because she wanted it too much. Bright dreams had the hardest edges, she knew; they cut too deep when they shattered.

Chapter Twelve

Shai slipped into Edren's council meeting only minutes in Emara's wake.

She hadn't wanted to. She had turned to leave, to sink back down into tunnels, so she might search for Xhea the way her grief and guilt demanded. Ease the restless anger in her hands, if not her heart.

Yet, hearing Lorn and Emara's conversation, she could not deny that there was more at play than just the attack on Xhea and Mercks, or the destruction of Edren's barricade. More threats, more people who might be hurt or die—and her own bright magic was at the root of it all.

There was no evidence that Rown's attack had been an attempt to steal the Radiant ghost spoken of in whispers on the Lower City streets. No evidence, either, that it hadn't. For all that she wanted to turn and run, Shai could not discount that Xhea may have been drawn into the underground as a means of capturing the ghost to which she was bound. After all, the dark magic boy had tried to grab Shai, and then only after killing Xhea to free Shai's tether.

She did not want Xhea to have died for nothing.

Such hubris in the thought—but it was enough, however briefly, to make her pause. Enough to force her to turn, for all that something in her screamed and cried and ached in the denial of her true desire, and walk through the wall into the council chamber beyond.

She needed to *understand*. Only then might her actions be worth more than the renai she generated.

Neither Emara nor Lorn's presence in council had been missed; the meeting was already in full swing. Around the table sat the full suite of councilors, the tall, knife-faced man who Xhea had said was Edren's old battle general, and a very angry Verrus Edren. Verrus was silent as others around him spoke in ever-louder voices. His hands were flat on the table, and anger seemed to shimmer from him like heat from a sun-baked stone.

Only Edren's old general—a tall, scarred, imposing man—sat unmoved, as if neither the arguments nor his leader's anger had any strength to touch him. The general, and Lorn. Even as Lorn came into the room and noisily took his seat, he seemed to lean into his father's anger rather than away, like a man braced against a storm wind.

"Enough," said Verrus. His voice was not loud, and yet it silenced the room, some councilors stopping speaking mid-word.

Watching, Shai moved from the back wall where Xhea had stood only that afternoon, behind the chairs toward the head of the table. The councilors did not seem to notice her presence, distracted as they were; only Emara, seated this time to Lorn's left, stilled and looked up, her eyes unfocused as she scanned the room. She looked, Shai thought, surprised.

"We have no other choice," the horse-faced councilor argued into that quiet. "Rown is preparing for war, Farrow has posted a heavily armed perimeter guard, and Orren has sent away our messengers unheard. We must move now, before they can gather their forces."

"Councilor Lorris," said a man down the table, "when we wish to kill our people with hasty, ill-conceived strategies, we will ask for you personally. Until that time, do us all the pleasure of shutting your twice-blighted mouth."

"*Enough*," Verrus said again. He leaned onto the table, atop which was spread a hand-drawn map of the Lower City in heavy black ink, accented with symbols in red and green. "The question is not whether we will respond to Rown's unprovoked attack, but when and how."

Unprovoked? Shai could have cried, could have laughed. Hysteria; she choked it down.

"About the girl, Xhea," Lorn interrupted, voice tight and words carefully calm. "If she's being held in Rown—"

Verrus barely glanced up. "The girl is of no importance."

Lorn took a deep breath. "With her abilities—"

"The abilities that patently failed to be as useful as either you or your wife argued?" Verrus's voice was cold, so cold. "Abilities that now allow her to provide information about our defenses to our enemy? I fail to see the benefit of your argument."

"We sent her down there," Lorn continued, clearly swallowing back an angry retort. "We have a responsibility—"

"Our first and only responsibility is the good of the skyscraper and its citizens. The girl is neither a citizen nor a valuable asset."

"Edren's resources are limited," added one of the councilors. She was a small, weedy woman who sounded as if she were repeating an earlier argument—one likely first voiced by Verrus himself. "Rown's target is larger than a single girl. We must focus on the true priorities."

Emara interjected, "Are you forgetting of her connection to the Radiant? Her continued presence is critical to—"

Verrus raised a hand. "Is the ghost still present?" he asked quietly.

There was a pause—a pause in which Shai wished she was somewhere else, anywhere else, so that the answer to that question might truthfully be "no." Lorn glanced at Emara and something unspoken passed between them, before at last Lorn nodded to his father. It was a slow nod, and reluctant.

"She's here," Lorn said.

"Then we have no further use for the girl." Verrus Edren turned away in dismissal.

Unseen, Shai could but stare. She felt too hot, too cold—she felt like smoke and light and nothing in between. It that moment, it didn't matter that Xhea wasn't waiting to be saved, that no rescue could claim her from where she had gone; only that no one cared. Verrus would just have left her there—*was* leaving her there, if only her fallen body.

Shai looked from Verrus to Lorn and Emara and the councilors around the table. Despite Lorn's obvious anger and Emara's carefully blank expression, no one mentioned Xhea again. Instead, they argued about defenses, offenses, scouting positions, spy reports—she knew not which. Didn't, in that moment, care.

Her head spun and she moved with it, pacing back and forth along the length of the boardroom as if motion might dispel her confusion or frustration or the anger that underlay it all. Were they concerned about the destruction of their barrier and the attack it presaged? They would have known of neither were it not for Xhea. What time they had to prepare for the upcoming aggression—time in which they might attempt diplomacy or court allies—was due entirely to Xhea's intervention. Though her discovery had been accidental, that fact in no way absolved Edren of their debt to her.

Shai wanted, for one crazy moment, to slap the woman who had spoken out against saving Xhea. As if her hand might do anything but cause the woman a moment's chill.

They might never know, she realized. If Edren did not investigate, they might never learn that Xhea had fallen. No chance of justice for her senseless death.

Shai watched as they placed metal chits on the map, marking out defensive points, places to assign their guards, places to set spells—she knew not which.

Forget understanding, she thought, suddenly, angrily. *Forget patience and politics and trying to stay calm. Just let them argue.* She knew little of the names and places of which they spoke anyway; it was easy enough to let the words flow over her, through her, as if they were nothing but the air of which they were formed. Easy, now, to turn her back on them all.

Gravity, she thought. She pretended the earth's pull had any claim upon her, and fell.

Floor after floor, Edren flickered through her, ground and ceiling, furniture and plumbing pipe, empty space and people. She hated the feeling—had avoided such drastic maneuvers ever since discovering that such things were possible, if only she dared try. Now it was just one more discomfort in a long list of hurts. She slowed to a halt underground.

Edren's basement level was cold and dark and so still that Shai's ears rang with the sudden absence of voices. There was no dread to slow her now, nor anyone injured. She sped past the barricade and down the hall marked with Mercks's blood to the place where Xhea had been killed.

Shai peered long and hard at those bloody scuffs in the dirt, as if she might read the meaning within them through will and attention. Looked, too, at Xhea's walking stick, abandoned in the dust. Nothing to learn there, she confessed at last—or, at least, nothing that she could see or understand. She turned her attention to the footsteps. There were so many.

It was clear that the attackers, whoever they'd been, had come here time and again long before she and Xhea had stumbled onto the scene. Shai was not a particularly good tracker—nor did she have Xhea's close familiarity with the underground—but the same prints made worn trails in the dust that led not just toward Edren, but toward the other skyscrapers as well.

The hall from which the attackers approached led to Orren and Senn, she found, and those skyscrapers' barricades bore signs of damage as well. Yet the most recent set of footsteps came from neither skyscraper; instead, the attackers had stopped in an alcove, just out of sight, as if they had been watching and waiting for Xhea's approach.

Shai shivered and turned away.

At last she found the attackers' path away, when they had been carrying Xhea's body. It was marked by a few widely spaced drips of blood in the dust.

Carefully, Shai followed the path to its source. That exit was not Rown's own barricade, as she had expected, but a subway station. She rose like a bubble to the surface, and stood blinking in the late evening sunlight, unseen in the bustling roadway.

Rown. The wide, squat skyscraper was fully visible before her, set like a dark shadow against the sky. Shai frowned. Given the distance, it would have taken the attackers at least ten minutes to walk to Rown from here; longer if they had grown tired of the burden of Xhea's body. Nor would that journey have gone unnoticed.

Shai turned—and there, not fifty feet away, was Farrow. There were no footsteps to lead her; she did not need them.

"Oh no," she whispered, staring up and up at the pale skyscraper and all its battered balconies, all its glittering windows.

She had no evidence—nothing she could see nor touch—but felt with sudden, perfect certainty that *this* was the skyscraper that had sent the attackers and the dark magic boy both, and the place to which they had returned.

It was Rown that Edren had aggressed upon, Rown whose territory Edren wanted and was preparing to claim, Rown whose symbol the bounty hunters had worn on their mismatched clothing. But Rown had not killed Xhea, nor caused the fall of the barricade.

Rown hadn't been behind the attacks at all.

She stared, horrified, thinking of the plans even now being made in Edren. *How many innocent people are going to die for their mistake?*

Something was happening outside the tall, pale skyscraper—there was a sound like cracking concrete, and people scrambled over the ground, yelling—but Shai paid them no heed. Instead she rose and flew arrow-straight back to Edren.

Neither Shai's absence nor her return was of any note to those in the council's war room. Though the council still argued, it was clear that their arguments were winding down, Edren's plans in their final stages.

A dawn attack on Rown.

Shai rushed to the map spread across the table—only to stop, blinking at its incomprehensibility. It was so far from the three-dimensional City maps that she knew—maps that moved as the City did, ever-changing—that for a moment she despaired of making any sense of it.

Then something shifted in her perception, and she saw past the flat paper with its crude, hand-drawn symbols to the shapes that they represented. There was Edren, which would make that shape Orren and that shape Senn . . .

Following the lines that marked roads and pathways, Shai found the square marked *Farrow*, already thinking desperately about how she could communicate her message. She could call forth a light, and make it blink; one blink for no, two for yes . . . or was it the other way around? And how could she possibly blink out the message that they were preparing to attack the wrong skyscraper?

Not blinks, then—could she write with light? She knew how to shape the energy into whirls and patterns—why not letters? Why not a word? There was no reason she couldn't make such a shape, and even hold it, using the simple light spell to make the word visible to Edren's magic-poor leadership. She had just never tried it before, living or dead.

Yet even as she started to form the spell-shape, planning out the lines of intent needed to bring even such as simple thing into being, she knew she was too late: one by one the councilors rose and began to follow Verrus Edren from the room.

No, she thought, willing herself to form the spell faster—but her sudden anxiety scattered her concentration like so much confetti. She, who could make pure magic swirl and dance through her fingers like it was an extension of her body, struggled again to make even the simplest of spells. She reached out as if she might catch the councilors as they passed, might hold an arm or grab a collar, might touch a shoulder—and felt her hands pass through them. Felt the cold of their leaving; felt the cold of sudden despair.

Only Lorn and Emara remained behind, waiting in silence until the last of the councilors had left the room and the door shut behind them. Waiting, Shai realized, to speak to her.

"Shai?" Emara asked. "Are you still here?" As before, Emara closed her eyes and raised one hand, trying to pinpoint whatever slight disturbance she felt from Shai's presence.

"She's here," Lorn affirmed. But even he took a moment to identify the general area in which she now resided, standing near the end of the long table, across from them.

"Shai," Lorn said in his deep voice. "I'm so sorry, I—"

She knew what he was going to say. Hearing the words, heavy with regret and anger and frustration, made none of it easier to bear.

Instead of listening, Shai kindled a light above her palm. It was just a point of pale gold little brighter than a candle's flame, like the one she'd used underground. The shadows in the empty boardroom barely shifted as it came into being. Even so, Lorn froze at the sight and Emara's breath seemed to catch in her throat. Both stared.

Knowing she was there, it seemed, was not the same as seeing proof of her existence. Nor, she realized, was it the same for her. As with Mercks, Shai found herself momentarily caught breathless, so shocked at the feeling of being *seen*.

"I'm real," she whispered. "I'm here." She did not know whether she meant the words for them, or for herself.

"Shai," Lorn said again, and his tone had changed. There was something softer, gentler about the sound. She flared the light brighter in response.

Then she let her power flow. It would not be so hard to shape the word *Farrow* in midair, surely; yet she struggled. She could form the shape from magic almost without thinking; she'd drawn magic-patterns as a way of calming and centering herself since she was a child. She could make a visible light and adjust its brightness with but a thought. But combining the two? The magic twisted and evaded her control as she attempted to change the light spell into something that she could shape with the ease of raw magic. The more she thought about it, the harder it became.

She suddenly felt so tired. Where was that strange calm, that empty flowing state she'd reached when she had healed Mercks? Gone now, as if it had never existed. *Simpler, then.* She just had to get her message across; she was not being judged on her ability with magic, no matter that it felt otherwise.

She let her half-woven spell go and brought the light toward the map until it came to hover above the shape for Rown, skyscraper Edren's intended target. Again Lorn started speaking, and Shai jerked the light to the side in quick and sudden denial. Whether he understood, she did not know; yet he quieted, watching. She made that quick movement above Rown, the light twitching back and forth like a head's shake.

"Not Rown," Emara said.

Shai moved the light across the map until it hovered above Farrow—drew the light in a circle about that shape, made the light shine brighter and brighter.

"Here," she said, as if words might somehow reach them if her frantic gestures did not. "They did this."

"Farrow took Xhea?" Lorn asked slowly, and Shai felt her stomach twist. Why couldn't she remember whether one or two flashes meant yes? Instead, Shai bobbed the light up and down in jerky affirmation.

Lorn swore and sank slowly into a chair. He put his head in his hands.

It was Emara who asked quietly, "Is she there now?"

Shai froze, and the light with her.

"Have they hurt her?" Emara asked instead.

How could she answer that? *Yes*, Shai gestured, emphatically, and watched their pained expressions with something like despair.

Lorn looked up, directing his quiet, bitter words to his wife. "It won't change anything. The attack and abduction are only his justification for the attempt to reclaim the warehouse district."

He turned back to Shai's light.

"Edren won't sanction Xhea's rescue, even with the attack on Rown. I was going to plan something anyway—I can't just leave her there. Except, if she's in Farrow . . . ?" He stopped and swore again, then rubbed at his face with one wide, tattooed hand.

How do I tell them that there's no point? It hurt to hear them talking this way, as if death were a barrier from which a loved one might simply be plucked whole.

Emara finished Lorn's thought, directing her words just above and to one side of Shai's light, trying to meet her eyes. She missed, of course, but Shai shifted just to have the illusion that someone could see her face.

"When Edren faced Farrow before, they—*we*—had allies. Edren had a close partnership with Orren until near the end of the war, and a truce with Senn. We couldn't have stood against Farrow alone. Farrow has more citizens, more territory, and far, far more magic—renai and spells both. For all the things one might say of Verrus and his leadership, he is not foolish, and he does not make decisions in haste."

"Attacking Farrow would be suicide," Lorn added darkly.

"Rown, on the other hand," Emara continued. "Edren has a score to settle with Rown, even after all these years—as much as Orren has a score to settle with us. I don't think much will turn Verrus's eyes aside. Even if the attacker was Senn or Orren . . ." Emara shook her head and sighed, her expression turned distant as if from some old memory.

It was Lorn who finally asked, "But what does Farrow want with Xhea? Or do they only want you?"

Shai did not know how to answer, only closed her fingers one by one, reabsorbing the magic until the golden light vanished.

After they left, Shai stared at the closed boardroom door. Absent gods, she felt like a fool. Flailing around with a pinpoint light, poor gestures with a spell so basic a child could master it in hours.

What good is power if you can't use it? She was the most powerful person in the Lower City—and it meant nothing, *nothing*, because all that power was the next thing to useless in her untrained, insubstantial hands. She was what she had been raised to be: a conduit for power, a magic-generating machine, nothing more.

And Xhea had died because of it. Already the guilt threatened to crush her; her fear and despair felt more tangible than the world around her, more real than gravity. One and all, they told her to sit down and let herself—her power—be used.

Maybe it wouldn't be so bad, being used. Maybe her magic might save lives. Maybe, somehow, Lorn could convince his father that they shouldn't attack Rown after all.

Slim hopes, all. But what other choice did she have?

Alone, Shai stared at her hands and the glow of magic within her. She thought back to the days when she and Xhea had hidden in the underground, always moving for fear of pursuit and the magic-poor bounty hunters on their trail. This must be what Xhea had felt, Shai realized, with her strange dark magic flaring entirely outside her control. Then, Shai had sat with her, taught her breathing exercises, and made her practice, practice, practice.

Had she truly believed that it would be any different for her? That an ability to not just shape her power, not just read existing spells, but to create spells of her own would just come to her?

She smiled sadly. *Yes.* Of course she had. As if an unpracticed talent might be birthed fully formed.

And why not? Though she had never been taught proper spellcraft, nothing more than the basics, what little she knew had come as easily as breathing. Now, in truth, it was little different: she lifted her hand, and a light appeared. A thought, and it vanished, only to be replaced by a filament of pure energy that wove through the air, forming the word *Farrow*, then *Stop*, then *They killed her*. That last message she held, letting her power shape the words over and over again until they glowed red before her eyes like an afterimage.

The few tricks she knew, she knew well. *Is it enough?* she asked herself. She opened her hand and released the power, letting the magic fade into the air.

Enough for what?

Not enough to help Xhea. Not enough to help Edren, if they even deserved her help. Not enough to stop this senseless war that threatened, curling and cresting on a tide of her power.

She would have to do better. She knew it and yet . . . and yet . . .

Shai realized: she was afraid.

Afraid she couldn't learn, or couldn't learn fast enough. Afraid that, when it counted, she would fail—as she had failed already. Afraid that the one spell that had worked, the strange spell-song that had healed Mercks, had been only a fluke, never to be repeated. Afraid . . .

She bowed her head. Afraid that this was a choice she should have made a long time ago, when she still had breath and blood within her.

For a long moment, the ghost of the girl named Shai sat curled, thinking of all the things that might have been, all the lives she might have lived, if only things had been different.

If only.

Then she lifted herself from the floor and rose through ceiling after ceiling until she was suddenly in clear air, up on Edren's rooftop. The sun had just gone beneath the horizon. Quiet and stillness spread through the Lower City's streets while the Towers above came alight. The City was always cast in a myriad colors that shifted and changed even as the Towers themselves did—but at night, they made the sky glorious. She looked up at a sky aflame with magic—magic like the power that ran through her, sure as blood.

That golden light, green light, red and blue, made the shadows shimmer and dance in the darkened alleys below. No one was out now, no one was moving. Only a few brave souls attempted to make their beds on sagging rooftops or concrete balconies rather than closing themselves away in stifling hot rooms, barred windows cracked in hope of a breeze. The walkers would be heading in from the badlands now, their steps slow and steady, their eyes blank, their fingers grasping at nothing.

She had seen it all. Night after night as Xhea slept, Shai had walked the Lower City streets, and caught glimpses of the thousands of small, dark lives lived down here in dirt and ruin. She'd been searching for her father.

Shai thought of the men and women who would be preparing, even now, for the dawn attack on Rown. She thought of her father walking somewhere in that darkness, thoughtless, uncaring. She thought of Xhea.

There was nothing she could do to help them, not any of them. Nothing to undo the mistakes she had made, nor their consequences.

But she would not stay helpless. Because in that spell that had healed Mercks was the answer to how to use her power. She had no known spells, learned and re-created strand by painstaking strand; she discarded her reliance on rules and old teachings and her belief in the way things had to be.

She had only years of knowing magic, feeling magic, having magic run through her like an unending river. She had to trust that, past the fear and uncertainty and near-crippling doubt, she would find her talent.

Trust. She wanted to laugh. But what had she told herself?

Don't think.

Shai spread her glowing hands before her and began to work.

Chapter
Thirteen

Ahrent Altaigh returned within the hour, knocking before
he opened the door. He did not check whether Xhea had
filled her pockets with small belongings. Any other time, that
would have been a mistake.

Xhea met his eyes, wishing she could achieve the
blankness of expression at which Daye so clearly excelled.
Her habitual façade of confidence felt far beyond her
reach—broken as surely as her knee. At least there remained
no sign of the tears she had shed unwillingly. That much
weakness, at least, she could hide.

"Are you ready?" Ahrent asked.

Xhea nodded. Whatever his payment—whatever the
truth behind his plan or the history of which he told—Xhea
wanted to know more. Wanted to *understand*—if only the
extent of his insanity.

A skyscraper rising. She would have laughed were it not for Ahrent's seriousness, the quiet conviction written in every line of his face.

Xhea made to rise—and only then, failing, did she wonder how she'd struggle out of the sagging couch cushions. Ahrent held out his hand. Xhea looked at him as if he had lost his mind, yet he did not withdraw the hand nor the offer inherent in the gesture.

Fine, then. Have it your way.

She grasped his hand and struggled to her feet, fighting her way out of the cushions' embrace. He did not flinch at her touch, only braced against it. She had to have hurt him, weak though she was, though he showed no sign of discomfort. When she looked at him, surprised, he only smiled.

Be careful, Xhea thought. She knew enough to be wary of those who could mask pain or joy or intent; she knew what a calm surface could hide. Torrence had taught her that much.

She should go now, leave as fast as her ailing legs could carry her. She knew it. And yet she walked in his wake through Farrow's halls, careful and slow, drawn forward by fascination and dread and her own terrible curiosity.

The first thing Xhea noticed about the floor to which Ahrent brought her was the quiet. The halls looked little different from the one that held her grandmother's apartment: closed doors and worn carpeting, walls dented and scratched and oft repainted. Here, as there, she saw no people; but this stillness had a different quality—one that she associated with spaces abandoned, ignored, and reclaimed by silence.

Not what she had expected, especially not in a skyscraper so desirable as Farrow.

It was only as they turned the corner that she saw they were not alone. A guard sat midway down the hall, an unsheathed knife resting across his knees. He had no book nor bit of carving nor any other distraction, only stared at the door across from him as if expecting it to open at any moment. As it was held shut with three heavy padlocks—newly added, given the sawdust and metal filings on the carpet—she rather doubted the risk.

The guard glanced up as they passed, sparing Ahrent only a terse nod and acknowledging Xhea and Daye not at all.

"Who's in there?" Xhea asked once they'd passed.

"No one, anymore," Ahrent said. "We'll be clearing the room out soon enough." His tone did not invite further questions.

Behind them, Daye said nothing. She said nothing very, very loudly.

Farther down the hall, Xhea heard noises: soft beeps and whirs and a slow, rhythmic rush of air. There was a smell, too, of bleach and plastic tubing and rubbing alcohol, sharp in her nose. She thought it might be Farrow's medical ward—yet if this was a medic's, either no one had died here or no one had remained behind. She felt not so much as a hint of a ghost's presence.

Ieren's been here, she reminded herself. The thought made her feel ill.

Ahrent paused beside a door. "This one," he said, and opened the door wide.

Xhea's first thought was that he had brought her to a waiting room. Mismatched chairs lined the walls, though the astringent smell lingered. On the room's far side was a narrow bed on rusted wheels, upon which sat an old woman in makeshift pajamas, her head bowed and bare feet dangling. She looked up as Xhea came cautiously closer, one limping step after another.

She was a large woman with a face marked deeply with lines that spoke more of laughter than anger. Her hair was a tangle of short curls of a shade that Xhea thought could be iron gray, or a faded brown, or something else entirely. Her eyes, though, were that particular mottled shade that she knew to be hazel, one clouded by a cataract.

Xhea's expression mirrored the woman's: brows creased, mouth slightly opened, eyes moving as if she might take in every detail at once. They stared, each at the other, in curiosity and confusion.

The woman drew in a soft breath. "Enjeia," she whispered, the word little more than a soft breath. Her face was transformed by wonder.

"Yes," Ahrent said. "But she goes by Xhea now."

The woman laughed at that, a sound full of gentle humor that was cut short by a wheezing cough that seemed to go on and on. Xhea winced. When she'd caught her breath again, the woman just looked at Xhea and said, "You never could pronounce your name. We called you Jeia most of the time."

It was not her name—but it was easy to imagine those shortened syllables mangled by a child's mouth and clumsy pronunciation. A memory came back to her, suddenly sharp for all that she'd not thought of it for untold years: crouching with Abelane behind their apartment, scratching the dirt with a stick as they attempted to figure out how to spell her name. *Zia. Zeeah. Shia.* She'd liked the look of *Xhea* best. She had written it over and over again until it felt like it had always been hers.

Xhea shook her head, pushing the memory away.

"Xhea, this is Marna," Ahrent said.

Her grandmother's wife. A woman who, that morning, had sat on her couch sipping tea, and now wanted to give Xhea her apartment while she . . . what? Underwent an operation? The unsettled feeling in Xhea's stomach returned.

"Hey." Xhea gave a half-hearted wave. She didn't know what to do, what to say, what to think.

Marna seemed not to notice Xhea's awkwardness. Instead she opened her arms to Xhea, her face lit with a wide smile. Xhea stared, confused. It took a long, uncertain moment before she recognized the gesture: Marna wanted to hug her.

"I—" Xhea said. "You can't—I mean, I don't . . ."

"Remember, she has her mother's power," Ahrent supplied quietly.

My mother? Again, Xhea wished for her lost walking stick; she felt like she might fall.

Breathe, she told herself, like she used to when high on bright magic. *Breathe, breathe.*

She didn't know why it felt like such a shock after she'd sat in an apartment where her grandmother had lived, and stared at the image of a woman who had loved her. But a mother? Xhea swallowed, her mouth gone dry.

"Oh," Marna said, and let her arms fall. "Of course. I'd . . . forgotten." A moment, then she patted the bed beside her. "Perhaps you could come sit beside me, then? Just for a moment."

Xhea felt sharp words in her mouth, begging for release; something, anything, to make Marna take an emotional step back. Yet she wanted, desperately, to sit before her legs gave out beneath her. At last she limped across the room and perched on the bed's far edge, as far from the woman as possible.

"I can't believe it," Marna said. She looked at Xhea and her eyes filled with tears. "Enjeia. Ahrent told me that he might have found you, after all these years, but I never truly believed it. If only Ennaline . . ." She shook her head. "Your grandmother never gave up hope of finding you, you know. She was sure you were still alive, somewhere."

"She was right." Xhea had been somewhere: underground. Living a life that she'd carved out of nothing with hands and will and talent alone. If her grandmother had been looking, it couldn't have been thoroughly nor well.

Anger flared hot—and brief. Xhea just looked at her, this strange woman who had been her grandmother's partner, and felt the silence resonate between them. So many questions unasked, so many things unsaid.

"Is it true?" Xhea blurted.

"Which part, dear? Your grandmother?"

Xhea nodded, though really she meant any of it, all of it.

"Oh, yes." She smiled. "Ennaline lived for you, especially after Nerra died. Your mother."

Your mother. Of all the words, why did those two spin around in her head like a terrible echo?

"How . . . how did she die?"

"Ennaline? Or your mother?"

Xhea shrugged. Either. Both.

"With Ennaline, it was heart failure, in the end." Marna closed her eyes for a moment, and brushed away a tear that slipped down her wrinkled cheek. "Your mother, though . . . it was her magic." Of course. A pause, then she added, "I think she was not much older than you."

Though more mature—or better fed—if she had been able to conceive and bear a child.

"Have you ever heard of anyone else with dark magic?" Xhea asked haltingly. She glanced up, including Ahrent and Daye in the question.

It was Marna who answered. "No, dear. Only Nerra. And we worked hard to keep her hidden, lest the Spire take her—though I'm told that her power was quite weak by their standards."

Weak? She was from the Lower City. What else would she be?

Xhea thought of what Lorn had told her earlier, before everything had fallen apart: the story of the assassin who had spread fear and death in equal measure, who had all but brought the Lower City's elite to their knees in the early years of the war. Farrow's masked assassin, a man with dark power.

Except that assassin hadn't been a man at all. They had only ever known one dark magic user, and that had been Xhea's mother.

Even thinking it felt strange—not her mother's role, but her very existence. To think of her mother as a person who'd had a life and death and a story in between; something more than a concept, forever absent.

"And my father?"

A pause. "Life here can be violent and . . . unkind. Though Nerra told us," Marna said carefully, "that he did not survive your conception."

That was clear enough. Xhea took a long breath and let it out slowly. It was a long time before she was able to reply. "Good," she said.

It was Ahrent who spoke then—and Xhea suddenly remembered that this was not why she was here. He had promised her answers, yes, but not about her life.

"I need to make sure that Ieren's ready," he said. "I'll be back in just a moment."

Xhea looked up. "But you said—"

Ahrent cut her off with an upraised hand. "I did," he said, knowing she wanted his promised explanation. Perhaps seeing how little she wanted to be left here with a stranger with tears in her eyes who said—who thought— she was family. "I will. A moment more only." He stepped outside and his footsteps receded down the hall.

Daye looked at Xhea for a long, weighted moment before she too stepped outside and softly closed the door, leaving Xhea alone with Marna.

Marna changed then, ignoring her tears and looking at Xhea with an expression turned fierce with intent. Even her clouded eye seemed to pierce Xhea in place.

"Xhea," she said. "Listen. Your magic will kill you, if you let it."

"I—"

"*Listen*. When you were born, your mother bound your—"

Footsteps outside. Marna hesitated, drew back—and suddenly looked no different than she had moments before: sad and gentle and old, hunching into her thin cotton pajamas.

Ahrent opened the door.

"Ready?" he asked, looking at Marna. The way he spoke, it wasn't really a question.

For a moment Marna seemed to show the weight of heavy years. Then she took a deep breath and smiled, face creasing into well-worn lines.

"Of course," she said.

Xhea retreated to a chair as an assistant came in and helped Marna lie down. He moved with practiced efficiency, swabbing the inside of Marna's elbows and her neck with antiseptic, and hooked up an IV, all without speaking. It was only as he brought out shears and made to cut away Marna's curls that Ahrent raised a hand to stop him.

"Later," he said. "The boy is here."

The assistant nodded and slipped out. Daye held the door open, and a moment later her partner and his charge arrived. Torrence's expression held no sign of his usual easy smile. He nodded to Ahrent, then to Xhea, murmuring, "Hello, darlin'." Only then did the edges of his mouth lift in the ghost of a grin.

He knew just how much she hated being called that.

Ieren stepped inside. He looked stronger now, happier; his eyes were bright and he broke into a wide smile when he saw Ahrent. He showed no surprise to see Marna lying on the bed, nor at the medical equipment that surrounded her. No, the only surprise was the ghost he dragged behind him at the end of a short tether.

The ghost was a boy little older than Ieren appeared to be, his face flushed and his lips cracked as if from long fever. The ghost did not walk but slid across the air in Ieren's wake, curled in upon himself and staring at the floor. When Ieren stopped, the ghost child glanced up anxiously, then scrambled into the room's far corner at his tether's farthest extent. Ieren ignored him completely.

New ghost, Xhea judged. *New and young and scared, with no idea what's happening.* She knew that look: the boy didn't understand that he was dead.

But neither was he hurting. For all that he was tethered to Ieren, he showed no distress not attributable to fear or confusion. She had thought—and now it seemed almost foolish—but she had thought that Ieren simply *ate* ghosts. As if any spirit that he dragged back would be half-crazed or half-devoured, like the one she had seen in Edren the night before. But maybe it was just the ghost's presence that helped steady Ieren and reduced the effects of his magic.

At the thought, Xhea touched the center of her chest where a tether had once been bound.

She'll be here soon, Xhea reassured herself. Even without the tether, Shai would find her.

"You look like you're feeling better," Ahrent said.

"Yep," Ieren said cheerfully. "We're doing another one?"

"And showing Xhea, here, how it's done."

Ieren turned, apparently seeing Xhea for the first time. "You stayed!" he exclaimed.

"Yeah, I was just having such a great time," Xhea muttered, "I couldn't bring myself to leave."

He smiled at that. "I know, right? And it gets better."

"If you don't need me, boss-man," Torrence said to Ahrent, "I'll just take a bit of a break now." At Ahrent's nod, he slipped out. Daye, however, stayed by the door as if she were a guard, watching not the room at large but Xhea, as if she expected her to bolt. As if she could.

Xhea watched as Ahrent went to the wall, stood on a chair, and drew down a bundle of wires from the ceiling. She went very still at that, staring—instinct running ahead of thought.

No, he wouldn't—

He can't possibly—

She was wrong. She had to be wrong.

Then Ahrent began attaching those wires to Marna's skin, hands and head and heart.

"No!" Xhea cried. She was standing and didn't remember struggling to her feet. She stumbled to the bedside as if her slight body might shield Marna from the rest of the room. "No, you *can't!*"

For she had seen a setup like this twice before, and if each had been vastly different she knew enough to see the similarities. A body lying prone. Life-support machines arrayed all around. Wires in one, binding that body to the storage coils nearby; spell in the other, connecting the body to the glass pedestal on which she lay.

The failed resurrection in skyscraper Orren. The failed attempt to bind Shai to Tower Eridian. And now this, here. How many times would her promise—*Never again*—be made a mockery?

Except this attempt centered not on a ghost, trapped or otherwise, but a living, breathing woman.

"Enjeia—Xhea," Marna said, and made as if to take Xhea's hand. She stopped before she touched Xhea's skin, but left that hand outstretched, earnest, reaching. "It's okay. I volunteered. My wife is gone now; I had no other family but her. I chose this. I'm old, my body's wearing out—what else can I give my people, my skyscraper, but this?"

"But to give your life . . ." Xhea started. Because that's what she was doing: they were plugging her into Farrow as if she were nothing but a battery, and she'd be worn down just as quickly. And oh, she could see why. The poor generated so little power, so little renai; most was used for a thousand small tasks, buying and healing and signing for goods, the very act of living itself. So little left for the skyscraper. Yet if they removed the burdens of choice and wakefulness—if they gave the work of living and eating to machines—all of a person's magic might flow to the skyscraper instead.

This was why Xhea was being offered the apartment: Marna would not need it. Whether she lived for a week or a month or longer, Xhea understood that she would not rise again. Would not wake. She would close her eyes, surrender to the drugs and the spells, and live only as long as her magic and her body managed to hold out.

They'd brought her to witness Marna's final moments of life. And for what?

All for the good of her people. She had heard things like that from Shai, trying to justify what her Tower had asked of her. Xhea had not understood them then, and did not understand them now.

"*Give*," Marna repeated, emphasizing the word. "A gift—and one that is mine to give as I choose." She smiled, her face creasing into well-worn lines. "I'll miss out on— what? A few years at most. But just think of what everyone here will get in return."

"A Tower," Xhea said softly, without thinking.

Again, that smile. "Yes. A Tower."

"But you—" Xhea started, and couldn't finish the sentence. She shook her head in denial, coins chiming.

Ahrent spoke. "Did you ever dream of living in the City, Xhea?"

She nodded mutely.

"Did you ever believe it might happen?"

Oh, foolish question. She had dreamed and planned and sought a thousand countless ways that she might somehow get herself into a Tower; but she'd always known that they were just that. Dreams. Still, she shook her head.

"It's the same for the rest of us. One may escape, if they're powerful enough. Lone individuals. The rest of us? Even the richest struggle, here. We fight for food and water, for shelter, for safety for our children. There is no way out of the Lower City.

"Our worth is decided on the day that we are born— earlier, even." Ahrent looked pained by the thought. "That worth is not in our skills nor talents nor our ability to work, not personality or perseverance. It's not our capability for love or joy or respect. Only generating capacity—or our lack thereof."

No value that was not measured in renai.

It was true; oh, there was no need to argue, for that truth was one that she'd been born knowing.

She thought of standing in Tower Celleran screaming before a crowd of City citizens. *You're not better than me*, she had yelled at them, so angry that the words had seemed ripped from her. *You're not better than me!*

But the City said they were, each and every one, because of their magic.

In Ahrent Altaigh's expression she saw that same knowledge, that same truth—the passion burning behind his words and work both. He was angry; she could see it in the line of his jaw, the set of his shoulders, the way his eyes tightened with the words. It was old anger, bone-deep, blood-thick.

"To the City, we're worth nothing. City citizens think we have no place among them. They say, if they think of us at all, that we deserve this fate—that we're just animals squabbling in the dirt and ruin.

"How long must we spend accepting their judgment as truth? Being thankful for their scraps, the disdain they call charity? I say that they are wrong. *Farrow* says that they are wrong."

"*I* say that they are wrong," Marna whispered. "We never deserved this, not any of us."

Xhea swallowed. She met Marna's gaze—one eye clouded, the other clear and sharp and perfectly sane.

"I understand what I'm doing, Xhea," she said. "I'm an old woman, and I'm sacrificing myself so that the children of Farrow can have the life that I never could. The life that Ennaline and I wanted so desperately to give to you."

Xhea stared at her, this woman who could have been her grandmother, who could have loved her, and now was a stranger trying not to weep and take her hand. A stranger about to die.

"It's my choice," Marna said then—softly, so softly.

Silence spread between them, broken only by the hiss of air through the overhead vents. Even Ieren was quiet, curled up in one of the nearby chairs as if this discussion did not, could not matter.

"May I?" Ahrent asked at last, gesturing to the wires. Marna nodded; Xhea's assent, unneeded though it was, came slower.

Was Marna really a victim if she went willingly? If Xhea fought back, if she shouted that people should never be used this way, should she direct her words at Ahrent and Marna—or at the City above? The City that spun on uncaring.

The thought came: *If Shai hadn't come to me, where would I be right now?* Not hurt and limping, no; but she would be in the streets, trying to find scraps of paying work, scraps of food. She'd be scrounging in the ruins for anything she could use or sell. Without power, it was the only life she was allowed. The life she had always accepted as her fate, her due.

No way out.

Xhea nodded, and watched as Ahrent affixed the wires to Marna's wrists, the side of her neck, and directly above her heart. His easy motions spoke of familiarity.

Marna reached out again, her fingers but a breath away from Xhea's hand. "I'm sorry," she murmured. "I'm sorry that I didn't find you until now. That I won't get a chance to know you, or get a chance to tell you . . ."

Ahrent touched Marna's shoulder—gently, Xhea saw, yet the woman went silent nonetheless. "Ieren doesn't have long," he said, his voice quiet. "Xhea?"

Xhea swallowed, then nodded and stepped back. Ieren, roused by his name, came to stand at the bedside as Ahrent did something to the IV.

"This is just a sedative," Ahrent told Marna. "You'll begin to feel sleepy in a moment."

"Tell me it won't hurt," she said softly.

It was Ieren who replied. "Okay," he said, cheerfully enough. "It won't hurt."

Marna closed her eyes. But as the sedative was taking effect she waved Ahrent closer, gesturing weakly until he leaned down and put his ear next to her lips.

"Did I do well?" she whispered, almost too quiet for Xhea to hear. Her slurred voice sounded fearful, needy.

"You did," Ahrent Altaigh replied just as softly. "All promises kept, all debts repaid." He took her hand and squeezed it. "Rest, now. Your part is done."

Marna's eyes fluttered closed and did not open again.

"Ieren," Ahrent said, and the boy stepped forward.

The wheeled bed came almost to mid-chest on him, and he stood on his toes in an attempt to look at Marna. Ahrent brought him a chair, and the boy clambered up to stand on the seat. Again Ahrent checked the IV and then the cascading wires with gentle fingertips, as if running through a mental checklist.

Ieren turned to Xhea. "Watch really carefully, okay? I'll try to do it slow."

"Do what?" she asked.

But she knew: this was the binding at which Eridian had failed when they'd stolen Shai; the binding at which Orren's casters had attempted so blindly in their resurrection. Spirit to body to the structure beyond.

Xhea was afraid. Yet she stood, holding the bed for balance, as Ieren raised his hands and began to work. She didn't see him call his magic—but she *felt* it. It echoed through her like the sudden sounding of a bell, and Xhea sucked in her breath in surprise.

She recognized the sensation. This was the feeling that had drawn her, once and again, in the underground; the feeling of magic, twin to her own. It drew her even now, the whole of her attention swinging to Ieren like a compass needle.

A moment later, that magic seeped from his outstretched fingers, soft and dark like a shadow in midair. Carefully, he touched each of the wires that ran from the ceiling in turn; touched, just as gently, Marna's flesh at the point where those wires joined. But it was only when Xhea shifted her eyes' focus that she could see what he was doing.

Thin tendrils of dark magic spun out from his fingertips and into Marna's body beneath, so delicate and precise that Xhea could but marvel at his control. His magic did not curl and coil like hers, with a restless movement like smoke, only unfurled like lengths of thin, dark thread.

As he wove those threads into a complex pattern, Xhea stiffened in recognition. She had seen spells like this before—spells that did not gleam with light, but were a cold, dark gray like lace woven from tarnished silver wire. Dark magic had woven the spells that had bound Shai to her body, and her spirit to life.

So, too, did these spells bind. As she watched, the end of those spell-lines created hooks that dug into Marna's spirit and drew it inexorably toward the wire—a wire that was suddenly as much a part of her as her hair or fingernails— tying the two together. Where the living spirit went, so too did the magic. Marna was not a rich woman, nor a powerful one; the flow of her magic was the barest gleam of light. Yet still it flowed, through her body, into the wires—and every last bit of it went into the skyscraper.

Soon, machines would need to take over the myriad small burdens of living. With Marna's magic no longer helping keep her body alive, she would need the battered life support equipment to keep her heart beating, her lungs breathing, until there was no magic left.

"Just like that," Ieren said proudly. "Did you get that? I can draw you the spell-lines, if you want."

Xhea opened her eyes, not knowing when she closed them, and blinked as if to clear what she'd seen from her memory. Movement did not change the sudden trance-like state into which she'd fallen, nor the feeling of calm that had swept over her as she'd watched Ieren work—watched that dark magic not hurt and destroy, as hers so often did, but bind, careful and delicate and slow.

She took a long, shuddering breath and looked at Marna's face. There was no pain in the woman's expression, no fear; only slack features. Xhea wished that unconsciousness looked like sleep, that she might pretend Marna was safe now in the embrace of some gentle dream.

"One woman?" she asked at last. Her words dropped into a moment of perfect silence.

For Xhea knew: no matter how long she lived, how much magic she had, one woman's power would never be enough to bring about the transformation that Ahrent promised.

"No," said Ahrent Altaigh, and showed her.

The next room was not empty.

There was no outside light here: the windows were bricked over—freshly so, from the smell of mortar. Beneath that were other, familiar smells: bleach and disinfectant and something that reminded her of the cheap, industrial soap so common in the Lower City.

Even before Ahrent turned on the harsh overhead lights—despite the quiet beeps and flashes from medical machines held together with tape and glue; despite the beds and the soft, rhythmic sound of breath—Xhea knew this was no medic's ward. Perhaps it had been, once. Perhaps the beds, pushed now to the far walls, had once been used for care; perhaps the machines had helped ease and tend and heal. Not now. Not, she thought, ever again.

For rising from each of the six beds and the figures that lay so still upon them were wires. Wires were bound to those bodies' hands and feet and hearts; wires were joined to electrodes glued to shaved heads, and they rose in a tangle toward the ceiling. Toward Farrow's walls and the great spells that lay within them.

She could feel them, those spells, now that she knew to look. Bright magic spells far greater, vaster, than the spells needed to run the skyscraper itself. A blink, and she could see them, glowing dimly within the walls and ceiling and floor. A steady stream of magic trickled through them like water. Farther, she could feel more magic, stronger magic— massive magical storage coils that lay somewhere nearby.

So much magic and power and wealth that was not being used—was not caring for Farrow's people nor running the skyscraper's core systems—but stored or funneled toward the transformation spells. More and more and more; the wealth of years. All that accumulated magic was nothing compared to a Tower's heart; and yet, even from another room, another hall, so much bright magic made her bones ache.

Xhea shifted her focus further, seeing only magic—and finally began to understand what it was that Farrow had wrought. She could see the light of magic rising from each of the six bodies, up and into the skyscraper, the myriad wires gleaming. She could see the spells beyond. And then, as she stared, the world fell away and she could see farther, through the barrier of the wall and beyond.

The room beside them was also filled with unconscious people wired into Farrow. And the room beyond that, and the one beyond that still. This whole hall, perhaps; this whole floor. She could see them, now; she could *feel* them, all those bright glimmers of light rising from their inert bodies like dust motes dancing in sunlight.

We have been preparing for this for years, Ahrent had told her. It was only here, with the weight of that magic pressing down, that she finally believed it. Finally understood.

"You don't have a Radiant," Xhea said. The words were simple, unadorned, and no less harsh for their quiet. Only fact.

"No," Ahrent said.

"But you have people."

He nodded. "And people, too, make magic."

So little, here—oh, so very little. But here they lay, hooked up to machines that fed them, that took their wastes, that perhaps even kept them breathing past the time when their bodies would have surrendered. This was nothing like the Radiants' glass coffins she'd seen in Eridian; she could only hope that these limp bodies that had once been people were turned and changed, their bodies washed and eyes cleared of the crust of tears.

Yet it was the same.

Magic stored and poured into Farrow itself, through its systems and wires and walls. Enough, maybe, to create a Tower's heart; enough, maybe, for Farrow to wake.

"Ieren can teach you," Ahrent said. "He tells me it would not be hard, even as weak as you are, for you to learn."

As if controlling her magic might ever be easy. Yet Ieren hadn't struggled or fought for control, only used his power with perfect ease and simplicity.

No more floods of magic, she thought. *No more accidental death or destruction.*

No need to be afraid of her magic anymore.

Xhea looked again at the people comatose on the beds. "They chose this," she said. "They came here willingly, like Marna." It wasn't in the end, a question—but she needed to hear the answer aloud to know it for truth.

"They did."

"All of them?"

"All of them."

Did that make it better?

No, came the thought. Willing death was still death— and enslavement? Was she supposed to feel okay, knowing that each of these people had willingly bowed their heads and held out their hands to accept the chains?

Another part of her disagreed. For each person made their own choice, and that some of the consequences were ugly did not undo that choice's validity, nor the benefits of sacrifice. Each of these people wanted to earn a better life, not for themselves but for their children, their descendants, their people, their friends. Their only coin—their only worth—was magic, thin and weak though it was. Who was she to judge that choice, that sacrifice, as unworthy?

Because there was a time when she would have done anything, *anything* to have a life in a Tower. Here, in the Towers' shadows, there was no other dream.

No way out but up.

"If we believe what those above say about us," Ahrent said softly, "the Lower City is all that we deserve. For too long we've lived by their rules and been grateful for their leavings."

He looked at each of the people who lay around them—and he seemed proud. His smile was edged: the smile of an unexpected victor, raising his blade to the crowd.

"The City creates the rules, and we choose now to defy them."

True citizenship—and not just for one person, or two, but *thousands*, now and in all the years to come. Xhea reeled at the implications. She wanted to flee from this place, these walls, and the terrible things done in the name of freedom. She wanted, too, to see them succeed.

Because for the first time she imagined it: that Ahrent might be right. She saw not the magic nor the spells but the transformation they would bring about. She closed her eyes and imagined an earth-bound skyscraper lifting slowly into the air.

Oh, she could not say yes to this, she could not possibly agree. And yet her "no" caught behind her teeth and stayed there, refusing to be spoken.

Whatever Ahrent saw in her expression, he seemed to understand. "You don't have to decide now," he said. "This is a lot to understand—too much—and it's grown late. Past sunset."

Night. She wouldn't be able to easily get back to Edren now even if she wanted to.

"Why don't you think about it, and sleep, and let me know how you feel tomorrow."

A long moment, then Xhea nodded. Everything would make sense in the morning.

Chapter Fourteen

In the hour before dawn, Shai sat in silence at Mercks's bedside, watching the wounded man sleep. It was quiet in his small room—no family, no sound of others' breaths, only the faint whispers of air through the vents and voices speaking someplace distant.

She should go, she knew; Mercks deserved his privacy, and his rest. He was healed—or healing. She didn't even know him. Yet she stayed, watching the slow rise and fall of his breathing, the twitch of his eyes beneath the veils of his lids.

"I . . ." she started, and fell silent. No use in speaking, for all that the words crowded on her tongue.

Shai ran a weary hand over her face. She wanted to curl up and lay her head on the mattress; wanted to have a soft sheet cover her, like Mercks did. She wanted to close her eyes and fall into sleep, or some quiet oblivion, if only for a while.

Anything to silence her thoughts or the chaos they left in their wake.

She'd thought using her magic was only a matter of practice. In life, Shai had avoided learning anything but the most basic of spells; there had been no need for her to do anything more. Yet in trying to work even the simple spells that children learned alongside the alphabet, she failed and failed again. It seemed she was years and millions of renai too late for *simple*.

Whatever instinct had enabled her to heal Mercks was likewise absent. It was only as she thought of the song she'd hummed without meaning to, and the memories the melody had conjured, that she made some small progress.

It wasn't the singing that helped, she found through experimentation, but the feelings behind the song. When she thought of warmth—of lying curled in her bed, pillows and blankets like clouds all around her, morning sunlight on her face—she could create a spell that generated heat. Not the most useful, given the stifling summer; but a similar memory, of sipping iced tea as beads of condensation rolled down the glass, could conjure a cool breeze from within her cupped hands.

It wasn't enough. Even those few successes had been clumsy and inefficient, the spells working only because of the sheer force of power that she'd pumped through them.

Shai looked down at Mercks's sleeping face, as if she might find comfort within the lines and shapes that living had etched on his skin, the patterns of a life well lived. Here, in the rise and fall of his breathing, was the evidence she wanted. His healed skin, the flow of blood within his body. If she could only work one true spell, at least it had been this one.

Her magic was dying.

That thought—that knowledge—had been echoing through her head for hours now, no matter that she'd tried to ignore it or push it aside. When her magic had failed in the underground, she'd thought its brief absence akin to magic shock—that she'd used too much power too quickly and had paid the price, improbable though it seemed. If she'd been living, magic shock might have given her a headache or made her feel sick; she might have ached, or become dizzy, or fallen unconscious. If she were poor, she might even have died.

What was a mere moment of confusion in comparison? What was a little tiredness? *Perspective*, she reminded herself. It didn't help.

Because her magic hadn't failed only that once, but again and again. Practicing on Edren's rooftop, spells had flickered and unravelled within her hands before completion; spells had faded like so much mist. Sometimes her power itself had vanished entirely for seconds or minutes at a time, leaving her bereft.

She'd always known that the Towers bound a Radiant's ghost to a living body to keep their magic flowing. Unbound, their power faded to nothing—but she'd thought it would leave her slowly, over the span of years. No, in truth, she had tried not to think of it at all, as if denial might save her.

No more.

Magic had defined her life as it defined her death; she'd only refused to let it define *her*. Or had tried. She'd always wanted—through blind optimism and determination alone, if need be—to be something more than her power. To be Shai, and not just a Radiant.

Now, facing the idea of an existence without magic, she could barely breathe. She shook her head, her blond hair falling forward like a veil. To just be Shai? *I don't know who that is any more.*

"Shai?" Mercks asked softly, and opened his eyes. Shai drew back, surprised. "That is your name, isn't it?" Mercks looked around his darkened room and laughed softly. "Still can't see you, but I . . . think I can feel you there, just a little."

Again his eyes closed. For a moment Shai thought sleep had reclaimed him.

"Thank you," he said. The word was the barest whisper, and this time his eyes stayed closed. "Thank you for the spell and for saving my life, but also for staying with me down there in the dark." He tried to say more, but it was as if the words stuck in his throat. Shai realized that he couldn't say more without crying, and he refused to let the tears flow.

It was a long moment until he could speak again, and then he said only, "Thank you."

It was the gratitude in his voice that broke her, let her cry the tears that he would not shed. So many tears: once she started, it seemed like it would be impossible to stop. Tears for Xhea and for her father, each absence a wound so large that she knew they would never heal. Helpless tears for herself, and her failures, and her inability to stop the attack planned for morning.

Tears to say all the things for which she had no words.

At last, her sobs eased. In that quiet, she knew one small truth: for all her failures, this man before her would be dead were it not for her. It wasn't just her magic but her actions that had saved him.

Slowly, Shai reached toward Mercks with a single shining hand until she could almost cup his cheek with her fingers. A gleaming tear fell upon him, and another; and if he did not feel her touch he felt her tears, filled as they were with magic.

"You're welcome," Shai said, knowing he could not hear her and speaking anyway.

She rose, slipped through the door, and fled.

On the skyscraper's main level, Edren's forces were completing their final preparations for the attack. Armed, armored, and in small groups, they would not wait for true dawn, but slip out as the sky lightened; the few night walkers left in the streets would pose little threat to so many.

They were not soldiers; they did not pretend to be. These, Shai had learned, were men and women trained within the walls of Edren's arena, their ranks bolstered by a few chosen veterans from the last bloody war in the Lower City streets. They were people trained to fight for the spectacle of spilled blood. She did not stay to see them off. She did not even want to think about what they were about to do.

Outside, the air was thick and humid, lying across the Lower City like a stinking blanket. Shai felt the heat, little though it could affect her. She moved quickly, heading away, away, sweeping past the buildings like an unfelt wind.

These streets, now, were familiar. When she had first begun searching the Lower City in darkness, she had stumbled about in confusion. She'd gotten lost time and again until she'd had to rise above street level to find her bearings once more. At first she'd searched only for the creature that had once been her father, but later she had returned and looked slower, longer, out of a late-birthed curiosity.

Xhea had showed her much of the Lower City, and yet there was so much more, some worth seeing and some very much not, and all so different from the world she had known. The wide and tastefully decorated rooms of her family home seemed impossibly far away; so too were the Towers themselves, for all that she had but to look up to see them.

The streets were poorly named: not so much streets as parts of a labyrinth masquerading as thoroughfares, narrow alleys and makeshift corridors, passages where once there had been buildings and buildings where there had once been passages, with laundry-lines and prayer flags and narrow rope bridges crisscrossing them all. The dirt was everywhere—dirt and refuse, thick gutter sludge and things Shai did not want to even look at never mind name, and all their associated smells.

If only Xhea had lingered behind, a ghost as Shai was. She could imagine them, two ghosts wandering the ruins. No—farther. Untethered, they could go past the ruins, past the badlands, and leave the City behind. There had to be something else out there, something in the world beyond. Dead, maybe they could have been the first ones to find it.

Shai's smile was fleeting, twisted by sorrow. She kept walking.

Shai told herself she was only wandering, distracting herself from the ever-tightening spiral of her thoughts. That, too, was a lie. For as the sun broke the horizon and the Lower City came to life—people rising, leaving their homes, shouting and laughing and calling to customers—Shai realized where she was headed.

Farrow.

And why not? Edren had turned its back on Xhea, and Lorn had his hands tied. Who else had cared for the small, sharp-edged girl? *At least I can find out why she died*, came the quiet thought. *At least I can try.*

For all that Xhea had named Farrow first among the skyscrapers—tallest and strongest and most populous—Shai hadn't been impressed at her earlier glimpses, even shadowed as they had been. Farrow had once been some shade of pale gray; it was streaked now, roof to ground, by years of soot and rainwater. Many of the glass-fronted balconies and wide windows that showed the vista of the city were gone now: patched or boarded over or replaced entirely. Many of the jutting, crumbling remains of those balconies were edged with rope or warped boards or nothing at all.

Morning treated its façade no kinder.

Yet as she made her way toward it like one of summer's oft-absent breezes, Shai saw it differently. Nothing had changed; Farrow was no cleaner, no whiter, in no better repair. Still it stood straight and tall, no dangerous tilt or missing floors like Orren; it was alive, busy and bustling, unlike Senn's tightly shuttered windows and guarded doors. She could see, too, not just what was missing, but what those myriad repairs meant: the skyscraper was not some crumbling hulk, but a place that others cared for.

It was their home.

A quiet voice asked, *How much of it will fall?*

She did not want this war; did not want even the threat of it. She had not chosen this—not her power, nor its use, nor its many cascading consequences. If she could, she would have discarded her magic and all that came with it like one kicked off an unneeded blanket in a sweltering heat wave: quickly, and without a second thought.

Only . . .

She hesitated, suddenly unsure. Looking not at the ruin, but at the repairs.

If things could be different—if her magic could be used not to threaten or dominate or control, but to make these lives around her somehow *better*? Even if her power was fading, and it was—even if she were to become no more than a shadow of her former self, her former radiance—it was more that many here had now.

If there was no war—

If Lorn were in charge of Edren—

If she could just choose how to use her magic instead of dumping it unthinking into unworthy hands, destroying more than she created—

Just think of what she might do. Her power had helped fuel a *Tower*; even diminished, she could barely imagine the difference she might make here.

Then again, she'd always been a dreamer. She'd dreamed once that her sacrifice—her life and magic and all the things each entailed—would change the lives of those in Allenai. That others would grow up happier, healthier, stronger because of her. That thought had helped her endure the pain. It was a gift, she'd thought, of plenty.

Plenty. She hadn't understood the concept, even though it was arrayed all around her in countless ways like a diamond's glittering facets. Hadn't understood that the poverty and lack that she'd witnessed above had, in truth, no claim to the words.

She hadn't understood at all.

Despite her illness, despite her death and all the pain and hardship that had come with dying, in so many ways her life had been easy. She saw that now in a way that she never could have before. Once, she'd wept for the fate she'd been born to; with time she'd committed to the necessary sacrifice. Now, with distance and years and her eyes opened to lives that were previously beyond fathoming, she knew that she'd been blessed. It wasn't just that she'd lived in a Tower; it wasn't about the things she'd had, or the places she'd been, or her countless experiences. It wasn't, in the end, about magic at all.

It was about choices. She'd had so very many; and if illness had closed some doors for her—if death had taken them all away—it did not change that those options had been hers to pursue or to squander, to take or to ignore.

At last, Shai drew close enough to Farrow to see what was happening at the skyscraper's base—the movement that she'd only glimpsed the day before. They were digging.

She had thought that the people of the Lower City did not often build or destroy, only tried desperately to maintain the crumbling infrastructure of the ancient city that had come before. Yet there was no word for what now surrounded Farrow but destruction: a trench dug around the skyscraper, close to its foundations. The sidewalk had been torn up and cast aside, dirt piled high nearby. Even a rare, sickly tree had been uprooted.

As she drew nearer, Shai could see dirt and rocks and chunks of concrete being lifted in buckets from the trench and carried to one of the nearby piles. The trench continued in a great ring around the whole of the skyscraper. In spite of herself, she was curious. *A defense?* If so, she couldn't imagine what would require such drastic measures.

Nor was the trench the only defense. Watchtowers were arrayed around the skyscraper, armed men and women inside. Guards, she thought—but not like Edren's black-clad security force, nor the teams that even now must be closing on Rown. There was something harder in their faces, something stronger in their stances; and Shai, who knew nothing of weapons or war, halted at the sight of their armaments. She saw the hilts of blades and the grips of guns, some holstered at belts while others were large enough to be strapped to a leg or crossed across a back. She saw something that looked like a whip, and a handle that trailed a long chain, and a row of spikes across one man's fingers that jutted like claws.

Had the attack force been carrying weapons like these? She could not turn toward Rown, dared not know more.

The weapons themselves only gave her pause; it was the magic that made Shai stop dead and stare. For each blade and chain-link and gun-barrel gleamed with spells—some brighter, even, that the magic of their wielders. They were crude spells, yes, broadly written with little grace. Crude, but effective.

She read the spells' lines of intent at a glance. A spell to silence sound, a spell to guide a projectile truly—these, at least, were no surprise. But the rest? She saw a spell for pain and a spell for fear, spells to tear flesh and speed bleeding, spells to pull magic from the victim's body in a single brutal swipe. There were more; Shai had to look aside.

She did not think it was possible for her to truly feel sick anymore, all too aware that she had no true stomach to rebel—and yet she had no other name for the feeling that churned through her but nausea. To see magic used that way—to see the light of life and living twisted into something so . . . so . . .

She could not finish the thought.

She knew that magic could be used to hurt, to attack and to defend; after all, she'd never seen a night that had not been lit with Towerlight—defensive and offensive spells alike, and spell exhaust set alight. She'd watched, too, as Towers joined in planned mergers and hostile takeovers—though neither process was exactly gentle.

Those were different. They were more civilized, more refined.

Or was it only that the violence she knew was a conceptual thing of position and politics and great powers moving, while these spells, these soldiers, promised something far more personal? Their glittering spells spoke of blood and pain—as did the blades upon which they shone and the scarred-knuckled hands that held them. It was easy to imagine the screams.

Shuddering, Shai turned away.

Ready though they were to attack or defend, they had no protection against a ghost. None noticed her as she slipped past the heavily reinforced doors and into the building beyond.

She looked around the entrance hall, blinking in the sudden dim. Beyond the bank of elevators before her, two halls stretched in either direction. She could hear voices from one, talking and laughing; the loud sounds of a busy kitchen from the other.

She paused, suddenly unsure what it was she should search for. Xhea's body, perhaps, or a conveniently overheard conversation. *As if you're going to find something just laying out, waiting for you. Maybe a nice stack of papers labeled Useful Evidence, opened to the relevant pages.*

Shai frowned and tried to ignore her doubt.

"It's better than doing nothing at all," she whispered. If only for her own sanity.

Maybe she wouldn't know what she was searching for until she found it.

After more than thirty stories of fruitless searching, Shai wanted to give up in despair—until she reached the thirty-fourth floor. After floor after floor of homes and offices and tiny stores, the silence of the thirty-fourth came as a surprise. No background chatter here, no doors opening and closing, no children running, no loud arguments little shielded by dusty drywall. Just stillness, broken only by soft beeps and a rush of air that sounded almost like breathing.

Familiar sounds, all. *A hospital.*

But when she peeked inside a room, something looked wrong. Felt wrong. Though people lay in hospital beds, magic glimmering in the wires joined to their bodies, she saw no attendants, no doctors or nurses—no sign, even, of what ailments might have felled so many. For there was room after room of patients, every one asleep and unmoving.

Farther down the hall, a guard sat outside a locked door. Shai couldn't help it: her heart leapt in sudden hope, and she rushed forward. *Xhea?* she thought, in spite of everything.

The guard, alone in the silence, seemed anything but relaxed. Three locks bound the door, at top, bottom, and middle, and the guard looked as if she expected them to open at any minute.

Shai slipped through the door.

Inside, all was dark. She found herself in a small room that seemed to have once been a person's entire living space. There was a narrow mattress heaped high with blankets, a battered portable stove with a single plate, fork and knife waiting nearby, and a bucket in the corner.

Strange things to leave with a prisoner.

"Xhea?" Shai whispered. The shadows shifted as she moved, the light of her magic flickering across the dented walls.

The pile of blankets moved.

"Xhea," she started—only to fall abruptly silent.

It was not her friend who now rose from the blankets, but a man. He looked starved and wasted: his cheeks were gaunt hollows, his lips dry and flaking, his bloodshot eyes wide. He pushed himself up with hands that seemed to be little more than skin wrapped over the ruins of his bones. Then he lifted his head, turned, and looked directly at Shai.

He could see her.

Worse, she knew that inhuman movement, slow and steady and deliberate. Knew, too, the way his head swung toward her on his unsteady neck, eyes wide as his pupils dilated in response to the light of her magic.

A night walker, she thought. *Here. Within Farrow's walls.*

Hard on the heels of that thought came another: *I know him.*

For as he stared into the light her magic cast, she recognized his face. Not her father—and thank absent gods for that—but a young man with dark hair and a sharp nose. She recognized his clothes, too: loose white cloth, like one might wear in a hospital—though so stained now, little of the fabric's original shade remained.

This was the man whose spirit had come to Xhea ranting and screaming around his mouthful of fingers—the ghost they'd seen pulled through the barrier and, she thought, half-devoured. There was no sign of that spirit now: no light in his eyes, no recognition, no surprise or thought or anger. The only sound in the small room was his slow and steady breathing.

"Oh," she whispered. "What happened to you?"

He was too weak to stand, she saw; too weak to do more than prop himself against the wall and stare at her. She looked around, thought of the locks and the guard and finally understood. They were starving him to death.

Shai, more than anyone in the Lower City, had seen the walkers. She'd watched them, night after night, as they came in from the ruins and roamed the deserted streets. Looking for prey, she'd thought; looking for anyone left exposed or unguarded. The idea that someone had lured him here, up to Farrow's thirty-fourth floor, only to lock him in a random room and starve him to death seemed ridiculous—and beyond dangerous. The only alternative— that he'd been transformed into a night walker here in this room—hardly seemed more credible.

"I'm sorry," she murmured at last. Because whoever he was, whatever he had done, he did not deserve this. No one did. "I'm so sorry."

She reversed step by careful step, slipped through the wall, and was gone.

For a time, Shai stared at the locked door, the guard restless behind her, unsure what to do next. *Pieces to a puzzle*, she thought, and knew not the picture she was trying to form. *Nothing to do but keep looking.*

Except even as she turned to continue her search, she felt something on the edge of her senses. She hesitated, frowning—and recognized the feeling. A crawling shiver down the back of her neck; a vice-like feeling in her throat that made her breath go short and her imagined heart hammer in her ears. Dread.

The dark magic boy was coming nearer.

"I can't . . ." she said, but already she had stumbled back an involuntary step.

Her thoughts tumbled over themselves: the walker, and the ghost of the man he'd been before, and the kid coming for them in the underground, and his dark spells, and—

"Your turn," he said, and she recognized his high voice. She would recognize him anywhere. "Come on."

Run, came the thought, echoing through her head like the memory of Xhea's voice. She could not let him see her, could not let him touch her. No matter what logic her mind might conjure, her very soul knew the truth: to let him near would be her end.

Surrendering to instinct, Shai fled.

Chapter Fifteen

When morning came, it was only the light streaming through the apartment's windows that woke her. Xhea cringed and hid her face; sunlight, she thought, had no place in her morning routine. Stretched out on the couch in Marna and Ennaline's apartment—her apartment, not that she believed it—she had slept; and if the sleep had been full of confusing, frantic dreams that she could not remember on waking, it was nonetheless her longest sleep in months.

If only it had made her feel better. It wasn't just her knee that hurt this morning, Xhea found, but the muscles all down her leg. Muscles, too, in her arms and hand—from where she'd supported herself with her walking stick, she realized at last; and muscles in her back, pulled when she'd fallen. It took a long time to push herself up and out of the couch's embrace; longer still to bathe and dress. She did not weep, but that was only a matter of will.

She'd thought, for a brief and glorious time, that Shai had healed her knee—that she was, if not wholly better, then well on her way. Would that it were that easy. Her knee was better than it had been; yet the pain was still enough to shorten her breath and make sweat bead her forehead, and it wasn't only her slowly rising magic that made her stomach ache and churn.

It's okay, she told herself. Even though her magic was returning, Shai could still help her. If Xhea could endure the daily pain of movement, surely she could endure the brief agony of magical healing. She just had to manage a little bit longer, and then . . .

What? As if life as she'd known it could resume.

Xhea looked around the apartment, her eyes skittering from the photos and drawings. If she were to help Ahrent achieve his goal—Farrow's goal—all of this would be going with her, or she would going with it, she knew not which. This would be her home. A skyscraper. A Tower.

And Shai? If Shai chose, she could join her, stay Xhea's friend—but why would the ghost want to return to the fate she'd so barely escaped? Was there an existence for an unbound Radiant, anything but countless twisting paths that all led back to the same destination?

Xhea took a long, shuddering breath. What was she doing? Oh, sweetness and blight, what was she *thinking*?

The payment Ahrent offered was beyond anything she'd imagined, all her heart's secret wants laid bare. Home. Family. A place, a *purpose*. As if such things could be bought or given.

For all that she cringed, it seemed daylight brought clarity, shining down on her in all her aching folly. Ahrent had said that she wasn't his prisoner, that he wouldn't try to keep her here. It was time to test the truth of his words.

As she stood, Xhea looked one last time toward that first photo, pinned once more to the wall. She stopped. Stared. She hadn't let herself look at the picture again, nor the myriad others that surrounded it, just tumbled onto the couch and into sleep. Now, looking at the pictures and the strange, familiar faces that looked out at her, she could not move.

There was another picture of the young girl, Enjeia. There was her grandmother and Marna, arms over each other's shoulders, laughing. There, a far younger picture of her grandmother with a different small girl swaddled on her lap. *My mother?* Dark eyes and skin and hair in two puffy, braided pigtails. Nerra.

Xhea turned away, leaving all the pictures behind. These people were dead, or as good as dead; their love as much fiction as the life she'd imagined among them. They had abandoned her as a child, willing or no; abandoned her again by dying before she could find them, before she knew even to look. No, of everyone, Shai was the only one she could trust.

But if Shai won't abandon me, why isn't she here?

Oh, traitorous thought. Yet all the night had passed, Ieren far away, and there was no sign of Shai.

There came a knock, and Xhea limped toward the door. Daye stood on the other side, a gift in hand.

"What's this?" Xhea asked, clinging to the doorframe.

Daye looked at her flatly and held out a cane.

Unlike the one the medic had provided shortly after her surgery, this cane was perfectly fitted to Xhea's slight size; unlike her lost walking stick, it seemed almost elegant. It was a simple length of twisted wood, like a tree's root, roughly polished and stained dark, and topped with a heavy metal knob.

No words: Xhea reached out slowly and took the cane, surprised at its weight, its stability. She leaned upon it gratefully.

No words: Daye did not so much as blink, only waited, as if the cane had always been in Xhea's hand, as if it had nothing at all to do with her.

Xhea followed her out into the hall.

"I need to see Ahrent Altaigh," she said.

Daye shrugged and led her onward, the sound of Xhea's new cane tapping against the carpet. They made their way through Farrow's halls—busier now, and far more alive—before returning to the silent floor she'd seen the day before. A new guard was posted outside the padlocked door, similarly armed, who spared them no more than a glance.

Daye opened one of the doors and held it for Xhea. Ahrent was not inside; only Ieren and the ghost of the young boy bound to him.

"You're here!" Ieren cried, as if he found her presence an unexpected delight. He rushed forward and grabbed her free hand, and it was all Xhea could do not to recoil and yank her hand away. Ieren's skin was soft and warm; it was a sharp contrast to her own chilled palm and fading calluses. To feel another's skin—to have him hold to her hand with his small fingers—

She did not know what to do, whether to hold tight or draw back in surprise and disgust, and in her moment of indecision Ieren clung tighter and pulled her across the room.

"Look," he said, tugging her to the side of another wheeled bed, another unconscious body.

Unlike Marna, this one had been prepared long in advance of Xhea's arrival. He was an older man with a shaved head, paler skin marking where his hair had been. The wires had already been attached—more, even, than

Marna had borne. Wrists and neck and heart, yes, but also all across his scalp and in the center of his forehead.

Again she made to draw away; then Ieren said, "Ahrent said I should teach you. We'll go really slow today, okay?"

"Teach me?"

"To use your magic. To control it, like I do." His voice radiated pride—enough, almost, to hide the condescension in the words. He was better than her, and he knew it.

Xhea hesitated, biting back an angry retort. She should drop Ieren's hand and turn away, just *go*—like she should have the day before. Yet she knew the damage her magic had wrought, the pains and fevers and the way it kept her knee from healing. *Your magic will kill you if you let it*, Marna had said, and Xhea did not doubt her. If death were the inevitable consequence of its use, she had no reason to learn more. But if she learned not just spells, but *control* . . . ?

She'd seen Ieren work his magic, those dark threads of power spinning out from his fingertips and woven together with ease. Knew, too, that she would find no other offers of training. She didn't have to stay long, didn't have to agree to Farrow's plan. But perhaps, if she learned just a little, it would be enough that her knee might heal.

Xhea swallowed. "What do we have to do?"

Daye left the room and closed the door behind her. Her footsteps had not been loud, nor did the door slam in her wake, and yet Xhea heard her disapproval nonetheless. *Like she's one to talk.*

"Here, look," Ieren said. "I wrote it out for you." He handed her a scrap of paper. Carefully, she unfolded it and peered down at the gray markings that covered the scrap from edge to edge.

Xhea had long prided herself on her ability to read—had practiced down in the dark and silence until she could read quickly and without moving her lips—but this? Xhea barely resisted the urge to flip it upside down. It was nonsense to her, all of it.

Her first instinct was to shrug and push the paper away dismissively. It was one thing to admit that she had things she needed to learn; yet even the thought of revealing such ignorance to this boy, this *child*, made her shoulders tense and her lips thin.

Xhea had never been a good student. Oh, she *learned*, but there were reasons that Abelane had often thrown her hands up and stalked out in the middle of one of their lessons. Many, many reasons.

She handed it back. "I don't know what it says," she muttered.

Ieren's incredulous reaction was just as unpleasant as expected. Once they got through the worst of it, and he had ascertained that no one had told her anything about her power—no, not ever, not even one time—seriously, Ieren, not even once—he sat her down on one of the chairs with a terribly self-important look on his face.

"He can wait," the boy said at last with a dismissive gesture to the unconscious man awaiting them on the nearby bed. If only she could wave away his smug look as easily. "Let's start at the beginning . . ."

With no anger to goad its rise, Xhea struggled to call her magic. Ieren's explanations made little sense; yet watching him as he drew power up from the core of himself, she could almost understand.

She'd always thought of her magic as a cold, dark lake—and that power, when it rose, raged through her like floodwaters. *Not a flood*, she thought now; what she needed was just a trickle of power, a thin stream of magic from that central pool.

A few dozen tries later and she had it: a thin curl of magic lifted from her palm like the smoke from an extinguished match. So little power—yet with it came a rush of perfect calm. All her doubts fell away, all her fears; there was only that moment, perfect and still, and the dark magic's gentle sway. Xhea took a long, slow breath, and another, feeling the power rise into the air. After so much hurt and fear and confusion, the magic's presence felt like a blessing.

Though she'd conjured a bare whisper of gray, Ieren was impressed nonetheless.

"I thought you'd be weaker," he said. "Old as you are."

He'd said something like that the day before, correlating her age with power. "What do you mean?" Xhea asked. "Weak magic means you live longer?"

He stared as if she'd grown a second head. "Uh, *yeah.*"

Ieren had pretended to be younger in an attempt, she realized, to impress her with the strength of his magic. And he'd already said that he was ill, little though he looked it today. *The more power you have, the quicker it kills you.* She looked at the thin curl of magic in her hand, suddenly grateful that it was not stronger.

But if Ieren thought that ten was old, and she was ancient at fifteen or so, then how long did powerful dark magic users live? Because she couldn't help but imagine little children with this dark and terrible power. A power, Ahrent had said, rarer and far more valuable than even a Radiant's.

Strong power—dark magic more powerful than mine— in the hands of a child? The thought was unsettling. What must it be like to grow up with such strength, unable to touch or reach out to anyone else, and to be fated for such an early end?

But she knew already, didn't she? She'd lived that life, or the Lower City version thereof; she knew how power and difference built walls between people. She also knew Shai—and though the Radiant's power was different, its ultimate effect was the same: death.

No matter how much light and magic and freedom it provided, the City's foundation was death; death its bedrock and the structure for its walls, for all that those walls floated airborne.

"What did you do?" Xhea asked slowly. "Before you came here. What did you use your magic for?"

Ieren shrugged. "Normal stuff, I guess. Bindings, mostly. Some prisoners. Nothing really good like a merger or binding a Radiant, but other than that . . . whatever the Spire needed me to do."

Xhea didn't flinch at the mention of binding a Radiant—but only just. Instead she asked, "The Spire?"

He looked at her with pity. "You really don't know *anything*, do you? The Central Spire. It's the big, tall—"

"I know what the Central Spire is," Xhea said acidly.

"That's something, I guess. That's where I'm from—where we're all from, all of us with dark magic. Except you." He nodded to the magic in her palm, that thin streamer still rising. "You going to do something with that, or just sit there looking stupid?"

The morning had passed, and a good portion of the afternoon, before Ieren judged her control good enough to work with him on what he called the bindings. Xhea looked skeptically at the bit of power that she spun from one finger to the other, that calm feeling of rightness swelling in its wake. It was not a thin, straight thread, like Ieren cast; more like a dark ribbon fluttering in the wind. Still, despite the magic's tendency to twist like smoke, it was her best attempt by far.

Time to go, Xhea thought, stood, and nearly fainted dead away. She clung to the chair and consciousness with equal desperation until the room stopped spinning.

"Why don't you have a bondling?" Ieren asked, unbothered. "Don't tell me you don't know about *that*, either." At her look, he tugged the tether that joined him to the little boy's ghost in explanation.

Except, it wasn't quite a tether; Xhea leaned in to look closer. There was something different about it, something—

Ieren jerked the tether, pulling both the line and the ghost at its end away from Xhea.

"Hey!" he said. "I didn't mean that you could take mine."

The dead boy had been huddled in the corner, and cried out as Ieren sent him sprawling. Ieren paid the ghost no attention at all.

Xhea swallowed her objection. She couldn't count the number of ghosts she'd dragged through the Lower City for an hour or a day or sometimes more, rarely with so much as a hello exchanged. No moral high ground there.

Still, she remembered how she'd seen Ieren in the underground: *Eater of ghosts.* Shai had recoiled from him— and severed her tether to keep from getting near. But the ghost now bound to Ieren looked as whole and sane as he had the day before, giving no sign that Ieren had done anything more painful than take him from his familiar surroundings.

He's not so bad, Xhea thought, looking at Ieren. Not the kindest kid she'd ever met, nor the most patient, but neither was he the monster she'd thought. Or if he was a monster, surely she was as well.

"You mean a ghost?" Xhea asked. "I had one, remember? You tried to take her."

"You said she wasn't yours!" Then he waved his hand. "Anyway, she's gone. You're going to need someone if you don't want to black out. You should have that woman take you to the medic's. Still, like, seven ghosts there." He made a face. "Just don't go for that crying woman, okay? *So annoying.*"

"I'm good," Xhea said. Already she felt steadier.

"Whatever. Come on, then, I'll show you how this works." Without waiting for a reply, Ieren rose and went to the bedside.

Just watch once more. Then go. It wasn't as if she was steady enough to leave Farrow yet anyway. Leaning heavily on her cane, Xhea limped after.

She'd been trying not to look at the man who lay drugged into unconsciousness, awaiting their attentions. *He volunteered,* she reminded herself. *He chose this.* But all she felt was the cold knot of her magic in the pit of her stomach, and longed again for its perfect calm.

Ieren bound the man, and Xhea understood more than she had when he'd worked on Marna. She watched him join those thin, dark threads of magic together, weaving small pieces into a complex whole. Yesterday, she'd been startled at his work and the ease with which he performed it. Now she thought she could do the same. Perhaps not quickly or well, not yet—but soon.

At what cost? asked a small, hard voice. She pushed it away.

"Your turn," Ieren said when he was done. "Come on."

The next room had six beds, all occupied, with a lone attendant carefully checking the ancient medical machines. Xhea looked at the wires that bound each prone form to the skyscraper's walls, but she saw no flickering light, no flow of power. Waiting, then, for Ieren. For her.

"This one," Ieren said as Xhea entered. He pointed to the woman on the bed before him. "Come on, you try."

Her skin was pale as clouds, her lips gray as shadow, and oh, she looked young. Yet Xhea's hands lifted as if of their own accord, wisps of dark already curling around her fingertips.

It didn't matter that she'd practiced; touching a living person's spirit with her magic felt different than she'd expected—sharp and intense and deeply personal. The world around her fell away, and there was only the power, flowing from her, flowing at her command. No torrent of black, this; it was something precise and careful and controlled. Even so, within moments she tired, and the magic curled and twisted once more, slipping from her grasp as she tried to bind spirit to wire. Ieren stepped in to finish the job.

"Not bad," he said, as if repeating words once said to him. "But I know you can do better."

Just one more, Xhea thought, swept up in the magic's tide. She'd already come so far, so quickly—she just had to learn to maintain her control. One more and then she'd go.

It was easier, Xhea found, not to look at their eyes. Lying there, the men and women were almost like dolls, their shaved heads and identical cotton shifts making them seem alike. No voice nor expression nor gestures to remember; only their flesh, steadily breathing, and the light of their magic—their spirits—inside.

Volunteers, she told herself those first few times. *They chose this sacrifice.*

Sometime during the afternoon, she stopped repeating the words. They simply vanished from her head, like water into steam, there and then gone.

She and Ieren moved from one room to another, dark magic twining through their fingers, bright magic shining in their wake. Xhea leaned more and more heavily on her cane, limped more, though she felt little pain. If anything, it seemed that she drifted in a trance, lost in a sea of perfect calm. For all her myriad hurts and fears, for all the things that had gone so terribly wrong, this at least felt right. The power in her fingertips, in her stomach, flowing through her flesh. It burned everything away—burned some part of her spirit, perhaps, or burned away years of her life—but left her feeling as if everything was real and true.

She had forgotten that magic made her feel this way. She forgot, too, why she hadn't wanted to be here, what had made her want to flee.

At last she sank into a waiting chair, her power as exhausted as her body. Her hands, clutching the metal-topped cane, trembled; and the world around her was spinning, spinning.

Ieren dropped into the chair beside her and peered at her without sympathy. "See," he said. "I told you that you needed a bondling." He shrugged. "But you did good. We got through lots of them."

"I need . . ." Xhea managed. "I need to go . . ." She could not stand.

She looked to the window, bricked over and solid—then looked through it to the world beyond. Dark now. Night. How had she let a whole day go by?

Wait. How did I—how could I see—

Only then did she realize that she was seeing with her eyes closed. Seeing magic, yes, but everything else too: all the world around her cast in a thousand shades of gray.

Eyes open. Eyes closed. It made no difference. Xhea held her hand before her eyes, and it looked no different, dusky-gold skin gray as always. The ceiling, Ieren's face, the magic flickering through the wires that led from the bodies to the skyscraper's walls: gray, gray, gray.

And farther? A whole world unfurled to her vision, if only she looked long and hard enough. The next room, and the room past that; the hall and the window and the whole City beyond.

"My eyes . . ." Xhea started. But what could she say?

Ieren leaned in, peering at her eyes. "Not blind yet," he said, "but almost."

"Blind?" The words seemed to come from very far away. It wasn't that she could see nothing, a landscape dark and blurred; it was that she could see everything. Things that eyes could not see.

"Sure." Ieren shrugged. "I've been blind since . . . forever. But you don't really need your eyes anymore, so it doesn't really count, does it?"

Xhea blinked and stared and the world spun around her and nothing made sense anymore. "I think I need to lie down," she said. But where—the floor? She clung to her cane and rested her head in her free hand.

"Okay, sure," Ieren said. "I'm going to check out the next room, see what we're doing tomorrow." She heard his footsteps, then he paused. "You did a good job today." The words had such overdone kindness she almost expected him to pat her on the head. Another time, she might have laughed, or scoffed, or spit. Now she just held her head and tried to think.

It was too much, too quickly, and she felt as tired as if she hadn't slept for days. And she was hungry. Funny that she hadn't realized it before. They'd taken a few breaks, eaten a quick snack or two—but now hunger roared in the pit of her stomach, loud and insistent.

Blind. It shouldn't have been a revelation. All the world seen only in shades of gray. Seeing underground—seeing in perfect darkness. It was clear that her vision used something that was not natural light—and yet she was *blind*?

Xhea remembered what she'd seen when Shai had performed her healing: not just color, as she'd expected, but a world gone blurred and dark. Her inability to focus, no matter how she blinked or squinted. Smeared vision that faded and returned to perfect, clear gray as the bright magic bled from her body. Was that smeared darkness all that her eyes could see when her magic was suppressed?

"Excuse me?" said a small, hesitant voice—not Ieren or Daye. Xhea forced herself to look up.

Ieren's bondling stood by the far wall. The ghost of the young boy stared at the floor, his hands pressed tight against his stomach. He glanced up, met Xhea's eyes, and immediately looked to the floor again, shoulders hunched and cringing.

"Yes?" Xhea said. In the doorway, Daye turned toward her in question—seeing, Xhea supposed, her talking to the wall.

It took the ghost a moment to work up the courage to speak again, and even then his words were so soft as to be almost inaudible. "He wants you to come see him. In the next room."

"Who does? Ieren?"

The boy cringed, ducking his head as if expecting a blow. A moment, then he tugged on his tether in reply.

"Okay," she said, though in that moment she didn't think she could manage to stand, never mind walk down the hall.

Still the ghost did not move, only stared at the ground as if he wished he could sink into it. Xhea looked at him carefully. He didn't seem to be hurt or injured—his hands were all there, and his feet, and he gave no sign of being dimmer or less real than he had before. Ieren wasn't hurting him, then; he'd just had a hard life that ended too soon. Nothing she did could change that.

Xhea wanted to just turn away, ignore the ghost until he left. But Shai, if she were here, wouldn't have turned away. She could imagine what Shai would say, her voice reproachful: *Xhea, he's just a little boy.*

It was true.

Xhea forced herself from her chair and tried to crouch down, struggling with her bad knee and her dizziness and ignoring Daye's look at her fumbling attempt. She extended a shaking hand. "Hey," she said—and the ghost flinched at her voice. "Hey," she said, softer this time, quieter. "Are you . . . okay?"

In the resulting silence, she couldn't help but think, *What a stupid thing to ask.* Of course he wasn't okay; he was dead. Dead and unhappy and in a foreign place, being dragged around by a stranger as if he was nothing more than a toy on a string.

After a long moment, the ghost glanced up. Slowly, hesitantly, he looked at her through the veil of his long, dark lashes. His eyes seemed almost black, his cheeks stained dark by the flush of the illness that had killed him. He blinked as he looked at Xhea, then flinched away as Xhea met his eyes. Seconds passed, then he again looked up cautiously.

Oh, sweetness, what do I say? Xhea had never been good with people, nor with easy kindness, neither given nor received. She fumbled for words.

"Is there . . ." she tried. "I mean, can I help you . . . somehow?"

The ghost's voice was but a whisper: "You won't hurt me?"

"No. Of course I won't." She felt the irony of those words, here in a room of people she'd help bind to a slow and unhappy death. Still she said them, because it was what Shai would have said—what Shai would have wanted Xhea to say.

Xhea reached out, slowly, slowly—and hesitated, staring at his tether. There was something different about it, she thought again, leaning to take a closer look. *It's not a tether at all*, she realized, as her hand hovered above it. She could feel a hint of its vibration against her palm. *Not a tether, but a spell.*

She stopped, frozen, as she became fully aware of the ghost. Suddenly, she could *feel* him standing there, feel the chill presence of a ghost in the room—and it was all she could think of. There was a roaring in her stomach and her head—a sound, a feeling that grew stronger with every passing second.

Wanting, *needing.* Hunger that grew and grew the closer she came to the ghost.

Xhea swallowed and tried to push herself backwards, push herself *away*, and yet she only trembled. Her hand reached out seemingly beyond her thought or control. Her magic reached with it: a current of dark that rose up through her body and out, twisting and coiling in midair as it stretched toward the ghost.

The boy made a noise that was too small and frightened to be a cry, curling in on himself and raising his little hands to ward off her magic. *Of course I won't hurt you.* The words echoed from impossibly far away, and Xhea wanted to laugh, or scream, or cry. She desperately tried to shut down her power, or draw back her hand, and could not.

"Xhea?" Daye asked, once and again. She knew the woman could see nothing of the ghost, nothing of Xhea's magic, only Xhea reaching for nothing, struggling against nothing as tears cascaded down her face.

Then a coil of dark magic touched the ghost and the tether that bound him. Xhea felt a short, sharp shock, hard enough to knock her to the ground, and she gasped desperately for air.

She heard Ieren's scream, even through the walls that separated them. It was the rage she heard first; the word came almost as an afterthought: "*No!*"

That Daye heard. She leapt to her feet and knocked the chair aside, pulling open the door with speed Xhea could only envy. When Ieren came barreling down the hall and through the door, Torrence was right on his heels.

"What did you—" Torrence began

Ieren screamed over him. "*You can't, he's mine! Mine, mine, mine!*"

Xhea recoiled from his blind rage.

"I didn't—" she started. "Ieren, I—"

The little ghost whimpered as Ieren turned on him. "Don't you *ever* talk to her!" The ghost curled in upon himself further, cowering at his tether's farthest extent. "Don't even speak," Ieren said, and the words had the sound of a command. "Don't say anything at all."

Ieren rounded on Xhea. His lips were drawn back from his teeth like an animal's snarl, and his hands, when he reached for her, were wreathed with black. "He's *mine!* Get your own bondling—you can't steal mine, you can't, *you can't!*"

He grabbed her by the shoulders, and Xhea cried out, for this time his touch hurt. Torrence tried to intercede and drew back, yelping, as if his hand had been burned.

Xhea could feel Ieren do something with his magic, and her own power vanished in response. She shuddered at the sudden absence and weakness, and fell the rest of the way to the floor. Still Ieren shouted, telling her that she was a thief and a liar and that she deserved to die. In his anger, his power flowed. She knew that strong emotion could bid the power rise—and that when it did, it felt like nothing in the world might stop it again.

No one could stop him, Xhea realized, if she could not; and she trembled helplessly on the floor. So much dark magic could kill—swift and sure, if not painless. Even the brief touch of that swirling dark magic against Torrence's hand had the man shuddering and shivering.

At last Ieren drew back, his breath rough in his throat. Only then did he seem to see the haze of dark magic that surrounded them like a cloud.

"No," he whispered, and for a moment he sounded afraid, so afraid. "Oh, no. I'm sorry. I'm sorry!"

She watched as he visibly gained control of himself, taking a deep breath and closing his eyes. His magic contracted, darkening around him like a living shadow before vanishing even from Xhea's sight. It was not enough. Ieren had started to quiver, and he swayed as she watched, suddenly unsteady on his feet. She knew all too well the pain that made his mouth turn down at the edges and creased those lines into his forehead.

Ieren looked at her, all anger drained away. "I don't want to die," he said, as if he'd heard her thought. It sounded like an apology. Then he turned, grabbed hold of the spelled tether that joined him to the ghost, and pulled the boy struggling toward him.

The ghost cried out—or tried to, his mouth opening in a silent scream. A scream, Xhea realized, that Ieren had commanded him not to voice. Even without the sound, there was no ignoring the pain on his face, nor his fear as he tried with insubstantial hands to push Ieren away. And for nothing. His hands passed through Ieren as if he, too, were nothing but smoke, just a shadow in all this darkness. Ieren seemed not even to feel his touch.

Instead, he pulled the boy nearer and nearer again, reaching not for his ghostly body but the line that joined them. And it was no tether, for Xhea watched as Ieren used it like a drinking straw, drawing hard, fingers grasping, as he began to steal the ghost's energy, his being, his very *self* through that line. She could see it go, a nameless *something* moving along the binding from the ghost to Ieren. Ieren absorbed it, drank it down.

Eater of ghosts.

She hadn't been wrong, hadn't been wrong at all, and that truth terrified her. Xhea tried to get to her feet, but her cane had rolled away, and she was trembling, horrified.

Ieren was not so much larger than the ghost, but he held the ghost effortlessly, despite the dead boy's struggles. As she watched, Ieren seemed to grow stronger, steadier— while the ghost faded, becoming paler and less real as he screamed and screamed in silence.

Not the blindness nor the magic-vision, not the skin that hurt to touch, not seeing ghosts—*this* was what she was. *This* was what her power did.

Oh, sweetness, Xhea thought. *Ieren's a monster—and so am I.*

Because watching him, beneath her horror and revulsion and sudden, desperate fear, she felt something else: hunger deep as her bones and as inescapable. While she cried out to even see the ghost so clearly suffering, some part of her was . . . envious. That was the most terrifying thing of all.

Through her mental turmoil, another thought surfaced—and it cut through the rest like a well-honed knife. *Why aren't you trying to stop him?*

Ieren dropped the ghost and turned his back as if the boy were nothing more than a wrapper for a meal he'd tired of eating. Ieren took one slow breath and another, and looked up. He seemed, if not healthy, then very much alive. His cheeks were flushed and his eyes were bright, and his movements came quick and easy.

"I'm sorry for scaring you," he said, all signs of both rage and weakness gone. Xhea, sprawled on the floor with both Daye and Torrence standing over her with knives drawn, could only stare. "I thought you were trying to take him. I'm sorry—I know that you wouldn't do something like that, right?" Ieren shrugged and smiled, as if everything were perfectly all right.

The ghost was weeping. Curled into a ball at his tether's far end, the dead boy clutched his head and covered his face as he sobbed and sobbed in perfect silence. When Xhea looked, the tips of those fingers tangled in his dark hair had begun to grow transparent.

Xhea's own hunger was little abated—eased, only, by the extra few feet of distance between her and the ghost. She shook, and her breath was short and shallow, and sweat beaded her forehead. She pushed herself back, reaching for her cane as she tried to rise, tried to get away.

Too weak to do either.

"Daye . . . ?" Xhea started, but could only reach out an empty hand as darkness returned to claim her.

Chapter
Sixteen

Shai had only just started her nightly practice when the screaming began.

After the long day, she had returned to Edren's roof to practice her spellwork—not out of any desire, but only because she couldn't think where else she could go, what else she could possibly do. Xhea's small room had been familiar, if not exactly comfortable; now, Shai couldn't bring herself to go near. The halls and common rooms were a hive of activity in the wake of the fighters' return; some gathered to tend wounds or mourn losses, while others laughed and drank and predicted Rown's eventual fall. In all the skyscraper, only the roof felt calm and quiet; only the roof felt like it was hers.

Later, she'd wonder if she would have heard the screams had she been lost in one of her spell experiments; as it was, the faint, panicked sound was on the very edge of her hearing. She froze, listening. For a long moment, there was nothing.

Then it came again: her name, shouted from impossibly far away.

Xhea? Shai reached for the tether. Habit. Her hands hit empty air and again she felt that sense of dislocation to find herself unbound and alone.

She spun, as if someone might have snuck up behind her while she wasn't looking, hid behind the stacked storage crates or slipped into one of the aircars parked beneath the canvas awning. But there was no one. Shai stepped to the skyscraper's edge and looked at the streets below, dreading what she might see in the shadows.

Her father wasn't—he couldn't—

But no, as she stared Shai realized that the sound was not coming from some distant, darkened street, but a window cracked open some floors below her. Realized, too, that she recognized the voice: Lorn.

She released her hold on the world around her, and fell. She didn't have far to go. One floor, another, and the sounds grew louder; Shai slowed, slipped through an apartment wall and out into the empty hall beyond. She heard clang of metal on metal, of grunts and scuffling feet and a body hitting the floor. She sped forward, turned the corner.

Chaos.

Three attackers were still standing, each clad in dark clothing, their faces obscured. One held knives; another wielded a blade long enough to be a sword, magic gleaming along its edge. Emara held off both, her own blades whirling, while Lorn fought another attacker in the hall's far end. Shai could just see a body lying behind him.

Closer, near the elevators, a fourth attacker had been cut down.

And oh, the blood. It should not have shocked her, given the chaos, but it did. The smears of blood on the wall's ancient wallpaper, parallel streaks of brilliant red across all those pale, faded flowers. Blood slippery across the floor, smeared by scuffling feet. Blood pooling, dark red and glistening, from the still figure near the end of the hall.

Through it all, she could hear Lorn's voice, shouting her name over and over.

"*Shai!*" he cried, then grunted as his attacker pressed close to grapple.

Lorn held no weapon. He wore only shorts, his legs and arms and the bare expanse of his tattooed chest entirely unprotected. Already he had been wounded: blood ran from defensive cuts on his hands and forearms, and a deep slice above his heart; blood mixed with his sweat.

His only defense was a spell, clearly woven in haste, held before his upraised hands. It was a protective spell meant to turn aside objects approaching above a rough force limit; but it was thin now, if it had ever been strong, and flickered around the edges. Flickered, too, every time the knife struck the near-invisible half-dome, and grew weaker with every strike.

Again his attacker tried to close, pressing in with both body and blade, and Lorn struggled under the onslaught. He was pushed back, muscles straining, his feet sliding across the floor.

Emara, closer, had no spells, no flicker of light around her hands—but she was armed. Like Lorn, she seemingly wore only the clothes she slept in, a light top and shorts, and from the way she moved Shai could only imagine that anything heavier would have been in her way. She held a curved blade as long as her forearm in each hand, shining silver moons that spun around her like extensions of her body. She was never still, the blades gleaming blurs that rose and fell—parrying a thrust, slicing at an exposed side, creating a whirling wall of steel past which the attackers could not pass.

Xhea had told Shai that Emara had been a fighter in her younger years, a gladiator in Edren's arena—and despite the woman's height and the muscled expanse of her chest and arms, despite the scars on her arms and the way that she moved, Shai had not truly believed it until that moment.

A black-clad figure fell at her feet, choking on blood, and Emara stepped back, making the other opponent climb over—or stand upon—his fallen comrade to come at her. She blocked the hall with her body and blades alone, protecting her husband and the body over which he stood.

They were not just attackers, Shai realized, but assassins—for it seemed that their only mission here was death. As Edren security arrived, shouting, shock sticks raised, Emara's second opponent did not try to flee nor turn to face the new threat, only pressed harder against Emara's defense.

"*Shai!*" Lorn cried again. "*Shai, here!*" His spell flickered and nearly failed.

He was not alerting her, she realized, but calling desperately for her help.

Shai rushed forward, through the attacker and his blade, through Emara, to go to Lorn. He must have felt her approach, for he suddenly fell silent and in his expression flared something that looked horribly like hope. Shai pushed aside the fear her heart birthed at that look, pushed aside the uncertainty, and moved to stand at his side.

Her only attempts at reinforcement—bolstering the faltering healing spells on Xhea's knee in the weeks past—had gone terribly wrong. Even when she'd managed not to twist the spell-lines or cause Xhea pain, she'd overloaded the spells, sometimes destroying them entirely.

She knew nothing of defensive spells; there was no time to learn. As she hesitated, Lorn's spell flared and flickered, letting the attacker's knife slip through to score a deep line across the palms of Lorn's upraised hands.

Don't think.

She touched the shimmering spell-lines. As the attacker's blade rose and fell through her, Shai remembered the feel of a thunderstorm surrounding Allenai, the night-black clouds and the harsh cut of lightning across the sky, the storm's fury against her window—and that window and the Tower walls holding it all effortlessly back.

She was the window. She was the wall.

Lorn and the attacker both cried out as her barrier flared into being, lightning-bright in the confines of the hall. It had taken the space of a breath—if that. Yet in Lorn's bleeding hands now gleamed a great arc of power, almost wide enough to span the hall from side to side. It glowed white gold, transcending the magical spectrum. The attacker flinched, shielding his eyes.

Leaving Lorn to hold back his assailant, Shai rushed to the man who lay on the floor—and it was a man, sprawled boneless as he had fallen. He wore a light robe, cotton pants, and a T-shirt. Pajamas, she thought—but she could not tell what color they had once been, so soaked were they with blood. The fabric was red and black and slicked to his chest, and a slim knife handle still jutted up from the arches of his ribs. But she saw the weak rise and fall of his chest, and she crouched by his side.

Looked down at his face.

And stopped, breathless.

Verrus Edren. They've tried to kill Verrus Edren. If the rough, wet sound of his breathing was to be believed, they might still succeed. In that single, frozen moment, Shai understood why Lorn had called to her so desperately.

Don't think, she commanded. *Act.* She reached out with glowing hands.

But how could she silence her mind's sudden clamor, or still the questions that whirled unanswered? She knew the importance of this life—here, now. She knew what hung in the balance.

Shai placed her hands above his chest as if she could touch him, feel his blood or the sodden weave of his shirt or the rise and fall of his stuttering breath. *Focus*, she thought—the same instruction that she'd so often given Xhea. But it was only now, her thoughts running circles as a man bled out beneath her intangible hands, that she understood why Xhea had struggled.

Blades clashed, and Emara cried out in pain, and there came a sizzle from Lorn's spell as the attacker tried to force his way past its weakest edges. Shai pushed it all away and focused only on the magic as it flowed from her hands, her heart, her self. Weaving that power on instinct, letting it sink into his ailing flesh to map out the injuries beneath.

Verrus's lung had been punctured and he struggled to breathe; blood frothed on his lips. So close, she could see his many stab wounds, like bloody little mouths gaping wide, on his arms and shoulders and neck. But it was the way the blood pumped from the wound in his chest that told her that the little blade had plunged deep enough to nick something important. Artery? Vein? Mind scrabbling at details, she couldn't remember the difference.

Doesn't matter. Yet when she went to set the spell-anchors along the deepest wound's edges, her magic seemed to slide off, entirely out of her control. *Steady*, she thought. *You can do this.* She tried again, and again her magic was repelled. And a third time: for whenever she attempted to push her power toward the wound and the knife within it, something pushed back. Pushed away.

Resistance.

Shai opened her eyes, not knowing when she had closed them, and looked down in surprise. Only then did she recognize the blade.

She had thought the knife small, especially in contrast to the heavier, longer weapons that the attackers now wielded. The knife's hilt was slender and bloody, the blade fully embedded in Verrus Edren's chest, but oh yes, she knew that shape. It was a narrow silver blade, an ancient thing that folded neatly into a handle inlaid with time-clouded mother of pearl.

Xhea's knife.

"No," Shai whispered, unheard. For she knew that Xhea had carried this knife in a jacket pocket above her heart for years; and that it had, over time, absorbed some shadow of her power. Now, searching for it, she could feel the knife's presence, the faintest pressure against the palm of her hand. The feel of dark magic. No poison, this, but something far worse. If her magic, bright magic, told things to live and grow and flourish, Xhea's magic said the opposite: to falter, to weaken.

To die.

The knife held little of that power anymore, but it was enough. Already the flesh still in contact with the metal was beginning to die—she could see it, *feel* it, as life and magic both began to slip from the cells that touched the silver blade.

Unthinking, Shai grabbed the knife to pull it from Verrus Edren's chest—she would deal with the blood as it came—only to have her hand pass through. It *hurt*, the knife hilt's passage through her reaching hand, hurt as nothing had hurt her since her death. Gasping, Shai drew back.

Lorn or Emara—either of them might touch the blade, if quickly—

Before she could do more than turn, Verrus began to choke. Blood spattered his lips and his chest heaved as he slowly drowned in his own blood. He coughed and gasped for air, mouth opening and closing like a landed fish. His eyes fluttered open as a look of pain and disbelief—and yes, fear—crossed his face. He made to speak, one hand reaching—

And then, nothing.

A last breath bubbled from his lips as his body grew still. He seemed to sag as his muscles went slack. A moment, and then his dark eyes, once so cold and hard, were simply empty, open, staring.

Lorn, Shai realized, was shouting, screaming—and not at the attacker, who had crumpled to the floor near Verrus's feet, and not at his father, but at her.

"Do something!" he cried. "Shai! Shai, *please*, why won't you do something?"

But she couldn't, no matter how much she wanted to, no matter how he yelled or raged or pleaded. And he did all three: Shai stepped back and back again, as if Lorn's hurt and confusion were a tangible force.

"I couldn't," she said softly. "The knife, it's the knife . . ." Knowing he could not hear her. Knowing there was nothing she could have done, no spell she might have wrought—and feeling the weight of guilt regardless.

Then Emara was there, cut and limping but whole, and she took Lorn's shoulders in her hands and drew him roughly to her. Her blades, Shai saw, had been laid aside still bloody. Of the two men that she had fought, one was on the floor unmoving, while the other was held by the late-arriving security forces, his hands bound behind his back despite an obviously broken arm.

I could try to heal him, Shai thought as she looked at the struggling attacker. Heal someone, anyone, if only to try to balance this new failure. But she did not move. Just stood, staring.

Emara murmured in Lorn's ear until his shouting ceased. He took a long, shuddering breath, looking from his father's body to the space of empty air where he felt Shai to be. He looked shocked, too stunned to believe what he saw, never mind cry.

Shai did not—had not—liked Verrus Edren, not from that very first moment. Something about him, the way he held himself, his cold words and colder expression, had made her feel mouse-like, as if cowering or running away were her only options. She'd liked him even less when he'd refused to rescue Xhea, choosing instead to knowingly attack a rival skyscraper with Xhea's abduction as feigned justification.

He was—had been—a hard man; and, from what she'd learned in her years watching her mother work as a key member of Allenai's council, a bad leader. He'd cared more for his own ideas and commands than reasoned decisions, and had surrounded himself with people more likely to bend to his will than oppose him.

But he was Lorn's father, and she had not wanted him to die.

Security was coming to them now, Lorn and Emara both, trying to take them to safety—wherever that might be. Where in this skyscraper would be safe if not here, outside their own rooms near Edren's top level? How had attackers possibly reached this far? Lorn waved them away, leaving Emara to give curt instructions for the remaining attacker to be locked up and watched until they were ready to question him.

Lorn knelt at his father's side, heedless of the pooling blood, and reached out to close his eyes.

"Who did this," he whispered. It wasn't truly a question.

Yet Shai knew; and after her hours of practice, she could at last hold her light spell in the shape of a word. She kindled a light, and let it flow between her hands, shaping it into the word she needed.

Orren.

Because Orren had taken Xhea's silver knife and not returned it. Xhea had explained what had happened in the time they'd been apart: her capture by Orren, her imprisonment and escape—and that there was a woman within Orren's broken walls who had seen and understood Xhea's dark magic.

A woman who knew enough, it seemed, to use the slim blade she'd stolen to achieve greater damage than could be wrought by a knife alone. Using the distraction of the conflict with Rown for Orren's own ends.

If Lorn or Emara were surprised at the sudden appearance of the glowing word, or that word's import, neither showed it. Too shocked, Shai supposed; too tense and shaken by the aftereffects of the adrenaline that even now must be burning from their systems. The only sharply drawn breath came from one of the guards behind them, and Shai paid him no heed.

Lorn simply nodded and looked back to his father's face.

"It was revenge," he said, and shook his head. "I told him, I *told* him . . ."

Emara put her hand on his shoulder. Her fingers, Shai saw, were quivering; that was her only outward sign of her distress.

Xhea had said that Edren and Orren had been allied for much of the earlier war, though she'd never mentioned how that alliance had ended. Shai thought of what she'd overheard earlier: that Verrus had ordered the slaughter of Orren's ruling family. Revenge ten years in the making. And if Verrus had killed the entire family, surely whoever in Orren now moved against them would not be appeased by the death of a single man. Lorn was still at risk, and Emara, and anyone else in this skyscraper in line to rule.

Oh why, Shai thought suddenly, hopelessly, *can't they just have elections like everyone else?* So much brutality—and for what?

"Sir?" a man said, coming up behind them. Not a guard; not anyone Shai recognized. Behind them, the bodies of the slain attackers were being searched, quickly and efficiently.

"Sir," the man said again, more insistent this time.

"What is it?" Lorn said at last. He did not sound himself. His voice, still deep and resonant, sounded somehow thin, empty. A shocked and desolate wasteland in those few words.

"Sir, with Mr. Edren—ah, that is, with your father . . . deceased, you are in charge. Sir."

Still Lorn looked at his father, until at last he seemed to see his own hands before him, resting on his father's chest. Saw the blood that patterned them, and their myriad seeping cuts; saw the blood and sweat on his arms. Lorn looked down at his bare, bleeding chest. There was a wound that scored a line across his pectoral muscle, and the tattoo written over his heart. *Addis.* The cut ran beneath the name as if in emphasis.

Lorn laughed then, and it was a sad, exhausted sound. He held his bleeding hand to his chest, seemingly pressing against that wound—but it was the name that he wished to cover, Shai thought. His trembling fingers pressed against those dark-inked letters as if he might push them through his skin to his heart.

Addis, once heir to Edren, raised and trained by his father to lead. Addis, dead these passing years—dead but living in a body not his own.

Lorn took a long, slow breath and moved his other hand from his father's chest. Looked away. He stood slowly and straightened his shoulders—took one of Emara's hands in his own and squeezed. Something came over his face, then, in a slow and subtle transformation.

"Yes," he said, once and again. "Okay."

He took a deep breath and stepped forward, leaving his father's body behind.

Chapter
Seventeen

Xhea quivered as she woke. She felt if she were rising not from sleep nor unconsciousness, but a deep pool of water, still and cold. She gasped as she surfaced.

She could not force her eyes open—exhaustion felt like an anchor, pulling her down—but she could feel the blanket on top of her. Not thin like she was used to, but thick and fluffy and warm. Pillow beneath her head, the couch on which she lay. A rasping sound nearby like stone on metal.

The morning before she'd thought her discomfort due only to overexertion and the lingering aftereffects of her injuries. Now, shivering beneath the blankets, she wasn't so sure. *The magic*, she thought, and did not know how to continue. For all the destructive force of her power, she did not know why she would only feel this way now.

And she was *hungry*, so very hungry, though the thought of food was enough to turn her stomach.

She opened her eyes. She was in her grandmother's apartment. She did not remember returning that afternoon, nor whether she had made it here unaided; she did not, in truth, remember falling asleep. Yet it was night now: full dark outside the distant window, Towerlight flickering overhead, and dim inside the apartment itself. Though she did not need the light, a candle burned on the table.

On a nearby chair, Torrence hunched over a bucket, a whetstone in one hand and Daye's long knife in the other. Carefully he sharpened the blade, his hands moving in slow and steady circles, water dripping to stain the floor around him. Closer sat Daye, arms crossed and eyes closed as she leaned back in her chair next to the door, the metal-topped cane that she'd given to Xhea against the wall nearby.

Seemingly casual, both of them. Xhea knew better. She could see their tension, that coiled readiness that no slumped posture or easy expression could belie.

Torrence looked up as Xhea moved, then dipped the whetstone back in the bucket with a splash. "Well, hey," he said. "You're not dead after all. Here I was starting to wonder."

"Sorry to disappoint," Xhea managed, barely getting the words past her chattering teeth. "What are you doing here?" She didn't bother to hide her hostility.

"Doing our charitable duty and visiting the sick, of course." He held up the knife and examined it in the candlelight with an easy, practiced eye.

Of course. Because everyone made secret charitable visits in the middle of the night, especially opportunistic bounty hunters. She glared at Torrence and the knife he held, not knowing whether that blade was meant as threat or warning. Not that she posed much danger to anyone at the moment.

"Why's it so cold?" she asked.

"It's not. We've got it hot in here as we can make it. You, darlin', are just suffering from the worst case of magic shock I've seen in a long time."

Xhea blinked, realizing that Daye was down to her undershirt, sweat gleaming from her muscled arms and from the ends of her short hair. Even Torrence looked mussed, and had his sleeves rolled up as high as they could go. Midsummer heat, and them running a heater.

It was hard to think; harder still to force her quivering lips to form words. "But," Xhea said, "but . . . I didn't even . . ."

"Didn't use much magic?" Torrence lifted the knife, dripping water, and tested its edge. "Tsk, tsk—it doesn't take much, you know that."

Except it didn't feel like it was overuse of magic that weakened her, but the hunger that had transformed her stomach into a painful, aching pit. Xhea knew hunger—and yet this hurt like nothing she'd ever known. It felt as if the shape of her magic were not that cold, dark lake she'd so long imagined, but an empty hole, black and endless.

A dark mouth, opening wide.

She could not stop shivering. The piled blankets, the heat in the air, were nothing to her; the cold had entered her bones. She'd felt warmer standing outside for hours in midwinter, with the wind biting through her clothes and the snow stinging as it drove into her face.

"Do I have a fever?"

"Oh, probably." Torrence tested the knife's edge again. "I think it's done," he said to Daye, offering her the knife hilt-first.

Daye didn't even open her eyes. "It's not," she replied.

Torrence sighed and looked to Xhea. "I'm telling you, don't ever lose a bet with this woman." He bent again, whetstone whirring against the blade.

In spite of everything, the comment almost made her smile. Torrence lost bets to Daye all the time, everything from card games to where they'd find the best salvage to how long they'd wait for their mark to come out into the alley to pee. The alley, of course, where they had been waiting with a black bag to cover his head and a startling unwillingness to take to bribes. Xhea's part in that job had been long since finished, yet she'd stayed, high on her payment and laughing at Torrence's increasingly ridiculous one-sided banter.

She missed that life sometimes, strange though it was to admit it. Not the lack of food nor the chill nor the fight for paying work; not the loneliness nor the times when the nights felt endless. But the rest. It hadn't always been a good life, nor an easy one, but it had been hers. Staring at her hand and seeing the shadow that lay beneath her skin, watching her fingers tremble, she thought, *It's gone for good.*

So, too, was that easy camaraderie with these two, no matter that she remembered better times. It would avail her little to forget what they'd done.

Even so, she couldn't help but ask: "What'd you bet on?"

Torrence snorted. "You."

"Glad that you lost, then." Xhea rubbed her eyes. "What happened, anyway?"

"Seems the magic got the best of you. Out cold for— what?—six hours now. Couldn't wake you if we tried. Which we did. Occasionally."

"How did I even get here?"

"That . . . ah. That was Daye."

Daye didn't move so much as a muscle, yet it was very plain what she thought of Torrence telling that part of the story. He would have more than a few more knives to sharpen in his future, Xhea bet.

It was hard to envision: Daye lifting her up, cradling her, carrying her all the way here. Even protected by the layers of their clothing—even though Daye and Torrence both had never reacted as strongly to Xhea's touch as some others did—she could only imagine her discomfort. And for what? Ahrent's instructions seemed to be for Daye to watch and guard Xhea, not care for her. Xhea couldn't imagine why she'd bothered.

Torrence rolled his shoulders and cracked his neck. "Well, then, if you're not going to up and die on us, we might all have a chance of getting out of this alive. Best news I've had all day."

"Don't tell me you're not having fun."

"Fun's when it's a challenge, fun's when it's all on the line. Here . . ." He shrugged. "Here it's just a matter of time." He held out the knife once more. "There, look at this. Sharp as my wit."

Daye snorted, but relented enough to crack open one eye, take the blade, and test its edge with her thumb. She nodded grudgingly. As Torrence turned away, Xhea caught just a hint of Daye's smile, there and gone so fast that she thought she must have imagined it.

Torrence dried his hands and pushed the bucket to one side, the plastic scraping against the wet floor. "You ever dream about your perfect job?" he asked. It was a stupid question; there was only one answer. Still, she nodded.

"This wasn't our dream job," Torrence said, "because we never had a dream this big. Renai, fame, all of it—that's one thing; the ultimate con . . . oh, that's another. But this? To do a simple job and be rewarded with citizenship—true citizenship?" He shook his head and Xhea understood; no words could do that idea justice.

"I didn't believe it, of course, and Daye walked out on Mr. Altaigh in the middle of a sentence—but he talked us around. Made us believe. Conning a conman—that takes skill."

Daye sighed, not seeming to listen to either one of them, then rose and crossed to the apartment's kitchen. There she turned on a small hotplate and filled a battered pot with water from another bucket off to one side. She stood before it, perfectly still and poised like a hunter, and stared at the water's surface as if daring it to boil.

Xhea looked from one to the other, not understanding. "You don't believe that Farrow can become a Tower?"

Torrence spread his hands. "I don't believe that it can now, here, no matter how many people that boy plugs into the wall like lamps. This whole thing is going terribly, terribly wrong—and the head man's doing everything he can to keep it all together. But you know what? He's just steering a crashing aircar. Thing's still going to fall."

Xhea had been in a crashing aircar before, and unpleasant though it had been, she'd survived. Maybe this was only another bumpy ride.

She shook her head. It wasn't that she didn't have doubts—but it was only the method of achieving that transformation that made her question. The method and the magic, bright and dark alike; she struggled to believe either would be enough.

She wanted to believe that Ahrent was right—wanted to see Farrow lift into the air, years of work and countless Lower City citizens rising in defiance of all that the City thought of them and their potential. Even the thought was glorious. But she'd stood in a Tower beneath its living, flaring heart, and for all the sacrifice and power represented in Farrow's attempt, she did not see how they could possibly compare. As if this, like everything else, could only be a poor Lower City echo of what those in the City took for granted.

She thought of Ieren, and the young boy's ghost—

Thought of those people, as still and helpless as Shai had been when she lay dying—

Volunteers, she reminded herself. It didn't make her feel any better.

"If that's what you think," Xhea said at last, suspicious, "why are you still here?"

Torrence shrugged. "We don't have a way out."

Across the room, Daye poured hot water into a glass bottle and a waiting mug she'd filled with leaves. Returning, Daye gestured for Xhea to sit up, and waited while Xhea first glared, then looked away, then at last relented. With quick, efficient motions, Daye propped another pillow behind Xhea's back, and wrapped the bottle of hot water in a blanket before nestling it at Xhea's side. Xhea blinked, wanting to protest the strange, sudden attention—yet immediately she could feel the bottle's heat, the first glimmer of warmth she'd felt since waking. She shifted it so that it rested directly on her stomach, only realizing belatedly that Daye still waited beside her, mug in hand.

Did Daye just make me tea? Even unspoken, the idea seemed incredible. A water bottle? That was like wound care, the necessary tending of an injured ally. Tea was something else.

Hesitantly, Xhea reached out, expecting Daye to just snort and turn away, taking the tea with her. Instead, she pressed the mug into Xhea's hands, careful not to let their fingers touch. The water, darkening to tea as the leaves circulated, splashed against the sides of the mug but did not spill. The rising steam smelled of mint.

Daye sat and looked directly at Xhea as if daring her to comment. At Xhea's continued silence, she turned away, looking bored.

Xhea tried to drag her thoughts back to the conversation, as if the sudden warmth against her hands and stomach didn't nearly take up the whole of her attention; as if a small sip of tea, sliding down her throat, didn't seem like the most important thing there was.

She had been going to say: *What's that to me? Not my problem that you got yourself trapped.* But she stared at her tea, her piled blankets and shaking hands, and could not say the words.

"You always have an escape plan," she said instead. "Or two."

Torrence nodded. "Or seven. Yes. Gone, now. Some jobs turn strange and you put the work in anyway, because the pay will be worth it, right? Some jobs go bad all at once, and you're left with nothing. Less than nothing." He shook his head and glanced at Daye. "Speaking of nothing, you could have made me some tea too, you know."

"No," she said.

"Typical." He turned back to Xhea. "If everything works out, maybe we'll still get the big payoff. Maybe. But if it all goes wrong, crashing aircar style? We're going with it."

"You know too much."

"Oh, blighted hell, yes. These last few days? Just a glimpse of the past month."

Xhea blinked at that. "Month? What did they hire you for?" Because she'd thought they'd been hired to kidnap her, and to guard her and Ieren both.

A nod. "That's when Ieren killed his handler—the man sent by the Spire to watch over him. The boy became unpredictable, his mood swings wilder. There was no one to rein him in when he got out of control. Those who tried, died. Until we got here."

Maybe she should have been taken aback by the thought that Ieren had killed—but she wasn't. Not after seeing one of his mood swings for herself. That much dark magic flying around in his anger? Even she'd felt it. And how could you stop a child having a tantrum when he could kill you on a whim?

"You want out, why don't you just go? You're Rown citizens." Surely that offered some protection, even if only within their walls.

"Rown who dances at Farrow's command? Rown whose barrier Ieren bored straight through, turning it to dust and ashes while we watched? Rown who barred the door when last we returned home, calling us spies? *That* Rown?" He shook his head. "We managed to grab a few of our things, but we can never return."

And oh, the bitterness in his voice—anger, sudden and sharp, to mask the grief. Rown had saved him, he'd told her once; taken him in when he was no one, just a scrawny kid too clever for his own good with a mouth that always got him knocked to the dirt. Rown had given him a chance when no one else had.

Xhea had never known how Daye had come to Rown, nor to stand at Torrence's side; there was no point in asking. But Xhea imagined that Daye's blank expression hid the same sorrow, the same pain of leaving. Even if they were to escape Farrow and any retribution, their lives would be forever altered.

No going back.

"So what are you saying?" she asked dryly. "That we should work together, just like we did before you abducted me?"

"Now, now," Torrence said. "You don't have to be like that."

Xhea's voice turned sharp enough to cut. "How else am I supposed to be, Torrence? Sweetness and blight, if you knew Farrow was doomed, why drag me here? You could have just left me out of it."

Torrence shrugged. "Sometimes you've got nothing but bad choices and worse, darlin' girl. You know that. Nowhere to run, Ieren with us . . . what would you have done?"

"I wouldn't have stabbed Mercks, that's for blighted sure. I wouldn't have pulled another person into this mess."

Again, that shrug. "And I wouldn't have gone underground at all, if I were you. But you did anyway. We all make our choices, darlin'. We're all stuck with the fallout."

It was true. *Run away*, the ghost had said. A ghost Ieren had sent to find her, and who had instead tried to warn her. A ghost that Ieren had devoured. She'd been warned; she'd just chosen not to listen. Anything, she had thought, to break the boredom. If only she could go back in time, she'd smack herself.

"You feeling better?" Torrence asked.

No, Xhea wanted to say, *I feel like I'm dying*—except she didn't anymore. Her hands, wrapped around her mug, were steadier; her mind felt clearer, and her teeth had stopped their awful chattering. She was still weak and feverish, and nothing—not the warmth nor the tea nor the distraction of their words—had touched the growing pain of her hunger. She nodded anyway.

"The lifting will be in a few days, at most. Not much time to get out. And you *do* want out, right?"

"I can leave. Ahrent said I could go at any time." Xhea looked to Daye for confirmation. She hadn't seen Ahrent, hadn't had a chance to ask him to let her go like she'd meant—but that didn't mean that she couldn't.

Daye just looked at her, slow and steady. She did not say anything; she did not need to.

"You're lying," Xhea said. "Both of you."

Torrence raised his hands palm up and shrugged. "We do have that tendency, I admit. But not this time. You can't walk out of here any more than we can."

"You left yesterday."

"Only on official business, and it's the rare mission where Ahrent lets both Daye and I leave Farrow together."

But that, Xhea thought, was their problem—not hers. Though it brought up the one thing she truly did not understand: "Why do you need me?" she asked. "Why are you even here?"

"Because, even injured as you are, there are things you can do that neither of us can."

She snorted. "You mean I'm leverage."

"No, I meant what I said—but you're leverage too, if it comes to it."

"Lovely."

Torrence smiled—yet for a moment, beneath the charming expression, he looked tired. "Just think about it." He turned to Daye. "You ready?"

A nod.

"We'll see you in the morning, then," he told Xhea. "One way or another."

Daye paused. She retrieved the cane from near her chair, and laid it by the couch where Xhea could reach it when she rose. Torrence, his hand on the doorknob, frowned.

"We can get her another cane," he said, as if Xhea wasn't there. "You don't have to give it to her."

Daye shook her head.

"Are you sure?" Daye just looked at him until he raised his hands in surrender. "Okay, okay, whatever you want." Shaking his head, Torrence left the room.

As Daye made to follow, Xhea whispered, "Daye?"

She spoke softly enough that Daye might have pretended she hadn't heard; yet she paused in the doorway, glancing back. There were so many things that Xhea could say; more, in truth, that she couldn't. Why did thanks lodge so fully in her throat, the words hard and round as stones?

"It was my mother's," Daye said, nodding toward the cane, and then closed the door behind her.

Xhea stared at the ceiling for a long time after Torrence and Daye had left. Despite the exhaustion that dragged at her limbs and eyelids alike, sleep seemed impossibly far away. She'd always thought better when she was moving, but she knew better than to pace. Or sit up. Or move at all, really.

Maybe they're right, she thought. *Maybe Farrow's attempt is destined for failure.* Still she imagined it: a skyscraper rising, leaving the dirt and the ruin of the Lower City behind. Not just one Lower City dweller escaping to a better life, but hundreds.

Xhea sighed, her feet restless, her hunger a painful ache. It was not that she wanted to stay, not that she believed all Ahrent had said. Wasn't even that she stood to learn more about her magic—good and bad and flat-out terrifying—within these walls. She shuddered, remembering Ieren as he'd consumed part of the young boy's ghost—and tried to push the memory away.

It was just—

Xhea smiled then, a thin and humorless expression. It was just that she did not know where she could go, what she could do if it were not this. Once she might have run from this place without a backward glance. Now, this was the only place where she was wanted, needed, and she'd abandon it for—what? Some cold, small room, hidden away. Limping the halls, day and night, tolerated only for Shai's presence. Xhea looked at her quivering hands, her weak and broken knee. She was hurt and feverish and dangerous.

Edren wants me. That was the lie she had been trying to tell herself. If not Edren, then Lorn, or Emara, or . . . someone. But if that were true, where was her rescue? Where was the sign that anyone had even noticed her absence?

Oh Shai, she thought. *Where are you?* The ghost should have found her by now. Unless, of course, she wasn't looking.

What if she just . . . left? Left Xhea; left the living world entirely. Xhea couldn't imagine which fate was worse. But no, she tried to reassure herself, Shai had been angry with her before they separated, little though Xhea had understood the cause—but surely not so much that she'd turn her back on Xhea altogether.

Xhea took a long, shuddering breath, trying to push away the fear and uncertainty. Ever since she'd understood how badly her knee had been injured, she'd felt like something had fled from her. Confidence, maybe; trust in her own worth. That feeling, however misguided, that she could handle everything on her own.

The ability to walk away.

She might as well have been bound, though she could not see the ropes that held her. Her past and her future, her needs and Farrow's, Ahrent's bold words and the dark magic that tied her to Ieren sure as any tether. Her fear. Her desire, in spite of everything, to learn more about the power that even now seemed to hollow her out and fill her up at the same time.

Xhea looked at the pale gray of the ceiling, the patterned gray of the aging walls. On the table before her, the candle burned out. She smelled mint and wax and the faint wisp of smoke—and beneath it all, the dust and rot of the Lower City itself. All the myriad scents of the people left to live and die and scrabble for scraps in the Towers' shadows.

Sweetness save me, she thought. *This? A blighted Tower?* If only.

But she didn't need to trust Ahrent's word, she realized; if he were telling the truth, the evidence would be written all around her. Spells upon spells within the walls and ceiling and floor—spells that she'd already glimpsed in passing. To bring this ancient hulk of concrete and rebar to life, power had to flow through those spells day and night. Even Ahrent's little metal sculpture, its core softly glowing like the heart of a living thing, had absorbed years of his magic.

Xhea refocused her eyes. A moment and then the grays vanished, replaced by a glimmer of light. She stared at the lone thread of a spell. Yet she'd no sooner begun to frown than she saw further, deeper, and gasped as layer after layer of spells were revealed. It took a moment to understand what she was seeing: the spells in the ceiling, and in one above that, all the way up to the skyscraper's top level, superimposed one atop the other.

Then she could only stare as the extent of the spells appeared before her eyes, unfolding like page after page of some dense novel written across the skyscraper's floors and ceiling and walls. However long its creation, Xhea had expected this working to be crude; massive, but crude. The reality, shimmering all around her, was enough to stop her breath, for what Farrow's casters had lacked in raw power they had made up for in complexity. It was beyond beautiful—it was a complex piece of art drawn across years, and it flared to life before her.

Viewed one atop the other, it was all but impossible to tell where one spell ended and the next began. She knew some small bit about reading spells' lines of intent, but this was far beyond anything she'd ever seen, ever known.

Deeper still, there were designs. Dim, now: the patterns glimmered on the edge of her seeing, faint but present. It was a charm, Xhea realized—the biggest charm she had ever imagined never mind seen. The lines of wires, of drawn patterns, of designs scraped and carved into Farrow's very bones, all held the shape of a spell where magic alone was too weak.

This was not the work of one man, no matter how passionate, but the work of generations. She could see the casters' signatures, many and varied, written in magic all around her.

She did not know how long she stared, watching magic flow through the building all around her, making her feel as if she were held in a cradle of light. Maybe Torrence and Daye were wrong. Her own earlier misgivings, too, seemed trivial—all her fatigue and worry and uncertainty— compared to something so vast and beautiful.

It will be okay, Xhea told herself. *One way or another.* At last, she sank into the couch's embrace and closed her eyes, banishing the vision.

Part Three

Chapter Eighteen

Daye came for her the next morning long before dawn, before Xhea had managed to force herself out of the couch's embrace. She had slept, but not deeply and not well, and was more than ready for the distraction.

"Ahrent Altaigh is waiting," Daye said in her strangely soft voice.

"For what?" Xhea asked, fitting the brace around her discolored knee. Her hands were still shaking. *Steady*, she told herself. *Steady*.

"You."

After three tries, Xhea managed to get to her feet and stood swaying, the cane's support the only thing keeping her up. Her vision, too, wavered. She kept feeling the sudden shift that she had oft thought of as refocusing her eyes to see magic, and suddenly the room around her would bloom with light and pattern, reflections of the spells beyond.

The depth—and the growing strength—of that vision surprised her. She was tired of being surprised, tired of being weak, tired of being *tired*. Oh, for the strength she'd once taken for granted. The strength to set her shoulders and shrug as if nothing in the world could touch her. The strength to simply stop caring.

Beneath it all was the weight not of magic, but the hunger its use had engendered—a feeling that went beyond hurt or desire into stark, cold need.

Xhea closed her eyes and swayed unsteadily, then took a deep breath and tried to push it all away. "Okay," she said. "Let's go."

They walked in silence to the elevator and then up to the skyscraper's highest floor, returning once more to the penthouse suite where she had first met Ahrent Altaigh. As the elevator doors slid open, Xhea spoke without thinking: "Something's changed."

Her words were meant more for herself than the man who once more stood across the room, looking through the expanse of windows—and oh, the exhaustion made evident in those spoken words, for who was she to express her thoughts aloud? Especially here.

Yet it was true, a myriad small things telling her their stories. Again, there was food on the table, but the plates were scattered as if left in haste. No places laid, no covered dishes; only the familiar: roasted skewers with scraps of unidentifiable meat, a tangle of cold, spiced noodles, and bits of day-old bread. Lower City breakfast. For all that her hunger roared within her, Xhea made no move toward it.

There were papers scattered over one end of the table, piled haphazardly as if they had been read, set aside, then read again. Half a glass of water dripped condensation on the table's surface, and from the sediment she knew it was unfiltered rainwater.

Not so fancy after all. She did not know how much of what she'd seen two days before had been truth and how much charade; but the charade, it seemed, had been discarded. Something had changed—including the man who had brought her here, not least of all his face.

For when he turned to her, Ahrent Altaigh, he might have been a different person. She recognized his dark eyes and arching brows, the sharp lines of his cheekbones. The stubble was new, and his silver-streaked hair was in some disarray.

But his expression? There was nothing she recognized there, no sign of the carefully crafted façade she'd seen before—even if she'd not known it as such before this moment. At their first meeting, she'd thought Ahrent a leader, then a spellcaster; during the long, quiet night that followed, she'd wondered what else he might be. Politician. Commander. Heir.

Now she saw all of those things, and none of them. She saw a man, just a man, strong and raw and somehow vulnerable.

He met her eyes, no hint of smile on that face. "Hello, Xhea," he said, then turned back to the window. No lift of his hand, no gesture, but she felt the invitation nonetheless. Xhea made her slow way across the room to the window by his side, grateful for the cane's support. The coins and charms bound into her braid-tangled hair made a soft, rhythmic music in the silence.

On the way here, she'd wondered what she should say to him, how to voice her questions and the fears that circled through her thoughts. She'd wondered whether to ask that she be allowed to leave—wondered how to demand the truth about him, about Farrow, about her abduction. She'd felt her anger rising, and with it rose her magic and the hunger with which it seemed entwined.

Instead, she stood at his side and looked out across the Lower City.

It was calm here, and dark. The sun had not yet risen, though it lit the eastern horizon with a wash of paling gray, erasing the stars. Below, the Lower City streets were shadowed black, everything poised and still. Seen from on high, the Lower City looked more like a picture than the home she knew so well; and, lightheaded and feverish, Xhea forgot to be afraid.

She looked up. The City glimmered, the Towers wrapped in veils of light, and she saw—

Xhea hesitated, blinked, and looked again.

The Towers above, always bright, seemed in that moment like brilliant pillars of light scattered across the sky. Looking down, she could see *people*—not in the streets, not yet, but she saw them as if walls were no hindrance to her sight. People sprawled in their makeshift beds against the summer's oppressive heat; people waking, rising, slowly moving. She saw them not as distant ant-like figures, but as lights, as if each held a glow in their head and heart—a glow sometimes so dim as to be barely visible, a glow that was nothing compared to the light of the Towers above, but a glow nonetheless.

Blind, Ieren had said. *Or almost.*

It wasn't true—not in the way it counted. It wasn't that she could not see, only that she saw differently. Magic, she realized. Gray upon gray: she didn't see light, but *magic*— and not just spells like those in the walls, not just power forced out into the world, but magic in its truest form. Magic running through a body sure as blood.

And she could see—

No.

Xhea looked away. Across the Lower City, Orren and Senn were too far distant for her to see anything but flickers of light—of magic—from their windows and roofs and from within their ancient walls. Beside them Edren seemed to blaze, magic shining from its windows, its walls, crackling like lightning from the peaks of its rooftop antennas. Not nearly so bright as the Towers above, but brilliant against the Lower City's firefly flickers.

Shai, she thought, shocked—but where had the ghost's Radiant power been flowing, day after day, night after night, but into Edren itself? Storage coils and structural spells could only hold so much; staring at that brilliant light, it was all too easy to see why Lorn had feared unbalancing the Lower City. Edren's very walls glowed with magic.

Xhea wished that she could reach across all that empty space and connect with Shai; her magic stirred restlessly at the thought. *She's okay*, she told herself, for surely Edren would not gleam so brightly were it not for the ghost's continued presence. Xhea's growing fear that Shai had, in fact, been lost from the world when her tether had been cut eased—and yet she did not like the thought that lingered in its wake. The thought that Shai had abandoned her.

I'm sorry, she thought, as if the words might traverse the emptiness between them. Whatever she had done, however she had hurt Shai—

She blinked, and swallowed, and looked away.

As for Farrow, Xhea could only imagine how the skyscraper would look to her now, viewed from afar. She wondered whether it too glowed like a beacon, lit by the spells woven though its walls—and by the magic even now being funneled into it from room after room of unconscious people, those connecting wires, that dark binding magic.

As Xhea turned to Ahrent, only then did she see that it was not Edren that held his attention, nor the skyscraper in which they stood, but Rown. Following his gaze, Xhea looked to Farrow's nearest neighbor: the wide and hulking shape of skyscraper Rown, with the low, flat buildings of the warehouse district at its back, stretched out like an army.

It was not yet dawn; so why, Xhea thought, did Rown seem to roil within? All the dim lights of their people did not rest nor sleep, but moved ceaselessly within the skyscraper's confines. If people at such distance were but ants, then Rown was the anthill, and it had just been kicked.

"I had plans," Ahrent Altaigh said quietly, as if these were not the first words he had spoken in many long minutes. "Careful plans, crafted and honed over many years. Good plans, even. Plans that were finally coming to fruition."

There was a span of silence. The rising sun's light turned the Towers into silhouettes against the sky's brightening gray, casting their shadows like seeds across some barren ground.

"Were?" Xhea asked at last. For what had she been doing if not helping with the achievement of those plans, in spite of herself?

"Are." Ahrent smiled, a faint and humorless lifting of his lips—though not at her, it seemed, but at his reflection in the window glass. At the Lower City beyond. "Plans are ruined, change, grow—even mine."

Something in the way he said it . . . "Is that my fault?" Xhea asked.

He glanced at her and laughed, the sound amused but not cutting, not cruel. "Your fault? No. No more than it is mine, or anyone else's. People never act quite as we expect, do they?"

You least of all. She felt a thin thread of fear at the thought, running like a cold rivulet down her back, and it was all she could do to suppress her shiver.

Run, she thought, *run away*—though she knew not what she feared. As if this fear was anything from which swift feet might save her. As if her feet might ever again be swift.

"Ah," he said. "There."

Again Xhea blinked, the focus of her vision shifting, and she thought—*No, he can't see it, he couldn't possibly*—

Only to realize what truly held his attention. For there, in the darkened streets, she saw dim lights moving—blinked, and had the lights vanish, only to see dark-clad figures in their place, creeping through the shadows.

Though she had once walked from Orren to Edren unprotected in the hours before dawn, the sight made her breath catch nonetheless. At night, the streets belonged to the walkers, no matter how well armed one might be. The span of risk that they called "night" only ended with true dawn: light bright enough to chase away the once-human creatures.

Yet these people did not move like frightened Lower City dwellers, in fear of their lives, but hunters, their movements cautious, economical, slow. At Farrow's peak, safe behind window glass, she was too far distant to do more than catch glimpses of their movement. Even so, she imagined she could hear the whisper of rough fabric, the slight crunch of boot soles against the rocky pavement, the creak of equipment.

There were so many of them—more, every moment that she watched. Ten turned to twenty, to fifty, and she traced their path back to its source: Rown.

"What are they doing?" Xhea asked quietly. But she knew. Of course she knew.

From her vantage their paths were laid out clear as any map: they arrowed toward the other skyscrapers, Edren, Orren, and Senn. As she watched, their numbers divided and divided again, groups taking different paths.

Ahrent Altaigh said, "The underground barricades are guarded now—more so, in some places, than the skyscrapers' main entrances. Open attacks, fighting in the streets . . ." He shook his head. "That wasn't supposed to begin for another week, at the least. But plans change. Rown has always been too eager."

"Rown fights at your command?" She didn't bother to hide her incredulity.

"One way or another."

"And you're in charge here?"

He raised a slow eyebrow. "Farrow is commanded by Alden Kian-Farrow, as it has been these past four years. Strong lad, spitting image of his father. Hasn't been seen much lately, though."

"Is he dead?" Xhea asked.

"Just an addict."

"A sad story, I'm sure."

"Heartbreaking."

"You give him his first taste?"

"Something like that."

Such honesty. There were places—times—when an admission of such magnitude would have been enough to see a man cast from the skyscraper in body and name. But there was no one here but her and him, and what were such admissions to either? In the Lower City power was no simple birthright, no mere gift of magic, but a thing made and held with iron-hard hands. If one could.

Xhea watched the hunters until they were hidden from sight, wishing that she might cry out in warning or stand in opposition; wishing that there was something, anything, she could do beyond stare as the rising sun turned the sky to ashes.

"Why?" she asked at last.

"Distraction," Ahrent said simply. "Farrow's transformation will be . . . messy, shall we say. Loud and explosive—the kind of thing that will attract attention. All before the skyscraper—the Tower—begins to rise."

"You started a war to hide *noise*?"

Ahrent Altaigh smiled thinly. "To distract from Farrow, yes. If anyone understood what we were doing before the Tower lifted, what do you think might happen? There would be a riot, Xhea—worse—as half the Lower City tried to climb on board before we went."

She heard him. She even understood his logic, no matter that some part of her cried out at its cruelty, its blatant disregard for life—any life, no matter how poor or starved or despairing. For he was right: were it known what Farrow attempted, they would be mobbed. All she had to do was consider what she might have done mere months before; his fears were not unfounded. In the Lower City, desperation was their salt.

You can't actually accept this.

But she stood at his side, unsteady hands on her cane and the windowsill to keep her balance. Listening. Looking down, despite her fear of heights. Watching. Waiting.

At last: dawn.

Sunlight struck the Central Spire first. Light glinted off its peak then fell downward like a curtain, touching the highest Towers, the ones so distant that they seemed like little more than stars—then lower, sparking off Tower sides and defensive spires until the whole City gleamed. Last of all, daylight touched the Lower City, the vast expanse of the ruins and the badlands beyond, chasing the darkness away.

It was not the Lower City that held Xhea's attention, but the Central Spire around which all the Towers spun. Now, watching, she saw only bright magic, only light; yet it was only as it stopped that she could at last be certain of what she had seen.

For as she'd looked out across the City in the predawn light she'd seen *darkness*. Not the black of night, that dark broken only by starlight, Towerlight—for what was darkness to her, she who had always seen in places where no light fell? No, it had been black that moved like a column of living smoke.

Magic. Oh, such familiar magic.

She'd seen little of it in the expanses of the City itself, mere wisps and tatters blown across the sky; but they gathered, closer and denser, as they approached the Central Spire, as if the Spire drew that power toward it like a shroud. The darkness had wrapped around the long, needle-like shape of the Spire itself, spiraling around and around—and it had twirled not up, not rising as the City rose, but *down* in a roiling column to blanket the Lower City below.

For a moment, it had seemed that dark magic hung heavy across the broken buildings of the Lower City like a bank of cloud that did not disperse, only sank slowly into the objects it touched. The buildings, the alleys, the streets.

The ground on which they all rested.

Blink, she'd seen it. Blink, and it was gone.

And again. And again.

Xhea took a long, shuddering breath. She'd never seen anything like it before. That falling magic had been beautiful, in its own strange way—beautiful and utterly horrifying. Even knowing what she did of dark magic and its consequences, she could only guess what that power would do to the Lower City and all of its people.

Except—she already knew, didn't she? For in the City above, there was nothing different about this morning; she might have seen the same thing any morning, if she'd only known how to look. And if the Spire poured dark magic on the Lower City every night, letting it seep into the people and the buildings and the very earth upon which they all rested, then the City was poisoning them, day by day. They created ground that was anathema to all those who lived upon it, that would sap their magic, their health, their lives.

Xhea tried again to push away the image and all the thoughts it conjured. *One thing at a time.*

Ahrent turned from the window. "We won't see more for a while," he said. "Are you hungry? There's breakfast." Xhea agreed, grabbing for the distraction.

She struggled into a seat and let Ahrent serve her noodles and water. Despite her hunger's roar, she stared down at the food queasily. Right now, in Edren or Orren or Senn, an attack was underway. Rown hunters—unstable at the best of times—were falling on those walls, disrupting their defenses, terrorizing their people.

She knew she should get up from this place, this table, this room; turn her back on all of it, as if even being here was some sort of betrayal. *How can you eat breakfast*, she asked herself, *knowing what you know? Why are you holding a bowl of noodles instead of trying to do something?*

But she knew, too, the futility of her efforts. It was as easy to stop Rown's hunters and trained crazies as it was to raise her hands and stop that dark magic from falling on the Lower City like rain. What might she do but limp in their general direction and wave her new cane like some bent-backed oldster? Shout and rant and get herself killed. However important, however necessary, any intercession was entirely outside her small power.

Yet if she stayed here, for this moment, she might learn more—*understand* more—and perhaps there would be something she could do that had nothing to do with her failing strength. She had never been one for sitting still, for talking and smiling when there were things to be done; she'd never had *time*. So it was with ill humor that she turned to her breakfast and tried to pretend that today the sun's arrival had heralded nothing but another stifling, unpleasant summer day.

Xhea took a bite—and gagged. She fought the reaction, choking down the food. She was hungry—but not, it seemed, for food. Oh, she could weep. Instead, she took another forkful of noodles and forced herself to chew and swallow.

"I was told that you did well yesterday," Ahrent said, seeming not to notice her struggle.

"Were you?" The words were flat and uninflected. Inwardly, she winced; she never could play nice.

"Indeed. Together, you and Ieren bound eleven souls—and that with your morning spent in instruction."

Eleven. It hadn't seemed—she hadn't thought—

Something in her expression stopped him; whatever it was he had been about to say went unspoken. Instead he sighed and placed his spoon deliberately on the table.

"I did this wrong," he said at last. "All of it. I should have never had you taken like I did. I should have asked you for your help from the first."

Xhea put down her spoon in purposeful mimic and raised a slow eyebrow. "You said Edren turned away your messages."

"They did. But I should have tried harder. Should have tried something *else*."

Not because of the violence, Xhea knew; not because of the fear that choice had caused, the hurt and death. Not because of what that choice had done to her, or to Shai, or even to Mercks. No, he regretted his decision only because it put him here, in this room with a conflicted and unmannered girl staring across the table at him—the unwilling key to his plans.

Ahrent Altaigh shook his head. "I am a caster, Xhea, not a leader. Not a politician. I have tried both, and found my skills little suited to either."

"You can't lie," she said; the words sounded almost like recrimination. "Not well, anyway." Something about his voice, the way he spoke, made even his truths hard to swallow. He should have asked Torrence for pointers.

"No," he said, almost smiling. "Not well. So no lies: I thought that even if we started out on the wrong foot, I'd have enough time to convince you—enough time to make you *believe* in what we are doing."

Some part of her already did. Yet the process, the awfulness of the coin with which they had to pay for this transition—what Ieren had done, what *she* had done at his side—repelled her in equal measure. She did not know what to think anymore; she did not know what to believe.

She was not so good at lying herself, it seemed; she felt as if her thoughts were written across her forehead in shining letters.

"You don't even need me," she said. "You have Ieren."

"Yes. But the Spire sent him to us years before I thought they'd accept our petition to rise—and Xhea, they don't give second chances. This is their test to see if we're worthy."

"The Spire?" she asked. "Petition?" The Central Spire was the heart of the City; it did not govern so much as set the rule of law within which all Towers had to operate, and punish those who stepped out of line.

It all comes back to the Spire. Ieren had named the Central Spire his home. And she herself, blinking in disbelief, had seen in that pre-dawn light—

Again she pushed the memory away.

"They control all use of dark magic, and thus the bindings that create the Towers' hearts. All dark magic users live and die under the Spire's control. All except you."

Which only cemented Xhea's belief that Eridian's attempt to steal Shai had been highly illegal, for there had been no dark magic user there at all, no one to assist Eridian's casters with the binding. She remembered, too, the awful mess they had made by trying—though she doubted that they would have faced any consequences for either the attempt or the mangling thereof had Tower Allenai not fallen upon them like a sword from the sky.

"Necessary, then," Xhea murmured. From Ahrent's look, she might win an award for understatement.

"Yes," he said. "Very. The Spire's approval is needed for any change requiring a spirit binding—connecting a Radiant to their Tower, birthing a new Tower's heart. In sending us Ieren earlier than we planned, they accelerated our timeline—and today, Rown has accelerated it again.

"When I tell you that we have put years into planning this transformation, I need you to understand that I mean years beyond the span of my own life. The spells that we're weaving even now into Farrow's walls and foundations were designed more than a hundred years ago. We train spellcasters—work in magic—only so that we'll have the people we need to complete the spell-work."

Xhea snorted. She'd seen the size and the complexity of the spells, yes—but a hundred years? "As if you've had this super-secret project for a blighted century and no one noticed. Especially with *everyone* working on it." She said this last mockingly.

"Not everyone," Ahrent said, "but the best of us. The ones with real vision. Some of the people we train go to work for the other skyscrapers, or strike out on their own—or even, sometimes, find work and citizenship in the City. Of course they do. But the best stay right here, working together on something that's greater than all of us combined."

Xhea shook her head and glanced away, made uncomfortable by his fervor. It was safer to look at her noodles, forlorn curls smeared with sauce; safer to lift her spoon and choke down another bite while her stomach churned and roared.

"As for Ieren . . ." Ahrent hesitated.

His hesitation made her look up; his expression made her go still. Suddenly she remembered all the things Ieren himself had said that she hadn't quite understood. Remembered the sight of the boy as she'd seen him when she'd first woken in Farrow's basement: wide-eyed, quivering and feverish, the energy of his words a stark contrast to his body's weary lethargy.

No ghost, then, to hold him steady. And now?

"Ieren's dying."

"Yes."

"How long does he . . ." She shook her head. "How long?"

"A few days, I think, at most. We're doing what we can, but . . ."

"Making him sleep in the *basement* is 'doing what you can'?" Xhea asked incredulously. "And do you prefer to hit him with sticks or with rods to ensure his comfort?"

"He's more comfortable there." Somehow, Ahrent managed not to sound reproachful. "He says the pain is less, and he can sleep."

Thinking of the way some unseen burden seemed to lift from her shoulders when she went underground, Xhea could almost believe it. Still, she shrugged. She didn't want it to be true; didn't want to think about the implications of that statement, of the dark magic seeped into the Lower City's deepest levels.

"Why are we sitting here, anyway, if timing is all so important?"

"*We* are sitting here," Ahrent corrected. "The casters on my team are most assuredly not. And I'm here with you because this discussion and the attempt to gain your willing assistance is worth more than any magic I might weave."

Willing assistance—for he had no way to force her. Not in the time he had, not given the nature of her magic. Disable her power, and she had no use. Attempt to force or torture or blackmail an angry girl with dark magic, and what would he earn but death?

It should have made her smile, that sudden understanding. The power truly was in her hands, and Ahrent was here to beg her assistance. It was what she had always wanted: to be the one not crouched and cringing, but making the decisions. The achievement felt hollow. Xhea took a long, slow breath and looked down at her hands. Hidden in her lap, they quivered even now—her body's betrayal of a weakness that she prayed Ahrent could not see.

Her bowl wasn't empty. Even so, she pushed it away. "I don't want . . ." she started, and didn't know how to continue. She realized that she had no idea what to want anymore, no idea what to do.

"Xhea," Ahrent said. "Please. We need you. Ieren's power is fading—and there's no one else who can connect the volunteers or reinforce the bindings when the transformation begins. You can support Ieren while he lives—learn from him. Help birth Farrow's living heart."

Xhea met his eyes. "Do you understand what you're asking? This work will mean my death."

If not now, nor in a week, then soon. If ten was old, then fifteen was leagues beyond; whatever time she had earned by suppressing her power for so long was surely being undone by her dark magic workings, now and two months past. The power of death, running unchecked through her flesh.

That's what she felt now, she understood; what she had felt each day and night since pouring the darkness inside her into Eridian's living heart as if she were bleeding into midair: the effect of dark magic on her body. Not just her inability to heal but the fevers, the exhaustion, the shakes . . . the desire to curl up somewhere cold and dark, and have the world pass her by unnoticed. The desire to simply *stop*.

And now, as she began to learn to use that power, the hunger.

"Yes," Ahrent said quietly. "I know."

It was a long moment before he found the words to continue: "I understand what I'm asking of you—but please know, in return I will grant you anything within my power. Truly, anything. You will have a place here, in Farrow with us, if you want it—and all that it entails. I will tell you about your magic, or the workings of the Central Spire, or the details of how a dead building becomes a living Tower. I can tell you of your history or that of your family, or the workings of the City itself. You have but to ask."

Knowledge. It was a coin that Farrow knew how to trade, and trade well. Spells and history and politics: Farrow knew them all. For all his dissembling and misdirection, this man, it seemed, was the true power behind Farrow.

Xhea looked up to meet his eyes. "Will you tell me why," she said quietly, "if you knew who I was and where I came from, Farrow just left me out there?"

A blink: it was not, she knew, the response he expected. Nor was she finished.

"Will you tell me why I grew up hungry and cold and alone if my family was within these walls? Will you tell me why I nearly starved to death on the streets if you knew I was born here, that I belonged here? Will you tell me why you only came for me—why you only *want* me—now?"

"Even that," Ahrent said at last, though they both already knew the answer. It echoed in the air between them, unspoken.

Say it, she thought to him across the table. *Say it out loud.*

Xhea held out her hand and smoke-like magic rose from her palm in a single swirling column, wisps of gray twining together into something thick and black. More power and more—more than she'd used the day before; more than she'd used ever, but for her attack on Eridian. Power enough that she knew it entered the visual spectrum, clear to see even if Ahrent chose not to look. The hunger rose with it—but also that perfect sense of calm, steadying her, giving her the strength to continue.

"Farrow has always valued magical talent, has it not?" Xhea said, looking upon the column of black that rose, spinning, from her outstretched hand. "The strongest and most skilled casters in the Lower City, all trained by Farrow."

"We did not think you had your mother's talent," Ahrent said. "Weak, latent magic that would kill you. Nothing more."

A sickly liability instead of an asset.

Xhea smiled, a thin curve like a knife's blade, as that pillar of dark magic rose between them. "I know," she said. And when she blew that power toward him like a kiss—when she let it wash across his face like smoke—he flinched.

Chapter Nineteen

There should have been more time, Shai thought, watching as Edren tried to recover from the assassination of their leader. Not time to mourn; no single day held time enough for that, no span of hours sufficient to even begin to find the edges of that loss, never mind understand them. Never mind heal.

Time, only, to lift the bodies from the floor and clean their mortal wounds. Time to put the bodies of their enemies to one side until they might be claimed or rejected by the skyscraper that had sent them. Time to lift their fallen leader, and wash the blood from his lips and chest and hair; time to begin to ask, "What happened? What did they do? What could we have done?"

For the attackers had entered Edren in silence and secrecy. They had not broken through any of the doors on the main level, nor disrupted the security perimeter; they had not come up through the tunnels below. Though there was talk that the attackers might have arrived via the roof, breaking through the peak defensive spell, Shai had been there and knew what the security tapes would show: nothing.

They had been waiting, she thought, within these walls. Waiting, perhaps, since the party two nights before; waiting only for their opportunity. It was as good a theory as any she heard whispered in Edren's halls.

But dawn when it came brought no rest, no easing of these sudden burdens; only more upraised blades.

At dawn, Rown attacked.

Shai had followed Lorn—and he still responded to the name, though Shai could see the change in him in every gesture and word. For a time he shook, seemingly uncontrollably; the aftereffects of adrenaline, of shock and fear. He worked through it, ignoring his shakes as he gave commands, and for all the unsteadiness of his hands, his voice never trembled.

He organized patrols, called in spies from across the Lower City or their reports where the people themselves were not available. It was, after all, before dawn, though only just; beyond the boardroom's dust-clouded window, the eastern horizon had turned blue.

As Lorn worked to understand what was happening beyond the skyscraper's walls, Emara took over the management of the skyscraper itself. Nothing, it seemed, was beneath her notice, from the kitchens to the repair crews to the combatants for that day's hastily cancelled shows. She woke the skyscraper's elite and put them to work, and made rules for everyone: no going outside, no sending messages beyond the skyscraper's walls. Stay in, stay quiet, and stay the blight out of security's way.

The ease with which they worked, despite their shock and the stunned expressions of many of the people called before them, spoke of long practice. So, too, did people respond as if familiar to their instructions. Shai had to wonder how much of Edren's day-to-day workings had already been in Lorn and Emara's hands, which small happenings had occurred beneath the notice of Verrus Edren.

There was nothing Shai could do to help, yet still she stayed, telling herself that every conversation taught her more about Edren and its workings; more, too, about these people to whom she had found herself tied. In truth, she just did not want to be alone. The sight of Verrus Edren down on the ground, the way his eyes went blank as he died—the screams of the attacker Emara had injured but not killed—and the blood, so much blood on hands and floors and walls—she saw it all, over and over again, anytime she let her mind wander. She knew that they could not see her, and yet they felt her there; they had nodded to her as she'd entered the room, and once or twice Emara had flashed a tired smile in her general direction. It was something.

Shai had only just begun to feel calm, if no less worried, when a harried young security guard entered the room, interrupting the conversations in progress.

"Sir!" he cried. "Ma'am! There are soldiers outside!"

"Explain," Lorn said shortly.

"Hundreds of them—right outside!" The young man's eyes were wide, his breathing short. "Please, come quickly."

"I'll get my father," Emara said and rose.

The guard led the way downstairs to the main security desk. At Lorn's urging, he quickly explained, fumbling over his words: the perimeter alarms had gone off shortly before dawn, first on one side of the skyscraper, then the other. They'd assumed the movement was due to walkers, late leaving the Lower City's streets, but when they managed to pull the images up on screen, they saw not lone walkers but armed and armored personnel moving to surround the skyscraper.

"They're everywhere, sir," he said as they came to the skyscraper's front hall and the chained main doors. Above the doors, the remaining windows gleamed with pale light. "They're all around us."

"Rown," Mercks said, and Shai started at the sound of his voice. The man sat behind the security desk, lit by the glow of dozens of security screens—though it wasn't just the light that made his skin look wan, nor his expression so tired. No bandages, no wounds, but it would take more than a day to recover from the shock and blood loss.

She looked behind him, and saw that every screen with an outside shot showed the same thing: dark-clad figures taking cover behind walls and fire barrels and low piles of refuse, targeting the skyscraper with both weapons and spells.

What had Verrus Edren called the other skyscrapers' behavior? Posturing. Mere threats and displays of aggression, any true danger weeks or months away—despite Pol's obvious disagreement. But now Verrus lay dead and the skyscraper was surrounded—and all the added protections that they might have enacted after Xhea had found the damage to the barricade were still undone.

A moment later, a display showed a heavily armed and armored woman walking up to Edren's front doors. She held a white flag in one hand and what seemed to be an envelope in the other, a tattoo of Rown's twisting sigil just visible on the back of one hand, mirror to the designs that ringed her left eye. She pounded on the door and then held up her hands, flag and envelope raised high, and declared:

"I'm here on behalf of Rown! We have you surrounded. You have no allies. I bring our terms for your immediate surrender."

Even on the grainy display, the woman's smirk was evident.

Once, when she was a small child, a beetle had made its way into Shai's home. In the Towers insects were a rarity—and a long beetle with a gleaming green carapace even more so. Shai had watched it run across the kitchen floor, scuttling on its tiny black legs—until her mother had knocked it aside and it had landed flat on its back. There it stayed, legs waving, until her mother brought her shoe down upon it with a crunch.

Edren was the beetle now. For all of Verrus's threats and attacks and use of the power Shai generated, Edren lay with their underside exposed and legs flailing, waiting to be crushed.

Shai turned toward the door, leaving Lorn and the newly arrived Pol and Emara in her wake, discussing their options. Beyond, they had monitoring spells and some few guards, but too little information and fewer options. Shai was not so hampered. She slipped through the chained doors and into the dawning light beyond.

The Rown hunter stood on the steps, waiting just before the twin lion statues that stood on either side of the door. The hunter wasn't that old, Shai saw, perhaps only a year or two older than she was—or, rather, than she had been when she died. It was only the facial tattoo and the rough, jagged cut of the woman's hair that made her seem older. The woman had lowered her hands, point made, yet that smug hint of a grin played about her lips. She was enjoying this.

Something in that expression made Shai pause. There were reasons to fight; reasons, too, that Rown would be here, on Edren's doorstep, armed and demanding surrender. She did not deny it. Yet to delight in the fear and the pain that such actions caused? To *laugh*? Shai wanted to rub that expression right from the woman's face.

Unseen, Shai stepped closer until she stood within the hunter's personal space, their noses all but touching. She did not move, nor speak, only stared as if through force of will she could make her presence felt. For a long moment, there was no reaction. A moment more and the smirk slowly slipped from the woman's lips. She swallowed, visibly attempted to suppress a shiver, and took a hesitant step back.

It was just a tiny step, but it was enough, for when the hunter looked at Edren now there was a flicker of fear in her gaze and no little caution. Shai was tempted to reach out, to hold her hand inside the other woman's heart just to see her flinch—and then she shook herself and recoiled.

You're not like them. Once it had been simple fact, no similarities beyond the basics of biology. To be like a Lower City dweller? The idea, had it even occurred to her, would have seemed absurd. Now there was no smugness in the thought, no reaffirmation of her superiority; merely a reminder, a plea. *You're not like this. Remember who you are.*

But it had felt good to watch the woman flinch.

Shai stepped out into the morning streets. Yet she could see nothing more than cameras and spells could tell those inside: she saw the same roads and alleys, the same ranks of hunters, the same spell-edged blades and pointed gun barrels. The only difference was that here, so close, she could see the light gleam in their eyes; she could hear their excited whispers as a minute passed and no one came out to answer their messenger's call.

They want to attack.

No, Shai thought. Not if there was another way.

She rose. Up and up, no floor beneath her, no aircar, no illusion that she was standing on anything but air. Up and up, beyond anything she'd ever thought—ever tried—to do before, to the height of Edren and beyond.

It was only from so high, the skyscrapers arrayed below her, that she saw the truth. It was not just Edren that Rown's hunters had surrounded, but Orren and Senn as well. They ringed each, using the surrounding buildings for cover, pinning in those that tried to venture beyond the skyscrapers' walls. Before Orren's front doors stood another messenger: a small shape that Shai thought was a man, a white length of cloth in one hand. As she watched, Orren's doors opened and someone stepped out to speak to him. She could not see Senn's doors from her angle, but could only assume that a similar scene played out there, in sight of the Lower City market.

She saw Rown hunters on nearby roofs, weapons trained on the skyscrapers; she saw Rown hunters in the streets, more and more of them approaching from the warehouse district, which they had defended the morning before. These were not soldiers. They moved not as coordinated units but clumps and groups that split and reformed as individuals chose their own paths, their movement speaking not of professionalism nor seriousness but a chaotic enthusiasm that made her more nervous than either.

Only Farrow was not surrounded. The men and women she could see all stood within the protective barrier of that strange, deep trench, and none from Rown came to aggress against them. Farrow alone stood aloof from this conflict, neither aggressor nor target.

She moved, trying to see more, though she dared not leave Edren behind. Of Rown itself, farthest away, she could catch but a glimpse—but it was enough. For atop Rown she saw a shape that caught the illusion of breath in her throat and left her gasping.

What had looked like little more than a hulking shape on the rooftop—one she did not remember seeing in any of the nights past—was revealed to be something like a great heavy gun, the black cover that had hidden it whisked suddenly aside. It was large and ugly, looking from a distance like a long-barreled cannon. Closer, it was clear that it was no common weapon at all.

Bullets, explosives—crude as they were, she understood the damage such basic weapons could wreak. Yet *this*?

"Oh gods," Shai whispered, shaking. "Absent gods save us."

Because she knew this shape, old as it was, rusted and battered and far from its rightful place. What had seemed to be a cannon was nothing but a solid, tapering length of metal, the spell-markings scratched into its surface just visible beneath the rust. Its cross-spars—its directional control—had been shortened to mere stumps. The whole had been mounted on what seemed to be some sort of swiveling turret built from scrap metal.

But nothing disguised what it truly was: a protective spell generator. Every Tower bore generators such as these in quantity, lengths of grown metal that often hid in the shadows of the Towers' main defensive spires. Most days they created only defensive spells: shields and protections. At night, when attacking, or when defending against an active encroachment, they projected the more aggressive workings—even the most basic of which was so far beyond anything they had in the Lower City that it defied imagining.

Towerlight, here. Sheets and waves of power. Magic strong enough to push a Tower from its place in the sky, magic subtle enough that each Tower had to constantly adapt their spells to compensate, defending one from the other.

She could not imagine how Rown had bought such a thing—nor what Tower would ever have sold one. But it, Shai knew with cold certainty, was the true threat. Not the people that crept through the streets, nor the weapons they bore. Not the spells she saw glittering in the hands of those few Rown attackers strong enough to cast a spell worth fearing. In comparison, they were nothing at all.

If a spell generator could destroy a Tower, what might it do to the Lower City?

That is, if Rown could gather power enough to fuel it.

That was her only hope—Edren's only hope, any of the skyscrapers' hopes at all. For if the spells a protective generator could produce were hugely powerful, it could not create magic out of thin air. The magic had to come from somewhere; and Shai could only pray, fervent and staring, that the impoverished skyscraper had not the power to make good their threat.

Shai turned and fell, streaking star-like toward the ground. Lorn had not gone far: trapped just inside Edren's main door, he stood in the ancient hotel's former lobby ringed by protective guards. There was still a spot of his father's blood, dark now and dried, beneath his eye like a blackened tear.

Guards surrounded him—and unlike the black-clad security members that Shai had, once and again, judged so harshly, these men and women looked dangerous. Gladiators, she thought, and having seen Emara move in the hall above she had sudden respect for these combatants. Emara herself was nowhere to be seen, but Pol, her father, stood nearby, watching the monitors and listening in a way that made Shai think that the man missed nothing.

Shai struggled to think what words she might shape in warning. Would he know what a protective spell generator was? Would anyone here? *Gun* was too simple—*weapon,* maybe? *Powerful weapon atop Rown.* Even after all her practice, it would take time to shape those words—and she knew that the warning itself, such as it was, was all but useless.

If only Xhea—

She cut the thought off. She would just have to find a spell that would give her a voice, that was all; and it mattered little that her attempts to date had ended in abject failure. Shai pushed toward Lorn, kindling a light to draw attention to her presence.

Again the hunter banged on the door, and Lorn tensed.

"Bring me their terms," he said at last. He spoke calmly, carefully, reasoned and in control—and in sharp contrast to his obvious rage in the last council meeting. He turned away from Shai's light, looking toward the door. "At least let us see what they want."

As a squad of four gladiators took their position behind a lone security guard, Lorn stepped out of sight, Pol following. One of his guards urged him to go deeper into the skyscraper, and he waved their words aside. No one spoke as the young guard unchained the doors. No one so much as breathed.

The doors swung open. No shots were fired, no knives came glittering through that opening. There was only the young woman—no longer smiling, no longer quite so calm—with that envelope in her hand. She looked at the young Edren guard who crept cautiously toward her, eyes wide and jaw set, as if he expected to be shot at any moment.

The Rown hunter cocked her head and looked at him, that smile playing about her lips once more. "Have you come to offer your surrender?" She held the envelope toward him almost as an afterthought, and used the white flag to dab sweat from her brow.

"We'll see," the guard said, and scurried back inside.

The doors slammed closed, but not fast enough to hide the sound of the young hunter's laughter.

When Lorn read out Rown's list of terms, Shai was not surprised at the very first item: Edren's immediate and full surrender of the Radiant ghost. And it was a very long list.

Lorn had to know about the spell generator, Shai thought, before he could make the right choice when it came to Rown's terms. If there was a right choice. To let the skyscraper fall without a fight? Even she could not imagine it. Yet he had to know the true consequence of saying no—here, now—when he knew not of the force that might be wielded against them.

Except Rown couldn't possibly power the spell generator; it had to be a threat, one on which they could never follow through. Of course, *she* might power such a thing . . .

Shai stopped.

No, she thought. *No.*

It didn't matter that the terms were addressed to Edren; seeing what she'd seen, knowing what she knew, she'd choose oblivion over turning herself over to Rown's armed and incapable hands. Shai set her jaw.

But Lorn was saying, "I can't accept these terms. I can't even accept a small fraction of them."

"Wait," Pol said, his quiet voice carrying. "They did not set a timeframe for a response. Stall. We need that time to prepare."

Lorn hesitated, nodded. He did not ask, *Prepare for what?* Already, the outcome felt inevitable: not whether there would be fighting in the streets, but when.

Shai re-kindled her light, not knowing when she'd let it go out, and made it blink until she caught Lorn's attention. She started her message: *Weapon—*

She got no farther. There came a sound of a commotion: distant voices raised, a shout of defiance, then the clash of blades. Confusion, inside and out, as they tried to figure out what was happening and where.

"Senn!" someone called. "Senn's fighting back!"

"*Senn?*" Lorn asked incredulously. In the conversations Shai had overheard, Edren's council had categorized Senn as the most eager to compromise. The only reason Verrus hadn't started his Lower City takeover with Senn, he'd said, was that they posed no true challenge, just administrative hassle.

It wasn't the first thing he had been wrong about, and she doubted it would be his last. *Though,* she mentally amended, *death might affect his rate of error.*

Outside, the streets surrounding Edren were all but empty. Though a few stragglers remained, resolutely standing around Edren, the rest of the hunters had turned and run toward Senn.

It was Pol who spoke first. "The situation," he said, "has changed."

When the first blast hit, they didn't know what it was; they only heard the sound of an explosion. The concussive wave hit a moment later, rushing through the streets in a thick cloud of dust, making those outside cringe and close their eyes.

"Bomb detonation in the market," came the shouted report.

But in that pressure wave, Shai had tasted more than thick summer air and dust and burning; she'd tasted magic, sharp like a lightning strike. It had flowed through the walls and doors where the dust and debris pinged like a rain of stones, and through her, hot and fast and stinging.

Bright magic could heal and shape and grow—but this magic had been warped and tangled into a wave of destructive force.

The market, she thought. *Senn's market*. She could only pray to absent gods that people had stayed inside this morning. Let no vendors have gone to open their stalls or spread their temporary blankets of goods across the cracked asphalt; let Rown's hunters have kept the shoppers at bay, none venturing out early for the best pick of the morning's food, aid to mend a broken tool, supplies for that day's repairs. *Let the market have been empty.*

But it hadn't been.

Not thinking, Shai rushed toward the market at the speed of thought, leaving Edren behind. Soldiers in the streets, and hunters, and some few scrabbling fights: she ignored them all. The first thing that she saw was not the debris scattered far and wide, not the tongues of flame that even now rose from the market's center, but the building close to the market's far edge, collapsed.

She saw the blood.

She saw the little girl lying sprawled on the broken ground, blood on her lips, blood in a halo around her head. Her hair, a tangle of tightly wound black curls, was matted to her forehead on one side of her face, and her dark brown eyes were open, staring. She couldn't have been more than four years old.

Shai raised her hands, magic flowing bright from her fingertips, but there was no use in healing—no use, even, in trying. The girl was already dead.

Beyond her, a man was splayed out on the ground. He looked fit and muscular, and he wore a blade at his side—and what use was it, what use was any of it, against an enemy that struck without warning? An enemy that targeted homes, that targeted children.

Shai walked, passing the little girl, passing the man who might have been the girl's father, and farther still. She walked as if she were in a dream, and the noises all around her—the shouts and screams and the wail of a siren, the roar and crackle of a raging fire—seemed distant, as if they echoed from impossibly far away. She took another step, sliding across air, and another.

Watching, waiting, to see someone rise from the rubble. But no one did.

When she reached the side of the collapsed building, she looked deeper; and while she could find the lingering warmth of bodies buried beneath that weight of brick and stone, she saw no flicker of magic. She saw no hint of life.

Shai turned. The market was burning. The stalls were scattered, a few left twisted or half-standing, the goods once stored within turned to so much refuse. But it was the main market building that Rown had hit, and the ancient mall that now burned hot and fast, sending a roiling column of black smoke toward the sky. Already people were running toward it with bowls and buckets, trying to form a line—and already the flames were a story high or more, and hot enough that the closest would-be rescuers cringed and stumbled back as the flames shifted in their direction.

It would spread, she thought, and fast. Through the fallen market tents and to the buildings surrounding them and to Senn itself; the wind was already fanning the flames.

Shai looked up. On Rown's roof, she could just see the point of the spell generator as the gunners positioned it for another shot. Only that broke her from her trance of disbelief.

"You will not!" she cried, as if it were a battle cry—as if anyone could hear. "You will *not!*"

Shai wept ghostly, magic-rich tears that fell glittering like stars as she raised her hands, fingers spread, and prepared to face the onslaught.

A shield, she thought, like the one Lorn had raised to protect his father's fallen body—but she had no warm, comforting memory to guide her hand in this shaping; no song nor imagined words, no image of light in the darkness. Just grief and rage, each as hot and fierce as the fires that even now rose around her.

The magic built in her and built, and she did not think nor tell herself not to, only let the power flow from her, light and life springing from her hands to create a great arcing dome over the buildings surrounding the market, over the people fighting the fires—even across Senn.

She felt the weakness then, a sudden wave of dizziness that sent the world spinning. She felt the magic in her hands pulse and flicker as she struggled to push that half-born shape farther, wider, as if she might save the whole of the Lower City from itself. She felt the rush of power slow.

You will not, she told her magic, as if it too were a thing she must fight. All her life her power had shaped her, had controlled her, had dictated her path and choices—and yes, even her death. But this time, it would do what she wanted, *exactly* what she wanted, and it would not falter, and it would not fail.

She would not fail. Shai stood, magic flaring all around her, as the next shot hurtled down.

There was pain, then. She had not often felt pain since her death, though she had tried, curious, to find things that might hurt her. She, who had stood within a roaring fire in one of Edren's ovens and felt nothing but the strange tickling movement of the flames, screamed as the magic struck her and her upraised spell.

Pain washed through her, sharp and searing, as the shot from Rown's spell generator blasted across the surface of her shield like a violent rainbow of blue and red and gold. In some places, her magic failed; again there was that terrible concussive boom, and again debris sailed skyward before falling in wide arcs to the ground below. Again flames shot up, burning furiously from the roof of a building that had been too far from Shai's shield to protect.

Still the weapon fired, the magic slamming into Shai and her shield with a force she could never have imagined.

Hold, she thought—repeating it, over and over as her knees bent under the pressure, and her arms felt like they would be crushed by the terrible burning weight. *Hold*, she told herself, screaming the word, screaming and screaming as if the sound might ease the pressure or take away the pain.

Hold.

It was not meant for such use, Rown's spell; the power flowed and flailed and overloaded, seeking a target it would never find, not here on the ground. It skittered across the surface of Shai's shield and rebounded—not a roiling column of power now, but like an explosion of burning ribbons, arcing up and out. Shai had no control over where they landed; only knew that those few that fell back toward the ground were flickering and fading even as they fluttered down.

She did not so much release her spell as let it collapse, and collapsed with it. She yearned for the feel of ground again, hard and real against her cheek; Shai could not fall, not truly, only hover aimlessly in a collapse that knew no end.

Where, she thought weakly. *How . . . ?* It had taken all of her strength, all of her magic, to repel that fire. *Where had Rown gotten so much power?*

So much power to waste on destruction. For she opened her eyes, and she saw burning. She saw people fallen, bodies empty and unmoving; she saw the Lower City's carefully preserved buildings crumbling, falling in on themselves, windows shattered, prayer flags fluttering limply across the ground.

Shai looked again to Rown. They did not have the power for another shot, she thought, watching the new stillness on that distant rooftop. She breathed a whisper of thanks to absent gods, knowing that if they had, she lacked the power to deflect it. Still, the market was burning.

She looked to her hands. They seemed to be only hands, with pale skin and short nails. She saw no glimmer of magic beneath, no matter how long she looked.

I have nothing, she thought. *I have nothing left to give.*

Even so, she forced herself upright, forced herself to move forward—because she would try nonetheless.

Chapter Twenty

Xhea looked away from Ahrent Altaigh to the wide windows behind him. Outside, the Lower City was burning.

She stared. It was not the smoke of cooking fires or Senn's generators firing up for the day, but smoke that was thick and dark and choking. *The market's on fire*, Xhea thought. She could see the flicker of pale flames, like tongues lapping at the smoke.

"Ahrent," she said—or meant to. Her mouth did not move, nor did sound emerge past the barrier of her lips. She just stared, and, staring, drew his attention.

He turned. Froze.

"They can't," he murmured, or something like it. "They can't possibly . . ."

Rown fired again.

Watching, at first Xhea did not understand what she was seeing; did not connect the roiling flow of magic that shot out sudden and powerful enough to make the early-morning streets seem bright as midday, to the fires she saw below. It came from Rown's rooftop, and in that moment she could see neither its source nor target, just the sudden surge of magic itself. The spell flew in a line, not arrow-straight but like a thousand winding ribbons of magic that curled and caught and twisted in midair, shining brilliant gray and white.

Her angle was wrong to see that magic strike the ground, but she saw its effect: the sudden spray of debris that arced skyward; a second spray of magic that glittered in the air; and then, suddenly, fire. A column of flame shot upward, blooming, and then came the smoke.

Farrow's windows rattled.

Xhea could not hear the screams. It was only her mind that filled them in and in her mind that they echoed. She wanted, suddenly, desperately, to cover her ears as if the gesture might silence her imagination. Silence, in truth, the sounds that must even now echo through the Lower City streets.

She looked to Rown and the shape that she could now just make out upon its rooftop, its cloth covering drawn aside. It appeared to be a long metal rod, reinforced near its base, with short cross-spars at irregular intervals down its length.

"What is that thing?" Xhea asked. The words were little louder than a whisper; it felt as if she could barely draw breath.

Ahrent didn't answer. "Go," he said, and if the request sounded like a command she was willing to let it pass. "Down to the thirty-fourth floor. I'll be there soon. Daye, take her."

Xhea turned, looking at the woman with something like shock. She'd forgotten Daye was there. Daye's face was as impassive as ever, as if there were no fire, no smoke, no future going horribly awry. She just waited in silence as Xhea struggled out of her chair and made her unsteady way to the elevators.

"But—" Xhea started.

Ahrent cut her off with a sharp gesture. "We're starting the transformation. Now *go*."

Xhea looked back once. Rising, the columns of smoke had begun to disperse, casting all the Lower City in a thick, dark haze. It was only after the doors had closed and the elevator lurched into movement that Daye spoke.

"It was a Tower's defensive spire," Daye said. She stared at the elevator doors, or perhaps their reflections, twisted by the scuffed and dented metal. "Ahrent bought three. Two are on Farrow's roof. One was traded to Rown as part of their agreement—but was supposed to be broken."

Xhea had never heard that many words from Daye, never mind in a row.

"A defensive spire?" she said, and oh, she had so very many questions. She asked the most pressing: "Why would they use it to *destroy the Lower City*?"

A fire of that size was always a problem—but now? For all the humidity in the air, it hadn't rained properly for weeks, and the sun had been merciless. Water stores across the city would be down to mere puddles. All those wooden slats and canvas awnings, rope bridges and makeshift shelter walls . . . they were going to burn, all of them burn, and Xhea could not think of a force great enough to stop them.

The elevator doors opened, and Daye led her down the hall without answering. A hall that Xhea almost didn't recognize. She'd been used to the hall's quiet, their only company the guard at the far end. The guard was gone now, and the quiet with him; the hall had become a hive of activity. All doors were open, and people rushed from one room to the other with quick strides that spoke of much to do and too few to do it. Xhea pressed herself against one wall to keep from being run down.

Word must have reached them about Ahrent's order already, for as she watched the casters' efforts redoubled. The transformation was beginning, he had said—days too early, if she understood truly. Perhaps weeks. Not enough time to finish preparations, not enough magic to birth a Tower's true heart—or was that only her fear talking, fear and uncertainty and the edge of panic that set her heart to racing?

Farrow offered escape, she knew that: escape from the realities of the Lower City, as well as from the chaos and destruction that even now raged outside. But was she supposed to just go on, binding people to these walls, and pretending that all she knew wasn't burning to ash somewhere outside? As if she could. Yet how could forcing the transformation be anything but another disaster?

"What about your plan?" Xhea asked. Whatever escape Torrence and Daye had intended, their timetable—like Farrow's—had just been accelerated.

Daye just gestured her inside one of the rooms at the hall's end. Xhea expected to find Ieren there with Torrence playing babysitter; instead, the room was empty but for the unconscious people whose weak magic trickled into Farrow's walls.

"We need to run," Xhea said. "Now, while we can."

Daye shut the door behind them and switched on the overhead lights. "Not without Torrence," she said quietly.

Xhea took a breath and tried to unclench her hands. "But—"

It was only then that Xhea recognized the woman in the bed nearest to her. She paused, turning. Marna's hair had been shaved since Xhea had last seen her, leaving her scalp pale and shiny. Her face was slack, mouth slightly open, dry lips cracked. Awake, she'd looked she'd looked vibrant; unconscious, with no hair to distract from her sagging flesh or the deep-scored lines in her face, she only looked old.

She was covered now with a thin, stained sheet; yet still Xhea could see the wires that connected to her neck and heart and hands. There were other connections now, too: the IV had multiple bags hung, dripping into the line in her arm; while stained plastic tubing seemed to handle her body's wastes. Though Marna, unlike the man two beds over, was not connected to a respirator. *Perhaps that's just a matter of time.*

Looking down at the woman's face, beneath her fear and anger and confusion, Xhea felt . . . what? She didn't even know. This woman was her grandmother, by marriage if not by birth; yet they had known each other for no more than a span of an hour. She was a stranger who had called Xhea family, but Xhea couldn't help but wonder what this woman might have meant to her had they known each other—or who she might have been had she been raised in Marna's care. She wondered, too, what Marna had been going to tell her before Ahrent had interrupted her urgent, whispered message.

Behind her, Daye dragged a chair across the floor until it was directly in front of the door and then sat down, leaned back, and crossed her arms over her chest. She looked at Xhea steadily, intent. Waiting.

Xhea glanced from the now blocked and guarded door back to Marna's body. "What . . . ?" she started, and let the question trail away. Daye would not answer her, not in words. This, Xhea thought as she looked at Daye's seemingly impassive expression, was the answer to a question she had not known to ask.

Xhea went to Marna's IV and fiddled with the controls until she had reduced the drip to all but nothing. Even so, whatever sedative they used would take a while to wear off. Instead of waiting, she leaned her cane against the bedside and reached out with both hands, holding one above Marna's forehead and the other over her sternum. She shifted the focus of her vision, and the world around her was reborn in light and shadow.

Clear as daylight, clear as fire, she saw the transformation spells running through the walls—stronger now, and growing brighter by the moment. Beneath her hovering hands, she saw the magic that ran through Marna's body and up into the wires, a thin trickle of light that merged seamlessly into the spells, Marna's life becoming the skyscraper's—the Tower's. There, too, were the bonds that Ieren had woven but two days before, the cobweb-thin lines that joined Marna's spirit to the wires, dark and gleaming.

As she stared, Xhea realized that she could almost see the woman's ghost itself, like a doubled image of her body, one lying atop the other. But though Marna's body was still, no movement but for the steady rise and fall of her breath, her spirit within was not nearly so calm. Held tight within the confines of her body—and bound tighter now by Ieren's dark spells—Marna's spirit thrashed.

Xhea did not move but still she reached, magic flowing at her command—slowly, gently, as Ieren had shown her the day before. Just a little bit of magic; just enough to loosen the tension upon the bindings without undoing them entirely. Then, not knowing if it would work, Xhea grasped the woman's spirit with her magic and moved her, bringing her ghost into alignment with her body.

Marna gasped for breath, shuddering beneath the sheet. A moment, then she opened her eyes.

Xhea drew back, watching as the woman coughed and shivered as she came back to herself, clearly fighting the drugs' effects. So, too, would the spells' pull on her magic have weakened her; even now, Xhea could see Marna struggle against magic shock.

Marna turned, and her gaze fixed upon Xhea's face. A moment of hesitation, then recognition.

"Enjeia," she whispered, slurring the name. "Xhea."

"Uh . . . hello." Now that Marna was awake, Xhea didn't know what to say.

"Is it over?" she asked slowly, clumsily—but oh, the yearning in that voice. "Tell me he failed, tell me . . ."

Marna lifted an unsteady hand and felt the bare expanse of her scalp—touched the wires bound to her at hand and neck and heart. Only then did she seem to see where she was, and what surrounded her: still bodies kept in poor comfort; a bare, echoing room; only a respirator's wheeze to break the silence.

"Oh," she said in a tone of defeat. She closed her eyes and shivered.

"Marna," Xhea said haltingly. "There was something . . . something you were going to say, before . . ."

Again the woman forced open her eyes, blinking once, twice, in an attempt to focus. "He has you working for him," she said slowly. She swallowed. "It doesn't matter now."

"It *does*," Xhea said. "Tell me. . . . Please."

Marna nodded, but it was a long time before she said, "Your mother, Nerra . . . she bound you. The last days of her life, those spells were all she worked on. Binding your magic. Keeping it down before your power truly developed." She licked her cracked and bleeding lips with a dry tongue. Belatedly, Xhea wished she'd had some water to offer. "I was supposed to tell you, if I could, that the only way to preserve the binding and extend your life was to use your power as little as possible. Too much pressure on the spells, and the binding will break."

Xhea stared at her, speechless.

Marna blinked again, and rubbed her eyes with the back of one shaking, wire-bound hand. "It already has," she said then. "It's already broken." It wasn't, in the end, a question.

Xhea nodded, because she remembered lying on the glass floor in Eridian, the Tower's living heart flaring beneath her, and *pulling* on her magic with all her strength. She remembered, too, the feeling of something cracking deep within her. She had come to believe that what she felt must have only been the glass floor upon which she lay cracking beneath the onslaught.

But every day since, she'd been weak and trembling, sometimes barely able to think for the fevers, never mind speak or laugh or walk. Magic shock. Too much magic for her body to handle, too much used too fast—blunted only, it seemed, by her bond to Shai. What was the word that Ieren had used? Her bondling.

Gone now, binding and tether both. Only her magic remained, and it was growing ever stronger. Even now, her stomach cramped in hunger—reaction to the dark magic that flowed through her.

"I'm sorry, child," Marna whispered. "We're both dying, you and I, aren't we? It's all just a matter of time. And neither of us gets the death we'd choose."

It took a moment for understanding to sink in. "Ahrent said you volunteered." Xhea realized she was all but pleading, wanting this woman to dispel her sudden fear. "He said you chose this."

Marna only laughed, a sad and defeated sound. "Of course he did. And you believed him." She shook her head, looking forlorn. "I'm sorry," she said, as if somehow this was all her fault.

"I—"

"We all have debts, child. Ahrent offered us a way to pay them off—a way that wouldn't see our loved ones on the streets when Farrow begins to rise."

"But, if they're citizens . . ."

Marna's voice was hard enough, dark enough, that Xhea finally began to believe their kinship. "As if Lower City citizenship can't be taken away at will. No, the deal was simple: if you could not pay the price of citizenship, you were out—unless someone was willing to give their life to pay on your behalf. All it took was one person's magic to pay the price for their family. A good deal, we were told."

Xhea looked around, thinking of the rooms around her filled with unconscious people. Not volunteers; this was a debtor's prison, the only escape from which was death.

The next thought came slower, because it was dark and heavy with a weight of stone. "And you?" Xhea asked, thinking of Ahrent whispering, *All debts between us are clear.* "Your family is dead. No one left to rise."

But she already knew the answer. Because hadn't there been more pictures on the apartment walls, newer children's drawings than the ones she might have drawn?

"My son," Marna whispered, "and his three children. I was old, but Ahrent accepted my sacrifice—so long as I helped you to understand Farrow's cause. He asked that I wouldn't tell you the truth when I could have."

Citizenship bought with life—with death—and silence. What could she say to that? She should be angry, she knew, if not at Marna then at herself. *Family*, she thought. She had no family but the one she chose—and her family in Farrow had abandoned her, once, twice, and again. There were reasons she had chosen to be alone.

"Put me back," Marna said at last. "Let me go, child. It won't be long now."

Only then did Xhea realize that it was not a reduction in the drugs that kept Marna awake, nor the conversation, but Xhea's magic. It was nothing more than a trickle, but still it flowed, holding the woman's ghost in alignment with her body. Pulling back against the bindings dug deep into her spirit.

She looked closer at the spells Ieren had woven—the spells he had taught her the day before and that she'd practiced, time after painstaking time, until she'd begun to get it right. There in the tangled lines of intent, she saw the truth: this was no temporary binding, no spell she might break with the ease with which it had been made, but one that dug deep into the woman's soul and grew stronger the longer it existed.

You saved Shai from this. The spells and fate to which they had been tied. *You saved her, and then you . . . and then these people . . .*

She didn't know what to say—all her words were gone, leaving only a terrible, echoing emptiness in her wake—and so she said nothing, merely opened her hands, released her magic and stepped back. Marna sagged into the bed's hard embrace, her eyes fluttering closed. They did not open again.

Xhea stared. She hadn't said goodbye. Hadn't let Marna—

But that's life, isn't it? came the thought, hard and angry. As if any emotion might overcome the guilt that swelled until it choked her. Even so, Xhea had to turn away; she couldn't bear to see Marna's face gone slack and empty once more.

"Why didn't you tell me?" she whispered, her eyes squeezed closed.

Daye replied, just as softly, "Why didn't you ask?"

"Then it's true? Their debts. Their families." That this was the way a person bought citizenship to Tower Farrow for their children.

"Why," Daye said—quietly, so quietly—"did you think they volunteered?"

Xhea swallowed.

"There are more, aren't there? More floors like this. More . . . people." Because she knew Shai's power. How many ordinary people did it take, how much magic, to equal one Radiant?

As if the thought were a cue, suddenly she could feel them—she could even almost see them, without wishing to. Not just the people in the room, and the ones in the rooms beyond that, but more. Xhea felt the pressure of the volunteers' magic, taken and gathered and sent flowing through these walls, like an ache above her, around her. Saw the light of their magic, long though she had pushed that glow away. Not just storage coils, not just spells, but floor after floor of bound people—people for whom today's forced transformation would surely mean their lives.

"Yes," Daye said.

Silence settled between them.

"I think I liked it better when you didn't say anything," Xhea managed at last, and then had to stop speaking lest she break down and cry. She grabbed her cane and clung to it as if it were the only stable thing left in the world.

This is what I helped create? The question seemed to echo through the empty reaches of her mind. She had been to the City, knew and understood the truth that lay beneath all the Towers' wealth and happiness, the foundation on which they'd built that life of ease. It was foolish, then, to believe that anything, even a new Tower, might be born with less pain and strife and hardship.

This is what I'm going to die for? Because her hands were shaking, and her legs, and the world had started spinning around her. She'd used just a little bit of her returning magic, and oh, now there was no pretending that it would be anything but the death of her.

The Lower City was burning, and Farrow was going to rise on the backs of its dead citizens, and the world around her was spinning, spinning, as if nothing would ever again be still or right or whole again.

Farrow shivered.

Even curled, shaking and shuddering, Xhea could not mistake the feeling for anything other than something outside herself. She went still—or tried to; pressed her hands against the cold floor, fingers splayed. Again the skyscraper shivered, a ripple of movement that ran through the floor and the walls and echoed all the way into her bones.

Xhea looked up. Beneath the sound of the ventilators, beyond the closed doors, she could hear voices. Terse, commanding. Beneath that ruthless efficiency: excitement. Somewhere, the sound muffled and faint but nonetheless audible, Ieren laughed.

"It's beginning."

Daye nodded.

Xhea could see no difference in the room or walls— yet already something *felt* different, even if she didn't know how to name that change. The air seemed almost energized; it vibrated, as if all around her echoed a sound just outside the range of her hearing. Goosebumps rose in response.

A song, she thought—and she knew that sound. It was the song of a Tower's heart, or the earliest notes of that song, struggling for harmony as the Tower itself struggled toward life.

She shifted her vision again. Before, she had seen the complexity of the spells and the charms running beneath; now, she was all but blinded by their light.

Magic flowed, not in a steady current but in pulses like a heartbeat. Already the main spells were all but incandescent, while the charms carved into Farrow's ancient walls caught the overflow and flared to life. As she watched, more spells burst into being, and more, layer upon layer until she could not see where one ended and the next began, never mind read their lines of intent.

She looked up and around and saw the whole of the skyscraper mapped out in power, the barrier of concrete and iron suddenly less substantial to her sight than mist. Above, she could see all the way to the shining spires of light atop Farrow's roof. Below, that power faded until there was no magic at all in the skyscraper's lowest levels. While around her, all around her, the Tower's heart was forming. It was no shape of pure magic—not yet, not so soon—yet already in the power's flow she could see the pulsing patterns that she had come to know in one Tower and another. Already she could feel the pressure of so much magic pushing against her like invisible hands, making her skin tingle and go numb.

It was so beautiful, Xhea could barely breathe for looking at it—and that beauty made her angry. Nothing born of death should shine so brightly.

For the magic that shone as it flowed lightning-quick through those patterns flooded in from storage coils, poured in from the hearts of Farrow's bound citizens. Even if it were not for the people that she and Ieren had joined to this working—even if it were possible for a person to give the whole of their magic without dying—the light she saw was a hundred years of the skyscraper's riches. A hundred years of magic—magic that could have been money, that could have been food, that could have been warmth in the winter and new clothes for its citizens; magic that could have eased pain or healed illnesses. Magic that had instead been hoarded away and hidden, saved for this very moment.

Xhea had not realized that she wished to place her hands to the wall and destroy it all—not until that desire died within her. Even without the strength of power she'd shown two months before—even if such a wild torrent of power would not cast her to the ground, gasping and shuddering, if not fighting death—she could have destroyed this working. Destroyed, if not the whole of it, then enough to compromise the rest—enough to keep Farrow earthbound, subject to gravity's dictates like the rest of them.

Destroy the work of countless people, countless years. *And how many will you kill in the process?*

For Xhea knew the dark spells that bound so many people's spirits to Farrow's walls; she had woven them with her own hands. There would be no easy escape, no quick cutting of those bonds—and a flood of dark magic would cascade down through those wires even in the attempt. The dark spells would hold their spirits still, trapped in their bodies, as Xhea's magic condemned them to oblivion.

But even if it were not for the people bound, willing or not, to these walls, she found she could not destroy what Farrow had made. For all his lies and misdirections, one thing Ahrent had said remained true: this was their only chance, their only way up, their only way to defy the fate, the life, forced upon them by the vagaries of birth.

She was angry, yes, but not just at Ahrent, not just at Farrow. At the City above them, all the countless Towers. At the Central Spire. But mostly at herself for so wanting what Ahrent said to be true—for so wanting to be needed—that she had tried to ignore all else.

Xhea pushed away the details of her magic vision, suddenly again seeing the small room with its beds and wires and unconscious occupants. Even so, the walls still glowed, sparkling and flickering in ways that hinted at the bright workings beneath. Across the room Daye rose from her chair and stood aside, no longer blocking the door, that movement slow and reluctant, as if she too had little desire to open that door, to step beyond, and face what waited there. A moment, then she squared her shoulders.

Xhea was slower and infinitely more awkward, pushing despair back into the corners of her mind as she grasped her cane and fought to gain her feet.

"Tell me we can run."

Daye just looked at her; no easy comfort there. Not that she had expected it.

"There are bombs below," Daye said at last. "We're blocked in."

"*Bombs?*" Xhea's voice all but squeaked on the word. Understanding came a moment later. "To free Farrow as it rises."

Daye nodded, and something in her expression said more: that their escape plan, whatever it had been, had used the underground routes. Routes that would now be blocked and inaccessible, if not destroyed entirely.

Xhea swallow. "Fine. What *can* we do?"

Daye closed her eyes a moment, as if steadying herself. But all she said was, "Be ready."

That shiver came again, rippling through the skyscraper like shock and aftershock.

Daye opened the door and stepped out, Xhea following unsteadily in her wake. In the hall, the activity had only increased. People shouted as they ran from one room to another, or stopped and pressed their hands to the wall, heedless of who might be passing. Casters, Xhea judged, as much for their intent expressions as for the sparks of magic that flickered about their fingertips.

There was chaos here, yes, but little fear. For all that both the Central Spire and Rown had pushed forward Farrow's timetable, this was the culmination of their life's work—and the life's work of people who had lived and died, their contributions written in the spells and charms and the song that even now rose around them.

With every step the air felt thicker, the magic within it stronger, brighter. Xhea's own magic rose in response—and with it came the hunger, roaring within her like an enraged beast. She stumbled to a stop, gasping, barely able to think; there was only the magic, clashing within and without, and the need beneath that raged stronger than all else.

Breathe, she told herself, and struggled to do even that.

A caster pushed past her, muttering something about her doing work or getting the hell out of the way; his words seemed distant and all too easy to ignore. Because she was suddenly aware of a presence before her—a presence she could feel through the walls and despite the increasing activity in these halls. A presence that called to her, urging her onward.

She took a step and the hunger roared its approval.

Daye had turned back to her, a hint of a frown between her dark brows. Xhea shook her head, clinging both to the wall and her cane as she made her unsteady way forward, step by step. The pain in her knee, her weariness and exhaustion—they were not gone, but suddenly seemed so distant to be unworthy of notice. So too did the pressure of the bright magic against her skin fade with each step, and she only noticed how blurred her vision had become when it suddenly cleared once more. The dark magic rose harder, faster; when she exhaled, her breath hung before her like fog.

Daye gestured farther down the hall, but no, that wasn't what she needed. Closer—another step, another, and Xhea stood in an open doorway, her hand on the frame for balance.

Ieren was there, and two casters who were weaving spells atop one of the unconscious forms; she ignored them all. Instead, she looked to the ghost of the young boy that sat, curled and cringing, in the room's corner. Xhea could not look away from the ghost—could not so much as think of anything else.

Ieren hadn't seen her yet, nor did he notice the sound of her cane on the floor as she moved toward his bondling. The ghost looked up as she came toward him, his dark eyes veiled by long lashes. For a moment, it seemed that he was going to smile at her approach, that shy and hesitant smile that she had seen so very briefly once before—and then he froze, eyes going wide. He pushed himself back, or tried to, but he already sat at his tether's end, as far from Ieren as he could possibly get.

No escape, came the thought from an impossibly distant part of her mind. He was so small. He was so young, or had been.

She wanted—she *wanted*—

Oh, she could not name it, could not so much as think of what she was doing. Yet her hand reached out as if it were a thing apart from her, magic swirling around her fingers like living smoke. Reaching as she reached toward the ghost.

Her finger touched the tether.

She sucked in a breath as she felt a sudden surge of power—a shock, hard enough to hurt, as if she'd brushed against a live wire. Ieren spun, screaming, at the same time as a sudden surge ran through the skyscraper, shaking it to its bones. Xhea, already unsteady, stumbled back and fell in a heap, cane clattering to the ground at her side.

This shudder was not in her mind, nor in the skyscraper's magical systems; the skyscraper around her shook as if in an earthquake. Xhea covered her face as a crack opened in the ceiling, raining dust and plaster. When the shaking stopped, she raised a hand to ward Ieren away.

"*I told you—*" he screamed.

"I fell," Xhea said quickly, desperately. "He's yours, I'm sorry, I didn't mean to—" Her words seemed to fall over themselves, tumbling and spinning as frantically as her mind.

Ieren hesitated, then glowered as Xhea fumbled for her cane and forced herself back to her feet. Behind them, the casters tried to call him back, but Ieren paid them no heed.

"You're sure?" he asked finally. "You promise?"

"Promise." The lie tasted like ashes.

Ieren smiled then, his anger vanishing. "Okay," he said. "We're almost done with this one. Isn't this exciting?"

Xhea shook her head, dispelling plaster dust and setting the charms in her hair to chiming. She took a long, shaking breath, trying to find some calm in the chaos. But even as she made the attempt, the skyscraper shook again, setting everything to rattling, while all around her the bright magic grew stronger and stronger.

"Yeah, sure," she managed. She took a careful step backwards, and another.

Something had changed, she realized, even with so small a contact. She'd barely touched the tether, but as she clung to her cane Xhea saw that her shakes had eased. Again she looked at the ghost boy, who sat curled in upon himself and whimpering, but she could not meet his eyes. The hunger was still there—still roaring, still rising—yet she was able to clamp down on it, hold it back with desperation and an iron-hard will.

Or at least she tried.

"I'll meet you . . ." she said, swallowing. "I mean, I'll be . . . somewhere . . ."

Turning, she fled the room and not even Daye's quiet voice calling after her, not even the pain in her knee, could slow her steps. At the hall's far end, where the guard's unoccupied chair sat outside the padlocked door, Xhea stopped and slumped against the wall, gasping. She could not catch her breath. It was only as she raised a hand to cover her mouth that she realized she was crying.

"Xhea?"

Not Daye, this time, though the woman stood nearby like a shadow, but Torrence.

She opened her mouth but all that came out were deep, wracking sobs. *Not the time,* she told herself; yet it was impossible to stop. Impossible to think of anything but the look on the ghost's face as she reached for him, that hesitant smile turned to horror and fear.

"Not to intrude, but whatever this is has to wait." No humor in his tone, only urgency. "Can you walk? We have to get to the stairs."

"Stairs?" Xhea managed, voice tight and aching. "But . . ."

This was the thirty-fourth floor. Farrow was—what? Fifty stories high? Sixty? There was no way she could handle so many flights of stairs—not in anything less than an hour, not unless someone carried her. Given the way her magic kept surging and flowing around her, fighting back the effects of the myriad bright spells, the latter wasn't an option.

"The charges on the foundations are set to blow at any time. We have to go up."

Daye raised an eyebrow—the same expression she might have made, Xhea thought, if Torrence had suggested that they all leap out a window. Yet she made no protest, only squared her shoulders as a muscle in her jaw twitched.

"But I thought . . ." Xhea hadn't taken their offer; she'd thought that they would leave her. Instead they waited as the skyscraper shook around them—waited for her, in spite of everything.

Xhea did her best to stifle her sobs. She staggered in the direction that Torrence gestured, trying to keep her head down, trying to heed his words to go quickly, quickly, before anyone noticed. It wasn't until they were on the stairs, tears still streaming down Xhea's cheeks, that she was able to ask, "Why are you doing this?"

The same question she had asked the night before. They didn't need her, not for this—whatever help she might have been in one job or another had nothing to do with their escape. If anything, she was a burden—and cause enough for Farrow's people to give chase. Let her go, when Ahrent had said that they needed her so very much? As if.

"Just go," Torrence said, urging her onward.

It was not so very many floors to climb, Xhea tried to tell herself, hauling herself up. But she could not stop weeping, and all around them the magic was rising, rising. Again, her vision seemed to blur, no matter how she blinked or tried to focus; glimpses of color flickered in and out of her sight. The warm gold of her skin, the dark green of Daye's pants, the brown and ember of her cane's wooden length.

Torrence was ahead by a flight of stairs or more, the sound of his footsteps loud in the enclosed space, but Daye kept pace beside her. Daye said nothing—and yet Xhea felt the woman's question nonetheless.

"I don't want to be like him," she said. The words came out quiet and despairing, for it seemed that she had little choice. *Hungry*, Ieren had said, and she'd thought little of the word or the drive behind it. She had thought she'd understood hunger's many facets.

This was nothing like going without food. She felt weakened, yes, fuzzy-headed and fixated on a potential source of nourishment—but never, no matter how hungry she had become, had she felt hunger could entirely control her.

This had been different. Worse—a thousand times worse.

Once she'd killed a man with her silver knife—shredded his ghost and body both to ribbons, to nothingness, and gone. It had been the worst thing she could imagine doing; yet her imagination had failed her—and oh, if only it could fail her again. For now, all too easily, she could imagine herself attacking other ghosts, not because she wanted to, but because she *needed* to, her body forcing her to act in ways she would never have wanted. Destroying ghosts, not with her silver knife, but with her hands and teeth like a starving animal.

Perhaps the reality wouldn't be so violent—but the image felt true.

For the first time, she was glad that Shai wasn't with her, because she was suddenly unsure of what she might do to her friend. Of what her magic might do, driven by that hunger.

"If you don't want to be like Ieren," Daye said, her voice just audible over the creak and groan of the skyscraper's movement, "then don't be."

Xhea shook her head, angry at the words, angry at Daye, angry at herself. But Daye hadn't seen—couldn't see—what she'd tried to do. What she truly was. *Eater of ghosts.* All the fear and revulsion in the thought was directed not at Ieren, not a boy who might not have known better, but at herself.

And what did it matter, anyway? Because Farrow was going to rise, or it was going to fall, and either way she might die. It was stupid to cry, just a waste of water and breath; it would change nothing.

Somehow, the thought gave her strength as she climbed.

Chapter
Twenty-One

By the time they'd reached the rooftop door at the top of the stairwell, Farrow was shaking hard enough that Xhea struggled to keep her feet. The vibrations came in waves in time to the wail of Farrow's half-born heart, the sound on the edge of her hearing.

Xhea clung to the railing, fingers white-knuckled as she hauled herself up one blighted stair at a time. Even in the dim stairwell, the light of the magic flowing through the building left her half blind and squinting, her own power pushing back against the onslaught. Cracks appeared in the walls, and spread, fast as thought. Xhea could only hope that the skyscraper could transform before it shook itself to pieces.

Torrence already had the door to the roof open, the aging lock little barrier to the slim tools he kept hidden up his sleeve. Xhea stumbled past him, panting, out into the sunlight. Or what little sunlight managed to reach the ground.

Outside, the air was hot and thick with smoke, even here, sixty stories up and blocks from the market fire. Except, Xhea realized as she stared out across the Lower City, it wasn't just the market that was burning anymore. She didn't want to go anywhere near the edge, that so-familiar terror gripping like a hand about her throat; even so, she could see the thick, black plumes of smoke were not limited to the span of Senn's central territory. Ancient structures of dry and crumbling wood; shacks and lean-tos and shelters built within the walls of buildings that were little more than leaning shells: all just fuel now to the flames that raged skyward, out of control.

They had to run; but for the first time Xhea wondered if there would be anywhere left to run to.

She coughed and tried to cover her mouth with her sleeve, not that it did much good. Torrence seemed not to notice the smoke or the distant flames, as if every breath did not make the back of his throat burn. Instead, he went to the garage on the roof's far side, and unwound the chains wrapped around the heavy doors. The lock had been sawn in two, as had a few sections of chain. In the shadows beyond, Xhea could see the shapes of aircars—not a collection of toys, like Lorn owned, but battered cargo vehicles and reclaimed City buses.

Old and mechanical though they were, she didn't much like the thought of riding in one. *We don't have to go far*, she reasoned, trying to smother her fear. *Just off Farrow's rooftop.* But the thought did nothing to banish the memory of her last aircar trip, all but falling from the sky as her magic destroyed the workings of the car around her. She shuddered and looked away, her hand gripping the top of her cane so hard it hurt.

Instead she looked to the two spell-spires now mounted on Farrow's rooftop, inset from opposite corners. They looked like nothing so much as tapered lengths of iron—and not smooth and well-cast, but metal dark and rippled and dented. Small, uneven cross-spars marked the spires' lengths, some half-melted, their ends rounded and bearing hardened drips of metal. Battered as they were, she would have thought them nothing but reclaimed junk were it not for the aura of magic that ringed them.

No spells there, nothing so complex; instead, pure magic flowed from each to travel down the spires' lengths in a lazy spiral of light. Not active yet, Xhea judged; though that power came faster, brighter, with every passing moment. Her own magic surged in response, making her feel weaker, hungrier, even as it protected her from the onslaught.

The skyscraper wasn't just waking up; it was preparing to fight its way into the sky. A Tower born of death and smoke and pure bright magic.

How fitting.

Xhea looked to Rown. Their own spell-spire, which they had used to fire upon the market, was hidden beneath a protective tarp. Broken, Daye had said—and, given Ahrent's shock, Xhea could believe it. That spire wasn't supposed to be functional for many long years, if she understood Ahrent's original plan: a payment with a greater future payoff, one designed to bind Rown to Farrow for years to come.

Instead, Rown had fixed the spell-spire and turned it on the Lower City. Who could have told them how to make those repairs but a Tower? Who else might have provided enough magic to fuel it?

The thought felt right—and yet there was not renai enough in Rown's coffers to pay for either. Poorest of the skyscrapers, with the smallest and most vulnerable territory, Rown had little power and less leverage. No, the only way Rown might have paid for the spell-spire's repair and the power with which to fuel it was with a coin with which Farrow was familiar: information. And the only secret that Rown knew and that the other skyscrapers did not was the truth, the timing, and the extent of Farrow's plan.

For Rown to be Farrow's ally now and as they rose meant securing an ally in the City—a trading partner that had access to resources the likes of which a skyscraper could only dream. Yet the future of any Tower was always at risk— especially the poorer, weaker Towers on the City's farthest fringes, which Farrow would most certainly become. In the City's center, surrounding the Central Spire, the biggest and most powerful Towers played out a delicate and complex dance of power, renai, and politics, mergers and acquisitions interrupted only by brief and brutal takeovers. Out on the fringes, the Towers' movements had all the dance-like delicacy of a drunken bar fight. Poorer, brutal, and often clumsy, Towers on the City's edges were always moving, always fighting, always looking for an advantage.

Slowly, Xhea looked up.

The Towers were cast across the smoke-stained sky, seemingly stacked one atop another. Even searching, it took her a moment to find them: Towers—poorer Towers, lower Towers—circling Farrow like crows. Fore-warned of Farrow's arrival, they waited—and as one Tower moved out of formation, shifting closer to where Farrow would rise, the others seemed to pause, looking for the thing that had caused the change. *Just carrion birds*, Xhea thought, for all that they looked like long, slender spinning tops, bristling with defensive spires.

"Rown sold them out," Xhea said, still staring upward. She watched as the Towers moved, circled. A new-birthed Tower would be an easy target for the taking.

Daye paused, followed Xhea's gaze, and nodded once. It was Torrence who replied: "We know."

The rooftop door banged open and Ieren stumbled into the sunlight.

"Xhea?" he called. "Xhea, what are you doing?"

Torrence swore and dropped the chains, turning toward Ieren.

Who was watching him? For him to vanish now, right when Farrow would need him most—she could only imagine Ahrent's reaction. Of course, she knew who was supposed to keep Ieren under control: Torrence.

"Ieren, my boy, listen—"

But Ieren paid him no heed. Instead he stumbled toward Xhea as if she were the only one there. "We need you," he said. "I've been looking—"

He stopped. Stared.

"You're leaving?" he asked, suddenly bereft. She knew that look, that feeling: the realization that you've been left behind. Abandoned. He came toward her—and then his ghost was dragged, struggling, out of the stairwell and into the open air between them.

Xhea could not look at the ghost—but she could not look at anything else. Her whole self reached toward him as if he were the only thing in the world.

"No," she whispered. "No, no . . ." But the hands she raised to ward away the ghost and block him from her sight were already dark with magic.

In a moment of perfect clarity, Xhea remembered Daye's words: *If you don't want to be like Ieren, then don't be.* She couldn't change what she was, nor what her power demanded—but she could fight both.

Her power surged and for a moment she grabbed control, thinking of her lost silver blade and forcing the magic into its image. She reached out and sliced through the tether that joined the ghost to Ieren.

"Go," she cried to the ghost, pleading, desperate—while Ieren screamed as if he were dying. "*Run!*"

Her magic came boiling out of her. Sweat and tears and ink-stained breath, dark magic reached for the ghost like a hundred arms formed of smoke. She could not hold it back, helpless against that sudden, overwhelming need.

But the ghost was not looking at her, nor at Ieren, but at the center of his chest where his tether had once joined. His face was transformed. There was no fear there, no pain or panic; merely a moment of perfect joy. Then he was gone, vanishing into the air as if he had never been there at all.

Xhea's magic writhed, suddenly denied its target, and she fought to regain her tenuous control. There was no denying: with every passing minute, her magic seemed to grow within her, becoming darker and more powerful even as it sapped her body's strength. Even as it killed her. She trembled, wanted to fall; but in that moment, she cared little for her weakness. The clear and evident failings of her flesh were as nothing; and her death, which threatened with every breath stained dark, seemed no more worthy of notice than the most distant Towers.

I'm dying. The thought brought no fear. There was only the magic's perfect calm, its feeling of wholeness and strength that filled her even as she collapsed.

Lying sprawled on the roof's hot surface, Xhea took a long breath and another, blinking as her vision shifted to see pure magic—black against glowing white—and back again. Everything was bright and dark: the spires spilling magic like fountains of light, Farrow below her shaking and shuddering as the spells within it grew. Her magic, and Ieren's. The flames of the distant fire, and the pillars of black smoke that stretched skyward.

If fear held no sway, logic could: her magic could still hurt Torrence or Daye. *Force it back*, she commanded. She pulled hard on that dark power, drawing it into her like a snail into its shell.

Ieren, too, had collapsed. He sprawled on the roof's gritty surface, twitching. Not dead, she thought, but nearly so. Torrence barely glanced at the boy as he stepped around him and came to Xhea's side. After a sharp, assessing look, Daye turned and ran to get the car.

"Are you okay?" Torrence asked, low and urgent. "Xhea? Can you stand?"

In all the years she had known him—in all the jobs they had done, all the tight spots they had gotten into—never had she heard his voice sound like that. Once she'd thought that if Torrence stood at the end of the world, he'd laugh to see it—maybe greet it with a mocking smile and a crude gesture. Now, he sounded afraid.

"Run," Xhea whispered. For what did it matter if she had fallen, or if she lay here on Farrow's rooftop as the skyscraper began to rise? She was going to die anyway, from one magic or the other, and the only way out would be for him or Daye to carry her.

"Stand," he countered. "Come on, Xhea. We need you."

But they didn't. She laughed at the absurdity; it came out as little more than a wheeze.

"Not to get away," he said, understanding her reaction. "After. We get you out, you get us into Edren—you see?"

She did, because he was suddenly an open book before her, all the hurt and desperation beneath his smiling exterior coming to the fore. Without Rown, without Farrow, they had nothing. While she had Edren—or so it seemed.

For it was impossible to imagine a life after this moment; impossible, even, to imagine living at all. She was weak, injured, failing—and her magic brought only death. Wasn't it better if that death was hers, here, now, rather than someone else's? Rather than ghost after ghost, person after person, destroyed to buy her a few more days? It was clear she could not control her power, nor the desperate hunger that drove it.

I don't want to die, she thought, and realized it was true. Not that she could stop it; but perhaps she could die standing. Perhaps she could look that death in the face— not just shake and shiver until the darkness came over her and swept her away. She could die like a true Lower City dweller: defiant until the end.

Unable to touch her, Torrence held her cane as she fumbled for it with weak, numbed fingers. The pain came then, pain and pain and pain, and Xhea laughed even as she cried out. She would stand, one way or the other. Torrence nodded his approval as he, too, rose.

From behind him, Ieren reached out and grabbed Torrence's leg.

Ieren's hand was so small, Xhea expected Torrence to just shake him off, swearing at the pain. Instead, Torrence froze. Every muscle went rigid, and the tendons in his neck stood out like wire cables. He barely seemed to be breathing, his chest fluttering with the erratic spasms of his diaphragm. Only his eyes showed that he was still conscious; they were wide and terrified, locked on Xhea's face.

"Torrence?" Her voice broke, and she struggled to toward him.

Ieren was faster. Weak as he was, he dragged himself toward Torrence with single-minded intensity, hand over hand as he used Torrence's legs and then arms to support him until he was standing, swaying, clinging to the bounty hunter as if Torrence were his last hold on life. And perhaps he was.

Ieren didn't hold to Torrence with his hands alone, Xhea saw, but with his magic. Dark power flowed from Ieren into Torrence, dark power that twisted and dug deep inside him like claws. Then he reached for Torrence's face, fingers spread. His power was a black rush that leapt across the space between them and into Torrence's eyes.

Torrence's own magic was but a flicker; beneath the onslaught, even that dim light faltered. But Ieren's purpose was not to drown Torrence's power. As she watched, Ieren's magic wrapped around Torrence's spirit, grabbed hold tight, and pulled.

"No!" Xhea cried, still struggling to push past pain and find the will to stand. For beneath her horror, she felt her own magic rise in response. It was all she could do to hold it back, to keep herself from reaching as Ieren reached, as if a living man were but a ghost in the making.

Hungry, came the thought, echoing through her like a bell. Her magic tried again to rise and she fought to hold it back—because she was not like that, she *refused*.

Ignoring her magic, she grabbed her cane and swung for Ieren's legs. The solid wood impacted hard against the boy's lower leg, but it did little to deter his attack; he clung to Torrence like a small, vicious predator with its jaws already locked on.

Torrence's eyes, still wide and staring, shone now, even wreathed as they were by the flow of Ieren's power. It took Xhea a moment to understand what she was seeing.

Ieren was ripping Torrence's ghost out of his body through his eyes.

Something screamed—a person's scream, an engine's scream—and a battered aircar flew from the garage and slammed into Ieren's side. The boy went flying, his hold on Torrence roughly broken. He tumbled like a rag doll, rolling, limbs loose and flailing, across the surface of Farrow's roof. He came to a stop face down near the wall that surrounded the skyscraper's edge, and did not move.

Torrence had taken only a glancing blow, but even that was enough to send him sprawling. The car skidded to a stop near his fallen body and Daye rushed out.

She was screaming. She, who Xhea had never heard raise her voice, screamed so loud that it suddenly felt like all Xhea could hear, all she had ever heard. The sound went on and on and on, seemingly ripped from Daye's throat.

Daye fell to the ground at Torrence's side, grabbing his body to cradle him roughly, and only then did she fall silent. Silence, Xhea thought, was worse. Daye bowed her head, her short tangle of dark hair falling over her eyes, and it did nothing to hide her grief or her rage or her pure, naked pain.

Xhea pushed herself off the ground and staggered toward them. Daye looked up, meeting Xhea's eyes.

"Let me help him," Xhea said. Beneath them, Farrow shook—not a small quiver, not a shudder, but what felt like an earthquake that rolled and rattled all around them. Xhea heard concrete crack, glass shatter—but she did not look away, only stared at Daye with single-minded intensity. When the shaking stopped, Daye nodded.

Xhea looked down at Torrence's unconscious body—
and unconscious he was, for all that his pale eyes were open
and staring. *Oh, let him be unconscious*—for she did not
want to think of why else he had grown so still.

As with Marna, she could see his ghost inside his body—
except that his ghost wasn't in his body anymore, not fully.
Where Marna's spirit had been an astigmatic echo of her
physical form, Torrence's spirit had been almost dislodged
entirely. Even now his open eyes seemed to gleam with
the energy that she associated only with ghosts and their
tethers.

If Ieren had succeeded in pulling Torrence's spirit from
his body . . . *A walker*, Xhea thought in dazed shock. *He
would have been a walker.*

Beneath it all, her hunger roared, demanding that she
finish what Ieren had begun. But she was stronger than
that; she had to be. If she had to do but one thing before the
power overwhelmed her, let it be this.

She reached out with hands and magic both, took hold
of Torrence's ghost, and *pushed*.

Hungry—oh, sweetness and blight, she was so hungry—
but she was not Ieren, would never be.

Never, she thought, *never, never, never*, and held to
the thought as tightly as she held to her magic. For it was
not a creature outside her—not a wild beast beyond her
control—but a part of her. A terrifying, horrifying part, yes,
but it was her nonetheless. Letting it dictate her actions?
No, that was a choice, and one she would fight with every
part of her being.

She felt the moment Torrence's spirit reconnected
with his body, and she drew back and pushed herself
away, putting as much physical distance between her and
Torrence as she could. Will could only do so much.

Torrence gasped and blinked, then flailed wildly in sudden panic. Daye restrained him, holding him until he calmed.

"Daye?" he said, and his voice was like a child's, pleading and broken. "Daye, I can't see."

Without speaking, Daye gathered him more fully into her arms and picked him up. Despite her size, and his, she did not struggle under his weight, only stared at his face as if he were the last person in the world. Step by careful step, she made her way to the aircar and lay him down in the cargo space in the back. She moved to the driver's seat, settled herself inside, and only then did she turn to Xhea and meet her eyes.

"I—" Xhea started.

Daye slammed the aircar's door closed and hit the controls, sending the vehicle rocketing upward without a backward glance. Xhea stared, open-mouthed. She could only watch as the car sped away, banking hard as it turned across the Lower City, the air in its wake shimmering with spell exhaust.

Xhea was too tired to laugh, too tired to cry; she just watched as the car vanished into the smoke and was gone. Only her magic held her steady. She had called it in her attempt to save Torrence, and now had nothing left with which to force it back. She held her hand aloft, her fingers silhouetted against the sky; it was hard to see where her magic ended and true smoke began. Both filled the air with darkness. Both made her eyes burn, and her breathing grow short.

Of course, she thought simply. *Of course this would happen.* That she would be left now, here, with no way up nor down, and all her bridges burned behind her. She looked to the garage and the aircars held within. Perhaps she could find one unlocked; perhaps she could get it started.

But flying it, like this? Impossible. That had to be why Daye had left; so much magic flowed from Xhea now that it had to have entered the visible spectrum, had to lift from her skin like steam and pool around her feet in a puddle of black. Too much magic for even a short aircar ride.

She knew it, and tried to pretend that some part of her didn't want to scream at Daye anyway. Still she stood—slowly, painfully, leaning heavily on the cane that Daye had given her—and started toward the garage.

A sound stopped her. A whimper.

Ieren.

No fear now, no panic; only the sound of her feet crunching against the roof's gritty surface as Xhea made her slow way to where the boy lay fallen. She, too, nearly fell, once and again as Farrow shook beneath her. Yet that movement was so constant now it was nearly beneath her notice; she had but to time her steps to the building's shudders.

Xhea lowered herself to the ground at Ieren's side. She could see the shallow movement of his ribs as he breathed, and a cut on his head seeped blood. His back might have been broken, or his neck. *Doesn't matter now.* Carefully as she could, she turned him over.

Ieren's face showed little sign of his injuries, only an abrasion along one cheek. But his eyes were distant; he blinked slowly, once, twice, and again, as the smoke-diluted sunlight fell upon his face. It took a moment more for him to focus on her. He smiled then, pale lips stained dark with blood.

"Xhea," he said. He raised one hand clumsily toward her. After a long, frozen moment, she took his hand.

His skin was cool and clammy to the touch. Yet though her magic still flowed, Ieren showed no pain. He was just like her—or she was like him. Perhaps it was the same in the end.

Though she looked, Xhea could see no flicker of his earlier hurt or sadness. It seemed not to matter how truly she had earned his hatred; he only smiled at her, closed his eyes, and tried to squeeze her hand.

A minute passed, perhaps two. Xhea realized that Ieren's breathing had stopped, and she did not know when. Still she held his hand.

Slowly she looked up at the Towers circling overhead and the smoke-hazed sky. Farrow's spell-spires shone brighter now, brighter and brighter until it seemed that her whole world was defined by that light. Somewhere below came a low *whump*, and the skyscraper shook—a different movement than all the ones before. Again, the noise came and the vibration—and again.

Explosions. They were setting off the bombs. Xhea took a long and shuddering breath.

Then, as if from nowhere, a tether connected to the center of Xhea's chest. Its impact against her sternum felt like little more than a drop of a pin, and for a second Xhea could only stare at it, disbelieving.

A span of a breath, and then her magic and the hunger beneath roared up like a tidal wave, hard and fast and inexorable. Darkness washed over her, and she collapsed.

Chapter
Twenty-Two

Rain, Shai thought as the flames grew and spread. *If only it would rain*. But the sky, behind the thickening haze of smoke and the shifting Towers, was a perfect cloudless blue.

The Towers themselves had water to spare, caught as rain or condensed from the humid air; she had never heard of a Tower's cisterns running low, never mind dry. Yet none, she knew, would open those stores to dump their water upon the Lower City below, no matter how high the flames reached, no matter how thick the smoke. The lives and deaths of the people on the ground made no difference to those above; they would suffer and burn and die, and in the City they would only complain about the haze and the harsh smell of smoke.

Once that would have been her. A myriad concerns filled her days long before the time when she lay dying, and never once had she thought to look down. Never had she wondered about the lives lived so far distant, scratched out of dirt and ruin.

Now she did what she could, little though it was. Her magic had all but vanished—and was exhausted seemingly as fast as it was generated. There were too many choices: did she battle the flames, or help the people who tried? Did she heal those on the edge of death, or spread her power thinner, helping dozens instead of one?

Wait, she told herself. *Let the magic come back first, let it get stronger.* But how could she let a hurt family pass her by, knowing that with a quick spell to aid that boy's fractured ankle, that mother's mangled arm, she could speed their escape from the danger zone? How could she not help the flagging people on the fire's front lines, knowing that even a little magic might strengthen their defense?

So, too, did she feel exhausted in a way that she had not experienced since her dying days. Sometimes she would find herself staring vacantly, as if her thoughts and will had vanished with her power. Again and again she shook herself and struggled forward, only to find herself drifting once more, as if her body was trying to slip from this world, her purpose done.

Rest, came the thought. *Just rest.*

"I won't," she said, pushing the idea away. Her voice was all but lost beneath the sound of the flames' roar and crackle. "I *can't.*"

The fire grew and spread despite all their efforts, despite everything. The market was gone, the assembled tents and ancient mall both, nothing left but burning wreckage and cinders. Heat beat against her face, intense even though it caused no sweat, brought her no pain; Shai could only imagine how it felt to the crowd trying desperately to fight the flames.

"Are you happy now?" she whispered to Rown. She conjured her cool wind, trying to keep the flames from spreading from one building to the next. Farther, another building collapsed in a sudden rush of burning timber and an explosion of skyward sparks.

Of Rown's hunters, she'd seen no sign. Neither had the skyscraper attempted to fire again; they had exhausted their unexpected power, or achieved their end, she knew not which. This, it seemed, was Senn's punishment for daring not to surrender—a punishment that might have come to Edren or Orren, had only the timing been different. But no matter who had stood up to Rown first, no matter whose territory burned first, all of the Lower City would suffer.

Suffer, if not fall.

There was nothing she could do to stop it. Her magic was gone now, she realized, staring at her hands. Gone or so weak that it made no difference. Her attempts to aid, to heal, to fight the flames did nothing now; and her hands, when she reached out, only passed through others unfeeling. She was just a cool presence, a momentary disturbance in the air; and who here, now, would sense such a thing?

No one saw her weeping.

Shai sank to her knees and then lay on the ground, wanting to sink into the earth, sink through the ash and the concrete, through the tunnels below, and be gone.

She had failed. Once and again she had failed, in spite of everything.

This is what you wrought, she told herself as the flames rose higher. *Your magic here, in these streets. Is this what you wanted?*

It didn't matter what she wanted; it never had.

I tried . . . But she could not finish the thought.

She only wished that she might have found out what had happened to Xhea, and why. She missed her friend. She missed having someone who could see her and speak to her, yes—but it was more than that. Xhea was the first person who had treated her like herself, neither intimidated by nor caring about Shai's magic until it had called Allenai and Eridian down upon them.

Xhea had taught her, in spite of everything, how to stand up for herself. How to fight for what she believed in, even when the odds were stacked against her. To try, because the effort alone had value.

"Xhea . . ." Shai whispered, thinking of her friend; thinking of Xhea's laughter and the edge of her sarcasm, her stubborn ways, her determination and her smile and the chime of her charm-bound hair . . .

A tether unspooled from Shai's heart.

Shai gasped, looking down at the near-invisible line that suddenly joined to her sternum. She felt the moment that the tether connected to its destination; it sent a shock rippling through her whole body. She felt the person on the other end of that line.

Xhea. Alive.

There was only time for that single, brief thought, before a sudden wave of magic knocked her senseless.

Her magic had been gone, fading to nothing—yet now it rushed through her, hard and fast. Shai struggled to cope with its sudden resurgence and the disorientation in its wake. There was so very much light.

At last she realized: a Radiant ghost had to be bound to a body for their magic to flow. She'd just never imagined that might mean a slender tether connected to another living, breathing person.

Hard on the heels of that thought came another. *Something's wrong.* She could feel a difference in the tether's vibration. Shai closed her fingers around that so-familiar line, frowning. No longer did it seem to hum against her skin in a low and steady tone, but surged and stuttered, almost fighting her hold. She might have thought it only a reflection of her own fading power; yet now that power shone from her, strong and steady like sunlight, as if it had known no break.

No: something was wrong with Xhea. They had done something to her, hurt her—and Shai hadn't been there, hadn't tried to stop them, hadn't even *known*. Ignorance, once more, was the root of her failure.

Whatever Farrow had done to her, she would not leave Xhea to face it alone. Trying not to yield to the screams and cries for help all around her, Shai launched herself into the sky and followed the tether's lead.

Within moments Farrow loomed before her, a pale shadow in the smoke. Of all the skyscrapers, it alone seemed unguarded, no armed or armored people threatening or defending. If anything, the streets around the skyscraper seemed unnaturally still compared to the chaos of the rest of the Lower City.

The building's only defense was the trench she had seen earlier. It was deeper now, and far more extensive, in places exposing the building's foundations, while the excavated rock and soil had been piled high in a great ring around the building. Were there any people close enough to attack Farrow, that pile alone might have been enough to keep them at bay. *A defensive moat?* As she watched, explosives buried in those depths detonated, one after another, shattering the concrete foundations.

They're going to bring the whole thing down, Shai thought in shock. *All those people . . .*

As she approached, the building shook and shuddered. Glass shattered in a line of windows along the skyscraper's farthest edge, sending shards raining down, glittering, to the upturned earth below. Farrow's concrete façade cracked, fissures spreading like lightning across the building's surface, while the makeshift barriers on the balcony platforms tore out from their moorings and fell away.

Farrow was destroying itself from the inside out. Except, as Shai drew closer, she saw that the air around the skyscraper had begun to shimmer, as if the whole of the building were surrounded by spell exhaust. No, more: light shone from the very walls, growing from a faint glow to a bright halo as she watched. A halo of magic.

Then the defensive spell generators on Farrow's roof came to life, like two fountains of pure bright magic. Shai hadn't noticed them, hidden as they were in the various antennae that bristled on Farrow's rooftop. These were not pointed at the ground, as Rown's had been, but upward, each mounted on opposite corners of the skyscraper's roof. Magic swirled and cascaded down around them in wide, glowing arcs as a defensive spell began to take form.

No, they couldn't possibly . . .

She pushed the thought aside and would have turned away, except that it was to that rooftop that the tether led. She had momentum now, traveling faster and higher almost as if the tether were dragging her forward.

And then: dread. The sudden feeling made her recoil.

The boy, she thought. He was there, with Xhea—for as Shai approached, once more she felt that sick churning fear in the base of her stomach. She forced herself onward, clinging to the tether with one hand as if it could steady her or slow the sudden pounding of her imagined heart. The fear only grew as she came nearer. Absent gods, she did not want to move closer; it felt almost as if her ghostly body screamed at her, having scented a predator that her conscious self could not name. She wanted to stop and run away as fast as she had come. Run and hide.

Like you did before? she asked, the words hard and vicious. *Just letting them take her?* Guilt was the goad that drove her forward when all else bid her flee.

A protective bubble of power arced up from the spell generators and over Farrow's rooftop like an umbrella, the magic flickering and fading as it attempted to cover the skyscraper's sides. Defensive though it was, Shai slipped through that barrier without pause, neither her magic nor her ghostly form hindered by the nascent spell. Only once she was through did she see Xhea.

The girl sat awkwardly on the skyscraper's closest edge, a cane by her side, next to the sprawled form of the dark magic boy from whom Shai had fled twice. The coins and charms bound into Xhea's hair glittered in the spells' light as they arced up and over her, bright despite the smoky haze all around her.

No, not haze: magic. A fog of dark magic to push back so much light.

Shai touched down on the building's flat rooftop behind Xhea and took a cautious step forward, fearing at any moment that the boy would see her. *Run,* her instincts screamed. For all her growing skill and renewed power, Shai knew of no spell that could keep her safe here. Still she raised her hands, magic shining about her fingers, and prepared a blast of pure magic.

Except the boy, Shai saw in dawning horror, was not moving. He lay beside Xhea, features slack, eyes wide and staring. The movements of his body were due only to the skyscraper's earthquake-like vibrations. There was blood on his lips—red, so red—and blood matting his blond hair dark. His hand, held in Xhea's own, was limp and pale.

And still Shai felt that fear, that dread and terror that crawled through her like something cold and wet and terrible—the fear that bid her flee.

"Xhea?" Shai said hesitantly.

Xhea turned. Her eyes were a pure and perfect black that did nothing to shadow the naked hunger in her expression. Shai stopped, stumbled back, and only then did Xhea blink; briefly, that darkness drew back from her eyes. No joy came in its place, no relief to see her: only fear.

"Shai," Xhea said. "Get back. Please." She shuddered then, and squeezed her eyes closed. Dark magic leaked from beneath her lids nonetheless, slipping down her cheek like tears before lifting into the air and questing toward Shai in thin, twisting tendrils.

Shai dropped her hands and the magic she'd held within them. Whatever was wrong with Xhea, she would not—could not—blast her friend as she might have blasted the boy. *Just a spark*, she thought, thinking of the myriad times she had helped Xhea regain control of her power with a little bit of bright magic—and dispelled the thought just as quickly. For never had Xhea's magic run so fully out of her control; it cascaded from her in heavy, black waves. Shai knew, too, the pain that even a spark of bright magic now caused.

Xhea would not look at her. "Go," she commanded. "*Go!*" She had dropped the boy's limp hand and clung now to the tether, her fingers white knuckled. She tried to sever the line that bound them once more, attempting to pull it apart or create a blade from her magic; but the tether resisted her movements, and Xhea's magic moved as if it had a mind of its own.

All of the dark magic did. It reached for Shai, curling toward her like countless reaching hands. Shai recognized it.

Ever since Xhea's magic had first risen, whenever Xhea slept or her attention had drifted, her magic had reached for Shai: gently at first, as if only curious; then stronger and more persistently as time passed. Driven, Shai thought now, by a need that Xhea had not known or acknowledged. In the past, Shai had used her own power to keep it back; yet that would not be an option now, not if she wanted to return to Xhea's side.

Xhea needed her. She shook and shivered as if horribly cold despite the summer day's dawning heat, and her face looked drawn, gaunt and exhausted. Abandoning the tether, Xhea grabbed her cane and tried to rise; and when that failed, she tried only to drag herself away, as if body lengths of distance might keep her from Shai.

Heedless of the magic that poured from Xhea and the bright spells that arced, glittering over their heads—heedless of the way Farrow shook and shuddered under them, growing brighter by the moment—Shai stepped forward, pursuing her. Closer, and closer again.

"Xhea." Shai tried to make her voice sound strong, confident. "You won't hurt me."

"You don't understand," Xhea cried. "I *will*. I can't stop it." Such fear in her voice; such loathing.

"You won't."

Fear bid her run. Shai refused. She had thought the boy a monster for evoking this very feeling; and perhaps he had been, or perhaps she had been wrong. It didn't matter now. All she knew was that, no matter what her dark magic did, no matter her basest nature, Xhea was not a monster.

Sometimes unthinking, yes; callous on more than one occasion. Frustrating, to be sure. But not a monster.

You trust Xhea, came the thought. *But can you trust her magic?*

Except, of everyone, Shai knew that they were one and the same. You could not separate a person from their magic any more than you might sever a brain from a body. Shai herself had lived her whole life—and yes, even part of her death—being thought of as only magic, power incarnate. But she wasn't: she was a person. As was Xhea. She could not have one without the other.

"You don't understand," Xhea said, her voice gone high and desperate. "I'll destroy you. I can't stop it." Still she scrambled back, her movements jerky and flailing.

Shai had to leave now, forever—abandon Xhea as so many others had before—or trust that, somehow, neither Xhea nor her magic would destroy her. Another step, another. It was a risk, yes—maybe even a terrible mistake. But Xhea had been hurt because of her, once and again. Xhea had risked everything to save her—even though Shai had already been dead. Could she truly do anything less?

"Please," Xhea begged. "Don't make me kill you. Not again."

Run away, Shai's fear shouted. Dread clotted within her, cold and hard. Still she stepped forward, staring not at Xhea but the dark magic that reached for her like a great, clawed hand.

"It'll be okay," Shai whispered, to Xhea, to herself. She walked into the dark magic's grasp.

There was only pain. Pain and pain and pain. There was not even space for regret.

A span of a heartbeat, and then something flared within Shai—something that beat back the pain and the desperation and the fear that underlay it all. Something pure and bright like sunlight.

Shai took a long, shuddering breath and opened her eyes.

She floated a hand's span above Farrow's shaking rooftop as if caught there, limp and unmoving. She shook herself, fighting a wave of disorientation.

Xhea had collapsed; yet even as Shai watched, she opened her eyes. Between them stretched the tether. The tether—and something else.

Shai could still feel that near-invisible line that she had created, but woven around it, through it, were countless tiny gray strands that shone like tarnished wire. Shai reached with a tentative hand and touched the binding.

She'd always felt the tether's vibration—heard it, when she thought to listen, like a single echoing note. If the tether had sounded a single note, this binding was a chorus: multiple notes all singing, rising and falling in a strange but perfect harmony.

One link was hers, a tether created by choice and need. The other was Xhea's.

Neither was a passive connection, not anymore, for Shai could feel Xhea drawing on her power—could feel something of herself flow out through Xhea's binding and travel down that length toward Xhea outside her control. Yet she felt, too, something flow back toward her through the tether that she had made—and if that power was dark and chill, it spoke equally of her friend.

"It doesn't hurt," Xhea said. Her voice was little more than a whisper; she sounded like she was going to cry in relief.

"What doesn't?" Shai asked softly. "Your knee?"

Xhea shook her head and carefully pushed herself to sitting. She looked at her hands, held steady before her, turning them over in disbelief.

"My knee," she said. "My head. My stomach. Any of it. The pain and hunger is just ... gone." She looked at Shai with naked wonder. "And you're not."

"See? You didn't even hurt me." *Much.*

"You're a fool," Xhea said, but she was laughing.

Shai was still here, and she was whole, but also ... changed. How was it possible to feel so strong and so weak at the same time? Despite the tether, despite the fact that she stood on air, as something of Xhea's power flowed into her Shai realized that she felt almost real for the first time in years.

Almost alive.

Shai looked down at her body. She was shining, she realized, radiating—but more strongly than she ever had before. All around her, it was so bright she thought that the fires must have burned down, that the air had started to clear—but, if anything, a glance told her that more of the Lower City was burning by the minute. Smoke rose in great clouds, thick and black and choking. Nor was the light from the defensive spells that even now arced up from the skyscraper's defensive spires.

It was her. Shai shone so brightly to dwarf them all, her radiance like noonday sunlight.

Magic also surrounded Xhea; but where her power had always moved like coils of restless smoke, this power was calm and steady like a living shadow. So, too, were Xhea's hands steady when she raised them before her; and her face had lost something of its pinched look, as if a terrible weight had been lifted from her.

And still the power flowed between them.

"Xhea," said a voice, soft and stern and completely unfamiliar. "Get in."

They looked up as one to see that a battered aircar had somehow navigated through the narrow space between the defensive dome and the skyscraper's sides and now hovered just above them. Beneath it was some sort of wide-webbed net that hung like a hammock, swaying with the aircar's movement. A small, hard woman looked out the open driver's side door, looking down at Xhea.

No, Shai realized, not just Xhea—for the woman looked directly at Shai, blinked once, and turned back to Xhea. Shai looked down at herself again, realizing that she shone so brightly that even her passive magic must have entered the visible spectrum.

"I can't," Xhea protested, looking at the aircar and the rope net beneath it. Her face was ashen.

"Get. In."

From beneath them came a great cracking sound, and then the rumble and rattle of falling concrete. That made Xhea move, when all else did not. She grabbed her cane and rose—and if her movements were stiff and she still favored her right knee, she showed none of the weakness she'd displayed but moments earlier.

"Sweetness save me," Xhea muttered as she grabbed the ropes. "Sweetness and blight."

The moment Xhea scrambled into the net, the woman slammed her door closed and the aircar rose, its movement quick enough to startle a yelp from Xhea. Behind them, the door to the skyscraper slammed open and a man ran out onto the rooftop, looking from the fallen boy to Xhea in sudden panic. He shouted something but Shai could not understand his words, not above the whine of the aircar's engine and the sound of shattering glass and falling concrete.

Shai turned and followed the aircar, watching as the woman navigated between the cascading curtain of the defensive spell and the skyscraper's edge—all without jostling Xhea or scraping the aircar against the shuddering building.

No, Shai saw as they entered the open air, Farrow was not just shuddering—but rising. The sound had been the final detonation that separated the skyscraper from the ground. Now, in defiance of gravity and the weight of stone, they hovered as she did, hanging above a pile of broken concrete and twisted rebar—and lifting slowly, slowly into the air. Shai, who had grown up in a Tower floating on air, watched slack-jawed as the tall, heavy building became airborne.

At last she turned away, speeding after the aircar as it made a slow and spiraling descent to the central edge of Edren's territory. When Shai reached it, Xhea was just scrambling out of the net and cursing all the while; she dropped to the ground, cane in hand, and looked as if she wanted to fall to her knees and kiss it, dirt and ash and all.

Nearby, a tall, sandy-haired man sat on the curb, his head in his hands, shaking with magic shock. Xhea stumbled toward him.

There was something about these two, something strangely familiar. Shai frowned.

"It's not safe here," Xhea was protesting. "You need to take the car out into the badlands."

The woman who had rescued Xhea from the rooftop just stared, her expression flat and unyielding. Xhea shook her head, grimacing, as if that unchanged expression had been response enough.

"Fine, then—but we can't just stay here."

The bounty hunters, Shai thought suddenly. The ones who had tried to abduct Xhea and take her away to Tower

Eridian—the ones who *had* abducted her, but days before. The ones who had stabbed Mercks and left him to die alone in the tunnels beneath the Lower City. Whatever she might have said or done as the anger welled within her was forgotten as a building only blocks away collapsed in a rush of smoke and sparks. Even from this distance, Shai could feel the heat—could smell the acrid smoke as it rushed over them in a wave.

Shai turned, Xhea and the bounty hunters ignored behind her as the import of what she had seen atop Farrow suddenly hit home: despite the combined efforts of the Lower City citizens, the fires were spreading. Without thinking, Shai lifted into the air, seeking a better vantage.

The fires to one side of the destroyed market were nearly under control, a wide, multi-laned street clearly helping slow the fire's progression. Closer to Senn, the flames raged hotter, higher. Those few who still battled the blaze could not get close; they fought now only to try to limit its spread. And what were a few buckets of dirty water against such flames?

People were fleeing. Children held in arms or on hips, older children leading younger, elderly folks stumbling along. Some held bundles of clothing or other possessions, but most held nothing at all as they ran, faces smeared with ash, coughing into dampened cloths that seemed no protection from the acrid smoke.

Where could they go? The ruins, or the badlands beyond. But Shai had seen those places, had walked them at Xhea's side and alone after night had fallen. No food, no clean water, no shelter awaited them; only the barest hope that the fire might not spread so far. And what would there be left to come back to?

Shai dropped back to the ground—but not only Xhea watched her fall, for still the light of her magic shone from her unthinkingly. Even the man was looking at her, squinting, his bloodshot eyes tearing at the sight.

"Shai?" Xhea said. She sounded almost uncertain, as if she had thought that Shai had been leaving her again. "We have to go below—find safety."

Shai just shook her head. "No," she said. "We have to help them."

"Shai, we—"

"*I* have to help them."

For already she could feel the magic within her—more magic than she'd ever held, more magic than she'd ever known, spreading through her ghostly body and out into the world. Brighter she shone, brighter and brighter; and she could already feel the spell that lay beneath that magic, and feel the rhythms of its song.

A spell for rain.

The very thought was absurd. There were no spells that could control the weather—or so she had been told. Too many factors, too large an area to influence—the reasons not to even make the attempt were many and varied. Yet she had also been told that spells had to be learned like careful recipes of pattern and practice, and that only a rare talent might create something new.

What was the point of power, of magic, if it didn't *do* anything? If it was used only to hurt and control but never to help? The Towers would never have wasted such untold fortunes as she now held on something so small as the lives and homes of a few thousand people down in the dirt.

Shai smiled then at the irony, for only now did she realize: her responsibility never should have been to her Tower, but to the *people.*

These were her people now.

She did not need a memory to direct the power, nor a mental image to shape it; only the feeling that rose now within her, a feeling so strong that she all but wept from its pressure. Fear and hope and a terrible empathy, growing as fast and as bright as her magic.

She felt, too, as the spell began to pull on the strange link to Xhea—the tether and spell both that joined them, one to the other. She did not understand the link that they had created, nor what she was drawing from Xhea; she only knew that she felt stronger, steadier, and more real.

She looked to her friend. "Will you help me?" she asked.

Xhea glared at her. "Of course I will. Do it. Whatever you're going to do, do it."

She touched their link. "I'm pulling energy from you somehow. Is that okay?"

"You're . . . asking my permission?"

Shai nodded.

"You have it. I . . ." Xhea shook her head, coins chiming.

"Tell me if I'm hurting you," Shai asked.

Xhea snorted. "You tell me if I'm hurting *you.*"

From the curb came a voice: "Whatever you and the dead girl are doing, now might be a good time."

Shai turned toward the fire and sent her magic cascading outward, as if mapping the world with its light. The buildings around her, the burning ones beyond; the skyscrapers and the people scurrying through the Lower City's streets; even Farrow, hovering now only a few stories in the air and struggling to rise ever higher. Then farther, out to the ruins and the badlands, up through the gap of open air that separated the City from the Lower City, and into the mass of Towers beyond.

It was not the people and structures themselves that Shai sought, but the water that filled the air all around them. Closest to the fire, the intense heat had driven away the moisture; but elsewhere the summer air was still thick with humidity. She reached as if that water was something she could gather with her outstretched hands, and drew it to her.

Even without letting the water fall, Shai knew it wasn't going to be enough. So she reached farther, and farther still, even the vast power of her newly strengthened magic growing thin as she reached and reached and reached. She reached into the Towers' water reservoirs and yanked them open; reached up and up toward the wispy clouds above. She felt as if it were not just her magic that was stretched so far but her very self, as if she had no ghostly body, only a strained kind of consciousness pulled taut and straining across untold reaches of sky.

Xhea was her anchor. Through it all, Shai could feel her: Xhea's magic and her presence, holding her steady and keeping her from flying apart entirely.

When she had reached her absolute limit, Shai pulled her magic and the water it contained toward her. *Cold*, she thought to it, thinking of the cool breezes she had created so laboriously before. No breeze this: as the temperature in the air she held dropped, the water condensed. Water droplets formed and were claimed by gravity.

Rain.

There, she said, directing its fall.

Shai had expected rain, called rain, shaped rain from the very air around her. Except what fell was a deluge. Water struck the burning buildings not with a hiss but a concussive shock. Water exploded outward, and steam rushed skyward—only to be caught again in Shai's shaping, cooled and condensed to fall once more. Beneath the onslaught, the flames began to die.

Shai released her hold on her magic, but still it rained. For all that Shai had dumped most of the water on the fire, the downpour even here had been like a spring storm at its worst. Water flowed in shallow rivers through the streets and sidewalks, poured from roofs, dripped from limp laundry lines. It was all she could hear, all she could see, in a Lower City gone still and silent in shock.

Not least of all herself.

Despite her power and newfound skill, Shai realized only now that she had expected to fail as she had failed so many times before. Yet the fires, where they still burned, were but weak tongues of flame amidst so much soaked rubble and smoldering ash—flames that would yield more surely to the Lower City dwellers' buckets and sand. Though she felt the strain of the spell in every part of her imagined body, her magic still shone; not just bright, but radiant in truth.

There was so much more to be done—so much that her mind quailed even from the thought. But here, now? This victory was hers. Shai found herself laughing.

Shai turned to Xhea, who stood unmoving beside her, water dribbling down her forehead into her eyes. She barely blinked.

"Xhea?" Shai asked, her laughter fading. She reached out, and touched Xhea's shoulder—and oh, to have someone she might touch again, if only so briefly. To know her words were heard.

Xhea did not respond to that touch nor the sound of her name, only stared.

"Xhea?" Shai said again, louder, more urgently—and found the sound echoed in the voice of the injured man behind her. He stepped forward cautiously, shielding his bloodshot eyes, the small, dark woman like a hulking shadow in his wake. Xhea took no more notice of him than she did of Shai—only stared, brow furrowing.

A moment, then without a word, Xhea turned and walked away.

Chapter
Twenty-Three

The Lower City was singing.

Xhea closed her eyes, opened them, blinking like she stood in the path of some strange wind. She shook her head, as if the sound might be shaken away with the rain that even now poured down her cheeks and dripped from her hair. Nothing changed the sound—the vibration—the *feeling* that seemed to rise from the very ground.

From the moment her feet had hit the asphalt, stumbling out of the net Daye had slung beneath the aircar, something had felt different. But then everything had been smoke and fear and the sound of distant voices screaming, the roar of the fire, the shifting glimmer of Shai's light. It had been easy to push aside the thought that something had changed, something far deeper than the chaos she'd seen all around her.

Only now she realized that there had been no change in the ground itself, not in the asphalt nor the tunnels nor the earth through which they wove. Only in her.

Even now, power flowed through her, the likes of which she'd never known. All the things she had once imagined—that cold, dark lake within her, the weight of darkness clotted beneath her breastbone—gone now, as if they'd never been. Not because the magic was gone, but the opposite: power flowed through her flesh with no start and no end.

More, she could feel herself drawing strength from Shai. It was not the horror she'd imagined, not the awful taking she'd seen from Ieren; for as she drew sustenance from the ghost, Shai also drew power from her. She did not understand quite what they had done, nor how they had done it; only that they had created a joining of binding and tether both, where Ieren had only had one. The energy seemed to flow between Xhea and Shai, quick and easy as breath, in an unending loop.

The ghost beside her shone brighter than daylight while she, living flesh and blood, stood like death incarnate.

It should have hurt; she knew that now. Knew the feeling of that power ripping through her, destroying her from the inside out even as it made her feel whole—knew the hunger that had driven her magic and actions alike. There was none of that now; only power, pure and black. Dark magic seemed to vibrate through her, sing from her very heart, stronger and louder with each passing moment.

And the Lower City responded.

Xhea was aware of the rain that Shai had called from the smoke-hazed sky; aware, too, of the flames still sizzling and dying under that onslaught. Yet none of it seemed real—not the heat, not the smoke and ash, not even the acrid smell—as if the world around her had become the memory of a dream.

There was only that sound that wasn't a sound, that strange and discordant song, calling her.

Xhea took a step forward, and another, leaning on her cane as she splashed across the street. She was tired in a way that neither her magic nor her binding to Shai could touch, a weariness of overstressed muscles and wounds half-healed—yet it did not stop her, only slowed her steps to something that even Torrence, half-blinded, could follow.

Follow he did—Torrence and Daye and Shai alike. Xhea heard as Torrence regained his feet, heard his swearing; heard what could only be Daye's footsteps, slow and steady as she supported him. Xhea could feel Shai's presence at her side, steady and calm, her anchor against the storm.

They called to her, shouted her name. *They can't hear it*, Xhea realized. Whatever the source of the song and the strange feeling that even now seemed to shiver through her, only she had detected its presence.

"There's something . . ." she murmured—but she had no words. Still she tried: "Something . . ." Her voice trailed away to nothing.

Xhea kept walking.

The feeling grew with every step, the song that was not a sound rising and falling all around her. It reminded her of standing beneath Eridian's flaring heart as the Tower merged with rival Allenai; it was as strange and beautiful and utterly inhuman. A sound that had nothing to do with her ears, the way her black-and-white vision had nothing to do with her eyes. But then, if one could see magic, why not hear it? Why not touch or taste?

The song led her toward the destroyed market and the smoldering remains of the surrounding structures. The dripping water was thick and black, the buildings still standing stained dark with ash.

When the sound had reached a crescendo, she stopped.

There was nothing here, Xhea saw as she looked around; nothing but another stretch of broken pavement, another block of old buildings burned, another ancient intersection. There were people here: Rown hunters, and soot-stained citizens; guards whose insignia identified them as being from Senn and Orren; children in their pajamas. Some milled while others argued, or pointed, or stared toward the place where so recently a funnel of water had seemed to appear from out of the empty sky.

No one else could hear the sound. None could sense the power that even now echoed all around her.

"Xhea," Shai said, looking around in clear confusion. "What is it?"

Slowly, Xhea looked up. Directly above her hovered the Central Spire, that impossibly tall golden needle that she saw as a bright, gleaming gray. From her angle she could only see half of it, from its downward point to the widest of its public platforms; the rest, tall enough to seem to pierce the sky, was lost to her vision. But it was enough—the Spire seemed to point directly at her, at this spot where she stood.

And that meant . . .

Oh, sweetness. Sweetness and blight.

For the memory of what she'd seen in dawn's gray light came flooding back. Of the Spire pulling dark magic from the City, all those wisps and clouds of black. Of that magic swirling around the Central Spire and pouring toward the Lower City in a flood of dark magic.

How long had they done the same, night after night? Power spilled like waste upon the ground and people below. Already she knew that her dark magic was not as strange and unknown as she'd once thought—merely rare, and closely guarded by the Spire itself. Dark magic spells seemed to underlie much of what happened in the City. She thought of those gray, wire-lace spells that had connected Shai to her Tower, and the way that Ieren had so casually spoken of binding Radiants. She thought of the walkers.

Xhea shook her head and looked around her—truly looked, as if for the first time. She let her eyes' focus change and did not force back the world that was revealed, no matter that it made her want to flinch.

It was not just her vision that made the Lower City look so dark; not just the falling ash and smoke stains and thick, black water, but *magic*. She could see it now—see it as clearly as she heard it, that song rising and falling all around her. The buildings seemed shadowed, as if a Tower or a cloud blocked the sun, dark magic having seeped into every brick and crack and stone. Those stores and windows she could see nearby, those homes and balconies, stained gray with power. The ground beneath her feet was darkest of all.

Xhea knew, then, what she would see underground.

Underground, where only those with little bright magic could stand to travel—and people like Xhea. Underground, where dark magic would surround them, pressing in from the very walls and floors and ceiling; every surface imbued with a power it hurt even to touch.

She thought of the way that plants struggled to grow within the Lower City core, while the badlands were nothing but green. She thought of these buildings here still standing—aged and marked, but standing, even whole— while the ruins beyond were succumbing to wind and time, the concrete marked with moss and mold and mildew, home to countless living things.

Not here. Nothing so small could live here. Nothing could thrive.

She thought of the people here, poor and ill and ailing, barely enough bright magic in them to live, never mind flourish. Sometimes someone came to the Lower City—a true City citizen, fallen on hard times—thinking that they'd stay only for a week or a month, just until they were back on their feet. Few ever left—for who could grow rich again, healthy and strong—who could even generate the bare minimum of power that the Towers required—when dark magic fell upon them every night, undoing all they had wrought?

Xhea stared and stared and stared, as if she might see something else that would make her understand why. As if understanding might strip away her horror.

How long has the City been poisoning us? She laughed then, the sound hard and bitter, for she already knew the answer to that: perhaps as long as there had been a City.

And from that poison . . . *this.* This song, this place, this feeling that echoed around her. Xhea remembered what Ahrent had said to her but days ago—days that now felt like years, with everything changed in their wake.

With enough magic and enough time, things begin to change—to become something more than they were. Eventually, even metal or glass or stone can begin to awaken.

She had thought him crazy—a fool to imagine that something constructed by human hands might ever be something more. Might live. But if he had been crazy to think his skyscraper could become a living Tower, she must have lost her grip on reality entirely.

For the Lower City was not just singing—it was singing to *her.*

As she'd approached, Xhea had heard surprise in that song. Surprise—and then, beneath that, welcome. Joy. It was foolish to ascribe emotions to a thing that she could not rightly name, never mind understand. But how else to describe the way the song shifted and changed with her every step until it seemed to reverberate in time with her magic, her bond to Shai, the very rhythms of her heart and breath?

"Hello," Xhea whispered. Then again, the words stained dark—imagining she could make her very magic vibrate with the greeting: *Hello.*

There was a pause, then the song roared up, so loud that she flinched from it—a rush of power that vibrated in joyous echo of that word.

No, not in echo, but in reply.

"It's alive," she breathed. "The Lower City is alive."

Alive like a Tower was—only not born of bright magic, but dark. Beneath her could only be its heart.

Shai said something, and Torrence, but Xhea heard neither. Someone screamed.

"It's going to fall!" a woman cried, her voice high with fear. "It's going to fall!"

Only then did Xhea realize that the crowd around her was gathered not just to put out the fires, but to look at the sky. She followed their gazes.

Farrow.

The skyscraper had risen as Ahrent promised it would. Yet this could not be the glorious transformation he had envisioned. So much power, so many spells, so many years spent planning—and Xhea could only think that they'd forced the transformation too quickly.

If transformation it was. Farrow looked worse for the wear: cracked and crumbling, once-whole windows shattered, holes in its side gaping wide like screaming mouths. It still shone, the spells were still working—and yes, it lifted slowly, slowly, into the smoke-stained sky—but it was no Tower, only concrete and stone.

Xhea had heard and felt Farrow's heart taking shape, yet it had been nothing compared to a true Tower's heart, that glowing orb of pure power on which every Tower functioned. It had been nothing compared to the song that resonated even now from the ground beneath her, different though they were.

Still she stared, as if by watching she could somehow change the inevitable.

Beside her, Torrence asked, "What's happening?" Xhea glanced at him; he shielded his eyes with one hand, blinking and squinting in Farrow's general direction. Not blind then—or not wholly so. "What *is* that? It looks like the moon."

"Farrow," Daye said. But she didn't look at the airborne skyscraper, only at Torrence in evident worry. Even Xhea's eyebrow rose—for how could Torrence, poor and all but magic-blind, see Farrow's light? Or perhaps he saw only the visible defensive spells that cascaded from the two spell-spires—though they had weakened, and were fading by the moment.

"Farrow's rising?" he asked incredulously.

"No."

And they weren't. Farrow's upward progress had halted in midair. *Planning their upward attack*, she thought. But as moments passed it became clear that they wanted to rise higher, and could not. The skyscraper shook and surged, looking for all the world like a broken-down aircar too weak to fly.

Strength left only to hover, and fight for a time. Strength left only to fall.

"I could . . ." Shai started, but it wasn't hard for Xhea to hear the uncertainty in her voice. Uncertainty that Xhea echoed, much though she wished it were otherwise.

For all Shai's power, that endless Radiant light, there were limits—and this went far beyond all of them.

"No," Xhea said. Only that.

"But I . . . I have to try."

"Try what?"

"I don't know." Shai sounded like her heart was breaking. Xhea reached out and took the ghost's hands in hers, lacing their fingers together.

Xhea had never asked Ahrent about Farrow's backup plans; somehow she knew that there were none. Perhaps they hadn't thought much farther than the moment of transformation itself. Higher, the poorest Towers circled their prey, waiting to swoop down and grab Farrow from midair.

Perhaps it's better that way. Better that than smashing on the ground.

Except that any takeover, hostile or otherwise, saw two Towers merged. Their grown-metal flesh went liquid and they joined, one into the other. If a Tower fell on Farrow, piercing the structure, it would only be to take what magic they could from its struggling newborn heart. There were no other resources there that a Tower might want, no matter how poor; no citizens worth enough to save and claim and feed.

This is your fault. The thought was heavy with recrimination. *You left them like this. You made it so they would fall.*

Except this was no small failure that might have been solved by binding the lives and spirits of another few people to those concrete walls. Everything—all those years and lives, all that magic and misspent renai—and for what? All it would earn them, in the end, was a broken building smashed upon the ground, lives ground to nothing beneath it.

Xhea watched as the skyscraper struggled again to rise and enter the City proper; watched them fail. Slowly, Farrow tilted from one side to the other like some unsteady top, objects and rubble tumbling from its balconies and the holes in its walls. She could not see the ground on which the skyscraper had once stood, but knew how it must look: that gaping hole so laboriously dug, bottomed now with the piled rubble from the detonations, rebar and plumbing pipe stabbing upward.

"Could we ... flatten Farrow's base somehow?" Shai asked, clearly struggling to accept the hopeless reality. "Cut off those ragged pieces? And make some sort of cradle for it to land in. And ..." Shai's voice trailed away as she thought through the myriad little details, none of which might be skipped. Because it wasn't just a question of power. If it had been, perhaps between the two of them they might have found a way—if they'd had days to plan and prepare. Perhaps.

One of the smaller Towers, already pushed from its previous altitude, dove toward Farrow, arrow-straight. Farrow, too, dropped—and even expecting it, Xhea's stomach clenched at the sight of the building dropping like a stone. Nearby, people screamed.

A moment, then the Tower pulled up with such speed that Xhea could only imagine what it was like to be a citizen inside. Its bottommost spires nearly scraped Farrow's rooftop as they swooped skyward once more. They didn't dare get so close to the ground, or the destructive power of the dark magic that pooled within it.

Though the attack had been aborted, Farrow's delicate equilibrium was broken. Spells flared around the skyscraper, but to little avail: they slowed but could not stop the skyscraper's descent.

Xhea squeezed Shai's fingers with one hand and gripped the top of her cane with the other. She couldn't watch. She couldn't look away.

She hadn't realized that her power still flowed—that her words and thoughts were being carried in the magic that filled her breath and tears—until she felt the Lower City's song change in response. No words, no thoughts, only a deepening of the song's resonance as its myriad melodies shifted: chords played in question and in sorrow.

Oh, what could she say? What could she do? How could she explain herself to an entity of living structures, of earth and street and broken concrete? How could she tell it what it meant for Farrow to fall?

Yet as she thought the name, *Farrow*, she felt the Lower City shiver.

Of course it would know. Farrow, so long a part of the Lower City, had changed in the span of a morning and been ripped away. Explosions in the ground, rubble left behind. The Lower City knew; of course it knew. Who would not know that they had lost a piece of their very self?

It was still hurting, she realized; hurting as much as the people here, the ones with their homes burned, their loved ones lost. Farrow's absence was part of that song; so too was the place where the market once stood.

Farrow slid sideways, sinking ever lower, and someone cried, "It's heading for the market!"

Whether their trajectory was guided or sheer accident, she did not know; yet Xhea heard the gathered watchers murmur thanks to absent gods that the skyscraper wouldn't crash somewhere that the buildings were still standing. Murmurs, too, of fear and shock, of what that crash would mean.

So much hurt. So much pain and death, with only the promise of more to come. While she—while they all—just stood here, helpless.

No, Xhea thought.

She released Shai's hand and her cane alike, and lowered herself awkwardly to ground. She placed both hands against the wet, ashy street, fingers splayed.

Help them, she said in word and magic both, pushing a torrent of black from her hands into that ground as if her message might be conveyed through sheer will alone. *Help them.*

She felt the Lower City respond, its song growing and swelling until it seemed her whole body vibrated with the sound. Above her, she heard her name—heard screams and cries as Farrow fell—

None of it mattered. There was only her and the Lower City and the power that flowed between them in this strange communion.

Xhea was not the Lower City—not the ground and the tunnels within it, not the ancient buildings perched atop; she was just one girl, small and dirty with braid-tangled hair. She was not the Lower City and yet she was, for as her power flowed into the ground like a gift, her senses expanded, out and out and out, echoing across the landscape.

She felt the skyscrapers—four, now, and the aching hole where once had stood a fifth. She felt the hurt of the market burned, and beneath that, the place where Rown's weapon had scored a line across the Lower City's living heart. The warehouse district, the broken highway overpasses, the arena, the wide and empty stretches where great houses once stood—the roads and the sewers and the pipelines beneath—Xhea felt it all, more and more until it seemed she could dissolve into it, soak into its bones like her magic itself.

Shai did not understand what was happening, that much was clear, and yet Xhea felt the ghost crouch at her side and pour her own magic into the link that bound them, letting Xhea draw upon her strength at will.

She needed it. The Lower City's need seemed endless—not for the magic itself, but for the understanding that laced it. No words passed between them, not even now; their languages had nothing in common. Yet understanding—urgency—*need*; such things passed between them at will.

Save them.

Xhea looked up, and with her gaze came the attention of all the Lower City. She looked to Farrow, losing its battle for altitude, and lifted her hand.

Hers was just a gesture skyward, fingers reaching as if she might pluck the falling skyscraper out of the empty air, the way a child might try to catch the moon. It was the Lower City who reached for Farrow in truth.

There came a great roar of sound: asphalt ripping, concrete cracking, buildings crumbling and collapsing. The ground beneath them shook, and onlookers screamed, stumbling back from the rush of dust that burst outward from the ruin that had been the market. Above it, a shape exploded, stabbing into the air in a perfect mirror of Xhea's gesture.

Farrow was falling, falling, and it didn't matter, for at Xhea's command the Lower City rose to catch it. It had not fingers, not a hand as she did, but a hundred twisting tendrils of rock and rubble, the broken pieces bound together only by dark magic. Where Xhea's magic was smoke and shadow, the Lower City's power was the deepest black, the cold and the dark that waited at the ocean's depth, the heart of flame unburning.

No, Xhea realized, holding her hand aloft as she poured all of her power into the ground beneath her to communicate her need. It wasn't even rubble, for as she watched the pieces blended and merged, one into the other into a strange whole. They were all a piece: roots and branches, each growing almost faster than the eye could track, twisting as they grew upward like a great, reaching tree.

The first branches reached Farrow's lower levels; they didn't wrap around the skyscraper but burrowed into it, digging deep into the concrete structure and sending yet more rubble raining down. The reaching branches reappeared from floors some distance up, bursting from walls and windows to wrap around balconies and grip the building's corners.

Some broke as the skyscraper's weight came down upon them. Even here, Xhea could hear the creaks and groans and crunch of crumbling stone.

It's going to be crushed.

But no: more tendrils burst from the ground and rose, wrapping around the trunk as it formed, reaching up Farrow's sides and gripping tight. The skyscraper shuddered and shook, and then came to a halt.

As the branches formed of asphalt and sewer pipe continued to rise and twist around the skyscraper, Xhea took a long and shuddering breath. It was, Xhea thought as she looked at the creation with an appraising eye, almost vertical.

Slowly, she drew back from the entity that was the living Lower City, and her awareness of that vast space—and the utterly inhuman intellect behind it—faded. But not before she understood some sliver of its song.

If it had words, the Lower City would have sung only this: *Home, home, home.*

A song of joy and welcome for the ones it had thought lost forever, snatched from the sky and the edge of death.

Within moments, the pale, rectangular shape of Farrow-that-was had all but vanished beneath the dark tendrils of the living Lower City. So, too, did Farrow's magic vanish. First the spell-spires atop the building sparked and fizzled to nothing; then the spells that lit the skyscraper from within flickered as they grew ever dimmer. It might have only been that the power was exhausted, as Xhea had been; that the newborn Tower was not gasping and dying even as she watched. But she did not think so.

"Xhea," Shai breathed. She stared at Xhea, at her upraised hand. "What did you do?"

Xhea looked at Farrow, a building held in a tree grown of ash and rubble, then up, up, toward the Towers cast across the sky. She licked her dry lips and swallowed.

"The Lower City," Xhea said slowly, carefully, "is alive."

It wasn't Shai that replied, nor Torrence, but Daye: "Yes." Her soft voice was weighted with finality, as if that word were the start and the end of the conversation.

It wouldn't be—it couldn't—but Xhea still laughed, little more than a small puff of breath. But enough. She lowered her hand, its weight suddenly like iron, and closed her eyes.

Her magic was all but exhausted, and in its absence she could not hear the Lower City's song. No vibration beneath her that was not from the people running; no thought or feeling that was not her own. Even her awareness of Shai seemed to be little more than it always had been: a link between them and the sense of the ghost's presence at her side.

All is as it used to be, she thought. *And nothing will ever be the same again.*

Again, she laughed.

Once Xhea would have fought her way to standing, forced her face to betray no pain. Now, it wasn't just her knee in its brace that stopped her, nor her aching muscles, but awareness that there were three people who stood beside her. Watching her. Waiting to help.

No need, anymore, to hide. No need to do everything all on her own.

"I think," she said at last, looking to Shai, "that I'm going to need help to stand."

As the people of the Lower City ran to where Farrow now towered—or fled from it as fast as their feet could carry them—Xhea walked back to Edren. Step by careful step, she limped with a cane in her hand. Torrence and Daye walked before her, Torrence clinging to Daye's arm as he too walked with uncertain steps. Shai stayed by Xhea's side.

At Xhea's pace, and Torrence's, it was a long, slow journey, but Xhea found that she did not mind. It was nice to let the world rush around her, and not think of anything that had happened. Only focus on the road before her, and her next step.

You're in shock, she told herself. Yet her hands were steady, and her heartbeat strong; and if her face was beaded with sweat, it was nothing more than was her right as the summer sun beat down. She was, she thought, simply tired.

At last they came to the ancient hotel that bore the Edren name.

Guards stood outside the doors, armed and armored and wary of Rown's hunters' return. But for all their readiness, they too kept turning to look toward the Lower City's center and the tree that now grew there, a skyscraper clutched high in its grasp.

I'm going to have a lot of explaining to do, Xhea thought with a sigh. But first: a nap, then a bath, then another nap. Maybe another nap after that. She felt she could sleep through to breakfast tomorrow, for all that the sun hadn't yet reached midday.

"Stop," one of Edren's guards said, raising his hand before Torrence and Daye could ascend the stairs toward the main door. Xhea didn't blame him: they still wore clothing that clearly identified their affiliation with Rown, and Torrence's infirmary said nothing good about their innocence.

Edren would need them, Xhea thought, little though any knew it yet. Magic-poor though they were, they were two hunters experienced with traveling underground. There were few who could withstand the dark magic underground; fewer still who might help Xhea in her new, self-appointed role.

Ambassador. Who else might connect to the Lower City's heart?

Xhea stepped out from their shadow, and everything changed. The guards called inside for support. A moment later, there came the sound of running footsteps.

"Xhea!" Mercks exclaimed as he hurried out into the sunlight. Xhea blinked, amazed, startled into a smile.

"Mercks," she whispered. "You're not dead."

Lorn was hard on his heels. "Is she with you?" he asked, before he had even come to a stop. "Shai. Is she okay?"

At the first question, Xhea's heart sank, that faint smile vanishing. *Of course*, came the thought. Someone else who wanted the ghost for her magic. But in his next words, she heard his concern: the whole Lower City burning and rising and ripping itself to pieces, and Lorn was worried about the girl who was already dead.

Xhea did not answer. Instead she turned to Shai as the ghost drew her power to her and let it flow, shining brighter and brighter until she was as she had been when they were first joined—bright as sunlight, and brighter still. Xhea knew the moment that Shai's light passed into the visible spectrum because Lorn gasped, and Torrence averted his eyes, wincing. Only Daye stood still and steady.

Lorn smiled then—a true smile. It transformed his face.

No, Xhea realized. Not Lorn—Addis.

Shai looked from one person to the next, her magic falling upon their faces, their ash-stained hands, and she smiled in kind.

"I'm okay," Shai said. "Truly. We're all going to be okay."

Only Xhea could hear the ghost, yet she remained silent. There wasn't, in the end, any need to translate.

Epilogue

For three days it rained, steady and soft. The rain didn't so much break the heat as sweep it away with the dust and the ash and the bloodstains, leaving clearer air behind. When Xhea stepped outside on the morning of the fourth day, it felt like entering a new world.

It was still hot, yes; it still smelled of sweat and garbage and ash long cooled. It was still summer in the Lower City. But the oppressive humidity had lifted and with it had gone some of the tension and fear that had bound the streets since Rown's attack and Farrow's rise and fall. People were outside again, walking, mending, arms heavy with belongings and building materials; and though their eyes were shadowed with pain and fatigue, they were there.

Xhea was there, in spite of everything. *Still standing.*

It took time to make her way down the steps; she did not rush. Did not, if she were honest, want to. Even in the street, she moved with none of her habitual hurry: only careful movements, steady and slow, taking the time to look around her as she went.

Within sight of Edren's main doors, young children played, laughing and shouting, as their parents and older siblings gathered to do laundry. Keeping pace with her, a bent-backed man dragged a cart laden with reclaimed tile toward where the market had once stood, the cart's wheels squeaking. Somewhere nearby, bread was baking.

It was not normal. Not even close. The heat had broken, and the fear, but not the anger. That simmered beneath every word and movement, the scents of everyday life and the light of the morning sun that cast long shadows across the ground. Even without looking toward the mess and ruin that had been Senn's territory—that had been the market building and the sprawling tents that had surrounded it in wide rings—she felt the difference. That anger was why Rown's doors were shut tight, its citizens glimpsed only through windows or on the opposite ends of weapons raised warily—those citizens that had not fled entirely.

Survival was the priority. Food and shelter, strong walls to keep the elements and the walkers at bay. Supplies for the coming winter. Lives and livelihoods rebuilt from the ground up. But that did not mean that the desire for revenge was not there. This wound was deep and fresh and would be a long time healing.

Time, Xhea thought, leaning heavily on her cane as she walked. The same word that she had been repeating these past few days—when she wasn't lost in an exhausted sleep. Time heals all wounds, wasn't that the saying? Except that it wasn't quite true.

Not for her, and not for the Lower City.

Oh, they could and would rebuild. New structures would take the place of the ones that the fire had destroyed, and if they had neither the height nor the strength of the ones constructed from the bones of the city that had come before, they would at least be standing. But even without the skyscraper that now loomed above the ashen ruin of the market, or the tendrils grown of asphalt and rebar that held it aloft—even without the unhappy turmoil between the skyscrapers themselves—the Lower City could not return to what it had been.

But maybe, she thought, it could grow be something better. Something more.

And Xhea? Without realizing it, she'd managed to deal with the reality of her injured knee only by reassuring herself that it was temporary. A wound, healing—and if her body failed to do the job on its own, she had put her trust in Shai. If one healing spell had done so much good, what might a second do, or a third? Especially given how much Shai had learned in the days that they had been apart.

Even so, it had taken three days in that so-familiar room on Edren's ground level for her to gather the courage to ask Shai to attempt a healing once more. She'd been surprised; Shai hadn't hesitated, only smiled as if she'd been waiting for the request.

That smile had faded when the ghost turned her attention to Xhea's knee.

"What do you mean it's already healed?" Xhea had whispered, after Shai had tried to explain. She'd asked—but she knew. Oh, she knew.

Shai had shaken her head, looking sad and guilty. "I did my best," she'd said. "Before. I tried, but I didn't know . . ." Again, that shake of her head, her light making the shadows around them dance. "I healed you, but I did it wrong. I'm sorry. I'm so, so sorry."

Once Xhea would have been angry; would have raged, if only in the confines of her heart. But there was no anger now, no more pain, only a kind of slow sorrow. It was only Shai's expression that hurt; Xhea had reached out and grabbed the ghost's hand.

"Don't you apologize," she'd said, for all that her voice had seemed to catch in her throat. "I wouldn't be able to walk at all if it weren't for you." Shai had come to sit beside her, and Xhea had leaned against her, they'd sat there for a long time, not speaking, not moving, supporting each other without words.

Xhea's knee would never work properly. She would never again walk unaided. Wounds healed; but some, in healing, left scars.

And what of it? If this was to be her life, her new reality, she would take it. She was *alive*. Even that seemed a gift.

Once she could not imagine what her life would be if she could not walk, if she could not run or hide or flee. But there were other lives than the ones she had imagined— other futures—and she was going to find them, one careful step at a time.

And she was not now, not ever, alone. Though no one walked at her side, she had both the tether and the dark spell that bound her to Shai, and Shai to her; she could *feel* Shai at the other end of that dual link. It was strange, that awareness, even as it comforted her. They had yet to understand the full nature of that joining—but that, too, would come with time.

Xhea paused for breath, clutching the top of the twisted wooden cane that Daye had given her. She reached up and touched the spell-bound tether. There was no need to yank to call for Shai's attention, as she'd done before; instead, she sent a faint surge of magic down that length, imbued with a quiet invitation.

As she waited, she looked slowly around. The ground before her was black and gray, and it was not her vision that made the expanse seem so bleak. The part of the Lower City core that had been the market and the surrounding buildings of Senn's territory had looked bad when they were burning. Blackened rubble, stumps of concrete walls, ash and wreckage: smoking, it had seem incredible. Now, damp and puddled from days of rain, it looked all too real.

Yet it was Farrow that drew the eye, the tallest of the skyscrapers made taller still, held within that tangled embrace. The skyscraper had shifted and settled and then . . . doors opened. Windows. People had begun climbing their careful way down the branches toward the ground, and building stairs and ramps for other, less adventurous types.

Life went on, in spite of everything.

Xhea felt as Shai arrived. It was not Shai's light, nor Xhea's newly heightened awareness of ghosts that alerted her, but something in their link. There was something of Xhea in the ghost now, something of her magic, even as there was something of Shai filling her, sure and steady as blood.

"I thought you wanted to be alone," Shai said quietly, coming to stand beside her.

Xhea smiled, and there was little in the expression that spoke of her habitual edge. "I think I've been alone long enough, don't you?"

For a time they looked at the ruin that had been the market, and Farrow, and myriad homes. A funeral procession passed, ringing bells made from scrap metal, singing in low voices. A scavenger crouched in the ash, sifting for nails.

"Walk with me?" Xhea asked.

As they walked through the streets, talking quietly, with every step, Xhea could sense the living Lower City beneath her. It had a slow thrum that echoed like a vast heartbeat and shivered against her boot-soles—an almost imperceptible vibration that only now could she hear as separate from the rhythms of life here on the ground.

It was quiet now, almost dormant. Healing, like the rest of them. She could, she knew, reach out to it once more—touch it with her magic and thoughts. Instead, she let it sleep.

For now.

Acknowledgments

There were times that I thought this novel would never be written. There were moments—days, weeks—during the writing process that I thought I should just throw everything away and admit defeat. Yet here it is, an actual book. I still don't quite believe it.

Huge thanks to:

Jana Paniccia and Jeanne Schriel, who read *Defiant* in all its unfinished glory and helped me make sense of the mess. (And oh, was it ever a mess.)

Greg Smyth, for enduring the craziness with love and patience, and for believing in me and in this book even when I didn't.

Jessica Leake, fellow adventurer on this publishing journey, for all the amazing comments—and for knowing *exactly* what I was talking about, every time. (Go #TeamTalos!)

Sarah Jane Elliott, Chris Szego, Julie Czerneda, and Michelle Sagara, amazing friends all, for helping *Radiant* find the right readers. (And, y'know, for putting up with me.)

Kelsie Besaw, Jason Katzman, Lauren Burnstein, and the rest of the team at Skyhorse for their hard work, support, and enthusiasm.

Sara Megibow, agent extraordinaire, without whom none of this would have been possible.

And you, the reader, for coming back for a second book. You make this adventure worthwhile.